RACHEL CAINE is the international bestselling author of over thirty novels, including the *New York Times* bestselling Morganville Vampires series. She was born at White Sands Missile Range, which people who know her say explains a lot. She has been an accountant, an insurance investigator and a professional musician, and has played with such musical legends as Henry Mancini, Peter Nero and John Williams. She and her husband, fantasy artist R. Cat Conrad, live in Texas with their iguana Pop-eye, a *mali uromastyx* named (appropriately) O'Malley, and a leopard tortoise named Shelley (for the poet, of course).

www.rachelcaine.com

Available from
ALLISON & BUSBY

The Weather Warden series

Ill Wind
Heat Stroke
Chill Factor
Windfall
Firestorm
Thin Air
Gale Force
Cape Storm
Total Eclipse

The Morganville Vampires series

Glass Houses
The Dead Girls' Dance
Midnight Alley
Feast of Fools
Lord of Misrule
Carpe Corpus
Fade Out
Kiss of Death
Ghost Town
Bite Club
Last Breath

Morganville Vampires Omnibus:
Glass Houses, The Dead Girls' Dance, Midnight Alley

a&b

Cape Storm

WEATHER WARDEN
BOOK EIGHT

RACHEL CAINE

This edition first published in 2011 by
Allison & Busby Limited
13 Charlotte Mews
London W1T 4EJ
www.allisonandbusby.com

A CIP catalogue record for this book is available from
the British Library.

First published in the US in 2009.

10 9 8 7 6 5 4 3 2 1

ISBN 978-0-7490-0994-6

Typeset in 11.5/15.75 pt Sabon by
Allison & Busby Ltd.

The paper used for this Allison & Busby publication
has been produced from trees that have been legally sourced
from well-managed and credibly certified forests.

Printed and bound in the UK by
CPI Bookmarque, Croydon, CR0 4TD

To Ter Matthies.
For courage, for peace, for sailing on ahead.
We'll meet on the shore.

What Has Come Before

My name is Joanne Baldwin, and I used to control the weather as a Weather Warden. These days, I can also control the forces of the earth, like volcanoes and earthquakes, and the forces of fire.

Sounds like fun, eh? Not when it makes you a target for every psycho crazy world-killing danger that comes along.

Good thing I've got my friends at my back – Lewis Orwell, the most powerful Warden on the planet; Cherise, my best (and not supernatural) friend; and a wide cast of sometimes dangerous allies who've got their own missions and agendas that don't always match up with mine.

And I've got David, my true love. He's also a supernatural Djinn, the fairy-tale three-wishes kind, and he's now co-ruler of the Djinn on Earth.

What I *don't* have is peace, because even while I walked down the aisle to get married to my true love, an old enemy totally ruined my chances for a happy honeymoon and possibly even my survival. I'm not just in danger now, I'm dangerous – to everyone I love.

I've got to go and fix this, before the whole world suffers the consequences.

Chapter One

I've had many *oh crap* moments in my life. If you know me at all, you can imagine how many of them there have been, and the rising scale of crapitude that these moments cover.

So when I say that I looked out past the Miami Harbor horizon to the east and saw the storm that was heading for us, and said a heartfelt *oh crap*, you'll understand that my concern was not so much for the state of my already disheveled hairdo, or my not-so-designer clothes, but more about survival.

And not just *my* survival. An ominous line of storm-black out there was spreading like ink, and it was already large enough to rain destruction all over Miami before it ripped through Florida's panhandle and blew apart into tornadoes, floods, deadly downbursts.

Hurricanes: the gift that keeps on giving.

I tightened my grip around a handy light pole as the

wind buffeted me. Rain had already started to fall, and although it was nearly midday, it seemed very dark. I couldn't see any hint of sun overhead, not even a pale shadow through the clouds.

Chaos ruled the docks, as shipmasters rushed to secure their vessels against the unforecast storm. Tourists scrambled for shelter. Locals resignedly broke out the plywood and hammers. I'd heard that the major freeways were jammed and that the hurricane evacuation plan had been triggered, but it was never going to work. The thing was simply moving too fast, and there wasn't enough warning.

And needless to say, all this was my fault.

I mean that literally. I'm supposed to be able to control the weather, and other elements at work on this planet; I'm supposed to be able to stop things like this from happening. I'm supposed to be the hero, dammit.

It came as a bit of a shock to be both helpless and – although no one knew it yet – a villain. As the storm came roaring toward us, I knew it was my fault.

I could feel it in the burning of the black tattoo on my back, high up on the shoulder. Not the normal tramp stamp you could get (with hepatitis on the side) at any corner needle shop; mine was courtesy of an old enemy named, appropriately, Bad Bob. Bad Bob had once gotten the upper hand on me, and I was still vulnerable to him in magical ways.

Ways that I was having a very hard time controlling.

The sickening thing was that as I studied the approaching hurricane, and felt the black torch on my back burn brighter, some part of me *wanted* landfall. *Wanted* to feel that awesome power rip into the fragile human community, twisting glass and metal, ripping wood and flesh, reducing all of this to a sea of wreckage and devastation.

It terrified me.

Focus, I told myself, and concentrated hard on pushing back against those impulses. I knew where they were coming from. Bad Bob was using the tattoo – no, the *mark* – to remake me in his image.

I had been denying it for days now, but it wasn't a tattoo.

It was a Demon Mark, put there by the scariest Demon alive.

And I really didn't know how to stop it.

'Jo!' A male voice bellowed in my ear, and I clawed rain-soaked hair out of my eyes and turned to look. It was my fellow Warden Lewis Orwell – the boss, actually. The CEO of magically gifted humans.

Panic didn't look good on him.

'It's not working!' I yelled back. The wind whipped the words right out of my mouth. He nodded and wrestled a yellow storm slicker around my shoulders, holding me steady while I put it on. There. I shivered in sudden relief as the rain pummeled the plastic instead of my skin, but it was just animal reaction. There was no such thing as true relief right now. 'We have to get out of here, Lewis! *Now*! This thing is after us!' Me. It was after *me*.

A bolt of lightning the thickness of a skyscraper tore through the false night, arcing over the bowl of the sky. It shattered into a thousand stabbing branches. In the glow, Lewis looked worse than I'd expected – tired, of course, and unshaven, but also pallid. He'd pushed himself to the limit, and it hadn't worked.

If the most powerful Warden on the planet, connected to a network of hundreds of *other* powerful Wardens, couldn't make this thing turn its course, then we were in for one hell of a start to our day.

'Get on the ship,' he yelled over the wind. 'We need to get it out of the harbor, *now*!'

I looked past him to the massive floating castle of the *Grand Paradise*. 'I can't believe we're stealing something the size of the frigging *Queen Mary*!'

'It's stable!' he shouted back. 'I'd take a destroyer if I could get my hands on one, but this'll have to do. It's fully provisioned and ready to go. It's our only option right now, unless you want to try to take this thing here!'

Yeah, I had to admit, our options were fairly limited. Die on shore or make a run for it and hope the storm wheeled to follow, sparing the city.

Still. A cruise ship? Granted, Wardens generally don't travel cheap. That's practicality. When you have the power to control the elements of the planet – like living things, geologic forces, wind, and water – and when those elements get *pissed* about being bossed around, you'd better have some room to duck and cover. And where do you get lots of room when you travel?

First class, of course. It's not all about the free champagne. Although that's good, too.

Taking all that into consideration, commandeering the *Grand Paradise* was still over the top, even for us. The ship mostly cruised the Caribbean, but it was still enormous, and it had originally been built to give the big boys some transatlantic competition, so it was tough as hell. It was the size of a ten-story building, ridiculously set afloat. The cheery paint colors on the decks and hull made it seem even more surreal.

The problem was that up to about an hour ago, it had been boarding for its normal, tame cruise business. Granted, the storm had reversed that process, but even so, it took time to de-board three thousand passengers, not to mention the thousand or so crew members. Police were on-site, guiding the confused, angry, terrified tourists out of the boarding area and off to waiting buses to take them to shelter. It was chaos, complicated by pile-driving rain and wind, and I expected it only to get worse.

I'd been watching the steady stream of humanity with a kind of stunned, detached disbelief. As a Warden, I would never pack myself into a ship so full of people and go out to tempt fate – not recreationally, anyway. It's a fact of life: Wardens draw storms, and not just any storms. They might start out as forces of nature, but they develop their own personalities once they reach a certain level of power.

And they develop intelligence. The one thing that seems consistent about storms is that whatever their origin, they seem to really *hate* Weather Wardens.

Lucky us.

It seemed counterproductive to be boarding a ship under the present circumstances, but Lewis knew what he was doing. *He* thought that the storm was being drawn here by the high concentration of Wardens, and that was partly true, although I thought it was mostly drawn to me; it also was feeding off the natural energy created by our presence.

If we moved, it would likely follow. Bad for us, good for the millions of people in the Miami area who were looking at a worst-case-disaster scenario.

A year ago, we would never have dared try to snatch a ship like this in broad (if stormy) daylight, but times were changing. The Wardens had been around since the last spire of Atlantis slipped under the waves, but they'd existed in secret, a kind of paranormal FEMA that was noticed only when it failed. Governments rose and fell, but they all worked with us. They all funded us.

They really had no choice.

Now, though, it wasn't all hush-hush and top secret. We'd come out to the public. We'd had to; we'd pushed the secrecy as far as it could reasonably go, and in an age when every person had a cell phone and a video camera our days of operating in deep cover were long gone. We were tired of exerting energy to keep people quiet.

The new strategy – of which I'd been a part – was to just let the chips fall where they may. Less work on our part, which was good, because our ranks had been thinned recently.

The upside of coming out in public was that when we said we needed the *Grand Paradise to* save the city of Miami, the government really had to make it happen, no matter what the fallout might be later on. Even if a good percentage of the population of the world thought we were a bunch of hoodoo con artists out to defraud them.

So – there had been a whole lot of orders issued from the highest levels of government, and cash passed both under and over the table by the Wardens to make sure that everyone bought in. All that had taken time, and lawyers, and paperwork, and we'd burnt up our safety margin in trying to make this happen in an expeditious fashion that didn't involve just storming the ship and pirating it away.

Hence the black morning, and the looming disaster. Sometimes, piracy is the only really efficient way to go.

Lewis took my arm and steadied me against the wind as we staggered down the harbor's spacious walkway – now crowded with confusion – toward the gangway. It still burped out passengers, though in uneven groups now rather than as a steady flow. The Wardens were clustered and ready to board. Standing at the mouth of the flapping canvas of the covered gangway was my best friend, Cherise, decked out in the latest in bright yellow hurricane-wear. She had a cute little clipboard, and she was checking off Wardens as they moved past her, flashing smiles and thumbs-up signs.

There were a total of one hundred seventeen Wardens gathered in Miami today. Not all of them would be coming with us on the *Grand Paradise* – Lewis was way too strategic to put all his eggs in one fragile, ocean-going basket – but we'd have a bigger force with us than I'd ever seen gathered in one place. Which – when you're talking about a group of people who have the ability to control the basic elements around us – is scarily impressive. Each one of us was capable of wreaking incalculable destruction, although of course we were sworn to *try* to avoid that. Our job was to make things better for humanity, not worse. Despite the wildfires and earthquakes and hurricanes, without us the human race would have been scoured off the face of the earth a long, long time ago – all because a few thousand years ago, by our records, human beings did something that annoyed Mother Nature. Nobody remembers what.

We're still waiting for her to get over it.

With enough of us aboard the ship, we were a

huge, juicy target, but we could probably defuse most anything that came at us.

Probably.

I hate qualifiers.

Lewis was about to lead a whole team of Wardens (and supernatural Djinn) into the jaws of death. I was really hoping that this plan worked out better than most of my *other* life-and-death adventures.

That triggered a sudden burst of anxiety in me, not to mention a jolt of guilt. 'Have you seen David?' I asked Lewis, pulling him to a halt.

My lover, David – leader of at least half the Djinn, the way Lewis was the head of the Wardens – had gone away some time ago to attend to urgent business, which probably involved some supernatural being throwing a hissy fit over being pressed into helping humans. Most Djinn had the power of minor gods and the egos to match; you could think of them as bad-tempered angels, or ambivalent devils. They weren't one thing or the other. Even the best of them could swing wildly from one end of the spectrum to the other, depending on circumstances.

As he'd left, David had told me that meant he'd be back. No time frame. I felt his absence like grief, although according to my watch, he'd only been gone for a couple of hours.

The dark part of me, the part still giggling maniacally over the approaching destruction, was glad he was gone. David could help me control the black tattoo – and of course it didn't want that.

Lewis shook his head, spraying rain in a thick silver spiral. 'Haven't seen him!' he said. 'Jo, we can't wait. He can reach you wherever you are, you know that. Get on the damn ship!'

I looked past the flapping canvas toward the storm front again, where lightning was ripping the sky open with vicious glee. My enemy was out there beyond this storm, with at least one hostage, and a whole lot of raw power in a form that was both invisible and fatal to the Djinn.

Bad Bob had bragged that he could kill the planet if he wanted to.

I was afraid he was right.

I was afraid he'd already started.

This was *not* the way I'd planned to take a honeymoon cruise to Bermuda.

Just when I thought things couldn't get any worse, a white-uniformed ship's officer with rows of gold braid on his sleeves came pounding down the gangway, avoiding departing passengers and arriving Wardens, to skid to a halt in front of Lewis. 'Sir,' he said, and nodded uncertainly to me on the off chance that I was equally important. 'We have a problem.'

Lewis dragged me into the cover of the gangway and pushed back the hood of his slicker. 'Of course we do,' he said, resigned. 'What now?'

'I'm very sorry. We're doing the best we can, but several of the first-class passengers have been . . .

reluctant to leave their onboard possessions. Several of them have valuable items in the ship's safe, and the hold. They won't leave without them, and—'

'I don't give a goddamn about their stuff,' Lewis interrupted tightly. 'I've given you all morning to make this happen. Get them off the ship, right now, or they're sailing out with us and they can take their chances. Understand?'

The officer – I wasn't familiar enough with shipboard command structure to know what he was, but I guessed maybe Executive Officer – straightened his back to full Navy-style attention, clasped his hands behind his back, and gave Lewis a long, steady stare. 'Sir, I recognize that this is a matter of urgency, but we cannot permit you to endanger innocent passengers. They must be offloaded before we can put to sea.'

'If we're still in this harbor in thirty minutes, you'll be sailing this ship as a fucking submarine!' Lewis snapped. 'They're already endangered. They get off the boat and run for their lives, or they come with us and we do whatever we can to protect them. Those are their choices, but we can't wait for them to call their lawyers to decide.' He looked past the officer to Cherise. My best friend – endearingly human, not magically gifted at all – gave us both a little half wave and kept checking off names 'Cherise! How many are we missing?'

'We're halfway in!' she shouted back. 'Better tell the rest of your folks to get their beach thongs in gear!'

She sounded incredibly cheerful. 'Hey, I hope I get to be Cruise Director too, because this is going to be the best world-ending crisis *ever*!' Cherise was being only faintly ironic. That was the great thing about Cherise; she could find a silver lining in a coffin, six feet under, without a flashlight. She was possibly the only person I could count on who wasn't supernaturally gifted, unless good looks and a wicked sense of humor counted. Cherise was regular folks, and I loved that she could hold her own with the not-so-regular crowd I tended to attract.

Lewis skipped right over Cherise's attempt to lighten the mood. 'Dammit, what's the holdup?'

'You're kidding, right?' Cherise pulled back her rain slicker hat, and her blond hair tumbled out like a flood of sunshine. She looked a little damp, but otherwise perfect, from her beach-approved tan to the hint of dark pink lipstick still kissing her lips. 'Getting Wardens to do *anything* on cue is ridiculous. It's like trying to pull Shriners out of an open bar.'

Those who thought Cherise shallow – which, taking one quick glance at her perfect features, perfect hair, and dazzling smile, one might – were in for a major shock once they got past her defensive dumb-blonde routine. She was a ruthlessly competent person, and if *she* couldn't get the Wardens organized, then it couldn't be done by any non-magical means.

I knew what was going on with the Wardens, and why they weren't on board. We're an egotistical, self-involved bunch – which is, sadly, not our worst feature. Each of us tends to think he or she knows better, no matter what situation we land in. You can call it absolute power corrupting, et cetera, but I think it's more that we all have to make life-and-death decisions daily, and that tends to make you confident, bordering on delusional. That's fine if you're operating autonomously, but in groups it can get in the way. It takes a strong personality, and a stronger grip on your temper, to bend Wardens to your will even in such a simple matter as *please board the ship now or we are all going to die*.

Lewis had trusted them too much.

'Fuck,' Lewis said. He had a tendency to be very Zen, but his legendary calm was showing significant cracks. 'Jo, I need David back here. Can you find him?'

'I can try.' I was glad for the excuse, actually. I stepped back against the billowing canvas wall, feeling the thump of rain like tiny body blows, and concentrated on the magical link that led from me to David. Up on the aetheric plane, the level of reality above the physical, the link looked like a gleaming silver rope, and it felt warm to the touch. It couldn't be seen here in the real world, but using Oversight – focusing my awareness into the aetheric, without actually leaving my body to go there – I could access it just a little.

Time to go, I whispered down the line, a pulse of

power that he'd know came from me. *You're needed, mister.*

And the answer came spiraling back, a surge of meaning without the framework of actual words to define it. He was coming, but there was some kind of complication. What else was new? Seemed like neither of us could take a breath without causing, or suffering, some kind of complication.

When I focused on the outside world again, things had not gotten better. In fact, they'd taken a significant turn for the worse, because Lewis's body language had moved from frustrated to outright furious, and he was fixed on the ship's Executive Officer like a cruise missile. 'What?' he growled. 'What did you say?'

The officer cleared his throat. 'I said that we'll need to have your attorneys draw up another set of papers to indemnify the cruise line if you sail with any – and I must stress *any* – persons who have not signed the appropriate waivers to—'

Lewis had a wicked bad temper, which was something few people had ever had reason to know because he had such a long, patient fuse. Once it blew, though, it was catastrophic; I remembered that once upon a time, it had nearly killed someone. Granted, that someone hadn't been exactly innocent, but still – it had been like using a nuclear bomb to kill shower mold. Once you pull the pin from Mr Grenade, he is no longer your friend.

I stepped up. 'Lewis,' I said, and drew his focus.

Some of the rage calmed in his dark eyes, but it was more of a move from full boil to simmer; the heat was definitely on. 'David's coming, but it'll take some time. Why don't we go round up the stragglers? Cherise can work on evicting the first-class stowaways. She'd love that.'

Cherise gave me a grin that assured me she would, very much. Give the girl a clipboard, and she became an unstoppable force. 'Damn straight,' she said. 'You two crazy kids go have fun storming the castle. I'll go schmooze the stars. Damn, was I born for that or *what*?'

Lewis looked at her helplessly. He couldn't yell at Cherise, and he had no reason to yell at me. I motioned for the remaining target – Mr Executive Officer Stick-Up-His-Ass – to back off, but if he saw the signal, he completely ignored it.

'The shipmaster is completely responsible for every soul on board,' he continued, as if he wasn't facing imminent grievous bodily harm. 'I can't permit this kind of violation of procedures to—'

'Procedures.' Lewis's voice sounded almost calm, but I had a bad feeling. 'Right. According to the papers I signed earlier today, you now work for me, not the cruise line. Are you aware of that?'

From the shock that flickered across the XO's face, he clearly hadn't been. He buried that quickly, though. 'No, sir.'

'Let me make this absolutely . . . perfectly . . . clear.'

I thought at first that I was imagining things, but then I realized that Lewis's skin had taken on an unearthly hot glow. So had his eyes. He looked about five seconds from detonation. I'd never seen a human do that. I'd rarely even seen a Djinn do it. 'That storm out there doesn't care about laws, or rules, or procedures. It cares about ripping apart everything in its path. And it's coming for *us*. So Get On. The. Fucking. Team. *Now*.'

The XO took a step back. Lewis's furious glow got brighter, and I saw it reflected in the man's wide eyes.

Then he saluted, spun on his heel, and marched back up the gangway without another word.

'Dude,' Cherise said in a hushed voice. 'That was *hot*.'

'Down, girl,' I said.

'Hey, can I help it that I find radioactive guys sexy?'

We both gazed at Lewis, who despite not having shaved, showered, combed his hair, or changed his clothes in an appallingly long time was undeniably hot, in a lanky, outdoorsy, glowy kind of way. He gave us both an exasperated look and stalked off to organize the Wardens on his own. The glow stayed on him for several seconds as he went out into the lashing rain.

'I'm surprised you didn't jump all over that,' I said.

'*Moi*?' Cherise pressed a small, perfect hand against

her breast and did a silent-movie face of astonishment. 'I'd never.'

'Since when?'

'I've got a sense of self-preservation. OK, granted, it's still in the original shrink-wrap, but I've *got* one if I ever want to use it. Besides. Dude is scary serious right now.' Cherise waggled her clipboard. 'Want to go with me? Terrify some mundanes? C'mon, it'll be fun! And I might need you to, you know, throw a lightning bolt or something.'

Well, I wasn't doing anything useful standing here worrying. I *could* follow Lewis out into the storm, but that didn't really have much appeal, his tension level being where it was. He was more than capable of scaring the Warden stragglers into line all by himself. I would only be collateral damage.

Cherise shed her rain slicker, revealing a tight baby-doll T-shirt with, weirdly, a cartoon drawing of a toaster on it, complete with toast. The toaster had some kind of bar on the side with a red glow that looked like an eye.

'Let me guess,' I said, and struggled out of my slicker as well. '*Star Trek*?'

She rolled her eyes. 'Do you not *own* a television? No. Not any flavor of *Trek*, and oh my God, what are you wearing? Oh honey. No.'

'Shut up. It's borrowed.'

'From who, a homeless person?'

'No, from the Jean Paul Gaultier fall collection.'

She accepted that with a straight face. 'Oh, that explains it. Homeless color-blind skank is so hot right now.'

We were jabbering because we were afraid. Because the world was coming to an end, again, and sometimes whistling past the graveyard is literally the only thing that gets you safely through the experience.

And I'm just talking about Fashion Week.

I looked down at my outfit, though, and acknowledged that Cherise did have a point. The white miniskirt was too tight and too short, even by incredibly lax South Beach standards. The top would have been rejected by Frederick's of Hollywood as too trampy, and by Wal-Mart as too cheap. The shoes were plain battered deck shoes, which at least were a safe choice, if not styling.

'They have shops on board,' Cherise assured me, and patted me kindly on the back.

'Cherise, do you *really* think they'll be opening the mall when we're running for our lives?'

'Why not? People got to shop. It's like breathing.' It was to Cherise, anyway. 'OK, fine. I'll tell myself that it's a costume party and you came as a drowned rat.'

I smacked her. She pretended it hurt. 'Cher,' I said, and put an arm around her shoulders. 'I really love you, you know. I don't know what I'd be right now if I didn't have you around to keep me sane.'

We weren't in the serious-talk business, me and Cher, but it seemed like this might be a good moment to make an attempt. She could have laughed it off; I wouldn't have been upset if she did, because I just needed to say it.

Instead, she fixed those deep blue eyes on me and said, 'I don't know what I'd be without you, either. Probably nothing half as good as I am.' She smiled faintly, and for just a moment, the storm lessened. Her smile was just that powerful. 'Love you, too, you skanky, no-style tramp.'

I smacked her again. Moment over.

We went to try to solve the first-class problem.

Chapter Two

The very rich are like everyone else, provided you classify 'everyone else' as 'spoilt rotten brats with vast incomes and little sense of responsibility.' There are exceptions, of course, but money gets you excused from all kinds of social constraints, just as fame does, and that never does a body good.

We had a whole cadre of spoilt rotten brats holed up, refusing to leave their stash of gold bars, drugs, or folding money – whatever they had stored in the ship's hold and safe. I wondered how they'd feel using it as life preservers.

The harassed Chief Steward pointed me toward the first-class lounge area, where apparently a lot of our troublemakers had forsaken their magnificently opulent cabins and gathered to jointly declare their displeasure at being inconvenienced. You'd think that *anyone* could see it wasn't a good idea to be riding out a storm on a boat, but then again, people do dumb crap all the time, and they always seem astonished that it turns out to be dangerous. Seriously. Look at YouTube.

My first brush with the Richie Riches came in the form of a *very* famous singer, with aspirations of being an equally famous starlet. She was actually obeying orders, believe it or not, and she was on her way out, practically clawing the expensively paneled walls with frustration. She was surrounded by a milling entourage who scrambled to juggle her coffee, BlackBerry, bags, appointment diaries, and small yappy dogs. She was scowling as much as Botox would allow, and had her Swarovski crystal-encrusted cell phone at her ear.

'I'm telling you, it's *outrageous!*' she was saying. 'I want a lawsuit in place before I hit the limo, do you hear me? I want to *own* this stupid ship, and then I want to use it for target practice. Just do it, Steve. And make sure that wherever I'm going, it's five star. I am *not* going to some shelter with cots! – What? I don't care what category the storm is, you find me a suite! What do I pay you for, idiot?'

I suddenly had a great deal more sympathy for the business-suited corporate drones who had no choice but to smile and take it for the paycheck. Once the flood of minions was past, I approached an immaculately white-uniformed steward who stood helplessly at the entrance to the first-class lounge, looking in.

'Joanne Baldwin,' I said, and presented ID. 'I'll

be taking the room that Botox Diva just cleared.'

He looked at me wearily. 'Ma'am? Why that room in particular?'

'Because she probably left Godiva chocolates and chilled Dom Perignon, not to mention random stacks of cash in the couch cushions,' I said, straight-faced. 'I'll guard it with my life.'

That broke the ice a bit. He even managed to produce an anxious second cousin to a smile. 'You're one of them, right?' *Them* presumably being the Wardens. I nodded. 'I hear you guys have some kind of, uh, magic. Would you mind . . . ?'

'What, working some on these idiots? Not sure you really want me to do that. It tends to not be so great at crowd control, unless you're trying to kill people or put them in comas. Better let me try the persuasion route first.'

'Be my guest. I hope you brought horse tranquilizers.' He gave me a bow and handed me the room. Cherise and I exchanged glances and stepped inside.

We stepped in it, all right. The place was complete chaos, which was odd, because it really was a room with all kinds of calm built right in. The designers had envisioned the space as a Victorian-style reading room, complete with expensively bound leather volumes and comfy couches and chairs. Nobody was enjoying the decor now, though. Middle-aged society matrons rubbed shoulders, however unwillingly, with young, vapid starlets (I might have recognized one or two of those, but truthfully, they'd all been sculpted and styled into the same person, so it didn't much matter). A thick cluster of black-clad people who I assumed were New York literary types clumped together like a dour flock of crows toward the outer edge. West Coast bling glittered in a group on the opposite side of the room. It was like a map of the wealth of America, from coast to coast – all arguing at the same time.

Another steward, looking not-so-crisp, was trying his best to calm people. They were ignoring him and all yammering away at each other, waving tickets, papers, cell phones and BlackBerries. The din was all focused on one thing: *I'm going to sue. I'm not leaving without my (fill in the blank).*

I beckoned the steward over. He came, looking grateful that someone – even a potential troublemaker – was paying attention to him instead of shouting at full volume. I could understand why; this room full of people, at least fifty strong, had enough clout to bury the cruise line in legal red tape for years, if not generations. 'We need to move these idiots out,' I said. 'It's time to go.'

I saw him swallow whatever he was tempted to shoot back at me, and try again. 'Yes, miss, I'm trying,' he said, in that smoothly patient tone that only the very stressed develop after years of therapy. 'I explained that if they didn't disembark, we couldn't wait for them to do so, but—'

'They called your bluff.'

'Exactly.' He swallowed and tugged a little at the white collar of his formal jacket. 'I've tried to get the captain, but he's busy with preparations to cast off.'

A woman of indeterminate age – indeterminate because plastic surgery, heavy makeup, and a forty-hour-a-week workout schedule had effectively rendered her a wax figure of herself – grabbed the steward by the arm with expertly manicured, clawlike fingers. 'What are you going to do about this?' she demanded. 'I demand to speak to the captain! Immediately!'

'Ma'am, I'm sorry, but the captain is occupied,' the steward said, and patiently removed her grip from his uniform sleeve. 'You must depart the ship immediately, for your own safety.'

'Don't be ridiculous. This ship was advertised as being able to sail through a hurricane without a wineglass tipping. It's the safest place to be! I refuse to be turned out like some penniless hobo into a storm. My people say there are no hotels, and no flights out. There's nowhere to go. I'm staying.'

'That's not an option,' I said. 'If you get your people and head toward the exit, you might still make it off the ship. Go. Right now.'

She fixed me with an icy stare. 'And who are you?' Her glance traveled over me, dismissing every item of clothing on me with ruthless clarity, and then summing me up and dismissing me as a whole, all over again. 'Are you with the cruise line? Because if you are, I will

have a word with the captain about the dress code
for—'

'Shut up,' I said. She did, mainly because I don't
think anybody had told her that in her whole life.
'Pretend there's a bomb on board. Now. What should
you do?'

She blinked. 'Is there?'

I stared at her, unblinking.

She lifted one heavily ringed hand to cover her
pouty lips. 'Is it terrorists?' Terrorists, the new monster
under the bed. Well, whatever worked.

'I can't confirm that,' I said, in my best poker-faced
government-agent style. Hey, I learnt it from television.
'You should go immediately. But don't tell the others.
We don't want to cause a panic.'

That was an added kicker, because by being told
to keep it secret, she felt privileged, and of course
that convinced her. She gulped, grabbed her personal
assistant in red talons, and whispered something
urgent. Then they hustled off, presumably heading for
the docks.

'One down,' Cherise said. 'Terrorists, huh?'

'The FBI can Guantanamo me later,' I said. 'It does
the job. You take that side of the room, I'll take the
other.'

And so it went. About three repetitions later of the
terrorists-but-keep-it-quiet story, I ran into someone
who demanded to know if I had any idea who he
was. I tried to control my instinctive awe and assured

him I did – how could I not? He seemed to like that, and especially the whole *I'm only saving your ass because you're so special* undertone. When he strode off, trailing employees like a comet, I turned to see the steward watching me with a look that was half appalled, half amused. 'What? Who is he?' I asked.

'I believe he's in the film industry,' he said. 'You're scary.'

'You should see her when she's *really* bothered,' Cherise said as she passed us, heading for her next victim. 'But I hope you won't.'

I felt the change in the ship before I saw the expression shift in the steward's face from nervous to outright alarmed. There was a deep, throbbing sensation coming up through the decks, transmitting itself all the way through my body.

'We're moving,' I said. 'Holy crap. Lewis wasn't kidding around.'

'Guess not,' Cherise said. We'd cleared half the room, but there were at least thirty of the first-class passengers still staging a sit-in, and we were out of time. 'Maybe we can toad them into lifeboats or something.'

'Cher, do these guys look like they'd let us put them into lifeboats?'

'I didn't say they'd *agree*. We could, you know, knock them out or something.'

'So we've moving up from threats to assault.'

'Oh, come *on*. Not like you haven't assaulted

anybody recently.' And Cher punched me in the shoulder for emphasis.

'It wouldn't do any good,' the steward broke in. 'In these conditions, we don't dare launch any lifeboats, not even the new speedboat type that this ship carries. We have to have relatively calm seas or there's a significant risk of the lifeboats being compromised.'

Compromised was, I assumed, ship-speak for *sunk*. Which was kind of where we were, from the standpoint of achieving our goal.

I looked around the room again. Thirty-odd people, of which approximately a third were the rich sons of bitches who'd refused to leave, aggressively arrogant and sure that the universe cared too much about them to put them in real danger.

The others were their hapless hangers-on, employees, and family members.

I hated having innocents in the line of fire, but they'd made their choice, and now I had to make mine.

'Let them go back to their cabins,' I said to the steward. 'Confine them to quarters for now. If they want anything, deliver it. Don't let them go roaming around. Let them whine all they want, but do *not* let them intimidate you.'

'Yes, miss.' He was glad to have a clearly defined order, and he signaled to a couple of discreetly suited security men standing in the wings. They were both impressive specimens – large, muscular, with the kind of no-bullshit expressions that only men who do violence for a living could afford to wear. I figured the bulges in their coats had more to do with weaponry than with overindulging at the all-you-can-eat buffet.

The steward stationed outside was waiting for us when we emerged, and he handed me a key card and a fancy colored map with something circled on it. 'Your cabin, miss,' he said, straight-faced. 'It's the least we can do in exchange for your help.'

I remembered my earlier snarky request. 'It's not—'

'Oh, yes, it is. A special thank-you from the captain. And if you can't locate any stray Godiva chocolates or Dom Perignon, please let me know. I'll bring some to you straightaway.' I shook his hand, held up the map, and waggled both in front of Cherise. Her mouth dropped open. 'You *didn't*.'

'Botox Diva's cabin.' I checked the details. 'Two bedrooms. Want one?'

'Maybe. And maybe I want my own swanky digs – you ever think of that?'

The steward cleared his throat very respectfully. 'The captain's ordered us to close off all non-essential decks. We only have enough first-class cabins for about half of your party. The other half will get our best accommodations farther toward the stern.'

Cherise gave out a sigh. 'OK, fine. I'll suffer with your guest room. You'd better not snore.'

* * *

We were about halfway to the cabin, according to the map, when I felt a flutter at the edges of my awareness, like a psychic breeze. It felt cool as a mint balm to my irritated soul, and I sighed in sudden relief.

David was back.

I turned my head to see him striding down the broad hallway, heading our way. He glimmered like a hot penny, even under artificial light – silky auburn hair, worn long enough to curl at the ends, perfect bronze skin that would make a self-tanning addict weep in envy. Behind round John Lennon glasses, his eyes sparked brilliant orange, like miniature suns. His eyes were the only thing that gave him away right now as being more than human. He was dressed in well-worn, faded jeans, a white Miami-weight shirt that fluttered in the air-conditioned breeze, and a ball cap advertising a local crab shack. He'd forgone his long vintage military coat, mainly because I'd lectured him enough about the unlikelihood of anyone except terrorists and flashers wearing coats in the Miami heat. Although the idea of David as a flasher – a private-performance-only one, of course – still lingered in my mind.

His gaze was fixed on me, and he crossed the distance fast, although he didn't appear to be in a hurry. Even so, it still seemed to take forever before his hands touched me – a gentle stroke from my shoulders down my bare arms, to my wrists, then back up to cup my face. My whole body hummed and relaxed into the sensation. At close range, David's eyes were both less and more human – less human in color and more human in content. He was worried.

He had good reason to be.

'How are you holding up?' he asked me. His voice was low and intimate, like the warmth of his body near mine. 'Any pain?'

'Nope,' I said. 'Nothing I can't handle.'

His gaze held mine, searching. Waiting. I was dimly conscious of Cherise standing a few feet away, doing the awkward dance of exclusion from an intimate moment. With no key card of her own, she'd have to wait.

'I promise, if I feel anything change, you're the first to know,' I told him, and put my hands on him, because I couldn't *not* put my hands on him. I stepped forward and folded myself against his chest, and his arms closed over me, holding me close. I felt his lips brush my hair, a butterfly touch that made my heart skip.

'Let me check the mark,' he said. I shook my head. 'Jo. Let me see it.'

'It's fine.'

'Jo.'

I sighed and backed up a step, then turned so my back was facing him. His fingers touched my shoulder and moved down and in, pushing back the fabric and moving the strap of my bra aside to look at the *thing* on my shoulder blade.

It looked like a black torch tattoo. I knew that, because I'd spent enough time staring at it in pocket mirror reflections. It was the parting gift of my old boss, Bad Bob Biringanine – or what was left of him, anyway, He'd once been one of the most powerful Wardens in the world, but he'd gotten it illegally, the way some athletes abuse steroids. His particular poison was a Demon Mark – he'd volunteered himself as a host for a gestating Demon, and in return it had given him all the power he needed.

Until it was done with him, at least. I wasn't sure that what was currently walking around in his skin had much in common with the original Bad Bob.

Bad Bob had also given *me* a Demon Mark – unwillingly – and eventually I'd gotten rid of it. I never wanted to feel Bad Bob's sticky, foul fingers pulling my strings again; the very thought of it made my skin crawl and made me long for a shower and a steel scrub brush.

David's gentle touch slid over the black torch mark, and it was as if his fingers disappeared as they passed across the dead space of it. I couldn't feel the pressure at all. Then his touch was back, real and warm, on the other side of the numbed spot.

'It's still contained,' he said. His voice was very quiet, meant only for my ears. 'If you start to feel anything—'

I already had felt something – that sickening longing for destruction as I'd watched the storm. I knew it was bleed-over from the black tattoo . . . but I couldn't make myself tell him, either.

'Yeah, I know, yell for help.' I hated being helpless. *Hated* it. But somehow, Bad Bob had found a way to strip away ray defenses, and I couldn't fight this thing. Not on my own. David could help, at least for now. He wasn't making any guarantees long-term, though. We needed to get to Bad Bob and make the evil old son of a bitch take the thing off of me.

Or kill him. That'd work, too. I hoped. Though I had to admit, it hadn't worked too well the last time I'd thought I put him in the ground.

I tugged my bra strap back in place and turned to face my lover. No – *husband*. I had to get used to that. *Husband*. We'd had the wedding ceremony, kind of. It had been interrupted by various attacks, but I thought we were married, anyway. I just didn't *feel* married. 'So, you've been AWOL most of the morning.'

'Busy,' he said, which was uninformative, as explanations go. His shoulders lifted and fell, as if he knew what I was thinking. 'Djinn business.'

Which meant none of mine. 'So what's the plan? You guys coming with?'

'Some are,' David said. 'This is obviously our fight as well as yours. He has Rahel prisoner. Even Ashan agrees that we can't let this go without an answer.'

Just as David was in charge of the New Djinn, the ones who traced their origins to human ancestry, Ashan was the Mack Daddy of the Old Djinn . . . who liked to refer to themselves as the *True* Djinn. You see where this is going, because if half the Djinn are 'true,' then the other half must be, well, 'false.' It's the equivalent of racial prejudice, among supernatural beings.

Most Djinn I've ever met are about seventy percent arrogance, twenty-eight percent altruism, and two percent compassion. David blew the curve; he was the least arrogant Djinn I'd ever met, and he maxed out on compassion. That made him incredibly hot to me, but it also made him vulnerable. Ashan buried the needle on the other end; he didn't know the meaning of altruism, and he couldn't care less about compassion. All arrogance, all the time.

He and David got along about as well as you'd expect, when they were actually talking at all.

'And is the great Ashan going to grace us with his presence?' I asked. I wasn't exactly looking forward to it.

'He'll be around,' David answered, which was a typically Djinn sort of evasion. *Around* could mean anything, and nothing. 'He's sending a delegation of four of his own, though.'

'*Four*? He did get the memo, right? World ending, danger, et cetera?'

'Four of his most powerful,' David clarified. 'One of them is Venna.'

Oh. Well, that was all right, then; Venna, I trusted. For an Old Djinn, she was a-OK; she even displayed an interest in regular folks, in the way a kid develops a fascination with an ant farm. She didn't consider us *equals*, but she thought we were kind of cool in a science-lab sort of way.

She liked to walk around in the guise of a child, but in no way could you classify Venna as vulnerable. Terrifying, yes. Frail, no.

David looked over my shoulder, and I followed his gaze. There at the other end of the hallway stood Venna, with three other, much taller Djinn. The expressions on the faces of the other three Djinn, whom I didn't know, were identical: pricelessly annoyed. Not here by choice, I gathered. Their smelling-something-bad scowls could have shattered titanium.

Venna, however, waved cheerfully. She was dressed in child-sized pants and a cute little pink top with a sparkly rainbow. She'd largely given up her predilection for dressing as Alice from *Alice in Wonderland*, but she'd kept the long blond hair and innocent blue eyes.

I waved back. Venna said something to her fellow Old Djinn, and the four of them promptly vanished, misted away on the air like a mirage. Heading for their own quarters, I assumed, if they cared about such things.

'I've brought ten of the New Djinn,' David said. 'In case something happens, I've also left someone at Jonathan's house who can take over as Conduit, at least temporarily.'

David, in other words, had made arrangements in the event of his own death. Jonathan's house – Jonathan had been his friend, and the leader of the Djinn for thousands of years – existed in a kind of pocket universe, apart from both the human world and the other planes of reality where the Djinn could travel. It was the equivalent of a defensive bunker.

If David thought this was dire enough to name a successor and stash him away in the ultimate Undisclosed Location, then things were really not at all good.

'David—' I didn't know what I wanted to say, except that I wanted it to all be OK. For *once*.

His fingers squeezed mine, very lightly. 'I know,' he said. 'But we're in this together. For life. Whatever may happen.'

He meant it.

My husband.

I blinked back a sudden irrational flood of tears and hugged him, hard, until the impulse to weep passed. 'OK,' I said, and cleared my throat to bring my voice back to its normal steady range. 'Want to help us out with something really, really trivial?'

'Always.'

'In the first-class lounge, you'll find a couple of stewards, a couple of security guards, and a bunch of very rich jerks who don't want to take orders and are probably giving the staff a very hard time. It might speed things along if they had something more to be afraid of than their platinum card getting declined.'

'You want me to intimidate them?'

'You betcha, buster.'

David smiled, and this time his smile had a whole different cast to it. Dark, powerful, frightening – even to me. His skin darkened and took on a metallic sheen beneath its surface, and his eyes glowed like storm lanterns. He looked fey and dangerous and oh my God, *hot*.

'I thought you'd never ask,' he said. 'Point me.'

We left the harbor before the storm made landfall, which was lucky for nearly everyone except, obviously, us. The *Grand Paradise* was a pretty massive vessel, but she also had considerable speed at her command. Ships didn't use old-fashioned screws anymore, but propulsion pods, and she was a lot more maneuverable than I'd suspected; we moved quickly but smoothly through the long navigation channel and out toward the open sea.

It was a good thing the ship was fast. That was all that allowed us to exit the man-made cut in time; otherwise, we'd have been boxed in, trapped like a ship in a bottle. And the bottle would have been smashed to smithereens.

Leaving port didn't mean we were free, though. Not even close. The storm wheeled like a flock of crows and came roaring after us, brushing Miami with the hem of its black skirts and probably creating another aneurysm for insurance adjusters, although it was nowhere near the destruction that could have rained down on them. The *Grand Paradise's* engines growled and throbbed, louder than I imagined they normally would be for pleasure-cruise speeds, and we took on extra speed, crashing through the choppy seas as fast as the captain dared.

The storm gained on us.

I stood at one of the thick glass windows in the first-class lounge and watched the trouble unfolding. The storm's outer bands had spiraled over the city, but through the driving rain I could see the lights of the towers. Power was still on, and that meant things weren't so bad. Miami was tough. It would make it.

I wasn't so sure, now that we were sailing full speed ahead, that the same could be said of the *Grand Paradise*.

After a quick Weather Warden meeting, we agreed that we would attack the storm as one unit, but we'd wait until we'd lured it out well away from the mainland and any populous islands before we started screwing with it. Deeper, cooler waters would slow it down, too, which was to our benefit. The *Grand Paradise* was fast enough to keep ahead of the storm for a few hours at least, though the margin of safety would be steadily eroding. The winds inside the eyewall were ferocious.

Effectively, that meant I had an hour off, more or less, so I went to my cabin.

Considering that we were sailing off on a potentially lethal sort of mission, it was a bit surprising to find that I was enjoying the moment a little. I hadn't been on a sailing ship in a very long time, and this luxurious-cruise thing was something I hadn't even dreamt about. *Dream honeymoon*, part of me sighed. *Except for the imminent threat of total destruction*, another part warned.

Yeah, so, this is my life.

No sign of Cherise, but the downstairs shower was running. I hadn't brought any luggage, so my unpacking consisted of trudging upstairs to the second level, and slipping off my shoes. My feet sighed, and so did I. The carpet felt like clouds exported from heaven in the ultimate free-trade agreement. I tried out the bed, and it was definitely from God's own bedroom, from the body-contouring mattress to the silken sheets.

Then I sniffed myself. 'Ugh,' I said, and fought my way back upright. It wasn't right, subjecting this kind of luxury to the stench of my body. Besides, I'd been craving a shower for days now, and being caught in the cold, pounding rain hadn't exactly counted.

The small bath proved to have a very nice shower, complimentary robes and slippers, and a variety of expensive shampoos and soaps.

Score. I spent a blissful half hour naked and slippery beneath the massaging showerhead, washing away the sticky exhaustion. When my fingertips started wrinkling, I finally shut down the water – honestly, it was better than a ride at Disney – and belted the robe as I walked down the curving stairs to the first floor.

The room was smaller than I'd expected, but still larger than many hotel suites, and it had all the good stuff even the most discriminating guest would demand. Polished mahogany, fine carpets, luxurious furniture. Genuine artwork on the walls. I was taking a disbelieving inventory when Cher came out of her own bedroom, dressed in a matching robe, toweling her blond hair dry.

'Dude,' she said. This particular inflection of that many-shaded word meant *I'm completely impressed*. 'This is straight out of *Titanic*. I'm surprised they didn't pipe Celine Dion into the shower or something.'

'Great. Now I'll *never* get that song out of my head,' I said with a sigh. 'How's your room?'

'Fantastic. Wait, check that. Why'd I get the downstairs room? Because I'm the sidekick?'

'Because you're shorter. I didn't think your little legs could manage the stairs.'

She stuck her tongue out at me. Sometime in the past few weeks, while I hadn't been paying attention, she'd had it pierced. A tiny diamond stud winked impudently at me in the butter-soft room lighting. 'Are you and David going to be love bunnies and keep me up all night?'

'Maybe.'

'Oooh, promise? Because the porn's all pay-per-view.' She fluttered her eyelashes. Cher was silly and goofy and endearing, and her silliness had a point; she knew how serious all this was. How dangerous. She'd signed up to go with me, knowing there might not be any coming back from it, and she didn't even have any superpowers.

Just courage.

Impulsively, I hugged her. 'Thank you,' I said. She wiggled free and flipped her damp hair back.

'First grope is free, but after that, you pay to play,' she said. 'I'm going to jump on your bed, for payback.' Halfway up the stairs, she stopped and turned back to look at me. Her face was very serious. 'We're not going to die, you know. You can smile every once in a while.'

I wasn't so sure about that, but I tried.

The *Grand Paradise* was a floating city. I studied the complimentary colored map as I paced the semi-spacious confines of the suite, occasionally stopping to stare out the large, very thick windows. Cher was fixing her hair, which I knew would be an hour-long epic struggle. I was content to air-dry. All the product in the world wasn't going to make my upcoming day any prettier.

The rain had stopped. The room had a sliding door and a balcony, and when I stepped out on it, salty sea air closed in around me like a hand. I felt a little stupid standing in the open in my bathrobe, but at the same time, it was a damn nice robe, and who was there to gawk? Dolphins? Let them look.

I put my hands on the cool railing and let myself float up and out of my body, which remained motionless at the rail. I moved up into the aetheric, where the forces that work on the world can be more clearly seen.

The storm, from this view, was even more terrifying. Most storms glow in the darker spectrums of power, and the worst of them take on an almost photonegative sheen. This one was all that, and a hazmat bag of toxic purple. It was also hungry, and angry. The menace and fury of it stained the entire aetheric like lethal radiation.

Bad Bob wasn't running the storm. He didn't have to. These things were sort of like the weather equivalent of a cruise missile – point, shoot, walk away. Sooner or later, they'll catch up to the target. He'd given it a taste of Warden power, and it wanted more. We were the best chance for it to indulge its cravings, and it would keep on coming.

It had a particular taste for me.

I studied the inner mechanics of the storm as I hung silently in the drifting pastel clouds far above it. I could see the bright flashes of other Wardens coming and going from the aetheric, and subtle smears of movement that I knew were Djinn, who were much more difficult to see. Humans barely registered, except as muddy outlines. The ocean itself lit up on this plane like a spiral galaxy, thick with auras and lights. All that rich diversity of life in it, trailing beautiful colors, pasts, emotions. Down at the bottom, the seafloor glowed with ancient history, steeped in bands of color and power. Mesmerising.

I floated weightless on the aetheric.

I felt a violent shove from behind, and turned just in time to be battered again – a flat force, like a moving wall hitting me. I bounced off and floated back. I saw nothing, but I could feel . . . something. A ripple. A breath of warning . . .

I twisted aside, and the shearing force just clipped me this time. That was worse, because it wasn't distributed evenly over my aetheric form; it caught my ghostly leg instead, and a bolt of pain lanced through me, odd and blurry.

I shouldn't be able to feel physical pain on the aetheric. And nobody should be able to attack like this. I'd never seen anything like it before, and I'd been around the block. Hell, I'd gotten body-slammed by the unexpected so often they'd probably named a whole wing of the Warden hospital after me.

I backpedaled, fast, and then dropped the concentration that held me so far up in the aetheric. My body was like a massive anchor, heavy without the use of power to hold me away from it, and gravity kicked in hard. I snapped and fell across thousands of miles of open water and air, and as I was pulled back toward my physical form, I saw something peculiar happen in the clouds.

I saw them turn a particularly poisonous shade of green, with jagged black edges. It was eerie and beautiful and alien, the green of a toxic emerald, and I wondered what kind of power could do that to a natural force.

Nothing I could wield, or would want to face.

I slammed back into flesh, and my knees gave way. The deck of the balcony was hard, and it hurt to hit it even though I grabbed the railing for support. *That's going to leave a mark*, I thought, but I was used to that, at least. I was more focused on the green color of those clouds, and then, belatedly, on the lancing pain that ripped through my left leg, from heel up to hip. I rose and put my weight on it, thinking it was some kind of cramp; the entire limb spasmed, shook, and gave way as if my electrical system had just cut out like a bad engine.

I clung to the railing, waiting for something . . . It reminded me of the sensation you get when your leg goes to sleep, but I didn't feel any tingle or prickling of blood returning to feed the nerves.

It was just numb.

Come on, I thought, exasperated. The exasperation faded. The numbness didn't. I kept trying to put my weight on my leg, and it kept folding up on me like cheap paper.

OK, now I was scared. *What the hell*? I plunked myself down on the balcony deck, legs extended, and massaged the numb leg, starting at my thigh. It was eerie. My fingers touched flesh, but that was the only feedback there was. It could have been someone else's leg entirely.

And then, with a snap, everything came back online, as if the nerve channels had just been switched on again. No slow awakening, just a sudden shock of pain and heat that made me cry out, and then it was all just . . . normal.

I stood up, clinging to the railing, and tested the leg. It hurt, but it held.

I limped back into the living area and stretched out on the sofa, probing my leg for anything that seemed oddly shaped, broken, or otherwise bizarre. Except for the continued random firing of pain through my nerves, everything seemed intact.

It faded, after a few minutes. I stood and cautiously walked around the room, careful to stay within grabbing distance of major pieces of furniture. *Walk it off, Baldwin.* I'd had worse. Hell, I'd had worse just *yesterday.* But it bothered me, because it shouldn't have happened. Nothing was supposed to hurt me in aetheric form, certainly not echoed down into my flesh-and-blood form.

Unsettling. It just didn't feel right.

I didn't want to, but I knew I had to mention it to Lewis. Every odd thing that happened to me increased the chances that I would end up confined to quarters, or tranquilized in the brig, if this floating casino had one of those. But this didn't seem like something I should keep to myself.

I checked the clock. I was due at the Wardens meeting.

'Cher!' I yelled to her closed door. 'I'm out!' I don't think she heard over the aircraft-carrier roar of her blow-dryer.

I put on my sadly wrinkled, salt-stained, and badly-in-need-of-laundering clothes, grabbed the map, and went to wage war with evil.

Chapter Three

The map was confusing. That was all right; there were plenty of staff members around. Seems that the cruise line and the Wardens had thrown around a hell of a lot of talk about triple pay and hazard pay and bonuses, and as a result, the current passenger complement was outnumbered by its service staff by about two to one.

Which I've got to say would have been potentially amazing had I not regarded every single one of them as another weight of guilt on my conscience.

Three staff members and three sets of directions later, I arrived at the ship's movie theater. I was late, of course, but not very. The lights were up, revealing opulently layered velvet curtains in the traditional dark reds and purples on the walls, some lovely Art Deco sconces, and seats for a couple of hundred people and their snacks.

There were thirty-eight Weather Wardens on board, and as I swiftly counted heads, I realized that I was one of the last to arrive.

Lewis watched me move down the stairs toward the stage, and I knew he was noting the way I slightly favored my newly funky leg. 'Did someone forget to tell you to watch your step?' he asked in an undertone. Not that anyone was paying attention. The Wardens were talking among themselves, probably arguing the finer points of weather control.

'Funny,' I said. 'Am I on time for the matinee of *A Night to Remember*?'

He wasn't sidetracked. 'What happened?'

'I got smacked on the aetheric. Hard. And I couldn't see anybody doing it – not a trail, not a wave, nothing. No trace. And it hurt.'

That got his attention. 'Hurt?'

'Like, *ow*, *crap*, *damn*. And when I came back down, my leg went out on me, like a power failure. It came back, but not right away.'

'Hmmmm.' Without the slightest self-consciousness, Lewis got down on one knee and put his large hands around my thigh. The conversations out in the auditorium came to a stammering halt, and I felt every pair of eyes in the place turn to focus on us.

I jumped a little, and there might have been a gasp involved, but he wasn't interested in naughty groping at the moment. I felt his power slowly filter into me, rich and warm as sunlight. It followed the nerves in a slow glide down my leg, into my foot, and out.

You could have heard a pin drop in the place.

Lewis finally sat back. 'I'm not finding anything except some strains in your muscles. Normal stuff.' He realized that everyone was staring and, for a moment, looked completely vapor-locked about it.

I cleared my throat. 'Thanks for the laying on of hands. You might want to stop now, being that it looks a little odd.'

'Oh.' He let go and rose to his full, lanky height. 'Sorry. Didn't mean to—'

'I know.' The other Wardens were *still* watching us, but after a moment they started whispering together again. Yeah, I could bet what they were whispering. 'Just be glad that David—'

'That David didn't see you?' That was David, of course, arriving in a white whisper of fog that poured itself into his human form in less than an eyeblink. He sounded amused. 'David did.'

'I'll take it as written that you said to keep my grubby hands off your woman,' Lewis said. David raised an eyebrow. '*Grubby* not strong enough?'

'Before you say that in the future, most Djinn find the concept of owning someone else slightly offensive,' David said, and I could almost feel Lewis's wince. 'Jo's her own woman. If she felt uncomfortable, she'd tell you.'

'Yeah, she always has.'

'Uh, guys?' I waved my hands. 'Thanks for the

macho plumage display, very attractive, but are we done? Time's a-wasting.'

David smiled. He wasn't competing with Lewis; he hadn't for some time. He was possessive, on levels that he would never let anyone but me see, but he was done with jealousy. We were bonded, in his eyes, for eternity, or as long as my human body lasted. He had absolutely no reason to worry. 'I came to tell you that the Djinn have completed preparations. We can begin anytime you're ready.'

'Let's not delay,' Lewis said, and stepped up to the edge of the theater's proscenium. 'Everybody focus. We've got work to do.'

There weren't five people in the world who could get thirty-odd Wardens to shut up and listen without arguing, but Lewis was one of them. I wasn't, so I shut up and paid attention, too. He'd taken his hour of downtime to shower, shave, and change clothes, and although he still looked exhausted, I wouldn't have bet against him in a fight.

Which was good, because we were about to step into the ring for the fight of our lives.

'David,' Lewis said, 'I need the Djinn to form a perimeter around the storm. Keep it from moving toward us. Try to hold it in place while we cut its generators.' By that, I understood that he was going to do the logical thing and try to affect not the storm but the underlying forces that fed its fury. There were relatively simple ways to do it, but out on the open ocean, they also required massive amounts of power. The less energy we spent chasing the damn thing around, the better.

David nodded. 'It'll stay as still as we can manage.'

That wouldn't be easy, but he had at least fourteen Djinn at his command – ten of his own, four of Ashan's. I didn't think there were many things that a couple of Djinn couldn't do, so fourteen seemed a pretty comfortable safety margin.

Still. I was getting a clammy line of sweat forming along my spine. *Bad Bob knows us. He knows how we think. He's one of us.*

I wished I hadn't thought of that.

Lewis paced, because that was what Lewis did when he was under stress. He prowled the stage, talking without focusing directly on anyone, even me. 'Four teams,' he said. 'Jo, you're heading the team that will focus on a rapid cooling of the water temperature directly beneath the storm and out to a margin of about half a mile beyond. We're shooting for a minimum drop of at least ten degrees.'

Someone in the audience whistled, and it was all I could do not to echo it. Ten degrees on the open ocean? Holy crap, that was hard. The amount of force it took to effect even one degree of change in that vast amount of water was astonishing.

'Ten degrees,' I said, and managed to keep the incredulity out of my voice. 'All right.'

'Pick your team.'

David watched me as I looked out over the audience and called names. I knew most of them, and more important, I knew their capabilities. I wanted raw power, and for this, at least, I wasn't overly concerned about fine control. There wasn't a single person out there I'd name my bosom friend, but they were all solid talents. Good enough.

Predictably enough, though, someone raised a hand. It was Henry Jellico, whom I *hadn't* picked. Henry was one of the worst know-it-alls that I'd ever met, despite being an overall nice enough guy. He'd studied hard, and dammit, he wanted every single person to know it. 'Excuse me, Lewis, but wouldn't it be wise to also match the cooling of the water with lowering the temperature of the exhaust process? Try matching it to the temperature of the eye to expand it outward?'

Lewis stopped pacing, but he didn't face Jellico. 'I believe I said four teams,' he said. 'Henry, you're in charge of team two. Exhaust process matched to the core temperature of the eye. Once you've got those equations balanced, try taking the whole thing down another five degrees.'

'*Five*?'

'Please.'

Henry Jellico wasn't in for any picnic, either. Lewis waited as Henry picked his ten Wardens, and then chose Amanda Chavez to head up the third team, which was smaller and focused on lowering wind speed. The fourth team batted clean-up, remaining in reserve and watching for any imminent threats, and it was headed up by Lewis himself.

I sat down on the edge of the stage, my legs dangling over the lip, and lowered my head in concentration. Out in the audience, all the Wardens did the same. We looked like we were engaged in prayer; in a sense, that was what we were doing, only on a slightly more active scale.

'Anybody got an eyewall wind speed on this beast?' someone asked.

'Approaching two hundred fifty miles per hour,' Lewis said. We had a moment of contemplation on that one. The storm was seriously powerful. The highest speed the Wardens had ever measured in an eyewall was two hundred fifty-five, give or take a bit. There was no such thing as a Category 6 storm, but if there was, this might have been the template. 'One last thing. There's been a report that our enemies might have the ability to strike us while we're on the aetheric, maybe even causing physical side effects. Watch yourselves, and my team will deal with any attacks that come at you.' That raised a few heads. 'Let's get it done. The faster we're in and out, the safer we are.'

I rose up into the aetheric, and the entire roomful of Wardens rose up with me. They were an army of glittering, powerful forms, shifting from the limitations of the physical to the more metaphorical shapes we registered on higher planes. I never knew what I looked like – none of us did – but I watched Henry Jellico morph from a mild little man into a bulky, muscular warrior who'd have been at home in *World of Warcraft* swinging a barbarian axe. Some Wardens didn't even keep human shapes; Greta Van Der Waal became a shining white dog that bounded and leapt through the clouds. We all had our fantasies, our true natures, and we couldn't really control how others saw us.

Lewis looked like himself. Always. He had a powerful aura, but the essence of him never changed, and that was both impressive and a bit on the scary side.

Speech wasn't possible on the aetheric – after all, no lips, tongues, teeth, or lungs – but the Wardens had developed their own methods of communication, mostly hand signals. I grabbed my team members' attention and arrowed up, fast and high, getting above the towering storm. It was like taking a glass elevator past a vertical oil spill. Nasty, and shiver-inducing. We went up almost ten miles into the atmosphere and leveled out at the top, where the storm formed a smooth dome. This was where the intake/exhaust process went on, dragging in warm air, cycling it down through the eye, breathing it out.

It was a living thing, after all, however strange it might be to our senses and logic.

The aura colors of the storm hadn't changed significantly from my first impressions – dark, shot through with photonegative spots and shapes, with livid purple around the edges. I didn't see any sign of that poisonous, otherworldly green that I'd glimpsed, though.

Good.

I felt a shudder running through the aetheric – a thicker atmosphere than the regular physical world, almost like matter caught in a phase transition from gas to liquid. Few things in the real world could stay at that balance point, but I'd always thought the aetheric was nothing *but* that – a place where everything, always, was transitional.

The shudder that ran through the aetheric came from the Djinn grabbing the storm and pulling it to a violent halt.

It fought them almost instantly, twisting, slashing back with waves of power. This was the dangerous part; if the forces got too far out of balance, things would happen that none of us could anticipate or control. We were dealing with the power of several nuclear bombs. Not the sort of thing where you want to apologize for a mistake to whatever survivors are left wandering around.

I signaled my team, and we took the express elevator back down, plunging through the storm and into the thick black water beneath it. The area directly beneath it was devoid of life; the residents of the sea that normally thronged the area had prudently departed. Good. I didn't want to be responsible for any massive fish kills, anyway.

My team – good people all – spread themselves out

in an approximate rough circle near the edges of the storm's fury, and each of us concentrated on a pie-shaped wedge of the water – not that water was static, of course, which was what made this so difficult. Water, like air, was always in motion. Unlike air, it had real density, and it took a lot more effort to really make a change in it on the molecular level.

Ten degrees. Thanks for nothing, Lewis.

I'd pushed my section down a solid eight degrees, but I could sense that there were massive imbalances emerging from the change. Some of the others were having trouble managing the temperature shift at all. Nobody had hit the ten-degree mark. To make matters worse, power was collecting in odd places, like pockets of gas in a mine. That was the risk of working with multiple Wardens.

I think I sensed trouble coming – an oddly thick ripple in the aetheric, maybe – and then I saw one of my Wardens spin helplessly out of position, losing control of her weather working. She vanished into the heart of the storm, and I felt her screaming.

Then I felt her stop.

Something was attacking us.

The fragile balances that the Wardens had built – layers of control, of forces, of risk – began to shatter like a glass tower in an earthquake. I desperately struggled to hold on to what we'd achieved. More Wardens were being attacked around me by invisible forces – battered the same way I had been earlier, but with far deadlier results. I could sense terrible things happening, but I had to hold on. *Hold on*. The strain increased. I was strong, but this was too much for any one Warden to hold on to . . . and then the storm ripped free of the Djinn holding it and began to move.

No way I could stay with it as it roared closer, heading for the *Grand Paradise*.

Something grabbed me as I faltered, but instead of bracing me, it dragged me backward, away from the fight. Up. Out.

I was just far enough away to survive what happened next.

The storm pulsed and shifted into that poisonous green color, shot through with drifting flecks of red and jagged cutting edges of black.

The power that the Wardens had been manipulating *exploded* in a brilliant burst of light, and I felt it rip through me, flaying apart my aetheric body. I re-formed, slowly and painfully, and fell with unbalanced speed back into my own body.

I jerked, gasped, and almost fell off the edge of the stage. David had me by the arms, and he dragged me backward into his embrace. He was seated on the stage, and I fell weakly against his chest. I felt broken inside, shredded, unable to think or feel.

My eyes focused slowly, and my hearing told me that people were shouting. Screaming.

Earth Wardens were arriving in the theater, summoned by emergency signal, and they were dragging limp Weather Wardens out of their seats and laying them flat for treatment. Lewis was already down there, holding Henry Jellico in his arms, pressing his palm to Henry's pale, high forehead. Henry was completely still. Lewis was gasping, shuddering, barely holding himself together.

'What happened?' I whispered. David's arms tightened around me.

'Don't try to move,' he said. 'You can't help them.'

'But—' I tried to get my body under control, but it was like swimming through syrup. Slow and cold and clumsy. 'They're—'

'Dying,' David said. His voice was low and hushed, and very gentle. 'Most of them are dying, and there's nothing you can do to help that now.'

'No!' This time I put real effort into the struggle. It didn't matter. It wasn't David's strength holding me back – it was my own weakness. I collapsed against him again, sweating and shaking, and watched as my fellow Wardens slipped away into the dark.

I'd been right. Bad Bob knew us.

In one stroke, he'd chopped down a significant number of the Wardens who could have posed a threat to him.

And I had no idea how he'd done it.

In the end, more than half of the Weather Wardens couldn't be saved. They'd been the closest to that blast of power, or they'd been drawn into the storm's hungry maw. Their aetheric forms had been completely destroyed, and there was no soul to come back into the bodies they'd left behind. Without that, the body stuttered and died, and there was nothing any Earth Warden, however powerful, could do to stop it.

That didn't mean Lewis didn't try with every last ounce of courage he had left before he collapsed and had to be carried away.

It was a dark, silent place after that.

I sat there numbed, watching as the dead were lined up on the stage. Most of my water team had caught the blast, or been spun into the center of the storm by invisible attacks. Henry's team, which had been mirrored above, had been a little luckier, but not that much.

It was a devastating blow.

'Sons of bitches were waiting for us,' I whispered. I didn't feel as shaky now, but I was still cold and weak. Someone had done me the kindness of wrapping me tightly in a thick thermal blanket, and my body heat was slowly coming back.

Cherise was holding my hand. I don't know who'd called her, but she'd appeared before David had let go of me, and I hadn't been left without human contact since. I wondered if they were afraid I would just dissolve without it, like those poor bastards we'd just led to their deaths.

David had gone to see to Lewis, though I doubted

that there was much that could be done for him, either. He was strong. He would survive.

It was our mutual curse, seemed like. Being strong.

'Somebody pulled me out,' I said. 'Was it David?'

Cherise's thumb rubbed lightly over my knuckles, and she squeezed my fingers. 'I don't know. He's not so sharey right now.' Even Cher's usual defiant good cheer was gone, replaced by a sobriety that was new to me. 'You just sit and rest.'

'The storm—'

'It's moved off to the west,' she said, which surprised me. 'At least, that's what the bridge crew told me.'

'You were on the bridge?'

She raised an eyebrow, and an echo of the old Cherise came bouncing back. 'Honey, there are men in uniform on the bridge.' She let it fade again. 'It looks like we're in the clear. For a while, anyway. Let yourself recover a little.'

I nodded, still feeling numb, and for no apparent reason, burst into tears. Cherise rubbed my back and murmured things that I didn't hear, a comforting sound like rain on the window. I wasn't the only person having a breakdown. At least three of the other Wardens had already been removed from the room, unable to stop crying and shaking.

'You should go lie down,' Cherise said. 'Nothing you can do here, babe.'

She was right, but with Lewis flat on his back, the Wardens needed a leader, and by default I was it.

I wiped my eyes, took a deep breath, and shook my head. I unwrapped the blanket and stood up.

Cherise took my arm, balancing me on my feet before stepping away and letting me go it on my own.

I found a knot of uniformed crew members outside in the theater lobby, whispering together. They fell silent when they spotted me – fear, or respect, I couldn't tell and didn't care. I suspected my blue eyes held something terrible, because none of them would look at me directly.

'What can we do, miss?'

'Body bags,' I said. 'I assume you have some on board. I'll also need some medical assistance, as we have some very traumatized people. Bring tranquilizers.'

They all exchanged startled glances. One of the female stewards nodded and stepped away to a phone. The response time for the medical staff was impressive, but then again, it wasn't like they had lots to occupy them right now. I followed the gurneys, doctors, and nurses into the theater, and went to consult with the next most senior Warden in the room.

That was a Fire Warden named Brett Jones. Brett was a big man, solid; I'd heard he played professional football, once upon a time, but he'd taken retirement before it had left him too busted up. He nodded when I approached him. The Fire Warden contingent of our little war party had been kept out of danger so far, but I could see that the losses had affected him just as deeply as they had me.

'What went wrong, Jo?' he asked. He sat me down next to him, angling to face me as much as a man that big could in theater chairs. 'Nobody can give me a decent explanation of what went on up there.'

'I'm not sure I can, either,' I said. 'There's something on the aetheric. I can't see it, but I can feel it, and it can hurt us. That's how it started. Then the storm itself – it was like it converted our power into something else. It changed, Brett. I've never seen anything like it.'

'I have,' said a childlike third voice, and we both looked up to see the Djinn Venna leaning over a seat in the next row, staring at us with unearthly calm blue eyes. 'Do you want to know what it is?'

We exchanged looks. 'Uh, if you don't mind?' Brett said. He knew what Venna was, and he was nervous. So was I, but for different reasons. Venna's small, pointed face screwed up into a frown. 'If I minded, why would I have offered?'

'Forget it, Ven. Tell us.'

The frown smoothed out into a bland mask. 'You shouldn't order me, you know.'

I felt a savage bite of anger. 'It's been a bad day. And I'm not too concerned about your fragile Djinn feelings right now. You'll live.'

From the disbelieving stare Brett was giving me, I could tell he couldn't quite grasp that I was sassing a supernatural time bomb of power this way, but I really didn't care. Venna wasn't going to hurt us, and I didn't want to play ego games.

She let it pass. 'A long time ago, there was a thing that happened. It doesn't matter what it was, but it left a kind of scar between the highest plane of our existence and another place. A bad place.'

'The place where Demons dwell,' I said. 'Right?'

'Oh no,' she replied.' Much worse than that. The Demons love aetheric energy, but really all they want is to eat their fill and go back where they belong. No, this is a place the Demons fear. We don't know what lives there, but it came through, once.'

'Came through,' Brett repeated. 'What happened when it did?'

'The universe died,' Venna said. 'I told you it was a long time ago.'

I stared at her, speechless. So did Brett. So did everyone else within earshot of this bizarre conversation.

She tilted her small head sideways. 'What?'

'Um – even you can't be that old, Venna.'

'I'm not. I read about it.'

'Where? At the Djinn Bookmobile?'

'Of course not.' She kicked her feet, just like a regular kid at the movies. 'In the stars. In the dirt. In the water. It's all around us. You can't see it?' She answered her own question with a shake of her head. 'Of course you can't. Even most of the Djinn can't see back that far. What we are wasn't always *this*, you know. Everything in the universe recycles. Universes expand, contract, explode again. But this wasn't from our universe. It was bad.'

'I'm – not sure how this is going to help us,' Brett said.

I was. 'You're saying that what's on the aetheric, what took over the storm, it's what came through last time?'

'No. I'm saying that it *started* this way, before. With the storm, and the power, and the ghosts.'

'Ghosts.' It was my turn to repeat her words. 'On the aetheric.'

'You can't see them, can you?'

'What kind of ghosts?'

'I can't see them either,' Venna said, 'but they're angry. They don't like Wardens.'

'Do they like the Djinn?'

'They don't notice us, really. At least, not so far.'

This was interesting, but it wasn't getting us where I needed to be. 'Venna, I need a way to stop this. Is Bad Bob behind it?'

'He was,' she said, and her eyes went unfocused and distant. 'He opened the door, but he's not interested in what's coming through. Chaos is what he wants. It's what he's getting.' She snapped back to focus with such suddenness that I flinched. 'You can stop it, but not if he keeps the gate open. You need to stop *him*, and then you can worry about the rest.'

'What about the storm?'

'You can't hurt it. You can only survive it.'

Kind of like this day. 'Venna,' I said, and looked right into her eyes. Not a comfortable experience, really. 'Can you kill Bad Bob for me?'

She considered the question for a long, silent moment. 'No,' she said. 'I could hurt him, but he could hurt me just as much. His power cancels mine in many ways, and I think he might just be worse than I am.'

'You mean he could kill you.'

'No, he probably couldn't. But I wouldn't like what was left of me, in the end, if I won.' She said it without much emphasis – just a calm assessment of her chances, nothing to be afraid of. 'It's better if you do it, anyway. Humans. You don't have the same vulnerabilities that we do.'

It was *very* odd to hear a Djinn talk about human strengths instead of considering us slightly less useful than a soiled tissue.

Of course, she ruined it by adding, 'And you're much more easily replaced.'

Lovely. 'Does *he* have any vulnerabilities?'

'Of course. He can still die,' she said. 'He can still feel pain. Part of him is still human. A small part, but it remains, and it feels things the way humans do. The way you do.'

I felt the ship's speed lurch, accelerating. Some of the ship's staff looked startled.

That wasn't standard procedure, obviously.

'I sped us up,' Venna said. 'We were moving too slowly. I don't want the storm catching us again. It would be inconvenient.'

Maybe, but now I could feel the thudding impacts of waves through the ship, and the very slight rolling had increased to a definite wallow. A ship this large dampened the usual motion of the sea, but in waves this high, at unnatural speed, we were going to be in for a rough ride.

I glanced at Brett, who was already looking distinctly uncomfortable. 'Better get the ship's stores to break out the giant economy-size Dramamine.'

He nodded. 'Anything else?'

'Yeah. Bad Bob was a Weather Warden, when he still had just his regular set of powers. Fire may be our best bet to overcome him – it's his biggest weakness. You get your guys ready. I want original ideas, something he can't anticipate or plan for.' I chewed my lip for a second. 'And whatever your plans are – don't tell me about them. I'd rather you keep it in your team.'

Whatever he thought of that, Brett nodded and left me. I sat, watching the dead Wardens being loaded into body bags, then trundled away on gurneys.

I looked at the faces of the survivors. Almost all the Wardens had gathered now, except those with specific duties related to the voyage or standing lookout up on the aetheric, and they all had a similar expression.

They were measuring themselves against the body bags.

I stood up and walked to the stage. I didn't go up, just stood in front of where the medical team was working. Venna turned in her seat to watch me, and all the Wardens did as well.

'OK,' I said, 'I'm not going to lie to you. We knew this trip would be tough, and today we got clear evidence of that. We made a mistake, and it cost lives, but those lives were not wasted. It's the duty of Wardens to give their lives in the protection of others. It's part of the oath we all took when we signed on to this job.' I paused and made sure that sank in. 'Now we know things we didn't know before, and couldn't know without triggering that trap. It sucks, yes, but our enemies aren't playing around. They want us dead, every single one of us. Every Warden and every Djinn. Once we're gone, there's nothing standing between them and the defenseless human beings of Earth. Once humans are gone, they'll strip this planet clean of every single thing with a connection to the aetheric – every animal, plant, insect, and bacterium. They'll devour all the aetheric energy they can get, and then they'll leave. It's what they do.'

The only sound in the theater was that of body bags being quietly zipped behind me.

'The Wardens were formed to save people,' I said. 'For thousands of years, we've tried our best to do that. Sometimes we've been better at it than others. Sometimes we've outright sucked, like lately. But we *can* save people. We *have to*. We're Wardens, and we cannot give up. Ever. Agreed?'

A few of them murmured or nodded. Wintry, unwilling agreement, but at least it was a start. 'So what now?' asked one of the Earth Wardens, holding the hand of a still-trembling and shell-shocked Weather Warden survivor.

'Now we get ready to kill us a Demon,' I said. 'And if you've got any good ideas, start talking.'

Sometime later – hours later, in fact – I realized that I was hungry, and so tired I was likely to doze off even if Bad Bob himself showed up and asked me to tango. Food wasn't an issue; the ship's staff brought us buffets, mountains of sandwiches and chips and drinks, entrees steaming in silver trays, sliced cheeses and elaborate desserts. I guessed we were getting first-class treatment. It tasted good, although I didn't linger after I got a turkey sandwich into my system.

I grabbed a ship's map and tried to find my way back to my cabin. The effort was marginally successful. Hallways were clearly labeled, but faded into one another with dizzying regularity. Add in the other decks, and I could see that I'd be getting lost for some time to come. That was something I really couldn't afford. You never know when you might need to get somewhere in a real hurry.

Following my map led me down a maze of corridors,

mostly deserted . . . whole decks were empty and lifeless now. Somehow, my exhausted brain betrayed me during some turning, and I found myself in an area that didn't match up to my less-than-expert map reading.

A housekeeper was just coming out of one of the cabins, and I tapped her on the shoulder. She turned, smiling. She was a cinnamon-skinned young woman with black hair pulled back in a sleek, lacquered bun, and warm chocolate eyes. Not very tall, but graceful. I could see her as a dancer, somehow, moonlighting as a maid.

'Miss?' she asked. 'Can I be of assistance?' She spoke excellent English, though I could tell it wasn't her mother tongue.

I held out my hand. 'My name is Joanne Baldwin. I'm one of your – ah – special guests. You're on staff, right?'

She looked at my outstretched hand, at my face, and slowly took my fingers to shake. 'Hello, Miss Baldwin. But I'm not staff. I'm crew.'

'There's a difference? Call me Joanne.'

'We're not allowed to use the first names of guests, miss,' she said. 'Yes, staff would be the people who work in guest relations areas. I'm a cabin stewardess. We're crew, not staff.' She read the expression on my face, and smiled. 'Ships are very tightly regimented, miss. We all know our duties and where we fit.'

'Trust me, the rules are going to be shredded on this trip. So I'm Joanne, and you are . . . ?'

'Aldonza Araujo,' she said, and her handshake grew a little more firm. We were about the same age, I thought. 'Aldonza, miss.'

I gave up temporarily on forcing informality on her. 'I'm looking for my cabin. I know I'm close, but—'

She got my cabin number and showed me the route by tracing a French-manicured fingernail on the map. I'd mirror-imaged my route, and I'd somehow ended up on the opposite side of where I should have been. Port, not starboard, in nautical terms. 'I'm afraid you'll have to go around this way,' she said.

I frowned down at the map. 'What about this way?' It was marked in featureless gray.

'Those are service areas, miss. You can't go that way.'

'I'm pretty sure that for us there is no such thing as off-limits. We're not regular guests. You know what I mean?'

She did, but her smile instantly froze solid. 'I – I am sorry, but I can't – we're not allowed—'

'Aldonza.' I interrupted her gently enough, but firmly, and took her hand in both of mine. 'You signed the waivers, right? The Wardens explained to you what kind of risk was involved in staying on this ship?'

She nodded mutely. I could sense that she wanted to pull away from me, but also that her curiosity was burning a hole in her head. Instead of asking, she just waited.

'The fact is, we're not going to be regular passengers,'

I said. 'Think of us as policemen, or military personnel. We don't need coddling, but we do need to know everything about this ship we can, from the technical stuff to the most insignificant details. It could mean the difference between life and death for everybody on board if things get worse.'

I watched that sink in, but Aldonza still shook her head in refusal. 'I can't let you in, not without someone telling me I can. It's strictly against regulations.'

'OK, you can tell me how to get there, and if I happen to stumble accidentally into the crew areas, then it's not your fault, right?' She hesitated. 'Please, Aldonza. It could be important. I promise, I'll talk to Security and to the Chief Engineer too, but in my experience, the bosses don't know everything. They *think* they know everything. You are the guys who really understand the ship.'

She actually laughed, covering her mouth with her hand, as if too loud a sound was definitely Not Done in the posh areas, at least not when wearing a uniform. 'That's true,' she agreed, but she sobered from her brief burst of laughter far too quickly. 'It's not possible for you to go through the crew area without being seen and stopped. The ship has lots of surveillance. Cameras everywhere. We all know each other. We have to, living in such close quarters. If they don't know you and you're in off-limits areas, they'll call security and escort you out.' She was shaking her head again, clearly talking herself out of even trying it.

'We have very good security people. It's not worth the risk. Talk to the captain or the Executive Officer.'

I tried to imagine any of the security people being prepared to deal with even a middle-grade Warden, much less somebody like me or Lewis or the Djinn. I failed. 'OK,' I said, because Aldonza clearly was feeling more and more uncomfortable. 'I suppose it's a bad idea anyway. I'll take the long way around. – But, just for future reference, what do the crew-area doors look like?'

Aldonza blinked. 'I thought you knew.'

Huh? My confusion must have registered, because she looked behind me at a simple door with a swipe card lock labeled PRIVATE.

'Oh,' I said. 'Right. Thanks.'

She clearly thought I was crazy, and she wasn't about to get fired over it. From the glances she threw back at me as she moved down the hallway, she was trying to make sure I wouldn't do anything wrong – at least not before she was safely away from the scene of the crime.

Couldn't really blame her.

I pretended to read my map, waiting until she'd had plenty of escape time. I marked the location of the crew door on it and noted the locations of the surveillance cameras, too.

I *could* pop the door right open, with a relatively minor pulse of power. I *could* fritz out the cameras, too.

But the truth was, I could do that anytime I needed to, and right now it wasn't my first choice. I just wanted to reach my soft, expensively appointed bed.

I looked up at the surveillance eyes focused on where I stood, sighed, and took the long way around.

I *still* got lost. This huge floating palace was like some creepily deserted amusement park – all the lights were on, but there seemed to be a faintly sinister edge to everything. It was made to be inhabited, to be full of life and fun and conversation, and instead there was just fear. The few people I spotted were staff (crew?) going about their business.

I somehow ended up on the Grand Promenade, or at least that was what I read on the map. It was the big railed expanse looking out over the ocean. Overhead, the sky was nail gray, and the water looked just as hard and unfriendly, with sharp-edged waves. The *Grand Paradise* was big and heavy enough to cleave its way through like a knife, even at the labored speed we were moving.

The promenade was deserted, too. I stood in the clammy wind for a while, watching the endless rolling of the waves, and then I yawned and felt my eyelids growing even heavier.

So tired.

At least, I was tired until I felt a hot, seductive tingle on my back, just over the shoulder blade. That jerked me back to full alert like a jab from a cattle prod.

I didn't make any more stops on my way.

Safely in the bedroom – no sign of Cherise downstairs – I sat down, closed my eyes, and focused on David. I can't really describe the connection between the two of us; the ceremony and the vows – even though our wedding had been interrupted by Bad Bob's attack, and technically not really finished – had pulled us together, bound us in ways that even now I couldn't understand, except that it made it easier to call him when I needed him.

When I opened my eyes, David was forming out of the air in a swirl of gray and gold. There was something blank in his eyes this time, as if I'd taken him away from something both terrible and important. He'd been with Lewis. I wondered how bad it was.

Then he took a deep breath and willed it away, whatever it was.

'The mark is burning,' I said, without any preamble at all. He took on human form and flesh and sat down next to me. He felt warm as summer, and he smelt faintly of spices and real, human sweat, deliciously male. His fingers unbuttoned my cotton camisole and pushed it down my arms, and then he unhooked my bra and slid it off. There was no seduction in it, or at least not as much as I'd have liked; he was very focused on the job at hand.

When his fingertips pressed on the black torch mark on my back, we both gasped. He spread his whole left hand over it, and the heat spread, increased to an agonising burn that felt as if it should come with the sound of sizzling. His right arm went around me, holding me up, keeping me from fighting him to get away from the pain.

With shocking suddenness, the fire turned to ice, a chill that ripped all the way through me, and I shuddered. When I exhaled, my breath frosted the air in delicate feathers that vanished in seconds.

I couldn't feel the mark on my back anymore, and that was a huge relief. But, as David trailed his fingers over it, I realized that I could feel less of the area around it, too. The numb spot was growing.

I turned to look at him, and caught the unguarded pain in his face before he could hide it from me. He was tired, and he was anguished. Worse, he was despairing.

'Stop that,' I said. 'What's happening?'

'It's getting larger,' he said. 'I had to expand the containment to keep it within the boundaries. You can't push yourself this hard.'

'I know that, and yet I'm not seeing I have much of a choice. How's Lewis?'

He didn't want to tell me, but I think he knew I wasn't about to let him slip away without an explanation. 'Fighting his guilt,' David finally said. 'He blames himself for the deaths. He feels he made a tactical error.'

That wasn't unexpected. 'He made the right choices at the time. We had to give it a try.'

'I know. He's afraid that he rushed into it. He's afraid that he allowed personal issues to color the decision.'

'That'll be the day,' I said, and then wondered what that meant. 'Personal, how?' Please, let it not be about me.

'Rahel,' David said softly. 'He can feel her suffering, just as I can. Bad Bob is making sure we can feel it.'

Bad Bob had a Djinn named Rahel in his clutches – one of David's New Djinn, and someone I could almost call a friend. He could do whatever he wanted to her – the curse of a Djinn being bound to a bottle, of having her will taken away. And she couldn't fight back. The nightmare dimensions of that stretched on and on into the darkness, because I knew how sick Bad Bob's imagination had been even years back. God only knew how much worse he was these days, with so much Demon in his body that I wasn't even sure the old Bad Bob was still around in any form I would recognize.

Rahel had done me some very kind favors in the past. She was never to be trifled with, or underestimated, but unlike a lot of the Djinn, she did care, however remotely, about the fate of individual humans – and the fate of the human race.

David, as her connection to the power source of Mother Earth, would feel every injury done to her. I wasn't sure, but I thought that her connection to Lewis was more about personal feelings than old-fashioned lines of fealty. She liked him. He liked her. Maybe it went deeper than that. He'd never felt the need to tell me, and I didn't ask. I had thought their relationship was more of a hookup than love, but I could have been wrong.

I put my hand on David's cheek and looked him full in the face for a long, long moment. 'How bad is it with her?' I asked him. I didn't want a kind evasion. I didn't want anything but the truth, the whole truth, nothing but the truth, and he could sense that from me. 'Is he going to destroy her?'

'Eventually,' he said, and gently took my wrist. 'There's nothing more I can do for Rahel just now. She would want me to focus on those I can help.'

'You've done all you can for me, too.'

'Yes,' he said, and I could see he hated to admit that. 'I'm slowing it down, but that's all I can do. It's deep, and it's still growing. But I intend to keep trying. I'm not giving up, not on either of you.'

He wasn't saying anything we didn't both know, but I could hear the frustration in his voice, and the anguish. I slipped my arms around his neck and the two of us cuddled close for a moment. His lips found mine, long and lingering.

'You're tired,' he murmured. Like the gentleman he was at heart, David slipped the bra back up my arms, turned me around, and fastened it for me. He even buttoned up my camisole. 'I want you to rest.'

I was more used to him undressing me. This

felt . . . warm. Intimate in a way that seemed more personal than unbridled passion. It was the kind of thing a husband did for a wife – an everyday kind of gentleness.

It made me crave him so badly.

'David?' My voice came out very small. 'I can't sleep. Will you stay with me? Just for now?'

His arms wrapped around me and his head rested on my shoulder. I felt a shudder go through him, some emotion I couldn't name. When he looked up, the intensity of it was enough to shatter my heart.

'I'll stay,' he said, and eased me down onto the bed. 'I'll stay as long as you're awake.'

'Big promises, Mister Big Shot,' I said. 'What if a cat gets stuck up a tree in Peoria? I bet you'd go running off to the rescue.'

'You know how seriously I take a vow. Unless I made one to the cat, you're my priority.' He tapped me gently on the nose, and there was humor in his face now. 'Clothes off or on?'

'Oh God, off. Off off off.'

We were naked before our backs hit the mattress, thanks to David's wondrous Djinn fabric-vanishing powers. The duvet settled over us like snowfall, but it was warm beneath it, so warm, and when his lips touched mine it was a dreamlike kiss, damp and gentle and sweet. I rested my head on the pillow of his arm and moved in closer, drawn without a word being spoken. His fingers brushed hair from my face and feathered it back, then lingered on my cheek, drawing heat down to my chin.

'Please,' I whispered. 'Please make all this go away. Just for a while. Can you do that?'

'I'm only a Djinn,' he said. 'Not God Himself. But I'll do what I can.'

His lips brushed their heat down, taking all the time in the world, pausing in unexpected and vulnerable places. The inner aspect of my forearms. My wrists. The delicate skin just beneath my breasts. He began to suck, drawing my blood to the skin with slow deliberation. He left a map of visible kisses down my body, a slow and thorough awakening of my entire body that made me writhe silently, sheets fisted in my hands.

Oh, I forgot. I forgot *everything*.

Gradually, his mouth became demanding. Challenging. Nips of his teeth, strokes of his tongue. My control slipped, and I made a tortured sound in the back of my throat, rising up to meet him. I didn't want seduction right now. I wanted to be ravished, and he could feel it echoing out of me like a ringing bell.

I could tell the exact second that his control slipped gears. His body language shifted, tensed, and he raised his head and looked at me. My already quickened pulse jumped, because the look in those Djinn-bronze eyes was feral. *Wanting*. I sat up and met him halfway through the space and devoured his mouth, hungry and desperate, full of feverish need and frantic energy. It fed back through the link between us, striking like lightning through a grounded circuit, shorting out whatever defenses we'd kept built between us.

When I pulled back, David's eyes were no longer bronze. They were fire, with pupils of absolute darkness. *Mine*, I thought incoherently. *Mine*. I didn't know if that came from me or from him. It had the force of a Djinn emotion, something vastly more complex than simple human possessiveness.

David growled and put a hand on my chest and pushed me all the way back full length on the bed. He followed, not quite putting his weight on me. Brushes of his hot skin teased and tortured us both. He ran his palm lightly over the rising tilt of my left nipple and flicked his tongue over the right, and the difference in sensations made me gasp. His hand was light, delicate, and burning hot; his mouth was heavy, demanding, and deliriously wet. I bit my lip and felt my whole body shudder in response. I heard an answering sound from David – need, lust, love, wordless reassurance.

We were both on the knife-edge of control. David had never fully let his Djinn instincts out to play before, not like this. I think he'd been too afraid – afraid of hurting me, afraid that I'd be shocked by the depths of his needs and desires.

I knew better. I put my hands around his face and held him still for a moment, staring deep into those inhuman eyes.

And then I nodded. No words, and none necessary.

His skin took on a dusting of gold, and then darker shades, until he seemed more metal than flesh – but it was flesh to the touch, warm and soft and firm. He tasted like exotic spices – cardamom, saffron, wild honey from the rocks. Everything about him was different, and yet everything was exactly the same.

His hand slipped lower down my body, into the slick folds between my thighs. The sensation was overwhelming – burning and cooling at the same time. His thumb pressed and stroked while his long, lovely fingers slipped within. His mouth closed over mine, cinnamon-hot, and I sucked his tongue and tasted fire.

Ecstasy to the power of infinity.

The old, wild magic spiraled up inside of me, exultant, slow pulses that built on each other. *Yes, God, yes* . . . When I came I did it silently, rigidly, holding the awesome force of it inside and giving it to David through the link between us.

It drove him beyond human disguises, and light exploded in the room. I heard him gasping, struggling to stay with me in flesh, because flesh was what we both needed just now.

He solidified again into skin, hot and firm against me. I rolled over and up to my hands and knees, and felt the fiery stroke of his hands over my back, down my hips, between my thighs . . .

I gasped and dropped my head to the pillow as the relentless pleasure of him filled me. Nothing mattered in that moment – only the need, the all-encompassing need to *feel*. Every thrust traveled through my body in shattering waves, as intense as any sensation I'd ever known. I heard David whispering in that liquid, sibilant language that I knew must have been his native tongue, the language of fire, of Djinn. I didn't know the words, but I heard the music – dark, delicious, and utterly abandoned.

He knew just the right spot to hit to shatter me completely. I screamed as another orgasm flooded me like boiling light. It spilt into him, triggering a matching explosion that rocked us both to the core.

The room was full of light.

I caught my breath to hold on to the pure, silvery perfection of that moment, riding the waves, feeling them slowly and gently diminish.

We hadn't said a word, not in English. David still didn't. He continued to move inside me – slow, gentle strokes – and kissed the small of my back. It was the gentlest gesture after such an aggressive, passionate coupling, and it promised me, without the luxury of words, that whatever boundaries we found ourselves crossing, he would always lead me back.

David eased down next to me on the bed, flushed and glowing and triumphant. Human, and not.

So much power and control, made vulnerable through me.

I felt a tingle of heat in my back. *No. Not now.* It faded, more like a warning than an attack.

I curled into David's body and recovered my breath. Despite everything the past few hours flooded back, bringing guilt and regret. *What right do I have to be happy?* I had none. Maybe I never would. *That wasn't safe.* I couldn't surrender control like that, not with Bad Bob's mark on my back. What if he'd taken advantage of that moment to strike? What if he'd taken control?

'Jo.' David's voice was rough, not quite steady. When I looked up into his eyes, I recognized the expression. 'I see I can't make the world stop for long. And you think too much.'

'I was just thinking what a terrible risk that was,' I said. 'Because—'

'Because of the mark.'

I nodded. He lifted himself up on one elbow and looked down at me, golden skin still shimmering in the light, flushed in all the right places.

'I know,' he said, and trailed his fingertips over the line of my collarbone. 'But you're my wife, and no matter what the risks might be, that matters more to me.'

'I love you,' I whispered. 'But you need to be careful. Especially with me.'

His smile was warm enough to light every candle in the world. 'I was, at first. But I fell in love with you instead. Now there is no safety from you.'

I burrowed close to him, and his arms wrapped around me, and for the moment it was all quiet. All peace.

'For as long as we live,' he said, and kissed the top of my head. 'Which means forever, if I have any say in it.'

Chapter Four

It wasn't heaven, but it was damn close. For the next couple of hours I slept, curled in David's protective arms, feeling safe for the first time I could remember. The motion of the ship was rhythmic and soothing, and for a little while the world did go away, after all.

I could almost – *almost* – believe it was a honeymoon cruise.

Right up until Cherise threw open the bedroom door and stood there, panting, staring at us with eyes that didn't really see us at all.

'You'd better get out here,' she said, as David sat up. I did too, swiping hair back from my face and grabbing at the thousand-thread-count sheets as they threatened to slide away. Cherise, shockingly, didn't seem to notice any of that – not even David's exposed chest, which frankly should have at least gotten a double take, or a stare, or a patented Cherise come-on.

She just delivered her message and dashed away.

'That's not like her,' David said, swinging his legs out of bed. 'Is it?'

'Nope. Clothes?'

'Closet.' He was already heading there. He pulled open the door and inside was a rainbow of choices, some for him, some for me. 'Underwear?' I asked.

He raised eyebrows. 'Is it absolutely necessary?'

'Right now? Yes.'

'Top drawer.' He nodded toward a delicate-looking dresser, something that would have made *Antiques Roadshow* stars buzz with excitement. In it, I found new bras, panties, stockings – pretty much anything I might need, or crave. Or David might crave. I picked out something plain and put it on. As I turned, David threw me a shirt and pants. Jeans, and a navy blue shirt that clung in all the right places.

He was dressing too, the old-fashioned way. As a Djinn, he could have easily just gone the magic route, but I stole a few precious seconds enjoying the sight of him wiggling into Joe Boxers, which might have been intended, from the smile he gave me.

Even with mutual appreciation, it took us only about a minute to dress, and then we headed down the stairs.

Cherise was there. So was Lewis. He was self-contained again, only the shadow of trauma left in his dark eyes.

'I need you,' he said bluntly. He turned and walked out of the cabin, moving fast. David and I exchanged a look and followed.

There was a dead body in the hallway. I stopped when I saw her, shock slamming through me. She looked like she'd been turned to crumbling clay, or ash – lifeless, a mockery of something that had once been real and vital.

'God,' I whispered, and slowly crouched without touching the corpse. Lewis knelt on the other side of it. 'Who—?'

'That's the problem,' Lewis said, 'I don't know. I think she's one of the Djinn.'

I looked up at David, who was staring down at the two of us with a frown. He focused on the body on the floor.

'That isn't a Djinn,' he said. 'I don't know what that is.'

He realized, then, what he was saying. Djinn couldn't *not* know, in the normal course of events; they could spool back the history of things. They saw *time* – it was a real sense to them, the way touch and taste were to humans.

The only way he couldn't know who this person was, was if this was a Djinn and the Djinn had been murdered by Unmaking, the special new weapon of Bad Bob Biringanine.

Antimatter. It was deadly to the Djinn in all kinds of hideous ways.

The next thought came to me with sickening speed and impact. *He had access to the ship.*

I snapped a lightning-fast glance at Lewis, and saw that this was not news to him. He'd already come to the same conclusion, presumably well before he'd come to summon us. David's reaction was just his confirmation. 'Fuck,' I said. 'He's been here, on board, or at least he's gotten one of his minions through our defenses. We should have known. Our early warning system—'

'Clearly isn't working,' Lewis finished. 'Which means he, or any of his people, could be here. This place is big enough to hide an army if they didn't want to be found.'

'But if hiding was the point, why leave this poor lady right here in the open?' I asked. 'They could have hidden her anywhere. Her Conduit wouldn't even know she was missing.' Which was the awful part of it. David, as Conduit for the Djinn, had a personal connection to each and every one he was responsible for. Ashan had the same connection to his half of their numbers. Bad Bob's weapon of choice did worse than kill; it erased. The Djinn couldn't recognize their own dead, or the weapons that killed them. The moment the victim died, it ceased to have ever been.

My nightmare was that it might be David lying here, with another Djinn staring at him in that same annoyed confusion, not even remembering his existence.

There was something so chilling in it that I had a hard time wrapping my head around it.

'That's not a Djinn,' David murmured. He wasn't trying to convince us, only himself. '*It can't be*.' We'd been through this. He understood, intellectually, what was happening, but this was a kind of phobia for the Djinn – a blind spot that left them vulnerable, one that couldn't be overcome by knowledge or experience. It wasn't seated in the rational parts of their brains.

'Count your people,' Lewis said. He said it quietly, a little regretfully, as if he didn't really want to know, either. David continued to stare at the corpse.

'Counting myself,' he said, 'fifteen Djinn are on this vessel.' In other words – exactly the number we'd started with.

I exchanged a baffled stare with Lewis. 'You're sure?'

'Of course I'm sure. Ten of my people, myself, and four of Ashan's. Fifteen.'

'Then where did this one come from?'

He couldn't answer that. It was like his brain locked up and refused to produce an answer. Instead, he shook his head, stubbornly unable to get past the paradox.

'Maybe Ashan sent another Djinn,' I said. 'A new one.'

'You're sure this isn't one of his four?' Lewis asked.

'I'm sure.' I'd seen the four of them, and Venna

had been the only one representing herself as female. While the Djinn *could* change sexes, in my experience they rarely did it without a damn good reason. 'This is insane. Can you get Ashan on the line and ask him?'

David's attention went elsewhere, but only for a moment, and then he shook his head in the negative. 'Venna's coming,' he said. Before he finished the sentence, I caught sight of Venna's sparkly pink shirt at the end of the hall: She didn't seem to be in a hurry, but in the next breath she was there, standing at David's side.

'What's this?' she asked, staring down at the dead Djinn with academic interest. It was creepy.

'We were hoping you could tell us,' Lewis said. 'Anything?'

She studied the body intently, then shook her head. 'No. I don't know what it is.'

I cleared my throat. 'Radiation?'

'Nothing dangerous left on the body,' Lewis said. 'It looks as if she died the same way the other Djinn did, from antimatter poisoning – but there's no residual energy. She's just – dust.'

There wasn't any way to resolve this, not through the Djinn, in any case. 'Thanks,' I said to Venna. 'Don't worry about it.'

She didn't give it a second thought. She skipped off down the corridor as if stepping around dead, dust-and-ash bodies was an everyday occurrence.

'I'll be back,' David said abruptly, and misted out before Lewis or I could protest. He was deeply bothered; I could see that, but there was no way I could help him. He'd have to come to terms with this, or not, in his own time.

'So what do we do?' Cherise asked. I'd almost forgotten about her. She was standing a few feet away, arms wrapped around her chest as if she was fighting off a chill. 'We can't just leave the poor thing out here. God. I can't believe this is happening. This is just awful.'

Lewis and I looked at each other, and I knew he was thinking the same thing I was: the way the body had disintegrated into dust and ash, I wasn't sure moving her was much of an option.

But it seemed like the only decent thing to do was to try.

'We'll save a sample,' Lewis said. 'Maybe we'll find some kind of clue if we analyze it in detail. But Cherise is right – we can't leave her here. And there doesn't seem much reason to store the body.'

No, because we both knew the body was going to disintegrate as soon as we started trying to move it.

We retrieved a shower curtain and repurposed it as a body bag. There was something very disturbing about having pieces of the dead Djinn break off and float away as we went about it, but we managed to get her scraped onto the makeshift bier and carried her away. Cherise didn't follow. She stood there, staring at the flecks and smears that littered the carpet. It looked like a spilt ashtray.

'Nobody even knows her name,' she said. 'That is just so – sad.'

Burial at sea was the best we could give our nameless victim. As Lewis and I tipped the crumbling remains over the railing, I felt we ought to say something, anything, but nothing came to my mind.

It did to Lewis's, though. 'You may be forgotten,' he said, 'but you won't go unavenged. I promise you that. We'll find out what happened to you.'

Her corpse disintegrated almost instantly in the pounding waves, returning to the embrace of nature. I hoped that the vast intelligence that made up this world remembered her, named her, gathered her close.

I hoped that her life had mattered to some human, somewhere, who still had fond thoughts of her.

White spray was soaking my thin shirt and leaving my skin cold and stiff. Lewis's warm hand touched my back. 'Inside,' he said. 'There's nothing we can do here.'

'I'm tired of hearing that,' I said. 'I'm really tired of being helpless. Aren't you?'

Turning, I caught the flash of outright rage in his eyes. 'Yes,' he said. 'And we're not going to be helpless much longer, I promise you that. Come on.'

He stalked away from the rail.

I followed.

* * *

'Where are we going?' I called, as Lewis's long legs pulled him several steps ahead of me. The hallways were narrow, even in these upper-class areas, but they were nicely appointed, with paneling and original artworks, some of them by artists I recognized. He wasn't giving me time to sightsee. I hustled past the art so fast that it could have been clown paintings, for all I knew.

He didn't answer.

When our little mini-parade came to the less exclusive areas, the design standards changed. Still nice but less art, more lithographs. Cheaper carpeting, and the wood was trim, not wall. I glimpsed a sign that said we were heading for the Main Gallery, whatever that was.

'Lewis, dammit, slow down!' I wasn't slow, but he was acting like this was an Olympic event. 'Where are we going?'

We turned a corner and stepped out into upper middle-class opulence. Maybe even nouveau riche opulence. There was a waterfall in the middle of the open space that spilt a graceful, sinuous wave over curved rock three stories tall, with lush tropical vegetation carefully complementing the lines of the design. Five levels of decks, all with railings circling this part of the ship. As I looked over, I saw that two of the dining areas were below, at the foot of the waterfall – one casual, one formal. All eerily vacant at the moment, except for some staff – I guessed they were staff – taking advantage of the slow moments to grab themselves lunch and drinks. A few Wardens were wandering around in groups of two or three, rubbernecking while they had the luxury of not being marked for death.

Somewhere in the back of my mind, Celine Dion was singing again, dammit. Well, one thing was certain, my heart would *not* go on, not if this voyage went badly, and I wished she'd just shut the hell up.

Lewis turned, leaning on the rail, with the waterfall as a backdrop. Its hissing rain formed white noise around us.

'I wanted to go someplace we could talk uninterrupted,' he said. 'And someplace it would be harder to overhear.'

'You think someone's watching us?'

'I don't think we can assume that our enemies are on the beach perfecting their tans.' He shook his head and leant against the railing, weight on his elbows. Mist from the impossible waterfall behind him made pearly rainbows around the lights. 'I'm sorry. I didn't want to do this. I'm really tried.' He sounded genuinely dispirited and angry about it, whatever it was.

'What are you talking about?'

'We're fighting shadows,' he said. 'We're guessing and flying blind. I didn't want to have to use the resources I knew we had.'

'What kind of resources?'

He didn't answer me, not directly. 'I've been thinking about Paul.'

The name hit me hard, in unguarded places. Paul had been my friend, my mentor in many ways, and somebody I'd thought I could always count on in a pinch.

But he had betrayed us, and I'd killed him for it. I hadn't meant to do it – it had been in the heat of battle, and my real enemy had used him as a human shield. I didn't know when Paul had chosen the wrong side, or how, or why; all I knew was that at that last, desperate minute, he'd been standing next to Bad Bob, and that had destroyed him.

I'd destroyed him.

'I'm wondering,' Lewis said, 'if Paul was really planning to funnel information back to us. He could have betrayed Kevin and Rahel anytime he wanted. He didn't. I think he was trying to do the right thing. Maybe he was still on our side after all.'

Did he think that made it any better for me, carrying around the memory of his death? 'I hope so,' I said. I really did. I'd much rather Paul died a hero.

'And now,' Lewis said, 'I'm wondering the same things about you. Whether you're really on our side . . . or not.'

I took a deep breath. It'd be too easy to turn this into a blame-fest, and the last thing we needed right now was to gouge pieces out of each other over nothing. Lewis was so exhausted I suspected he'd welcome a fight, just to keep his pulse moving, but I'd hurt enough people recently.

'You don't think I'm loyal?' For answer, Lewis reached over and put his hand on my numbed shoulder. I shook him off with a little too much anger. 'Screw you, Lewis. I'd *die* for these people. Hell, I *have* died for them!'

He held up a hand to stop me. 'No offense, but in a certain sense, if I tell you what I'm thinking or doing, I may be whispering it in Bad Bob's ear. You know that, don't you? Can you guarantee me it isn't true, or it won't be tomorrow?'

That was a cold, hard slap of reality, and I smarted from the impact. He was right, of course – the black torch on my back might be controllable for the moment, and I might be convinced that I was my own person, beyond Bad Bob's reach for now, but I couldn't really *know*. I also couldn't guarantee that it would stay that way five minutes from now, much less tomorrow.

'So now I'm the enemy,' I said, and tried to keep my tone as dry as a good martini. 'Fine. You know a good Demon tattoo-removal guy? And can we work in a day spa visit, while we're at it?'

He didn't laugh, and he didn't take the opportunity to lighten up. 'I wanted to tell you that if I think you're slipping away, I won't hesitate. I'll kill you. I'll have to. Understand?'

I did. There was no room for misunderstanding in

this. We both knew the stakes, and we both knew the consequences.

'Yeah, I understand,' I said. 'You're sure you can take me if you have to?'

'I can,' he said. 'And I will.'

I took a deep breath. 'OK.'

'The problem is, it would probably kill us both in the end, and we both know that's not a good outcome.'

'I promise not to fight back.'

'You can't promise. That's the problem, isn't it?'

'So what are you asking me, Lewis?'

'I want to put in a fail-safe. I need your cooperation.'

Fail-safe.

This was something I'd heard about, rarely. It was generally used on Wardens who'd demonstrated behavioral problems – those who were mentally unbalanced. A crazy Warden was a very dangerous thing, and fail-safes were sometimes the only way to be absolutely sure you could stop a Warden before it was too late and the body count was too high.

I'd never thought I'd be facing the possibility myself.

'Fine,' I said, and my voice sounded thick and strange to my ears. 'Do it.'

'I also need your consent.'

I rolled my eyes. 'Didn't I just say *do it*?'

His smile was very thin, and not at all happy. 'I need you to say more than that. Informed consent.'

'What, you think I'm going to sue? Fine, here's the cover-your-ass speech: I hereby authorize you to put a fail-safe switch in my brain, to be under your sole control, which you can use to shut me down if I present a clear and present danger to those around me.' I heard the sharp, angry edge in my voice and tried to moderate it. 'I give you permission to kill me. How's that for consent?'

He gazed at me with compassion, and a good deal of resentment. 'You know I hate this, right?'

'Yeah. I'm not a big fan of the concept either, but I get why it's necessary, so let's get it done before David finds out what you're thinking about.'

We probably looked like we were just meditating together, in front of the peaceful roaring waterfall. Two friends, standing calmly together, getting our Zen on.

Lewis held out his hands, palms up. I put mine over them, palms down.

I had to stand there, open and horribly vulnerable, as Lewis's Earth power moved slowly through my nerves, climbing my arms, my shoulders, lighting a bright fire at the base of my neck and spreading out over the cap of my head.

It sank in like a net of light. I couldn't see what he was doing, but I felt it – a sharp, bright spark deep in my brain, quickly contained. My whole body jerked, and my eyes flew open, but I couldn't see anything.

It took several seconds for my vision to come back.

Just shadows at first, then smears of color, then a gradual definition to the edges of shapes.

Lewis's face, intent and focused.

He sighed, and I felt the power drain away from me, heading toward my feet. It was a little like being embarrassed in slow motion, a wave of heat traveling through flesh until it terminated through the soles of my shoes.

'Done?' I asked. He nodded. 'How does it work?'

'It's a signature switch. I'm the only one who can trip it, and I have to do it a certain way, in a certain sequence.'

'And if you do, it's lights-out in my head? Instantly?'

'Yes,' he said. He sounded beaten and very, very tired. 'Lights-out.'

'No pain, though.'

'Very little. About like a pinprick. It's over in about three seconds.'

'I can't believe we're even talking about this,' I said. 'What's to stop me from undoing it, especially if I go all Team Evil on you? And once I know, Bad Bob could know. He could just disable the kill switch.'

'I know,' Lewis said. He looked very sad, and very guilty. 'That's why I had to get you off alone before I did this. I needed to be sure I was the only one who knew about it.'

I didn't get it. 'But *I* know about it.'

He just stood there watching me, and the look in

his eyes was intensely strange. 'I need to say this,' he said. 'Just this one time. I love you. I've loved you for half my life, it seems like. And I always will love you, even though I know it's not possible for you to love me back. If you hadn't met David, it might have been – things might have been different. But I know when I'm beaten.'

I was stunned. Lewis, of all people, was not a confessor. He didn't blurt out his emo secrets, not to anyone, *especially* not to me.

'I . . . have no idea what you want me to say,' I said. 'You know how I feel about you, you're – you're *Lewis*. God, why are you telling me this *now*?'

'Because I can. Because you won't remember anything about it thirty seconds from now,' he said, and reached out and touched his finger to the exact center of my forehead.

'No—'

The world exploded into jagged shards.

What the hell had I just been saying?

I'd somehow managed to hypnotize myself by staring at the waterfall for too long. I shook off the blurring fascination and gave Lewis a doubtful look. 'Jeez, I just spaced like mad,' I said. 'I'm really tired. What was I saying?'

Lewis was leaning on the railing, staring into the falling curtain of water. 'You were saying you'd die for us,' he said. 'For the Wardens.'

You'd think I'd remember that. 'Damn straight I would, bucko. Anything else?'

He seemed tempted to say something, but then he shook his head and shifted gears. I could tell from the way his body language changed, from contemplative to decisive. 'Yes. I want a thorough check of every Warden. Make sure there are none of Bad Bob's crew in our particular woodpile. When you're done, interview the passengers and crew. I want everybody, absolutely everybody, checked out by you and David.'

So much for sweet, sweet bed rest. 'That's going to take all night.'

'Oh, at least. Let me know if you find anything.'

'You are *such* a bastard.' I sighed. 'Is that all? Want me to build the Sistine Chapel out of paper clips in my spare time? You know, you didn't need all this hush-hush privacy to tell me to do your scut work.'

'I know I didn't,' he said. 'I just wanted to show you the waterfall.'

I glanced at it. 'Pretty,' I said. 'Anything else, O Lord and Master?'

He continued to lean on the railing, staring into space. 'That'll about do it.'

I walked away still wondering why the hell he'd dragged me here. Maybe he'd been about to ask me something personal. Maybe he'd been about to declare his undying love for me. *Yeah, like that would ever happen.*

Whatever it had been, he'd chickened out, and I could only think that was a good thing, given the circumstances.

I had a lot of work to do.

Sitting the Wardens down for their loyalty checks was easier than I figured it might be – mainly because they were shell-shocked after the disaster of trying to control the storm. Even the Fire Wardens, notoriously temperamental, and the Earth Wardens, notably hippie-nonconformist, decided to play nice.

I found nothing. If any of them were lying about their allegiances, it was beyond my ability – or David's – to discover. If Bad Bob and his crew could go that deep cover, there was no way we were coming out of this alive, so I decided not to worry about it.

That left some thirty-odd rich folks who were confined to their cabins – hopefully – and a whole bunch of ship's staff and crew.

It was going to be a long stretch. Luckily, I had David along with me, which meant he was paying more attention to my energy levels than I was, and after thanking the last eerily compliant Earth Warden and shaking hands, he steered me in the direction of the only open restaurant.

'I'm not hungry!' I protested. He raised his eyebrows. 'I can't eat now. I've got work to do. Besides, I ate at the buffet when we had the meeting.'

'You ate a turkey sandwich. Before you dumped all

your energy into the attempt to control the storm.'

David had a point – I'd burnt profligate amounts of power, all day long, and now that I thought about it, my muscles had that oddly shaky feeling that meant I was about to crash. My head hurt, too.

I tried rejecting the whole problem again, but David knew when to press, and before I knew it, we were taking the big, sweeping gallery stairs down to the restaurant. It was called Le Fleur D'Or, and it was one of the smaller eating places on the ship – kind of an intimate date-type restaurant, with lots of dark woods and plush carpeting.

The hastily printed menu featured sandwiches, which I figured wasn't the usual fare. The place (and the staff) looked more used to handling lobster and exotic salads than BLTs. They couldn't resist foo-fooing them up by cutting crusts off the bread and making little triangles, but a sandwich is still a sandwich, even if it's on challah bread. I think I ate a dozen, making sounds that probably would have been more appropriate in bed than at the table.

David didn't need to eat – Djinn don't – but they like to eat, to take advantage of all the human senses they assume in human form. So he had some kind of pasta thing and a glass of red wine. Could Djinn get drunk? I'd never really considered the question before. I tried to imagine David intoxicated; he'd probably be a sweet, sloppy drunk, not a mean one, I thought. He'd be throwing his arms around Lewis and mumbling about how much he loved the guy in no time.

Well, maybe not, but it was an intriguing fantasy.

'Thanks,' I said, pushing back from the crumb-dusted plate and swigging half of my iced tea in convulsive gulps. 'I didn't know I was that bad off.'

'You've got limits,' he said. 'You should learn to pay attention to them occasionally.'

'Hey, that's not fair. I see the blur as I blow past them.'

He came around, pulled my chair back, and handed me up to my feet in a courtly Old World gesture, very appropriate to this hushed, romantic restaurant with its subdued violin music. He combed his fingers through my curly hair in a slow, gentle gesture that left it straight and shining in the wake of his touch. 'I was thinking more of actually staying within them.'

'Funny. So where do we start with the rich folks?'

David turned to the waiter still hovering near the table, eager for any chance to break out of his boredom. 'Do you deliver room service?'

'No, sir, the cabin stewards do that.'

'Do they ever tell you about the difficult passengers?'

That got a big fat silence. I could imagine that passenger gossip was one of those major disciplinary no-no things.

'We won't say who it came from,' I promised, and

gestured to David, rubbing my fingers together. He reached in the back pocket of his pants, pulled out a wallet, and peeled off a hundred-dollar bill, which he placed on the table as a tip.

The waiter's eyes widened. 'Cabin seventeen in first class,' he said. 'If you're looking for the biggest jerk.'

'That's what I'm talking about. Mr Prince?'

David offered me his arm in another of those dashingly gallant gestures. 'Mrs Prince,' he said. 'Cabin seventeen it is.'

Cabin seventeen was located only a few doors down from my own spacious digs. As we headed in that direction, I saw Aldonza, the cabin stewardess, closing the door to room twenty-two. She had a tray of used dishes balanced in her hands. I waved. She gave me a professional, polished smile in return, as impartial as a Swiss banker.

'Aldonza,' I said, 'can I ask you a question?'

'Yes, miss,' she said, and tried not to stare at David too openly. 'Of course.'

She was carrying about twenty pounds on that tray, and she was a slight little thing. As I glanced at David, I saw he'd already reached the same conclusion. He reached out and took the tray from her, despite her shocked gasp.

'To the restaurant?' he asked. She gave him a stunned nod.

'But, sir, you can't—'

He could. David was quite enjoying being free of the Djinn secrecy restrictions; he misted away with the tray in full view of Aldonza, and her pretty face went pale with shock. She crossed herself and murmured something in Spanish.

'He's OK,' I promised her. 'More like an angel than, you know, the other thing.' She stared at me blankly, shaking her head as if she simply wanted the whole thing to go away. 'I need to ask you about one of your guests. Cabin seventeen?'

That snapped her out of her fugue state. Color flooded back into her face, and then she made a visible effort to stay calm and professional. 'Mr Trent Cole,' she said.

'Nice guy?'

'I can't talk about my guests, miss.' Her lips twitched. 'Not even about you and the angel.'

'Eh, don't worry about us. You can talk all you want. We've been on CNN.' She snorted, then covered her mouth with her hand as if she was appalled at her bad behavior. I winked. 'Look, about Mr Cole – I'm about to go talk to him. Anything you can tell me about him that might help me decide if he's a threat or not?'

She hesitated, and I could see the good-girl/gossip-girl conflict being played out for a solid three seconds before the gossip girl pulled a smackdown. 'He has a gun,' she said. 'I saw it. He put it in the pocket of his bathrobe. He doesn't like anyone coming into his room, and he's very rude. He doesn't let me do any cleaning, and that makes it so hard, because he can complain that I'm not doing my job, and if a passenger makes a complaint like that I can be fired and left at the next port—'

Man, when Aldonza decided to talk, it was hard to stop her. 'What kind of a gun?' I asked. She looked puzzled. 'Small? Big? Revolver? Automatic?'

'Big. An automatic.'

'OK. I just want to know what we're dealing with,' I said. 'Aldonza – did Mr Cole threaten you? Hurt you?'

From the rigid set of her posture, I thought he had, but she shook her head. Maybe not even her gossip-girl side could voice that complaint. At least, not to a mere passenger.

'OK,' I said. I felt David coming back, and saw her eyes shift and widen as he whispered into existence behind me. 'Thank you very much for your information. David—' I did the finger-rubbing thing again. He produced his wallet, Aldonza got a hundred-dollar bill, and as we walked away, David handed me the wallet. 'What?'

'I just thought it might be more convenient,' he said. 'In case you want to bribe anybody in cabin seventeen.'

'I want to intimidate the holy living shit out of cabin seventeen,' I said. 'How would that be?'

He gave me a slow, evil smile. 'You only love me for my ability to terrify.'

'And your ability to produce money out of thin air. That's important, too.'

'I'm glad I'm well-rounded.'

'In oh so many ways.'

Mr Trent Cole, aka Cabin Seventeen, decided that he wasn't going to submit to answering any questions, no matter how nicely we asked. In fact, Mr Cole wouldn't even open his door.

Yeah, like that was going to keep us impotently standing outside.

'We're not Housekeeping,' I called through the door. 'Open it or we're coming in anyway.'

'Like hell you are! I know my rights!' Mr Personality screamed back at me.

David moved me out of the way – my own personal Djinn shield – and put a single finger on the surface of the glossy wooden door. When he pushed, the lock snapped and shattered like glass.

Nice. I liked the economy of his violence.

He stepped over the threshold, and Trent Cole fired three bullets into his chest, point-blank. He did it like a guy who'd had practice, but when David didn't fall down – didn't even flinch – Cole's expression turned from murderous to completely confused.

David stepped forward, took the gun (Aldonza was right, it was a big black semiautomatic), and handed it to me. I dumped it in the ice bucket on the bar, after burning my fingers on the barrel. If David was bothered in the least by someone trying to kill him, he didn't let it show in his cool smile, or the absolute ease with which he stiff-armed Mr Cole toward the sofa.

Cole met the cushions at speed, and toppled like a tortoise onto his back, an awkward position at best. He was dressed in one of the ship's fluffy robes, his big feet shoved into slippers that flopped around hilariously as he tried to right himself. He struggled up to a sitting position as David shut the door behind us and repaired the lock with a minor pulse of power.

There was a bottle of Perrier-Jouet champagne sweating on the coffee table, along with two full flutes of sparkling liquid.

'I see we're in time for happy hour,' I said, and settled myself in the tapestry armchair across from the sofa. I poured myself a glistening flute and then appropriated the second one for David. We sipped. Mr Cole, a bulky sort, grabbed at the flapping hem of his robe to avoid giving me a Full Monty as he swung his feet to the floor. David settled himself in one of those intimidating poses the Djinn had perfected several millennia ago, literally guarding my back.

Cole, uncertain what to do, leant back on the sofa. Slowly. 'You can't just barge in here,' he said. 'I've got rights, whoever you think you are.'

The champagne really was excellent. 'You think those rights include shooting anyone who walks through your door?' I asked him. I craned my neck a bit to look up at David. 'Speaking of that, you OK, honey?'

'I'm fine,' he said. He held out a fist. I opened my palm, and he dumped three perfect bullets into it. 'Souvenirs.'

'For me? Thanks.' I fluttered my eyelashes at him, and got a slow, hot smile. We both loved this part. I focused back on Cole, who was staring at us like we were straight out of a big-budget special-effects movie. 'You need these back? Maybe you recycle?'

He shook his head. I put them in the pocket of my jeans. You never know when you'll need a good bullet.

'Now,' I said. 'Thanks for seeing us, Mr Cole. We'll only be a minute. First question: Why do you feel the need to go all Wild West Show on friendly visitors? Bonus question: Why are you still on this ship? Because I think anybody who doesn't have to be here must have a really good reason to be staying.'

Trent Cole was not accustomed to answering questions of any kind, much less from a plebeian like me. He struck me as nouveau riche, probably something to do with hedge funds or stocks or porn. Someone who had a lot of cash and was tremendously impressed with it.

He kept darting admiring looks at David. I was familiar with that. I just wasn't so familiar with seeing it in a man.

'I was just defending myself,' Cole said. 'I'm sorry. I got rattled.'

While he was speaking, I allowed myself to drift just a bit out of my body so I could examine him in Oversight. His aura was muddy and indistinct – so, a genuine regular human-type guy, no surprise there – and bloody around the edges with guilt and nerves.

'Rattled?' I repeated. 'You looked pretty calm to me. Good grouping on your shots.'

'Center mass,' David supplied. 'Very well aimed.'

Cole looked, from one of us to the other, then fixed on David. His whole body relaxed. 'You're wearing a vest, right? Of course.'

For answer, David unbuttoned his shirt and displayed part of his bare chest.

'David, stop teasing the man,' I said. *And me.* 'Mr Cole. Look at me, please.' He did, not with any great pleasure, and I deepened my focus to get a better look at the inner Trent.

Not a terribly good experience.

'You're protecting yourself,' I said aloud. 'That's why you didn't leave the ship. You know you're an obvious target if you do. You're running from something.'

He flinched, but he didn't move otherwise. 'What the hell are you talking about?'

'Do you know a man named Robert Biringanine?' This was the money question, but I got nothing from him. Just a continuing roil of anxiety and fury.

He didn't know Bad Bob, at least not by name.

David took his cue. 'He looks like this.' And he transformed himself into a perfect replica of Bad Bob, from his flyaway white hair, bloodshot blue eyes, and pug-Irish nose to his bowlegs. In fact, it was so good that I pulled in a startled breath and clenched my fingers on the arms of the chair, then deliberately relaxed. It was just an image, nothing more, and David dismissed it with a flick of his fingers when Trent Cole shook his head.

'OK,' I said, and tried to slow down the fast beat of my heart. 'Who's after you?'

'None of your business,' Cole barked.

'It is if you plan to go around shooting anybody who looks at you funny on this ship,' I said. 'Let us help you. There's no need to be afraid. Not now.'

Cole stared at me with a perplexed look on his face. Clearly, I wasn't fitting the pigeonholes he was trying to stuff me into. I was used to that, actually.

'Who are you?' His gaze leapt from me to David, and then back again. 'Are you with the government?'

'Yes,' I said. In fact, that was sort of true. And sort of not.

'I'm calling my attorney. He's kicked the ass of everybody in the Justice Department, from the attorney general to the janitorial service. He'll make short work of you two jokers.'

Cole reached for his cell phone.

It disappeared. Cole stared at the place where it

had been, slapped his hand around, and looked at me with comically big eyes. 'What the hell?'

David opened his right hand, and there was Cole's cell phone. 'If you want it back, play nice,' he said. Cole's mouth dropped open, and he surged to his feet.

'Hey, fucking David Copperfield, give that back!' His face turned brick-red, which I was pretty sure wasn't an indication of his general good health. 'You sons of bitches, my life is in that phone!'

'Then I hold your life in my hand, don't I?' David pointed out mildly. 'Sit.'

I wasn't sure if it was a suggestion or an order, but Cole's ass hit the sofa cushions pretty quickly. His high-blood-pressure blush was already fading, as he realized that his biggest problem might not be in retrieving his contact list and scandalous text messages. 'What the hell do you people *want*?' From Cole, that actually sounded kind of subdued.

'We want to be sure there's no more trouble,' I said. 'So we'll be taking your gun. Anything else contraband in here we should know about? Purely for safety?'

His gaze flicked away from me, racing toward the sweeping staircase, and then returning just as fast. In the aetheric, his aura whispered a fast rainbow of anxiety and guilt. I sat back and looked up at David, who nodded and disappeared, taking Cole's cell phone with him.

'What—' Cole's mouth had dropped so far open

that I could see all his impressive dental work. I guess he'd figured out that David might share a first name with a famous magician, but he was far, far more impressive. 'What *are* you people?'

'Who said we were people?' I smiled coolly at him. That flummoxed him for a full ten seconds.

'Look, I'm not some terrorist or something, I'm just – OK, I took some money. A lot of money. From some people I worked with. And they're trying to get it back from me, that's all. It's just business.'

Business mob-style, I gathered. Which explained why he wanted to hole up in his suite with a warm gun, and why he hadn't disembarked with the others. A common criminal.

I could live with that.

David ghosted back into view behind me and dropped a hand on my shoulder. I twisted to look at him.

'Boyfriend,' he said. 'Up in the bedroom. He had this.' David deposited another gun in my lap, a match for the semiautomatic we'd confiscated from Cole. 'Do you want to take a look?'

'Why, is he naked?'

It's hard to get a complete double take from a Djinn, but I managed. 'I didn't notice,' he said. Which was, no doubt, a crushing blow to Mr Cole. I was sad for him. 'What do you think? Pass?'

'Pass,' I said. 'Whatever problems he has aren't any concern of ours. Mr Cole, we're done here. I'll be taking your guns with me, though. If you have intruder problems, David will be happy to come to your rescue.' I batted my eyelashes again. David didn't look pleased with being volunteered. 'Thanks.'

'Thanks for what?' Cole asked, mystified. I walked over to the bar and retrieved the second pistol from the ice bucket. Nicely cooled down.

'Not shooting me, too,' I said. 'That would have been awkward.'

'No,' David said. 'That would have been fatal for Mr Cole.'

I gathered that Mr Cole was a man of few boundaries, but he recognized that one, and he nodded. 'It won't happen again. Sorry. Eh – what's your name?'

'I'm David Prince. Her name is Joanne Baldwin,' David said. 'But you can call her Mrs Prince.'

I got a shiver out of that. A nice one.

We left Cole on the couch, still grappling with the utter destruction of his worldview.

All in all, not a bad first interrogation. Then again, my standards are pretty low. If I survive it, it can't be *that* bad.

Chapter Five

After Mr Cole, the others seemed meek as kittens. Spiteful, furious, spitting, hissing kittens with needle-sharp claws and biting teeth. Each cabin seemed to come with its own particularly darling set of divalicious problems. Take Holly Addams, the model . . . She had two employees, one of whom was solely occupied in making her disgusting-looking smoothies whenever she got hungry. They must have been made out of cardboard and water, because she had less body fat on her than your average piece of dry bone. She also had a trunk full of illegal and controlled substances, which explained why she hadn't left the ship when ordered. Her employees were just hapless and cowed. I tried not to traumatize them any more than I had to.

Three bankers in a row, two male and one female, all of whom had refused to leave out of lapdog-like devotion to star clients. These were rich people in their own right, but they'd gotten that way by single-minded dedication to that art of brown-nosing, and they weren't about to stop the habit of a lifetime now. No connection to Bad Bob that I could find for them, their assistants, or (in the case of one of them) his mistress, who was ensconced in the downstairs bedroom.

And then we ran into Cynthia Clark.

'The Cynthia Clark?' I asked Aldonza, who was still hustling clean towels around the hallway. She nodded. 'Isn't she making a movie?'

'She was,' Aldonza said. 'But she quit. I don't know why. Now she's here.'

Cynthia Clark was an old-school star – glamorous, beautiful, icy cool. If Grace Kelly had ever had a rival, or Audrey Hepburn had ever worried about being upstaged, she was the source of their anxiety. Her 1960s-era films were classics. So were her '70s efforts. By the '80s she'd transitioned from starlet roles to tough matrons, and still did it better than anyone else.

Then she'd had a well-publicized marital disaster, some alcoholism, some rehab, and a whole lot of plastic surgery. Now she looked frozen at the age of fifty, although the twenty-year-old ice was beginning to crack under the strain.

She occupied cabin thirty-two, along with a European maid and a personal trainer, who I suspected doubled as another kind of workout partner.

I knew the minute we entered the cabin that something was off. David did, too. No bullets flying, no obvious signs of danger, but there was something very wrong with the feeling of the whole place. I couldn't put my finger on it.

Maybe Miss Clark had been in the middle of a knockdown, drag-out fight with her assistant. That would have explained the feeling of tension and anger that saturated the air.

Miss Clark was seated, like Mr Cole, on the grand sofa, but she was wearing a pair of pencil-legged white pants, very '60s nautical, paired with a blue-and-white-striped knit shirt. Her eyes were the same blue as shallow Caribbean waters, and if her hair was dyed that lustrous shade of blond, I couldn't tell. Even with the makeovers, she had seriously fierce DNA at work.

I felt as if I should genuflect before taking a seat in the side chair that she offered with a gracious nod. David remained standing, but he didn't resort to the intimidation stance this time around. More of a tranquil stand-at-ease type of thing.

Clark's trainer and maid busied themselves in another part of the room. I barely registered them as background noise, because La Clark simply drew every bit of attention to herself just by sitting there.

'Thank you for seeing us, Miss Clark,' I said. 'My name is—'

'Joanne Baldwin, yes, I know,' she said. She had

a contralto voice, and she used it the way a master musician uses a violin, conveying all shades of meaning in one brilliant stroke. 'You represent these Wardens I've been hearing so much about. And your companion?'

'David Prince,' he said.

'You're one of the . . . Djinn?' She tried the taste of the word, and I could tell she liked it. When he nodded, Clark's eyes drifted half closed, and she sat back against the cushions, studying him. 'Extraordinary. I thought there were no surprises left in the world, but here you are. Like something straight out of a fairy tale. The old kind, of course. The frightening ones.'

She offered us coffee, tea, drinks. Neither of us felt thirsty, but I accepted a delicate little teacup steaming with French Roast, just to make this more of a social call. Being able to say *I had coffee with Cynthia Clark* didn't factor into that decision at all. Well, not much.

Clark blew on the surface of her own brew and studied us both with X-ray eyes that had reportedly once made Steve McQueen swoon. 'How can I help you?' she asked.

'Just a few questions, and then, I promise, we'll certainly be out of your way,' I said. 'First, can you tell me why you didn't leave the ship before departure, as you were asked to do?'

'Well, you're direct,' she murmured. 'How very refreshing. It's all a bit embarrassing, I suppose, and it's going to make me seem like a horrible tyrant. I was terribly tired, and I left strict instructions not to be disturbed for any reason prior to departure. I'm afraid my employees might have taken those instructions a bit too literally. When I finally rose for breakfast, I was informed of the evacuation order, but it was too late for us to make our arrangements and leave.'

There was something odd about Clark's aura. It seemed very calm, swirling with neutral blues and soft golds, but it also felt *artificial*. 'What kind of arrangements? I'd think you'd want to get out as quickly as possible.'

'I really can't go into details,' she said. 'But it was entirely accidental that we ended up staying here, on the ship. We won't be any trouble to you. I'm quite content to stay in the cabin.' She gave me a cool smile. 'It's so difficult to find privacy these days out in the real world.'

I wondered, because a curl of hot magenta drifted over her aura. Resentment, maybe. She wasn't the It Girl anymore when it came to the paparazzi, and she knew it. It probably took a great deal of effort to get herself photographed at all, except in retirement magazines talking about how she was 'still young at sixty-five.'

'Routine questions, Miss Clark. We just want to be sure we're aware of any problems that might come up,' I said.

'Such as?'

'Oh, I don't know . . . Trouble between you

and another passenger, maybe a stalker? Business disagreements?'

'Alas, I don't have that many enemies, Miss Baldwin. I'm sure I'd feel much more important if I did. No, I have no fears, and I'm sure that none of my little party represents any sort of difficulty for you.'

I wished I could figure out what was bothering me. She just didn't seem . . . *right*. Was she scared? No, not really, but when I concentrated on her aura, I saw flecks like floating ice. I wasn't sure what it meant, but I *was* sure that it wasn't normal.

I let the silence go on too long. 'Is that all?' Clark asked, suddenly a good deal less welcoming. 'I have a strict meditation schedule. Yoga. It keeps me toned and flexible. I highly recommend it.'

'May I speak with your employees?' I asked her.

'No,' Cynthia Clark said. Just the one word, cold and final. I blinked and glanced at David, who was staring at Clark with very dark eyes. I didn't know what he was seeing, but it wasn't good. Not good at all.

Then he looked from Clark to where her two employees stood at the other end of the room.

'Jo,' he said, and touched my shoulder. 'You should go.'

'I – What?'

'Now.' The touch turned into a painful squeeze. '*Now*.'

I stood up, but it was too late. I barely sensed the

snap of power coming before it hit me like a pile driver to the chest – not just on the physical plane but on the aetheric, too. I knew this sensation.

It had hit me before. It had killed a whole lot of my friends.

The blitz attack sent me into the air in a tumbling, twisting heap. I flew across the cabin and slammed into the solid wall with a wood-cracking thump. I hardly had time to process the shock of pain before pressure closed around me, deep as the black depths of the ocean, and drove all the air from my lungs. I felt my entire nervous system flickering, overloading, on the verge of burnout. There was an unearthly shrieking roar in my ears, like a mental institution on fire, and everything felt *wrong*, so wrong.

I fought. I flailed, trying to throw it off, but I couldn't, because there was nothing to grab hold of. I blinked away darkness and saw David moving like a streak of light toward the two at the far end of the room, but he was too far. It was happening too fast, unbelievably fast . . .

I was going to die, and he wouldn't be able to stop it.

You can stop it, Joanne. All you have to do is let go.

The thought bubbled up on some black, greasy tide from the depths of my soul. It was solid as a life preserver in a storm, and I grabbed it, desperate to stop the pain, the shrieking, the sickening and inevitable feeling of every cell in my body being crushed into slime.

You have to let go, it told me. *Let go, Joanne. You can save yourself if you choose.*

With the weight of mountains on my chest, with my entire body screaming for release, with my bones turning to powder inside and my nervous system frying like a bumed-out bulb, I believed it was the only choice.

Then I felt the eager, hot twinge of the black mark on my back, and I *knew* where that thought was coming from.

No.

Time had proceeded only a tiny fraction of a second.

David hadn't even reached the far end of the room yet, although the Djinn could move at the speed of thought. I was being crushed into greasy paste by a force so vast it felt like Earth herself had landed on me, and the idea of waiting an instant, a single breath, for help was almost impossible.

Save yourself. You can. It's easy.

Yes. All I had to do was shatter the containment that David had put around the black torch, and it would burn away all my problems.

Forever.

I held on. I don't know how; it wasn't inner strength, it wasn't courage, and it wasn't anything I could be proud of. Maybe it was just paralyzing terror. The instant passed, and even though I felt death's breath on my lips, the taste was all that lingered; David reached Cynthia's personal trainer, and that man – whoever, *whatever* he was – had no more time for killing me.

I gagged in a trembling breath, rolled on my side, and sobbed in agony. My nerves continued to burn, and the entire circuit board of my brain seemed on the verge of overload. I hadn't been hurt that suddenly, that *deeply*, in a long time. The taste of mortality is ash and blood, and I coughed until I could stop gagging on it.

Getting up was like free-climbing the Empire State Building in a hurricane, but I used an overturned table for support until I could feel my legs. They weren't quite right, somehow. Most of me wasn't, at that moment. This was going to hurt later. A lot. For a long time.

I forgot all of that when David screamed, 'Jo! *Cover*!'

Fire rolled out from him, blistering white, and I lunged for the sofa, where Cynthia Clark still sat frozen in shock by the explosion of violence. I shoved her down into the cushions and threw myself on top of her. I couldn't reach the other innocent in the room – her personal assistant – but I extended the fastest, hardest shield of interlocked molecules I could over the woman's prone body. She'd sensibly dropped to the floor and curled into a ball on the rug.

No time for any other defenses. Whether David had called the fire, or his enemy had, it filled the room like an airburst of napalm. I felt the back of my clothes and my hair smolder, and smelt instant, toxic charring of plastics and carpet and furniture. The flame would have incinerated all three of us if I hadn't shielded us; mortal flesh would have burnt off like flash paper.

It *had* burnt the flesh off of David's opponent.

The blast flamed out, leaving a thick swirl of smoke, and I raised my head to see my Djinn lover facing a skeletal, blackened *thing* that was certainly not human, never human – something that should be dead, and yet was still standing. It wasn't a Demon, though it had some characteristics that reminded me of the way a Demon's bones curved and spiked.

It looked like it was made of glass. In fact, only the smudges and soot that clung to it made it visible at all. I blinked and clicked into Oversight.

It was *invisible* on the aetheric.

Ghosts, Venna had named them.

The forerunners of the end of all things.

David let out a wordless roar of fury and fastened his hands around the creature's throat. He was glowing like liquid gold, dripping with living fire.

But where he touched this thing, his fire went out. And darkness began to creep up his arms. No, not darkness – oh *God*, I knew what that was.

Ash, and dust.

He was being destroyed, just like the Djinn who'd died in the hallway. The touch of this thing was toxic to them. That Djinn must have come across it somehow, maybe even been sent by Ashan to warn us of the danger – and it had killed her.

It had *erased* her.

Just as it was trying to do to David.

'Let go!' I shouted, and rolled over the top of the couch to land on my feet. I staggered, but I didn't have time for weakness. 'David, back off!'

David didn't want to, but he did, breaking away and lunging to his left as I strode forward, gathering up raw power in both hands. As I moved, a silver sword formed in my grip – not metal but ice. Hard as steel, reinforced with a binding that left the cutting edge as thin as a whisper.

If this thing could survive David's heat, I wanted to see how it felt about chills.

The blade hit, bit, and cut, slicing through fragments of muscle and cooked skin, through crystalline bones that glowed blue where the ice slashed.

I chopped right through its neck. I paused, holding in my follow-through, to see what would happen.

The creature's head stayed on. As I watched, it wobbled a bit on the skeletal column of glassy vertebrae, then settled back into place.

It smiled with needle-sharp crystal teeth. If it had ever been human, other than a casual disguise, it certainly wasn't playing at it now. This was something out of a big-budget nightmare, and I took a step back from it, fast.

'David, get everybody out!' I yelled. I could sense this thing orienting on me, predator to prey. The last thing I needed right now was mortal trip hazards and speed bumps; it was going to be all I could do to protect myself, much less Cynthia Clark and her employee.

I sensed David grabbing up the noncombatants and hustling them to the door.

The creature facing me opened its mouth and flicked a tongue like a whip at me. It was more like an icicle than living tissue, but it moved like a cobra. The end was as sharp as a needle, and I barely avoided the stabbing turn of it in midair. A return stroke with my ice-knife passed through the tongue without any effect at all.

Damn. I couldn't hurt this thing, at least not with these weapons.

I retreated. I changed out ice for steel and tried again. This time, I sliced a piece out of the tongue, which fell to the floor and writhed like a slug in the sun. Whether that hurt the creature or not, it charged me, and I tried to make like a matador. That didn't help. It had reach and speed, and what had been its fingers in human form were now claws, diamond-sharp and lightning fast.

I felt the slices like chilly tugs on my side, but there wasn't any pain, not at first. I didn't allow myself to look down, I kept moving, turning, keeping myself away from the razor-edged whirlwind that was hissing through the air in pursuit.

Then I hit a corner, and there was nowhere left to

run. I slashed, trying to slow it down, but the creature was just too damn fast, and too damn powerful. It smashed through the shield I put up. I didn't have time to try any Earth powers; fire wouldn't work, and weather tricks wouldn't buy me more than another fragile breath.

I was going to lose.

A small, white ball of light hit the thing from the side and plunged beneath the crystalline structure. It lit the creature up like an arc light from within. I couldn't even estimate the heat; it felt like a nuclear bomb compressed to the size of a baseball, forces well beyond my ability to summon, much less command.

All I could do was duck and cover. Again.

The creature shrieked in that horrible, soul-destroying range again and became a photonegative blast of flame that cooked everything within a foot of it – but not an inch beyond. The inverse flame became white flame, then reversed itself into a tiny, glittering spark . . . and the creature was gone except for a shower of glittering crystalline powder.

A wave of intense pressure passed over me and shoved me hard into the corner.

The white ball of light expanded into a softer glow, and as the wave passed over me I squinted into it and saw the Djinn Venna standing where the creature had been, her pink *Hello Kitty* sneakers buried in half an inch of crystal powder.

She looked worse than I had ever seen her: pallid,

trembling, *afraid*. She sank down into a crouch, just a frightened little girl, and I couldn't help but move toward her. I picked her up in my arms, and she shuddered and buried her face in my chest.

Her warmth changed, cooled, became gentle against my skin. I felt my wounds starting to heal, though very slowly. My body began murmuring a shocked report of damages, but I told it to be quiet. Shock felt nice, at the moment. Soothing. I'd take whatever comfort I could get just now.

David reached us a second later, wrapping his arms around us both. 'All right?' he asked, and looked into my eyes. He didn't like what he saw there, clearly, but he liked what he saw in Venna a whole lot less.

I didn't blame him.

'It's one of them,' Venna said. 'One of the ghosts. It didn't belong here. It can't *be here*.'

The confidence of the Old Djinn in their well-ordered universe had just been shattered, and beings that had never feared much in their long, long lives looked into the abyss that humans faced every day – the dark chasm of uncertainty of the future.

'It's OK, Venna,' I said, and smoothed her long blond hair. 'You did great. Ghost or not, you completely kicked its ass.'

'I can't do it again.' Venna looked at David and took a deep breath. 'It took part of my ass with it. And I don't think I can get any of that back. Maybe ever.'

* * *

Cynthia Clark hadn't boarded with a personal trainer, as it turned out. In fact, she didn't remember a thing about the entire incident. There didn't seem to be much point in trying to convince her that she'd been hypnotized into covering up for some otherworldly demonic glass monster. She wouldn't even believe that David and I hadn't set her room on fire deliberately, so I figured the whole monster thing was right off the table.

I staggered away to the nearest public lounge while David tried to settle things to everyone's satisfaction. I was checked out by a small army of Warden medics and Lewis himself – none of whom were happy with me, or my descriptions of events, come to think of it – and eventually was told that I was in no imminent danger of death or coma, but healing was a long way off.

I was still lying there, feet up, grateful to be breathing, when I spotted Aldonza hurrying past, rolling a luggage cart. She did a quick jerk of surprise when she saw me, and loitered. 'Are you OK, miss?' she asked, which told me just how terrible I looked. 'Can I get you something?'

I didn't raise my head from the leather pillow. 'I'm OK, Aldonza. Sorry about the cabin.'

'The cabin?'

'Miss Clark's cabin. It's – ah – kind of a mess.'

Aldonza got a blank, terrified look on her face and hurried on. I could hear her horrified cry all the way down the hallway.

A half hour later, a whole phalanx of stewards rolled by, carting La Clark's salvaged baggage and armloads of expensive clothes. They were moving her to a new cabin.

They moved her into mine, as it turned out. I didn't find that out until I struggled up from my temporary resting place and met Cherise in the hall, dragging her suitcase and looking half-mournful, half-impressed. 'Did you know that *Cynthia Clark* is going to be sleeping in your bed?' she asked. 'That's kind of awesome, in a sucky kind of way. Anyway, we're down the hall, and *Moses on a motorcycle*, what the hell happened to you, bitch?'

I was better, really I was. I was limping – broken bones had been repaired into merely cracked and hurting bones – and I was singed and bloody and looked like some Halloween fright mask, but hey, I was breathing, upright, and thinking straight again. 'You should see the other guy,' I said, and coughed. It turned into a lung-bursting hack like a fifteen-pack-a-day smoker's. I could still taste that awful taint of death, even though I thought that it was all in my head now.

'Uh, thanks, I faint at the sight of gross anatomy. Come on, sweetie. You need a bunk.'

I didn't argue about it. I'd been inclined to think I could walk it all off until I'd walked about ten feet, and then priorities had shifted again, drastically.

Rest seemed like a very good idea. I accepted

Cherise's support, staggering the rest of the way to our new cabin.

'Ouch,' Cher sighed, as the door swung open on a cramped little room with two narrow beds facing each other. 'Looks like we've been bumped to coach. Or maybe servants' quarters.'

'Don't care.' I sank down on the closest flat surface – luckily, it had a mattress – and covered my eyes with my forearm. I needed to think. *How* had that creature gotten on the ship? And why? Was it just biding its time, waiting to kill as many Wardens as possible?

Had it killed the nameless Djinn we'd found in the hallway?

Most importantly – were there *more*?

David had sensed it, though not with any accuracy. Venna had been able to nuke it, though only at a drastic cost to herself.

We just couldn't fight an army of these things, and I had the sense that these were just incidental players in Bad Bob's upcoming melodrama.

Crap. Why did this keep happening to me?

'Jo?' The mattress dented on my left side as Cherise perched on the edge. 'You crying?'

'No,' I lied. 'Fuck.' I swallowed hard. 'I can't do this. *We* can't do this. We're sailing away into the middle of nowhere with a bunch of innocent people and we're all going to die, Cher. I can't stop it. God, we've screwed this up.'

'Hey.' She moved my arm away from my eyes and

looked down at me with such gravity that she didn't look like Cherise at all. 'What's going on?'

'Did you hear me? We just about got our asses kicked!'

'But you didn't,' she said. 'You told me before we got on this ship that it was going to be hard, and people were going to die, because you can't go to war if you don't expect casualties. You didn't want me to come with, remember. You wussing out on me now, Rambette?'

I sniffled. 'No.'

'Good, don't even. You're a Warden. You don't let *anything* stand in the way of what you think is right. You have the most lustworthy guy I've ever seen madly in love with you. You have fabulous hair. You're strong and beautiful and smart and evil pees itself when it sees you coming. So don't you fold up on me, Jo.' Cherise's mask slipped, just a little. 'Because if you do, I don't think I can keep it together on my own.'

'Bullshit,' I said. 'You're way tougher than me.' I hugged her. 'I'm just so tired. I just want to rest.'

'Then rest,' she said, and let go. I settled back on the bed. 'But don't you dare think you're not up to this. You're a hero, babe. Heroes don't wuss.'

'Do they whine?'

'Only to their bosom sidekicks.' She flashed me her bosom to prove she had the cred. Cherise, motivational speaker to the stars.

I managed a weak laugh. I didn't feel like a hero,

not at all. I didn't think Venna did, either, and I *knew* David didn't. He was too worried for me, and his anxiety was feeding mine, like a deadly and accelerating loop.

I took some deep breaths. Then I took some more, and let myself drift away from the pain and fear. I imagined myself floating in water, in a sparkling blue pool, with calm clouds whispering by overhead. The sun was warm and soft and kind, and I had on the perfect blue bikini that David liked so much.

The *Grand Paradise*'s rocking motion lulled me into a mindless calm, and as I hung there, suspended, I felt my body reaching for relief. It healed itself, bit by bit, cell by cell, using power drawn from the energy around me. The temperature of the cabin lowered in response, and I heard Cherise get up and check the thermostat, then break out the blankets. One settled over me, thick and soft.

'You OK?' Cherise whispered. I didn't open my eyes.

'Yep,' I murmured. 'Check it: Heroes don't wuss.'

I was hoping that Venna had been wrong about her damage. I mean, shock, right? But no. Venna had been not just injured but *diminished* by the battle in Clark's cabin.

When David told me that, sitting on the edge of my narrow bed in much the same way Cherise had earlier, I could tell that he was trying not to give away how much it disturbed him. He had on his *just-the-facts-ma'am* face, and he'd damped down the link between us to a low hum, suggestions of emotion, nothing more.

That was as close to cutting himself off from me as he could manage, since our wedding ceremony had joined us together on that powerful level.

I didn't like it.

'She's all right,' David told me. He was looking at me, but not – eyes unfocused, and miles away. 'Physically . . . aetherically . . . she's all right, she's just . . . less than she was. As if pieces of her had been burnt away.'

'Or eaten,' I said.

'You're thinking of an Ifrit,' he said, and the focus sharpened in his eyes. 'That wasn't an Ifrit.' No, it definitely had *not* been an Ifrit. Those were Djinn, badly damaged and transformed, yes, feeding on their own kind, but still recognizably of the Djinn DNA family.

This thing . . . not so much.

'What if it was part Ifrit?' I said slowly. I struggled up to a reclining position, with my pillow bracing my aching back. 'Part Demon, too? Some kind of hybrid?'

'That would be bad,' David said, very softly.

'Yeah, it'd suck like an industrial-strength Hoover. Demons are hard to kill; Ifrits can consume pieces of other Djinn, right?' As I understood it, Ifrits were the result of damage occurring to a Djinn's ability to process energy from the aetheric. Starving and desperate, they did what any living creature might do to survive; they turned cannibal, stealing energy from their own kind. Dark, nightmarish vampire Djinn, usually with a nearly complete lack of higher mental faculties. Maddened by hunger.

Marry that to a Demon, and you've got a truly terrifying weapon against the Djinn, not to mention anyone else who gets in the way, like Wardens.

In a word, one of Venna's ghosts – invisible, deadly, and adaptable.

'Can she recover?' I asked, thinking again of Venna. David gave me a highly suspect shrug. 'Check that – can she recover in time to do that again?'

'I don't know. I'm not her Conduit.'

'Cop-out.'

'Hey!'

'You know. You may not be able to help her, but you know whether or not *Ashan* can help her.'

'Ashan isn't saying much,' David said. 'You know how he is.'

Oh, I knew. We'd hit the same brick wall when trying to help another of Ashan's Old Djinn, a particularly arrogant specimen named Cassiel who'd pissed the old dude off and been cast out to fend for herself for her troubles.

She hadn't *quite* become an Ifrit. Instead, she'd decided to go the less conventional route of binding herself to the Wardens for her daily dose of life energy . . . and I wasn't at all sure that had been a good idea, still. Thank God, she wasn't here with us, causing trouble. Wherever she was, I hoped she was doing better than we were.

Ashan had refused to talk about that incident, too. He wasn't, in general, the chattiest of all my many enemies. He'd read the guidelines for villainy, the first one being *Don't monologue*.

'Is she staying?' I asked. Because Venna being Venna, she could stay or go, exactly as she pleased. In her place, I'm not sure I wouldn't have gone off to the Djinn Day Spa for the next several millennia, and left us human idiots to our own devices.

'Of course she's staying,' David said, and smiled just a little. 'Venna's more like you than she'd like to admit.'

'Apart from being cuter.'

'Debatable.'

'I don't have any *Hello Kitty* shoes.'

'Could be remedied.' He lifted my hand to his lips, and I shivered at the gentle touch, not to mention the look in his eyes. 'I'm sorry about earlier. I realized I wasn't helping you recover. It's hard to remember how much we share now. I don't want to add to your problems.'

'You were worried,' I said. 'Hell, join the club. We have T-shirts and free-drink coupons. Open bar every Wednesday.'

'Come here.' He folded me in his arms, and I let out

a long sigh. Most of my remaining tension went with it. 'You did very well back there.'

'What, getting myself backed into a corner to be chopped up by the walking meat slicer? Yeah, spectacular job. Mom would be proud.'

'I don't think many humans could have stood against it at all,' he said. 'Fewer still would have tried. I talked with Venna about how she destroyed it. She vibrated it. I think you could do the same?'

'Vibrated—' Of course. Crystalline structure in its bones and claws and teeth. Strong, but hit it with the right oscillated frequency, and you could hurt it, maybe destroy it. 'I'd need to experiment to get it right. I don't suppose you have any remains . . . ?'

For answer, he reached in his pocket and pulled out a single crystal tooth, about the size of a small switchblade. He held it in his palm for a moment, weighing it, and then handed it to me. 'Careful,' he said. 'Sharp.'

He was right; it still held a wicked edge. I wrapped it in handfuls of tissue paper from the box on the nightstand and put it in my own pocket for later study.

'Do we know if there are more on board?' I asked. 'Because we really don't need another ugly surprise.'

David got up and opened the cabin door. In walked another Djinn, a brawny, bald-headed sort who looked like he might have moonlighted on a cleaner bottle from time to time. His skin was a dull metallic gray, and his eyes were the color of rust.

He looked around the sparse cabin with an expression like he'd bitten a bug in half, then dragged over the small side chair. Cherise wasn't in at the moment, for which I was grateful; she'd gone off in search of medicinal ice cream. I could imagine her running commentary on this scene.

'This is Lyle,' David said.

'Seriously?' I blurted. They both shot me an odd look. 'I mean, come on. *Lyle*?'

Lyle smiled. He'd filed his teeth into sharp little points. 'You got a problem with that?' He had a surprising Deep South accent, slow and warm. It didn't sound artificial, as if he was mocking me, either.

Another oddity.

'Uh, no, no problem,' I said. 'It's just not exactly the kind of name I'm used to hearing from supernatural beings. A little too—'

'Human?'

'Country,' I said. 'Not even a little bit rock and roll.'

David decided it was time to intervene before my conversational skills cost me a bruise or two. 'Lyle became a Djinn during one of the World Wars.'

'Which one?'

'They come so close together,' David said. 'First?'

Lyle nodded. 'I kept my human name. A lot of Djinn don't bother. Sorry it doesn't meet with your approval, Warden.'

'No, you're not,' I said, and he smiled again. This

time, he'd put away the scary teeth, and his dentition was blindingly white and perfectly human-normal.

If anything, that was weirder.

'Lyle was checking for energy signatures,' David said. 'Did you find anything?'

'Yes. Weaker than the one you two tripped across, though, and well hidden.' Lyle's rust-colored eyes darkened just a shade. 'They're hiding as humans.'

'How many?'

'Two.'

'Two *more*?' My throat threatened to close up around the words, and Lyle sent me a sharp look. I needed to work on my poker face. 'What do we know about them?'

'They're wearing skins,' Lyle said. 'The skins used to be people, so they have history and weight in the aetheric. They took care not to kill the skins. I think they knew it was a good disguise. Good enough to fool most Djinn, even.'

He was trying to describe something that I was trying equally hard not to imagine. 'These people – can we save them?'

'Not people,' Lyle said. 'Like I said, they're just skins now. Nothing inside.'

I wished he hadn't said that. Or at least, hadn't sounded so matter-of-fact about it.

'Why haven't they attacked us already?' I asked. 'They probably know their big brother's gone, right?

What are they waiting for, the all-you-can-eat-buffet light to go on?'

'They're definitely waiting on some type of signal, if they haven't struck at us yet,' David said. 'They can afford to bide their time. We don't even really know what they're capable of doing, not yet.'

'No,' I said slowly. 'They did strike already. They killed the Djinn we found in the hallway outside my old cabin. We just don't know why, because we can't figure out who she was or what she was doing at the time.'

It was the perfect dead end, and it was wasted on David and Lyle, who looked at each other as if silently thinking that I'd gone just slightly nuts. *Humans*, Lyle's shrug said. *Who knows what goes on in their tiny heads?*

'We need to backtrack and figure out why they felt threatened by that Djinn,' I said. 'Or why they had to stop what she was doing. David—' He was still giving me that blank look. 'Never mind. I'll figure it out. Anyway, one good thing about it – they're probably worried about how we managed to kill their strongest monster already.' I swallowed. 'Please tell me that it was the strongest one.'

'It was,' David said. I heaved a deep sigh of relief.

'We should kill them now,' Lyle said.

'How? Just one of them was capable of nearly killing me, fighting David to a standstill, and halfway destroying Venna,' I said. 'So I'm not feeling real good about our chances with taking on two of them at once. Any other options?'

Lyle cocked one thin eyebrow. 'Swim back to shore.'

'Just run away.'

'Unless you want to wait for them to strike first.'

'You weren't serious about the running away, right?'

'Oh, he was,' David said.

Lyle nodded. Lyle was turning out to be the least confrontational supernatural being I'd ever met. Under normal circumstances, that would have been a refreshing change, but considering that I wanted a bunch of fire-eating, hard-charging badasses to back me up right now . . . not so much.

We both looked at David, who seemed to be half a world away. He dragged himself back with an effort. 'We bide our time,' he said. 'It's too dangerous to go after them right now. Venna can't be used against them again, and we need to know more than we know now. Joanne—'

'Yeah, got it. Find out the right frequencies to do damage, and get everybody up to speed on the info, quietly. Oh, you probably should tell me just who I'm avoiding, here. Not Wardens?' Because I'd hate to have missed that in my initial checks.

'No,' Lyle said, relieving me of screwups. 'One is crew, an engineering mate below passenger decks. The other is hiding as a stowaway in the ship's hold. He will be difficult to reach, and harder to trap.'

'Let them hide for now,' David said. 'Watch them. Any change, any indication something's happening, report it as soon as you can. If they try to sabotage the ship—'

I hadn't even thought of that, and the idea twisted me deep in the gut. 'Could they?'

'Of course. But not easily, and probably not fatally. With the Wardens and Djinn aboard, most damage can be repaired immediately.' David sounded a lot more confident than I felt at the moment. I guess I was glad somebody was. 'If you need help—'

Lyle gave a very human-sounding snort. 'Why would I?'

'Because Joanne's right,' David said. 'One of these things nearly won against two Djinn and a powerful Warden. Don't let your confidence blind you to the possibility of losing spectacularly.' At that moment, I thought he sounded a whole lot like his predecessor, Jonathan – calm, acidic, absolutely in control. And Lyle must have thought so too, because he inclined his head a bit and looked contrite.

'Their names,' I said.

'What?' Both Djinn looked at me.

'The people. I'd like to know their names.'

'Why does it matter?' Lyle asked. 'They're skins. I told you, they're empty.'

'You also told me the skins used to be real people. Real histories. Families. Friends.' I held his gaze. Good thing I'd had practice with that, because Lyle had the eerie Djinn thing down pat.' I want to know because it's the only way we can honor their memories.'

He seemed to understand that. 'The engineer's mate is Jason Ng. He joined the crew twelve years ago. He had a wife and three children in New Orleans, and a mistress in Brazil. The other was once named Angelo Marconi, from Naples. His sister owns a restaurant there. His family thinks he's still away at school.'

'School,' I murmured. 'How old—'

'He is dead, Warden.'

'How *old*?'

'The skin is sixteen,' Lyle said. 'I'm sorry. But you can't let what they're wearing fool you into hesitating. You know that, don't you?'

I knew. I also knew that if push came to shove, if I had to stand there and sling fire at a sixteen-year-old boy, I wasn't going to be very good at it.

But I knew someone who would be.

I found Kevin Prentiss on the ship's main promenade deck, standing at the railing. He was watching the thick gray foaming clouds and the iron-colored water with its lacings of white, and he looked – as always – like a punk streetwise kid who needed to learn the concept of personal hygiene.

The difference these days was that Kevin had pulled himself together, to a greater extent than I'd ever thought possible. He'd earned himself some respect from his fellow Fire Wardens. He'd learnt something from his apprenticeship to Lewis. He still looked greasy, but it was mostly hair product and deliberately baggy clothing. He had at least a handshake acquaintance with regular bathing.

However, Kevin *still* hated me. The look he sent me as I approached was a shot across my own personal bow, warning me to steer clear. I ignored it and took up a post at the rail beside him, leaning on the wood and bracing myself against the rise and fall of the deck with my feet well spread.

'You look like shit,' Kevin said, and flipped half a lit cigarette into the air. Before it hit the water, it had burst into flame. Nothing but ash to litter the ocean. 'Congratulations on the improvement.'

'Well, you know me, I'm all about the cutting-edge fashion trends.'

'What, beat to shit is the new black?' Kevin abandoned the ocean to turn and face me. He still needed a haircut, but his pimples were mostly gone now, and he'd filled out while I wasn't looking, turning from a skinny beanpole to something closer to lean and hungry. I supposed some girls went for that.

Like Cherise, now that I thought about it. The kid was legal age. I knew she'd originally been attracted to him because he was needy, broken, and bad; I also knew that she'd been the perfect foil for him, to remind him that he had better things inside.

Kevin liked to put on the badass hat, though. And always would.

He studied me out of the corner of his eye. 'You want something,' he said.

'Why would you say that?'

'Because you never talk to me unless you want something.'

'So not true,' I said. I held my breath for a second, then let it out. 'OK, I want something.'

He didn't even have to waste his breath on an *I told you so*. 'Big or small?'

'Pretty big.'

'And I'd do it for you because . . . ?'

'Because you're a good man, somewhere deep underneath all that greasy stupid kid disguise,' I said. 'Because you want to be, or you wouldn't be out here on this insanely stupid trip. And because you don't want anything to happen to Cherise.'

He straightened up. He was getting taller all the time, and now his body language reminded me less of skate parks and more of Lewis in a really foul mood. 'You should never have dragged her off with us.'

'I didn't. Cher goes everywhere with her eyes wide open, you know that. I'm just saying that of all of us, she's the least able to defend herself if something bad happens, so she's a good reminder note, because we both care about her.'

Kevin muttered something impolite under his breath that I pretended not to hear, and turned back to glare at the ocean. Steam rose from a couple of waves before he got himself back under control. I was impressed. A few months ago, he'd have vaporized a few metric tons of ocean in a fit of pique.

Of course, *not having* a fit of pique would be better still, but baby steps.

'What do you want?' he asked, in a different kind of tone than before. Actually asking for information instead of confronting. Good for him. And good for me, of course.

'I want you to make friends with a Djinn named Lyle,' I said. 'Pick a team and stay alert. You may have to react quickly.'

'Lyle?' Kevin let out a braying laugh that got whipped away by the fiercely driven wind. I licked my lips, and tasted salt and metal. 'You're shitting me. OK, never mind, I won't even ask. React quickly to what?'

'He's going to be keeping watch on a couple of people who aren't supposed to be here.' I reached out and grabbed Kevin's shoulder, turning him toward me. 'Kevin. Pay attention. This isn't a joke. These two are very, very dangerous, even to the Djinn. Even to you. So don't get cocky.'

'Me?' He gave me a look so ironic it was practically tipped over into sincerity. 'You're not telling me something. Or, like, anything.'

'I told you they're dangerous.'

'How, toxic body odor? Really sour attitudes? Can they kill me with their brains?'

I gave up, and held on to the rail as the ship took a particularly hard dip into the water, almost a bounce. The waves were getting thicker and deeper, and the storm behind us was finding gangs of friends to our port and up ahead. It was going to hit us sooner rather than later.

'They're not human,' I said. 'They're fast, they're deadly. Think *Alien*, made out of indestructible crystal, only with human skin.'

'Wouldn't that be *Terminator* or something?'

'Enough of the movies. This isn't funny, Kevin, it's serious. The one in the ship's hold is wearing the body of a sixteen-year-old boy.' There, I'd said it.

And he understood it. 'And that's easier for me, right? Because I won't see him as just a kid. I see him as more of an equal.'

I nodded unwillingly. 'I'm not putting you out there alone,' I said. 'But I know you. I know you won't hesitate if—'

'If I have to kill somebody who looks like he just got passed up for his junior prom? Yeah, I'm definitely that guy.'

I didn't answer that, because there was a new note in his voice: self-loathing. Kevin hadn't lived an easy life.

He was more pragmatic than most kids I'd ever met, and tougher, too. But that didn't mean he wanted to be, even though he wore his damage like a badge of honor.

'I'm sorry,' I said, finally. 'I wish I didn't have to ask you.'

'I wish I wasn't the go-to guy to kill monsters dressed as teens, but there you go.' He shrugged. 'At least I've got experience.'

And that was the heart of it, at last. I'd come to Kevin because I'd seen him kill without hesitation, and without remorse. Granted, he'd had plenty of personal hatred built up, but it took a special kind of detachment to do what he'd done and never suffer much guilt about it. He mostly resented the fact that we all knew about it – not that he'd been forced to do it.

'I'm not your pet psycho.' I flinched, because Kevin could have been reading my mind. 'But yeah, I'll find Lyle and do this. Just don't put me on speed dial the next time you have to push a school bus off a cliff or something. So. What's our approved monster-killing technique?'

I pulled the tissue-wrapped crystal tooth out of my pocket. 'Let's find out.' The thing glittered like a diamond in the dull light.

We took the fragment with us, found a crew member to open up the gym for us, and moved equipment to get clear floor space for our experiments. Kevin took to the scientific method with enthusiasm, because there's nothing a teenage kid likes better than trying to destroy something that's indestructible. Kevin tried so many kinds of fire that even I was impressed with the variety and breadth of control he had over it, especially since he didn't kill us in the process.

Except that nothing worked, and eventually Kevin tried stomping on the thing in frustration. That didn't work so well, either.

'Let me,' I said, and crouched down across from where the glittering crystal shard lay between us. Kevin mimicked me from about four feet away.

'No fair using Earth powers,' he said. 'I'll call bullshit.'

'You'll be working with an Earth warden, idiot,' I said. 'Watch and learn. I'm going to start with super-low frequencies and work my way up. You watch the structure with me. If you see any response at all, tell me.'

'If I'd known this favor of yours would mean sitting around watching you use a vibrator, I would've said hell yeah earlier—'

'Bite me,' I said. He flipped me off. I ignored him – mostly – and paid attention to the structure of the crystal.

It took the better part of an hour, but we pinpointed the frequency range that had the greatest effect on the thing. I couldn't get to Venna's epic pulverising effect, but I figured that anything that cracked and shattered the bone would do. At the very least, it would distract the holy living hell out of the enemy.

'Yeah, that's great,' Kevin said, as I wrote down the numbers. 'Big problem. I can't do that, genius. It takes a tree hugger.'

'And I'll get one for you,' I said. 'But I wouldn't call her a tree hugger if I was you. She'll make your face grow backwards if you piss her off.' I wrote down the name – Maida Manning. Three hundred pounds of extremely sarcastic Earth Warden who wouldn't take any of Kevin's bullshit. Maida also had a vicious sense of humor. I could see a beautiful friendship developing, unless of course they managed to kill each other first.

I'm so public-spirited.

'Give her this,' I said, and handed him the written instructions. 'Tell her I'll give her a raise if she manages to not kill you before you kill the bad guys. But whatever you do, wait for Lyle to give a signal to move. Got it?'

'Of course I've got it. I've got an IQ above your dress size.' He paused. 'Then again, it might be the other way around. I mean, do they even make dress sizes in the hundred and fifties?'

Cherise was having a terrible influence on the kid. I decided that one of us really needed to stay focused on professional dignity, and so I settled for a rude gesture instead of a comeback.

'Score,' he said. He walked away, just another bad-attitude teen from his messy, uncombed hair to his dragging, world-weary sneakers.

It takes a special kind of courage to know your own darkness, I thought. I wished he didn't have to be such an expert, but as long as he was, I had no choice but to take advantage of his skills.

Lewis was going to take my head off for it, too.

Chapter Six

Passengers – even me – weren't allowed on the bridge. Apparently, that only happens in the movies, or to Cherise. I helped Lewis get through the rest of the passenger and crew interviews in neutral, nonsecure locations. No real surprises: a couple of drug smugglers, some embezzlers, and a few people who had raided the cabin steward's closet for illegally obtained soaps and pillow mints. Other than that, we were clear of evil influences . . . except for the two we already knew about.

And me, of course. I was acutely aware that the tingles from the numb area on my back were coming with more and more frequency.

By late evening, I was feeling exhausted and even more sore than I'd anticipated. Cherise forced sandwiches on me, and then a glass of scotch, and I dozed off curled up in the corner of a sofa in the first-class-lounge area, listening to half a dozen Wardens debate the logistics of creating a clear course for us to follow. I was wishing that David would drop in, but I knew all too well that Lewis had other plans in motion – plans that specifically excluded me, thanks to the Bad Bob mark on my back. Need to know, and all that.

So I napped.

Lightning flared, startling me, and when I opened my eyes, I was somewhere else.

No . . . I realized that I *wasn't* somewhere else. My body was still huddled on the sofa, still watched over by Wardens and Djinn alike. Protected.

But I was *also* standing in a small concrete room with bare, dusty floors and a few battered old chairs held together with wire and tape, and it was nowhere near the ship that still held my physical form.

It's not real, I thought, but it felt damned convincing.

The door opened on howling darkness, and I could feel the blast of sea-salted air that rolled through the room to stir up debris.

When the door closed, a bandy-legged old white-haired man moved into the pallid circle of overhead light, Bad Bob, in the flesh. At least, I presumed it was flesh. I was starting to wonder how real the real world actually was, in relation to what my former boss could accomplish these days.

'Look who dropped in for a visit,' Bob said, and

pulled up a rickety chair. He flopped into it – risking total collapse of the ancient wood – and sat there smiling at me as if I were a favorite niece come for the holidays. Honestly, that was the worst thing about him. You couldn't really tell how crazy he was at a glance.

Or how vile.

I could hear the wind howling and it grated on me, and I wanted to lift my hands to cover my ears – only my ears weren't physical. *I* wasn't physical. I was a spirit in the aetheric, and there was simply no way that Bad Bob could see me, or that my spirit could walk around like this in the real world. Surely this was a dream. No, a nightmare. Except it felt real, from the gritty concrete floor under my feet to the demented shrieking of the storm winds outside.

'I thought I'd give you guys a chance to surrender,' I said. My voice sounded distant and disembodied, and I wasn't sure he could hear it until his smile widened. He was an evil old man, but he still had a charming smile. It went well with his apple-red cheeks and blunt little nose. 'I'd hate to skip the niceties. Courtesy is so important.'

'You're playing my song, sugar,' he said. 'You're also playing my game. I wonder why?'

I smiled to match him. 'Guess.'

'If I have to. Well, you found my little friend on board your ship – I felt him shuffle off this mortal coil. Good for you. Bet you can't do that again, though.'

He studied me with those fluorescent eyes – almost Djinn eyes, these days, brighter and more intense than they'd been in the old days when he'd been my boss, a genuine Warden hero. 'I have to hand it to you, I figured you guys would argue until doomsday about what to do about me,' he continued. 'Seriously now, a *cruise ship*? I didn't see that coming. Beautiful. I thought maybe a yacht, or a freighter. But putting all those people in the line of fire? You're growing a pair, sweetness. I like that.'

I waited. Bad Bob always had liked to hear his own voice more than anyone else's.

'But you know what I think?' he continued, right on cue. 'I think it's so showy that it's desperate. Like dressing up in neon and waving look-at-me flags while blaring Tchaikovsky's Fifth. You really should study magicians. Misdirection, that's the key to a good trick.'

'You think I'm tricking you?'

'You're not that subtle,' he said, which stung because it was true, mostly. 'But there's somebody else on board that ship who is.'

We both knew that he was talking about Lewis. 'You've still got a chance to end this peacefully,' I said. 'Let Rahel go. Give up. It doesn't have to be Armageddon: Atlantic Edition. We can find a way to make this work, Bob. Or whatever you are.'

'I'm still Bob,' he said, and winked at me, just the way Bad Bob would have back in the old days. 'I'm just Bob plus. And I don't think we're going to come to any nice, peaceful settlement, princess. This isn't about dividing up territory or setting boundaries. This is about me, wiping all of you off the face of the earth, and then my, friends coming in to take everything else. It's nature's way, you know. The strong eat the weak. The many eat the few. And I am about to eat *you*.'

He smiled, opened his mouth, and his jaws gaped hideously wide, like a snake's. If this was a nightmare, it was a first-class effort out of my very darkest subconscious.

I stepped back from him.

His jaws re-formed and closed. The Cheshire Cat smile remained. 'Don't look so scared,' he said. 'You wouldn't believe the stuff I can do with my tongue. Bet I could make you forget all about that wimpy little Djinn boy you're so taken with. Give me a chance – No? All right, then. I guess I'll just have to settle for something else. Thanks for being so accommodating and wandering on over here, by the way. I figured you might, sooner or later. The torch has that effect on people. It just draws people to me, whether they like it or not.'

He took two steps forward, thrust out his hand, and put it all the way through my ghostly, insubstantial chest. Unsettling, and a little uncomfortable, but I actually felt a little spurt of triumph. *Not as easy as you thought it would be*, I was about to say, when I realized that he'd reached to a very specific place.

To the ghostly mark on my back. The black torch. His fingertips brushed against it beneath my translucent skin – I could feel it, even if I couldn't see it happening.

All of a sudden the room was far too small, like a trap, and I wanted to leave this place, now, before something happened.

Too late.

I felt my physical body, still far away on board the ship, writhing in its sleep. I felt the hot tingle of the black torch begin to spread across my shoulder blade.

I'd lost David's containment, and because I was asleep, he might not know it.

Bad Bob removed his hand from my chest, shook it as if he was flicking something nasty off his fingers, gave me a feral grin, and walked away, I struggled to figure out what was holding me here, in this place, pinned like a bug to a board. *The mark*. He was right. Until I figured out how to turn it off – if I could – he could keep me here, out of my body. I knew that the longer I stayed out, the worse it was going to be when I got back.

I remembered the Wardens, lost in the storm. If my spirit was shredded, my body would just . . . stop. And they would never know why.

Outside, a truly ferocious storm raged. I felt the hot, damp blast of air burst into the room, stirring grit and pushing the rickety sticks of furniture in random fury. Lightning flashed like strobes, turning Bad Bob's pale hair and face into a fright mask.

He reached outside, and when his hand came back through the doorway, it was holding a spear. I recognized the thing – it was thick, and it sparkled with bursts of something that wasn't color, wasn't darkness, wasn't anything human senses could identify or codify. He'd refined his weapons, I saw. This spear had started out life as a small chunk, grown in the dying body of a Djinn, and Bad Bob had given it enough care and feeding to make it a seven-foot-long, wickedly pointed expression of his own appetite for destruction.

The Djinn called it the Unmaking. It was, as best I understood the physics of it, stable antimatter, capable of destroying anything he wanted to destroy.

Including removing Djinn from the fabric of the universe.

'Oh, Bob, that's just sad,' I said. His grin broadened. 'Seriously, why can't your type ever grow a discus for a weapon, or the world's largest potato? How come it's always so – phallic?'

Bob ignored the opportunity to banter, and stepped out into the storm. He looked up at it, into the heart of it. I knew what he was seeing – the raging engine of destruction, the primitive mind forming behind it. This was a living thing, this storm – a predator, yes, but a natural one, like a tiger or a puma.

He ground the butt of his spear against the dirt, and a blinding pulse of something that wasn't light, wasn't heat, wasn't *right* went up from the pointed end of the spear into the storm.

Again.

Again.

With every thump of that weapon against the earth, I felt the world itself shudder. On the aetheric, muddy red waves spread like blood from a mortal wound.

The force emitted from the spear had a sickening feel to it, and the color – if you could call it a color – was a poisonous, pallid thing, like the glow given off by decay.

The storm's lightning suddenly flashed, but it wasn't light.

It was *dark*. Photonegative energy, but here on the real world. He'd infected the storm itself, made it a force for destruction far different from any natural predator.

And then it flashed that unearthly emerald green.

'Almost ready,' Bad Bob said, and reversed his grip on the spear. Handling that much anti-energy couldn't have been pleasant, even for him; I could see the skin blackening and flaking away where his hand touched the surface. 'Ready for the cherry on top?'

He pointed the spear down at the ground, and drove it in. It went deep, even though he didn't use any real force – as if it tunneled greedily on its own.

I felt the earth shriek in real pain beneath my ghostly feet, and the whole building shook. Grit filtered down in feathery whispers, and then the *real* lurch came.

The building exploded as force traveled up through the ground, pulverising layers of granite into dust. The cinder blocks of the walls buckled, ground themselves into powder against each other, and the ceiling crashed in a twisting, tearing mass of wood and metal that was snatched away by the wind.

Nothing touched me.

I stood exactly where I had as the building disintegrated around me, ripped away by the howling Category 5 winds. The ground lurched like pounding surf underneath me.

Bad Bob rose up into the air, holding to the end of his spear. He kept rising.

The spear grew, and grew, like some poisonous tree with its roots sunk deep.

He broke it off at ground level. It shattered at the stress point with a musical, glassy sound I heard even above the shriek of the storm.

A palm tree toppled and rolled toward me. Through me. Bad Bob landed on the rippling earth in front of me, appallingly normal in this terribly destroyed setting, and used the remaining part of his spear as a walking stick. *Thump. Thump. Thump.* It echoed through me like the beating of Poe's telltale heart.

Around us formed a little circle of clear air, stable ground, like the eye of the hurricane. It expanded, and other people appeared out of the chaos. Wardens, once upon a time. I recognized many of them, at least by face if not by name. His pets, his converts to his righteous war against the Djinn – not that Bad Bob cared a bean about killing the Djinn to benefit humanity. Oh no. Bad Bob cared only, and always, about his own ends, and whatever these pathetic, deluded people thought they were getting out of fighting on his side, they were bound to be disillusioned.

I assessed numbers. Might as well, since I was stuck here. It did occur to me that Bad Bob was showing me only what he *wanted* to show me, of course, but for all that, the guy who keeps showing off will eventually show you something he doesn't intend to.

Bad Bob was one hell of a chatterbox.

Sixty of them. My spirits sank, which was no doubt what he'd counted on. He had numbers. Of course, we had more, but add to that Bad Bob's Demon-derived powers and the neat trick of handheld antimatter that the Djinn could neither recognize nor defend against, and we were well on the train to Screwsville.

'You still think you can win?' he asked me. I didn't answer, because I wasn't sure I dared tell a lie right now, and a lie was all I really had. 'Scared little Jo. It was always going to end like this, you know. You against me, and you never could take me.'

'I did take you,' I said. 'You sadistic old bastard.'

He lost his smile and pointed the spear at me. 'Wonder what happens if I give it a taste of you in your aetheric form?' he said. 'Bet it'll hurt like fuck.'

'Bet you don't want to be around when I survive it and come to kick your sorry ass off the face of the planet.'

He laughed and grounded the butt of the spear again. 'I always did like that about you. You got sand, I'll give you that.' He leant forward, eyes avid and wet. 'Fight me, Jo. I love it when you fight me. It won't matter in the end, but it'll be damn fun. You thought by dragging the Wardens away from all those innocent people on shore you'd save lives, but I think you just made my job a whole lot easier. See? You were already working for me. And now you're going *to really* draw your paycheck, peach.'

'Like hell,' I said.

He blew me a kiss. Back on the ship's sofa, my body continued to twitch and writhe. Cherise sat down next to me, putting a hand on my forehead, then calling for help.

The sensation of her hand against my skin was just enough to form a link – a way back. I pulled. The black mark felt like Velcro, sticking me here to this spot, but I ripped and tore at it, struggling, and with a hissing snap I came free.

I called lightning.

A white blast of energy erupted out of the clouds overhead – clean, pale energy, not the poisoned kind he'd poured into the storm – and struck me squarely in the top of my insubstantial head, flooding through my form in a splintered glowing ladderwork, then blasting out into the ground.

It shattered the remaining connection that held me at Bad Bob's command, and I flew backward through the screaming darkness, whipping past pitch-black writhing ocean, over half-seen bits of island, into calmer seas.

Into the massive, smugly sailing bulk of the *Grand Paradise*.

Into my body, with a lurch like a slap.

I came awake with a gasp that felt like a shriek. My back was burning, on fire, and I tried to lunge to my feet. It felt like my entire nervous system cut out, faulty wiring shorting and sparking.

I pitched off the sofa to the carpet and got a taste of rug.

Cherise was instantly on her knees beside me, trying to cradle me in her arms. I couldn't let her touch me. Everything felt wrong, strange, bad, vile . . . and I wasn't sure that it wasn't contagious.

'No,' I panted, and crab-crawled back to jam myself against the bottom of the sofa. 'No, leave me alone!'

'Help!' Cherise shouted. That got the attention of some passing crew members. A passing steward – I still didn't know his name, but he was the one who'd been trying to manage the First-Class rebellion before we'd set sail – shoved aside the coffee table and reached down for me. 'Miss, are you all right? Should I get medical help?'

I wrapped my hand convulsively around the white lapel of his jacket, and where my fingers gripped the fabric, it started to smoke and hiss.

He exclaimed and tried to claw his way free. I couldn't let go. My hand didn't seem to be *mine*, exactly; it was moving, and I could feel what it was doing, but it was holding him in place.

Part of me wanted to destroy him. A big part of me, and it was growing larger as the broken containment on my back allowed the poison from the torch mark to flood into me. The dam was breached.

I was being swept away.

The steward struggled, panted, yelled for help, and finally managed to slip out of his jacket, which remained clutched in my fist as it burst into full smoking flame. I heard other voices – Wardens? – in a rising babble. Somebody tried to tamp down the fire that was bubbling up from my fingers, but I couldn't stop it. All my nerves were fried, useless; all my control had gone with them.

The jacket caught the rug on fire.

Someone hit me with a good old-fashioned fire extinguisher, but as soon as the icy foam stopped blasting, fire erupted from *both* my hands, crawling up my arms like snakes, twining around my body in living veils of flame.

I could feel other things happening inside me now – fire was always the easiest of powers to call, because it was virtually unstoppable even in natural form, but now I could feel my other abilities stirring, too. Something inside me was rifling through my mind, my soul, shuffling aside unwanted things to find the most devastating things on offer.

I was an open doorway, and *something was reaching through*.

I think I might have screamed, but if I did, it was just in my head. My body stood up, dripping flame as my clothing burnt away, leaving me draped in living energy. I could see myself reflected in the lounge windows – a pillar of fire, a pagan goddess, naked and primal. My hair didn't burn, but it rose and fluttered on the waves of heat created from my skin.

My eyes were Djinn eyes, flaring gold, and where I touched, things blackened and smoked and charred into ruin.

'Back!' someone snapped to the growing cluster of onlookers, and a hardened bubble of air formed around me, thick as steel. The fire erupting out of me consumed the available oxygen in seconds, then began to gutter and fail as its fuel ran out.

I felt nothing, except that all-consuming heat exploding from the black torch on my shoulder. It seemed to be getting worse, not better, as if someone had injected me with acid. If I'd had control of my voice, I'd have been begging for it to stop.

The cold, blackened part of me inside still had control, but it allowed me to collapse into a naked, smoking heap inside the air bubble. I struggled to breathe, but there was nothing left to fill my lungs that wasn't toxic.

Someone stepped up on the other side of the bubble.

Lewis.

The darkness in me took over, but it did it in a horrifyingly clever way.

I lifted my hand and slapped my palm flat against the bubble, pleading for mercy. My fingernails were turning a delicate robin's-egg shade of blue. I must have looked completely pathetic and weak,

I wasn't. Not at all.

There was something very strange in the way he was looking at me. Something my grandmother used to say. *Tombstone eyes . . .*

Lewis's head snapped around, not fast enough, and something collided with him. A streak of bronze light that froze into the form of David, on the other side of my invisible prison.

I watched Lewis's lips move. He was yelling at David, telling him not to be a fool, not to fall for it. *He knew.*

He needn't have worried. David might be passionate, but he was no kind of a fool. He crouched down and put his hand flat against mine, separated by five inches of thickened, impenetrable, interlocked molecules. His face was a mask, his eyes dark and secretive, but not quite managing to hide his fury – at me, at himself, at Bad Bob for putting us here.

I smiled, tasting his despair – it felt *good*.

The talisman burnt into my back hit a white-hot peak, and I felt my Weather powers flooding out of me, battering at the prison holding me. Lewis was incredibly strong, maybe the strongest Warden who'd ever lived, but I was damn close on this front. I hadn't always been, or at least I hadn't always known it, but I was afraid that very strength was going to be my undoing now . . . because I could feel my powers eating away at the force he'd set up to keep me contained. Once it broke, there was no telling what I'd do. What I *could* do. Possibilities raced through my mind, each worse than the last – poison gas drifting through the sealed corridors of the ship, killing everyone it touched. Or maybe I'd just blow a gigantic hole through the bottom, sending this beautiful floating coffin down to join other famous wrecks. I could almost see that one – the foaming rush of the sea through the shattered hull, the rooms filling up, all these people trapped and dying . . .

God, I wanted to do it.

I couldn't let this happen. I couldn't be the cause of so much death.

Bad Bob had done one thing for me, thanks to this little exercise in hellish torment; he'd shown me how to break loose. I wasn't trapped in my body; my body existed separately from my spirit, connected only by random impulses and autonomic functions. I pulled away and stretched to the limit. I arrowed up into the aetheric, feeling the bond stretch and pull, thinner and thinner. At the top of the aetheric, there was a flickering white milky light – the boundary of another world above that one. Another plane of existence. The Djinn could pass through it. Humans couldn't, not even Wardens.

I touched it, trailed ethereal fingers against the barrier, and looked down. Distances and heights didn't mean the same things up on the higher planes, but in this sense they did – there was a form of gravity, and momentum, and forces that translated from the aetheric back to the physical.

I let go, turned, and put all my power into an accelerated dive back to my physical body. Instead of letting myself *fall*, I *raced*, gathering as much force along the way as I could. Pulling it directly from the aetheric, like the wake from a speedboat. I'd never tried this; I knew that there were Earth Wardens who had, who'd managed to get a power boost through this technique. It wouldn't last, and it came at a heavy cost, but it was at least something to try.

They never told me how bad it would *hurt*, though.

Hitting the physical form of my body had a psychic shock wave, like slamming head-on into a bank vault at eighty miles per hour. Then the aetheric wake slammed in behind me, temporarily compressing me inside.

I blew it out through the mark on my back, channeling it through the black lines. It overloaded within an instant, shocking the mark into silence, sending it back into its containment state.

I raised my head and looked David in the eye and mouthed *Help*. I didn't know if he'd believe me or not – I almost hoped he wouldn't – but without him, I knew that sooner or later this was going to end in my death.

My whole body was trembling, anoxic, on the edge of unconsciousness. I couldn't create oxygen from the toxic soup of molecules left inside this bubble; I'd have to break the shell, get some kind of feed from the outside.

Or maybe I'd die. That wasn't a bad solution, all things considered. Not my fave, admittedly, but it would save innocent lives, and—

David's outstretched palm pushed through the hard shell of air. Stress fractures formed as white cracks around his fingers, and then he broke through, and a rush of delicious air fanned my hair back from my face. The bubble disintegrated. I dropped facedown to the floor.

A weight settled on top of me – David, straddling me. Slamming his hand down on top of the black mark, and if I'd thought that sucker was painful already, this was a thousand times worse, so bad that I couldn't stop screaming, writhing, trying to claw my way out of the pain.

'I'll kill you!' I was screaming. And worse. And I meant it.

Lewis took my wrists and held me still. Somebody else grabbed my flailing legs and anchored them. It was like old-style surgery without the benefit of anesthesia, this feeling of something vital being cut out of me, bloody and dripping . . .

And then it stopped.

I collapsed, sobbing helplessly. I couldn't feel David's hand on my back. I couldn't feel anything from the nape of my neck to my waistline; it had all gone icily numb.

'Mother of God,' someone among the onlookers murmured, and the tone was so appalled that I wondered just what he was seeing. I didn't care. It was enough that it didn't hurt, just for a few precious breaths.

'Get the medical team,' Lewis said. His voice sounded strangely rough, low in his throat. When I turned my head and focused on him, his eyes were red, lids swollen. There were tears tracking down his cheeks.

He was still holding my wrists in a brutally tight grip.

'I'm OK,' I said. I wasn't. I felt hollow and odd, as if I was floating several feet from my own emotions. 'Hey. Don't worry. I won't go nuclear on you.' I didn't think I had anything left, anyway. 'I'm losing, you know. Can't hold it.'

Lewis let go, very slowly, and swiped his arm across his eyes. He sat back on his haunches, and his gaze moved away from me, up and behind.

Locking eyes with David, presumably.

I felt David's warm hand touch the back of my neck. 'Don't move,' he said. He sounded almost as odd as Lewis. 'I need to tell you something.'

This didn't sound positive. 'What?'

'The mark. It's gone.'

Wasn't that good? 'And?'

There was a short, heavy silence. David said, 'It burnt off your skin, all the way down to the bone in places. I've tried to close the wound, but—'

'It won't let you,' I finished for him. That explained the emergency numbness covering my entire back, and the shocked trembling of my muscles. I felt cold, too. My body was trying to marshal its resources against a life-threatening crisis. 'It doesn't matter, the mark's still there. It's buried inside me. I can't burn it out. Was anyone hurt?'

David let out an uneven breath. 'Other than you?' I felt his weight ease off of me, and then he moved into view, kneeling next to me. Lewis moved out of his way. 'No. You didn't hurt anyone. You fought it off.'

'No. Not really.' I swallowed and tried to order my drifting, scattered priorities. 'I saw Bad Bob. He has sixty former Wardens with him. I can tell you where.'

'Jo—' That was Lewis again, soft and almost regretful. 'We can't believe you now. You understand that, don't you? You can't know that any of what you saw is real. He could have put it there. He's a manipulative son of a bitch. Even if it was true, he'll move before we can get there.'

'He knows,' I said. 'He knows we got one of the skins. He'll be activating the others. You have to move, now. Stop them.'

Lewis tore his gaze away from me. 'David, I'm going to need you.'

'No,' David said.

'If this ship goes down, she still dies. Is that what you want?'

David's eyes flashed – not fire, not bronze, but white-hot, like the flash from the sharp edge of a diamond. 'I'll give you all the power you need. I'll assign Djinn to you. But I won't leave her. Don't ask me again.' The edge to his voice scared me, and I reached out to touch his hand.

'No,' I said. 'I'm not dead, I'm just massively screwed up.' I sucked in a deep breath. 'Help me sit up.'

David didn't like the idea, but he saw that if he didn't, I'd flail around and do it anyway, probably hurting myself even more. 'Wait,' he said. 'Bandages.'

I suppose the medical team had arrived, because I was lifted up to a sitting position, my arms were raised, and I got wrapped up like a mummy, from waist to just under my armpits. It was a very odd sensation – I could feel every bit of the pressure and texture on my front and sides, but the bandages simply disappeared when they touched my back.

It took care of half the problem that I was naked in the middle of a crowd. Somebody brought in one of the cruise line's fluffy guest robes, which took care of the other half once I'd gotten it on and belted.

When I faltered getting up, Cherise ducked in and braced me, arms around my waist. David held me up on the other side. 'I'd carry you, but—' I understood. There was no way for him to do it without putting pressure on my ruined back.

'It's fine. I can walk.' I wasn't sure I could, but damned if I wasn't going to try. As I stood there catching my breath and my balance, though, I took a look around.

I'd pretty much managed to trash the first-class lounge. The sofa was a skeletal wreck, burnt through to the springs. The carpet where I'd been standing (or lying) was melted and blackened into a tangled knot of ash and acrylic fibers. Add to that the still-lingering smoke that curled blackly around the room, seeking exits, and the general reek of burnt flesh . . . Yeah. That security deposit was gone for good.

'Sorry,' I apologized, to no one in particular, and concentrated on putting one foot in front of the other on the way out of the room.

I heard a dull *boom* from below us, somewhere in the bowels of the ship, and looked at David's tense expression.

'It's not your problem,' he said.

Whether it was or not, he wasn't going to let me claim responsibility of any kind.

'Are we sinking?' I asked.

We were sitting on my narrow bed – me lying on my stomach, David propped on the edge, looking down at me. The ship was rocking much worse than before, slamming into waves with such force that I swore I could hear metal groaning somewhere in the bowels of the vessel. Of course, that was stupid; big as this thing was, I'd never know if something was going catastrophically wrong. The iceberg that had killed the *Titanic* hadn't even knocked over glasses in the dining room.

Of course, the *Titanic* hadn't been wallowing in massively turmoiled seas, beset from all sides, and between being driven toward an even worse predator. We were like a whale being stalked by a school of sharks. Sooner or later, they'd take out enough bites to make a difference.

'No,' David said, and stroked my hair. 'No, we're not sinking.'

'You think the mark's gone,' I murmured, and closed my eyes. 'It's not. I can still feel it.' My mind kept wanting to shut down, lock itself off, focus on summoning up its strength for healing, but I couldn't seem to let it go.

David shifted. He probably touched my shoulder,

or at least the bandages over the open wound, but I couldn't feel anything. 'I know,' he said. 'I can see it on the aetheric.'

'It's bigger.'

'Yes.'

'I said I'd kill you, didn't I?' He didn't answer. 'I meant it. I really did, David. The only thing that's stopping me is the containment. You understand?'

'I do.' He brushed fingers gently over my forehead. 'It's not your fault.'

'It will be,' I said. I felt a distant, inescapable grief, but like everything else, it was arm's length from me. I really couldn't *feel* anything. 'How's Kevin doing?'

David was silent for a long enough minute that I had to fight to stay awake to hear the answer. 'He's doing well.' My lover sounded surprised. Well, I supposed I was a little bit surprised, too. Pleasantly so. 'One of the skins has already been destroyed. They're hunting the other one in the hold. They're getting close.'

'No problems?' It was odd to be worried by that, but I was. Things never went that easily, did they? Not in my experience.

'If there are, it's for someone else to handle,' he said. 'Rest. We'll see to things.'

He seemed confident. I went over that in my head like a string of worry beads, and finally said, 'You did warn Lyle, right? Not to take the skin on directly?'

David frowned. 'I don't know what you're talking about.'

'Don't you remember?' I rolled over on my side to stare up at him. 'These things are lethal to Djinn. David, you have to pull the Djinn back. Let the Wardens handle this one.'

'I will.'

Was he just humoring me? It was understandable if he was; I wasn't sounding overly competent just now. Too tired, too sick, too much in shock. Besides, I was compromised. Even burning the tattoo right off my body hadn't destroyed the link between me and Bad Bob. I wasn't sure anything, short of my horrific and gruesomely painful death, would. That meant I couldn't really count on my mind being my own, or be sure that Bad Bob wasn't hooked into me like some kind of long-distance spy bug. I'd be perfectly placed for that kind of duty. He could use me, and there would be nothing – *nothing* – I could do to stop him.

Bad Bob could use me as the hammer, to shatter the entire Warden organisation, not to mention the Djinn. Through my link to David, I compromised their safety, too.

'Jo.' David must have known what was going through my mind, because his tone and his touch were both gentle. 'You're alive. Don't underestimate your ability to come through this. I don't.'

'You want to be there, with them.'

'My place is here.'

'Your place is at the front of the battle. You're not Jonathan. You don't sit things out.' I couldn't quite suppress a smile. 'Being the Boss of Bosses doesn't really suit you, you know. You're more of a hands-on guy.'

'I'm not sitting anything out. I'm a Djinn. I don't have to be physically present to make things happen, you know.'

My brain drifted away, randomly connecting things. Wardens didn't have to be present to make things happen, either, although for Fire and Earth Wardens it was certainly a whole lot easier to be in close proximity – which was why Fire Wardens had a tendency to die fighting their fires . . .

My eyes opened. 'David,' I said. 'Who's with Kevin?'

'Don't worry, Lewis sent a whole team. Kevin's only part of it.' He thought I was worried about Kevin. I struggled to sit up, but my arms felt like wet spaghetti. David helped me. 'What?'

I didn't know exactly, but I *felt* something. 'I need to get to them. Right now.' A building anxiety. A conviction that something was very, very wrong. My arm's-length emotions were rapidly closing in on me.

'No. You're not going anywhere,' David said. He was right, horribly right; I couldn't summon up the energy to make it off the bed, much less carry on to a fight. But my heart was pounding, my palms sweating, and I could feel dread boiling up from the pit of my stomach. 'What is it?'

'*I don't know*! It's just—'

The whole ship shuddered beneath us. I looked at David, horrified, remembering the lessons of the *Titanic* all too clearly. I could see the same thing reflected in his face.

'Stay here.' He flared white and disappeared.

The *Grand Paradise* groaned like a living thing and heeled ponderously to starboard, rising and then settling back to vertical. Our little cabin didn't have the luxury of a balcony, but it did have a small reinforced porthole. I dragged myself off the bed and shoved aside the single guest chair to reach it.

I was staring at water. That wasn't possible. The deck we were on was far above the waterline – six stories above it, probably. How could I be looking at the water?

Were we sinking?

There was chaos outside. Shouting, screaming, rich people boiling out of their cabins and demanding to see the captain, which was their standard response to everything from being out of toothpaste to a terrorist attack. I kept myself upright by sheer force of will, edging along the wood paneling, heading for – what? I didn't know. I just knew I needed to get there.

Two people were in my way. I blinked, because quite frankly, the last two people I expected to see holding on to each other were the cabin stewardess Aldonza and movie princess Cynthia Clark. Their body language wasn't what I expected, either – no subservience from Aldonza, no arrogance from Clark. They were just two women, staying together for support and comfort.

They turned and looked at me with identical expressions of surprise that turned into concern.

'What the devil happened to you?' Cynthia Clark asked, and grabbed my left arm to support me. 'Mrs Prince?'

That still sounded odd to me. 'Oh, hell, call me Jo. Everybody does,' I said. I felt sick and dizzy and a little bit high. 'Aldonza. I need a door to the crew area. Right now.'

'Yes, Jo,' she said. Finally I'd made her give up the formality. Just in time for disaster. 'This way.' She took the lead, glancing back to make sure we were struggling along in her wake. The ship seemed to be wallowing more and more now, side to side. Lights were flickering.

I looked at Clark, taking the bulk of my weight, who seemed composed despite all the chaos around us. 'Thanks,' I said.

'You seem to be one of the people who can make sure we survive this,' she said. 'It seems reasonable to be sure you get where you're going.'

'Can I have your autograph?'

She smiled, and even now I couldn't see the strain. What an actor! 'Maybe later,' she said. 'I'll have my assistant drop some photos by. I hope I can sign them: *To the woman who saved my life.*'

'Well, if you can't, I'll let you off the hook for the headshots,' I said. I was shaking off my shock and weakness, though not quickly; I felt more alert, steadier on my feet. Good enough for shopping, maybe, if not fighting evil.

Too bad I was heading for the latter.

The subdued, elegant lighting in the hall flickered again, buzzed, and then died. After a heart-pounding five seconds of absolute blackness, emergency lighting clicked on with a hiss – glaring white halogens, not flattering to anyone's complexion, much less when people are distorted with terror. And somewhere in the back of my mind, I kept seeing water rising, rushing through corridors . . .

'Yeah,' I muttered to myself. 'Wish I'd never seen that damned movie.'

Aldonza paused at a simple metal door labeled PRIVATE, with a key card reader to the side. She swiped a card that was hanging from a pull cord at her side, but nothing happened. Of course. Emergency regulations – all electronic locks would have popped, allowing for easy evacuation. I grabbed the knob and turned it, and opened the door on a different world.

It was as startling as opening up a broom closet at the Ritz – all of a sudden, there was no expensive thick carpet, no indirect lighting, no artwork. Just metal, some indoor-outdoor carpet for traction, and plain fixtures that wouldn't have been out of place on a fish trawler. Aldonza stepped over the watertight lip of the door and gestured me inside. Clark tried to go with us, but I stopped her with an outstretched hand. 'No,' I said. 'Get to the lifeboat stations. The captain's probably going to try to get you off as quickly as possible.'

'In this storm? How?'

'Trust me. He'll find a way.' I shook her hand. 'Love your movies, by the way. Sorry about incinerating your cabin.'

'These things happen,' she said, deadpan. 'And I hope you find a way to stop this before it goes any further.'

Me too, I thought, but I didn't even really know what I was heading toward in the first place.

Aldonza shut the watertight door and spun the locking mechanism. Nobody would be getting in that way, not now.

'Come on,' she said, and offered me her shoulder. 'You want the hold, yes? Where your friends went?' I nodded, and off we went.

The hallways here were narrow industrial constructions, and as we passed larger open spaces they were uniformly workmanlike. A TV lounge area big enough for a few dozen, with comfortable but un-fancy Sears-style furniture. A computer area with banks of monitors and keyboards. A mess hall with all the charm of mess halls everywhere.

The place was deserted. 'Where is everybody?'

'Duty stations,' Aldonza said. 'Organising the passengers.'

All of them? I supposed that made sense; we were heading down now, flights of narrow stairs descending into the emergency-lit bowels of the ship. Stairs. Lovely. *Feel the burn, Baldwin.*

I wondered where David had gone.

'One more,' Aldonza murmured, when I had to stop for trembling breaths. 'You're sure you want to do this?'

'No choice,' I said, and coughed. 'Let's go.'

The bottom of the stairs opened into another hallway. This one held crew quarters – four narrow bunks to a room, top and bottom on each side, with small lockers in the middle on the far wall. Most had homey touches – photos of family home, friends. Magazines to read, or books. Colorful nonstandard blankets and pillows.

Aldonza stopped.

'What?' I asked. She let go of me and took a step back. I braced myself on the metal wall, looking first at her, then down the hall.

Lights were going out, one by one, marching up the corridor toward us.

'Which way to the hold?'

'That way,' she said. 'Straight on, then go left when you must turn. The crew entrance to the hold is there.'

'Get out of here,' I said. 'Run.'

She stared at me in confusion for a few seconds, then she must have seen what was happening inside me.

She backed away and ran.

And I went toward the darkness.

And the darkness went into me.

Chapter Seven

The danger sign was that I felt . . . better. Calmer. Steadier.

I shouldn't have, not at all. I was operating on threads, and yet suddenly I felt assured, in control, and *powerful*.

The containment was leaking. Leaking badly. I was starting to turn around again, and I needed to do what I'd come to do before that happened.

I wasn't totally blind. Earth Wardens can sense heat, shapes, all kinds of frequencies not usually accessible to other regular folks (or Wardens), and with my night vision, I could see the hallway, the cool shapes of closed doors, and a long empty stretch.

The hallway ended in a blind T-shaped intersection, and I turned left as Aldonza instructed. At the end was a big double-sized watertight door with all kinds of warnings and crew restrictions blazoned next to it.

I spun the wheel and pulled. The air on the other side felt heavy and thick, unpleasantly stale. No fire, at least. And no ocean flooding in, which made me wonder why we were sitting so low in the water.

The hold was massive, a cave of treasures that would have taken months to map and explore. Cargo containers were stacked in neat, symmetrical rows that glowed cool greens and blues in my night vision.

And I saw the bright red and yellow flicker of bodies up ahead.

None of them were moving.

I struggled with a fiery hot pulse of primal satisfaction, of pleasure. I pushed it back.

I limped ahead, stopping for breath when I had to, and the scene slowly came into focus. There, near the center of the hold, were cages where I supposed dutyfree items like liquor and expensive perfumes were kept. There was a massive freestanding safe, too, which no doubt held all those precious goodies the rich passengers had been so loath to leave behind. I wondered how much of it was drugs.

Standing, sitting, or lying in a circle near the safe were bodies. Some had the white-hot glow of Djinn, some the merely warm spectrum of human flesh, but none of them were moving by so much as a breath.

Still alive, though.

Not for long, the darkness inside me whispered, and purred. I felt it stretch its claws.

I limped as close as I dared before I felt something

tingling along the edges of my nerves. There was some kind of energy field here that I really didn't want to encounter directly.

This was the team, Wardens and Djinn, that had come here to fight the skin. I didn't sense the signature of the one they'd been hunting at all, though. Instead, I saw a broken heap of crystal, and some slagged flesh.

Score one for the good guys. So what had gone wrong?

Kevin was standing only a few feet from me, frozen in midstep. Up on the aetheric, I could see his fury boiling like lava, so he was aware, if unable to move.

'Hey!' I yelled. One of the Djinn – Lyle, with his lead gray skin and rust-colored eyes – was closer to me than the others. 'Lyle, can you hear me?'

'Yes,' he said. He couldn't move, but he could speak.

'What's happening?'

'We are all that's holding the ship out of the water,' he said. 'We have to hold our concentration, or the forces won't balance. This deck will collapse. The ship will sink.'

Instead of merely being frozen, the Wardens were in danger of being smashed, because there was a force *below* us, rising up from the blackest, coldest depths of the ocean . . . and it was pulling us down.

That was why the ship was riding low in the water.

It was caught in a downward suction, like a ball at the end of a vacuum hose.

If the Djinn let go, it wasn't just the team of Wardens who were fatally screwed.

We all were.

Good. This time, the darkness pooled in my guts, warm and velvety, and I had to choke back a sob. It would be so easy to let go. So utterly easy.

There was a grating sound in the hold, something scraping over metal. I crouched down, making myself as small a target as possible, as the voice echoed off of metal, wood, and immobile bodies. I heard the shuffle of footsteps, and saw an odd shape moving among the stacked cargo and luggage. It had the outward shine of a human form, but it was like a superimposition – beneath it lay something dark and twisted.

The skin. It had created some kind of decoy, which was what the pile of glass was not far from Kevin, for the Wardens to chase while the rest of the plan had gone into motion.

Great. We might have killed the powerful one first, but this one was the clever one.

The skin ducked behind a parked, covered Porsche, then flitted around some hanging chains and weights, more like nightmare than human form.

It paused long enough in the glow of an emergency light for me to get a good look at it. The body it wore was one of those fresh-faced kids who looked like they'd be more at home in a television ad for soap than running around murdering people. He was almost as pretty as a Djinn.

'Angelo,' I said. 'Angelo Marconi?'

It just looked at me. I could see now that Lyle was right – it was literally just skin, stretched like a Halloween mask over the darkness inside.

Like you, laughed my dark side. *Like you are becoming. Not long now* . . .

The skin flitted out of the light and into the darkness.

I had no idea what I was going to do if it came to power-on-power, because I was barely staying on my feet.

Ten feet away, the frozen statue garden of Wardens and Djinn glowed steadily in my night vision. I caught a moving glow, much cooler than the others, blue instead of yellow or white.

Angelo darted into the middle of the standing figures. I switched back to regular sight, and saw him put his hands on one of the Djinn. One of Ashan's, who snarled and struck back with invisible force that bounced off of Angelo's body like the impact from a water balloon.

Angelo's skin blackened, crisped, and flaked away, revealing the crystal underneath, as the Djinn fought him. I felt the ship lurch sharply downward as the Djinn's attention was pulled away from the task of holding the opposing forces in balance.

The Djinn began to turn a soft ashy gray. Rotting

from the outside in, the way the Djinn who'd died outside my room had ended her life.

I settled my back against the cold metal of the safe. If I was going to do anything at all, I didn't want to worry about falling down while I was about it. If what Venna had said was right, this thing was the forerunner of something much bigger, something that devoured on a universal scale. I thought about all those lifeless planets spinning in space that our telescopes and probes had found. How many of them had once been like us? How many had fallen prey and been wiped clean of life?

Why fight it? It's nature. You are all aberrations, a momentary mistake in the plan of the universe. Let go.

The ship bounced and settled deeper in the water. I heard the almost-human groan of the metal around me. It couldn't withstand this strain, not for much longer.

And neither could I.

I closed my eyes, visualized the frequencies I needed, and began to set them up in a tightly enclosed ring around the skin and his Djinn victim.

Nothing happened.

The Djinn struggled now, no longer interested in maintaining the balance, but he'd waited too long. He couldn't break free of the crystal claws that were digging into him, siphoning away his power and his life. He was losing.

I shifted frequencies.

The Djinn shrieked in unworldly agony as his body began to crumble away. The dark part of me met that with trembling eagerness, drinking in every agonized second of it.

I shifted frequencies again, blind to everything but the dance of molecules, the music of the energy being expended and absorbed.

Come on . . .

It wasn't strong enough.

Venna had been able to blow her victim to kingdom come, but she was Venna, a power of the ages. I was just a wounded, exhausted Warden up against something I didn't understand.

I was losing.

The Djinn who'd screamed was no longer recognizable as a Djinn at all. It was a pile of disintegrating ash and dust, sliding away from cohesion to scatter on the deck.

And I felt everything slipping away inside.

The ship groaned again, and I saw metal buckling, vast rivets ripping out of place, and the first jets of water blow through into the open space of the hold.

We started sinking again.

The skin turned to the next Djinn. Lyle.

I felt the shift of power in the room. The water stopped rushing in. The metal sealed and strengthened.

Where David walked, the world mended around him.

'No,' I whispered, but he wasn't going to stop, not for me. Not this time.

He wasn't going to allow Lyle to die.

Another watertight door opened on the other side of the hold, and a swarm of Wardens poured in, led by Lewis. In seconds, they had the skin surrounded.

But the skin had its claws buried in Lyle's chest, like some giant parasitical tick.

I switched frequencies one more time. Lewis saw what I was doing, and joined me; the other Earth Wardens quickly supported us, creating a resonance that was so powerful it began to shatter glass and crystal stored in the crates. Someone's eyeglasses broke under the strain.

I felt feedback – the exact frequency that this creature's bones sang to. I began to focus harder, refining the sound until it was at a lethal intensity. I could see the waves now, a standing well of ripples in the air around the creature, battering it from all sides.

'Jo, let go!' Lewis shouted. 'Drop out!'

I couldn't do that. Instead, I reached inside and came up with more power than I'd thought was hiding down in the empty storehouse of my gifts.

Because it felt so *good* to kill.

The vibrations ramped up into a shriek of power, and instead of Lyle dissolving into ash, the skin that had been Angelo Marconi blew apart into glittering crystal dust.

Lyle sagged and hit the deck, too weak to continue, but David stepped into his place and froze, concentrating.

The ship leveled out – still fighting the downward force but no longer being pulled down.

As quickly as it had come, the extra power I'd found was gone. Vanished. I was just me again, frail and fragile and ready to drop. If Angelo hadn't been a pile of ragged flesh and demonic parts on the metal floor, he'd have had an easy meal of me.

Lewis reached me a few seconds later, as I slid down to a sprawl against the safe. 'I told you to step out!' he snapped, and touched my forehead. 'Damn it. What the hell did you do?'

I struck out at him. I couldn't help it; his anger woke the beast inside, the one that had patiently stalked and laughed and waited.

I couldn't hold it back anymore.

I burnt him.

If it had been anyone but Lewis, I'd have killed him; I wasn't pulling punches, and the fire that boiled out of me onto him was thick, plasmatic, and clung like napalm. It flickered with a sickly green tint.

Lewis reacted instantly, stepping back from me and concentrating all his will on putting out the fire before it could eat him up. He succeeded, but my attack left him with nasty third-degree burns on his hands and arms.

I laughed.

David called another Djinn to take his place in the fragile power structure that held us above the waves, and flashed across the hold toward me. As he did, Lewis blocked him. 'No,' he said. His voice was ragged with pain. 'Don't touch her.'

David looked like he was considering touching Lewis, in a very hostile manner, but he took the advice. He pulled in energy and ignited a small golden ball of light in the palm of his hand. It was cozy, warm, and gave me a false sense of security. The glow woke shades of orange and red in his eyes, made his face into the image of a classical bronze god.

Next to him, a faint mist formed in the air. It didn't bother to take human form, and it didn't need to; there was a *feeling* that came with it, oppressive as the ocean depths, and just as cold.

The Air Oracle. She – or he? – was the Djinn equivalent of an archangel, both supremely powerful and unknowable. Even as Conduit for the Djinn, David couldn't order an Oracle; he could only petition.

He'd obviously petitioned, and now the Air Oracle was here, looking at me out of a body that barely registered in the world at all. There was communication going on between David and the Oracle. It wasn't civil, from the look on David's face.

This was a perfect moment to see just what I could do with all this power.

As I summoned it up in a roiling boil inside me, thick and hot and dizzying, the Air Oracle's attention focused on me with a snap, and I was driven to my knees.

The Oracle seemed surprised that I hadn't been driven into tiny little fragments identifiable only by DNA. Very surprised. *You're going to get a lot more shocks, bitch*, I thought, and smiled.

David was far sneakier than I gave him credit for. Instead of coming at me directly, he used his link to me, sending a massive burst of power through the aetheric connection between us.

It blew me out of my body. I fell, stunned, and waited for the end. The Air Oracle was no friend of humans in general; I was no better than the slime at the edge of a pond to her. But she didn't act.

She just left.

David bent and took me in his arms as if I weighed less than my equivalent in feathers. His lips brushed my temple. 'Forgive me,' he said. 'It's better if you sleep.'

Before I could even think about protesting, all the light winked out, and I was drifting away into warm, dark, safe eternity.

When I woke up, it was because David could no longer afford even the small pulse of energy it was taking to keep me unconscious.

I swam up out of the thick darkness to the sound of alarms, screaming, and the gale-driven shriek of wind. The air smelt of metal and salt and fear.

Heavenly, that smell.

I opened my eyes on darkness, but in the next second a lightning bolt split the sky above me in half, miles across, like a hot purple zipper letting in the darkness.

It lit up low, thick, black clouds that fired rain down like arrows from the battlements.

I was on my back on the deck, reclining in a white padded chair that was made for lounging. It slid hard to starboard, and I jerked and rolled off and to my feet before it slammed into the promenade railing. My bare soles hit cold, wet wood, and I shivered. I was soaked to the skin. How had I gotten here? And why? And what the *hell* was going on?

Nothing good, obviously. The deck was thick with uniformed crew and a chaotic swirl of passengers. It was too dangerous out here, but that didn't seem to be stopping anybody; I wondered why they hadn't taken refuge inside, but some practical knowledge finally kicked in, and I knew.

Either the crew understood that there was an excellent chance that this ship was going down, or there was something below that was even more dangerous than the storm. Either way, not good news for me or anybody else.

'Jo!' Cherise. I barely recognized my best friend, because I'd rarely seen her look this – well, bedraggled. Drowned-rat wet, pale, and shivering with cold. 'God, I thought you'd never wake up. Come on!'

She dragged me off in some random direction. No one had told her that I was prone to irrational bursts of killing fury, I supposed. *Good*. That would make it easier.

'We need to get to the lifeboat—'

My senses were coming back online, all of them, and in Oversight I saw the thick red streams sweeping around us, closing in.

The storm that Bad Bob had dispatched, the one powered by the Unmaking he'd pulled out of the spear, was almost on us, and it was devastating.

Cherise's words were lost in a fresh blast of wind, a gust so flat and hard that it slammed her bodily against the metal wall. I suppose that in better times I might have tried to help her. Instead, I just clung to a metal stanchion and watched her struggle.

I saw one of the heavy lounge chairs topple right over the railing and disappear as the ship lurched to starboard again. We were heeling around, getting hammered by churning waves like a punch-drunk boxer.

The ship was still stuck in one spot, anchored by the suction coming from deep beneath the ocean. I could feel it, and it was growing stronger, not weaker.

The Djinn were losing the fight.

'Hang on!' Cherise screamed, and another gigantic wave crested and fell, pounding us with spray like nails. 'We have to get off the ship, *now*!'

How exactly that was going to be accomplished I

had no idea, but I nodded. In the brief lull between lashing waves, we staggered to the next handhold. Along the way we ran into more castaways. I barely recognized a sopping-wet Cynthia Clark, who surely hadn't been this miserable since she'd made that epic disaster movie with Gene Hackman, back in the day. I also recognized Cho Chu Wing, one of our Weather Wardens. Cho was a tiny little thing, skinny as a restaurant greeter. She'd managed to keep herself mostly together; her black hair was pegged back in a tight ball, and only random strands of it clung to her damp face. She'd worn a storm slicker, neon orange, and beneath it she seemed to be drier than any of the rest of us. She waved us frantically toward the bow of the ship. As we slipped and fought our way through blinding spray and stinging, whipping rain, we gathered Weather Wardens in ones and twos, until there was a tight knot of them linking arms together, like a rugby team in a scrum.

I stood apart from them. Remote, even in the midst of my fellow Wardens.

'We need to get a bubble!' Cho screamed. 'Focus on giving us clear water for a hundred feet in every direction!'

That wasn't as hard as it might seem; it was basically wave cancellation, which is a fundamental principle of the physics of anything that moves as a unit – sound, water, a rippling flag. You need to find the specific frequency of the wave and cancel it out, and move the energy elsewhere. Normally that was the tricky part; bleed-off energy could destabilize everything, and whip up a whole mess of side problems you'd never anticipate.

In this melting stew of uncontrolled energy, another few mega joules in the wrong place would hardly matter.

'Tornado!' someone screamed, and I looked up to see the approaching black arms of the hurricane sweeping in like scythes. There were bulbous eruptions forming in the trailing clouds, swelling and then narrowing into cones. Forming tornadoes have a lazy look, almost tentative; they bob and weave and seem impotent at first, until they get their strength consolidated.

I'd never taken time to admire their elegance before. *So beautiful. So deadly.*

Cho was shouting something at me. She wanted my help.

Well then.

I gave it. I gave it to the tornado, and laughed as it gobbled up power like a greedy shark.

Cho must have realized what I was doing. She stepped up and gave me a sharp elbow to the back of my neck, sending me reeling into another Warden, who put me down on the deck and pinned me, yelling for Djinn.

My pet tornado collapsed – no great surprise, they always were fragile constructs, by the very nature of the physics that drove them – and the waves that battered the *Grand Paradise*, heeling her violently from one side to the other, eased to merely heavy instead of psychotic. I felt the waves' pounding rhythms begin to ease, like a racing heart slowing as adrenaline faded.

'You can't stop it,' I told Cho, who was taking advantage of the breathing space to stare into the heart of the storm. 'Everybody dances with the devil.'

I knew the storm was watching too, this monster of a thing that Bad Bob had imbued with life and cunning and cruelty, and a particular kind of insanity. I could feel it gathering itself, studying us. *Planning*.

It could feel that I was an ally, if only it could reach me. I could have done more, but I felt lazily content to wait.

No hurry. I was enjoying the panic too much to end it quickly.

The ship lurched – not side to side, but *down*, as if a giant hand had suddenly grabbed the hull from beneath and pulled it straight down. The ship sank like an express elevator, and I watched the ocean pour in over the railings on the decks below, then come for us in a foaming, deadly rush . . .

. . . and then the force let us go, and the ship's buoyancy popped us violently straight up like a cork from a rubber band. I don't think the *Grand Paradise* quite came out of the water, but there was a sickly sense of utter stillness as momentum fought gravity and gravity's patient pull won.

The ship crashed back into the water and settled. We were sprawled like ninepins all over the deck – Wardens, crew, staff, hapless passengers. The screaming sounded thin and lost.

'We're loose!' one of the Wardens shouted. 'Get everybody on the lifeboats!'

'No!' Cho snapped. 'We're getting control! We'll stand no chance at all in the smaller boats!'

'Are you?' I asked. 'Getting control? I don't think so!' It felt like the kind of adrenaline rush you get from hurtling down a mountain on skis, straight for a killing drop, knowing it may destroy you but there's nothing so beautiful as that moment when death means nothing, nothing at all . . .

The Warden holding me down – I realized it was Kevin, as I focused on his face – gave me a solid right cross, trying to put me out. 'You'll have to beat me harder than that,' I told him, very seriously. 'Come on, Kevin, dig deep. Hurt me like your stepmother taught you.'

He went pale, and I felt his grip on me loosen. Too easy. I threw him off, not particularly caring where he landed, and stalked to Cho.

Before I reached her, we all staggered as a massive subsonic *boom* rocked the decking.

Far beneath the *Grand Paradise*, the seafloor collapsed into a massive trench, sending a crush of seawater flooding downward to fill the sudden mile-deep gap. For a moment, a significant section of the sea dipped into a concave bowl – not by much, distributed over such a huge and adaptable area, but enough.

And a wave formed, rushing over the depression, gathering strength and speed and energy.

Rushing straight at our port side. It would take a minute to get to us, maybe more – not much more, though. We were in deep water, not shallows; that was the only thing that might save us. To survive, the ship had to turn into the wave.

I needed to stop it from turning.

'Jo.' That was Cherise, laying her hand on my shoulder. 'Jo, stop.'

I turned to look at her, and I saw fear ignite in her eyes. 'Oh God,' she breathed. 'Oh my *God*—'

She was so fragile. So *easy*.

Cherise's fear was like incense rising on the air, and I wanted more of it. All of it.

Every last, red drop.

She raised her chin, and the fear faded.

'This isn't you,' she said. 'And I think you can stop it, Jo. You're the hero.'

She was wrong. I wasn't the hero now – if I ever had been. What I'd done to Lewis was proof of that. What I'd tried to do with the tornado.

Part of me still liked Cherise, but it was a small part, and it was getting smaller all the time, like a tiny island of color in an inky flood.

I didn't hurt her. I'm not really sure why.

I felt the shudder beneath my feet, as the *Grand Paradise*'s enormous bulk began to make its ponderous, city-blocks-wide turn toward the wave that was sweeping closer.

I looked up, drawn by a pulse of power, and saw Lewis and David standing on a balcony above us. Arguing. David tried to turn away.

Lewis grabbed David by the fabric of his shirt. His lips moved.

David disappeared. No misting, no sense of transition, just . . . gone.

And Lewis didn't look surprised. I was – not just by David's sudden vanishing act but by the sensation that rippled through me, liquid and hot and wrong.

What just happened?

Lewis shoved something in his pocket as he vaulted the balcony railing. He landed flat-footed, keeping his balance on the still-lurching deck with one hand on the railing. 'Get everybody inside!' he yelled. 'Everybody!'

Cherise turned and began pushing people to the nearest entrances. People seemed more than motivated to follow instructions, for once – in fact, there was a traffic jam until officers began funneling people to other doors.

I didn't follow. I stood at the railing, hands folded, calm and content. It was all unraveling around me.

All I had to do was enjoy the ride down.

The ship had managed to slew around at an

impressive rate, but the waves kicked up as the Wardens' fears eroded their concentration. It significantly slowed our progress.

Lewis joined me at the railing, far enough away that it indicated he knew what a risk it was to be near me.

'Where's David?' I asked. I looked over at him, noting the healing burns on his hands. I wondered if it hurt. I certainly hoped so.

'Where you can't hurt him,' Lewis said. 'I know what's happening to you.'

I shrugged. 'So you know,' I said. 'Can you stop it?'

'Do you want me to stop it?'

I laughed. That was probably enough of an answer.

On the horizon, there was a mountain. One big rising mass, heading for us. At this rate, we didn't have another minute. Maybe thirty seconds, I was guessing.

Maybe less.

'The ship will capsize,' I said. 'You can't turn fast enough. Where are the Djinn?'

'Gone,' Lewis said. 'For their own protection. We're all alone now.'

David wouldn't have run, not to save himself. He was foolish that way. 'You've done something.' He didn't deny it. It was big, whatever it was; it was more than likely an unforgivable sin. But Lewis was the sort to make that choice, if he had to. Or thought he had to. 'Something to David?'

He didn't answer me directly. 'We're going to capsize, even if that wave doesn't hit us broadside.' And it probably would. We just didn't have enough time to hit it bow-first.

'You could turn it,' I remarked. He locked stares with me, and his eyes were bleak, tired, and frightened. 'No, I can't,' he said. 'You can.'

I smiled. 'I won't.'

I felt the front of the ship dipping down, and then rising, more like a speedboat than a giant of the seas.

Lewis seemed very calm. Very tall and still, hair ruffling in the wind. There was a glow about him, a power that I couldn't remember seeing before.

As the mountain of water roared down at us, I turned and walked calmly toward the nearest door.

Cherise and one of the white-coated officers waved me urgently on. Cher grabbed my arm and pulled me over the high threshold, and the officer slammed the door shut and turned the locking mechanism.

'Hatch twenty-three sealed!' he shouted into his radio, in the high-pitched voice of utter panic. I took a moment to look around. It was a bar, large and casual, but all the bottles and glasses had been stowed away, and the place had an unfinished look to it. The room was packed with refugees, some of whom were gazing longingly at the bar as if they wondered where all the rum had gone. I spotted Cho Wing and three other Wardens, all seeming tense and expectant. They knew what was coming. The civilian passengers seemed confused and a little bored.

The bridge officers assuredly knew that their worst fears were coming true; they could see it from their windows.

Cherise was chattering at me, trying to get me to take cover. I shook myself free. She gave me one last, despairing look, then wedged herself in a corner and tipped an armchair over herself.

I heard the wave coming, even through the steel plates. I felt the rumble of it.

The bow of the *Grand Paradise* lifted sharply, and kept rising, rising. Tables and chairs started sliding, and people screamed and clung to whatever was within reach, stable or not. I heard glass crashing; that was probably unsecured stock somewhere under the counters.

A huge wooden cabinet, designed to look primitive and rough-hewn, began to topple down from one wall. There were six people beneath it. I watched with placid interest.

Cho yelled a warning. One of the Earth Wardens flung out a hand and stopped the falling cabinet. Disappointing.

A racing bite of energy spread over me like a hot blanket of fire, concentrating on my back and then flowing down my arms and into the core of my body. I went down to one knee, bracing myself as the horizon continued to rise toward the sky. People slid past me, screaming, flailing. I didn't pay much attention.

'We're going over!' someone shouted amid the chaos and crashing furniture. We were still climbing. The floor passed a forty-five-degree upward angle, heading for vertical, and I felt the whole ship slip sideways, twist, and start to tumble out of control.

We were falling.

Then we stopped falling, and the ship's torturous descent changed, smoothed, and entered an eerie kind of calm. The ship slowly drifted back to a stable, horizontal line, but it didn't feel like we were in flat seas. It didn't feel like we were in the water at all.

I rose and walked to the large picture window that commanded a view of the promenade.

Lewis was standing just where I'd left him, at the railing, and his glow was Djinn-bright, the color of soft morning sunshine against the blackness of the storms. Yes, the storms were still there, whipping around us in a frenzy, but we were floating in a bubble of force that stretched all around the ship in a perfect sphere. *Ship in a bottle*, I thought, and for just an instant I was too angry to think properly. No Warden could do this, not alone.

Not even Lewis.

We were floating on the storm in our own little self-contained pocket universe of calm sea and air.

I tried to unlock the watertight door, but it seemed stuck. I sent a snap of Earth power from my fingertips out through the metal, realigning the surfaces, and when I turned the handle again, the door slid smoothly open.

'Jo!' Cher was right behind me. Her eyes were huge and frightened. 'What's happening?'

'I'll find out,' I said, with utter calm. I felt alive inside, manic with glee, but I didn't want her to see that. 'Wait inside.'

'But—'

I slammed the door between us and hit it with the heel of my hand, hard enough to make a hollow *boom*. 'Lock it!'

I heard the heavy clash of metal engaging, and then I turned toward Lewis, standing like a misplaced figurehead at the rail.

He opened his eyes. I could see the energy spilling out of him, a raw wound that split him open to the core.

He was bleeding on the aetheric. Bleeding himself to death.

'How?' I asked, and leant on the railing. He didn't answer me. Couldn't, perhaps. His nose was bleeding, and his eyes were flushed red under the stress of what he was doing. Fifteen Djinn and four times as many Wardens hadn't been able to stop the storm, but Lewis was somehow fighting it, toe to toe.

Not winning, though.

Not hardly.

'You'll kill yourself,' I commented. 'For God's sake, Lewis, what does it matter? What does any of it matter? Just let go. The ship will get torn apart. People will drown. Life will go on, for a while, until it doesn't.' I shrugged. 'Just let go. It's that easy.'

Lewis let out a gasping sob. His knees buckled, but he held fast to the railing.

He held the bubble of force against the storm.

'You aren't doing this alone,' I said. 'But you didn't have time to get the other Wardens to help. And even if you did, they're not capable of this kind of power. Not alone—' I paused, because I finally worked it out. 'But you're not alone, are you?'

Lewis's breath was coming in short, desperate gasps now. Nobody could sustain this, not even the most powerful Warden in the world.

Not even one with a direct connection to the aetheric.

Which was what Lewis had. He'd always been close to our temperamental Mother Earth, but this was beyond that, way beyond. The power that poured through him to fill this shell of force was like a geyser, tapping directly into the heart of the planet herself.

Only the connection between Lewis and a Djinn Conduit could do that.

He'd claimed David. He'd put David in a bottle and made him a slave, and he was using him to open this portal directly into the lifeblood of Earth, to save the ship.

It would burn Lewis out before David, but not much before.

They'd both die.

Some part of me was screaming inside, begging me to stop it. But that was the very last tiny foothold of the old Joanne drowning in a sea of darkness.

I closed my eyes and sighed. All I had to do was . . . wait.

I felt a warning tingle in the still, calm air, and as I looked up, I saw a tornado striking down at us from the clouds that writhed overhead. Lightning snaked around it, living barbed wire, and it hit the curved surface of Lewis's protective bubble around the *Grand Paradise* and began to probe for weaknesses.

Then it bombed us.

I saw the metal shape hurtling down at us through the oddly clear eye of the tornado, that empty funnel space where the cold air and the warm air cycle to fuel the beast's engines. I didn't know what it was at first – wreckage, maybe a mass of siding or a barn, or—

No. That was a *ship*. A whole, intact *ship*. A small fishing vessel. The black-painted bottom was heavy with barnacles, and as lightning flared brighter I saw the name on her rusty bow – *Abigail*.

There were living men on board. I could see their terrified faces at the railing as the ship dropped toward us in free fall, her weight turning majestically in the air and driving her nose down like the tip of a spear.

'No,' Lewis moaned, but he didn't drop the shield. He couldn't.

The *Abigail* hit his protective bubble and exploded

into shrapnel, scrap, and bodies. I flinched – instinct, not sympathy. The ship's fuel tanks burst, slopping marine diesel in a wave across the invisible wall.

Lightning ignited it, and flames sheeted over us in a semicircle. It didn't last long. Nothing to burn once the diesel had flamed out.

The wreckage of the *Abigail* was gone in even less time, along with her crew. Even if there'd been a chance of saving them – which, after the fury of that crash, I doubted – there was no way to reach them without dropping our own protective shield.

Bad Bob really was bringing his A game.

The tornado's sloppy mouth slithered over Lewis's shield for another few seconds, and then it withdrew up into the clouds. Not gone, just reloading. I could see this storm sweeping its way from Bad Bob's location to ours, picking up ammunition along the way, like a boy collecting stones to throw. Congested shipping lanes out there. Naval vessels flying under various flags. Pleasure craft and yachts and sailing ships and cruise ships smaller than this one . . .

Lewis's strength gave out, and he lost his grip on the railing. He fell to his knees. I could feel David's agony rippling through the connection between us. This was tearing them both apart. Lewis's body was surrendering under the strain.

I reached out and put my hand on his sweat-matted hair.

Finally, he turned his head and looked at me. Just

one look, not very long. Bone-deep exhaustion in him, and just a tiny trace of regret.

'Jo, you have to stop yourself,' he said. 'Please. Stop yourself.'

'Too late,' I told him, and took control of the bubble away from him.

It was a shock, how much power was involved. Even with the enormous flood pouring in from the storm, from Bad Bob himself, the force that hit me was staggering. A normal Warden, no matter how accomplished, would have been shredded in seconds.

Lewis collapsed limply on the deck, rolled away, and began to crawl slowly.

I rolled him faceup, and held him in place with a foot on his chest. I turned my face to the storm, looking into the abyss.

Nietzsche was right – it also looked into me.

'Stay put,' I said to Lewis. 'I want you to see this. You used to be an altruist, but I watched you change. You turned into such a realist, with all your cold win/lose/draw equations. You just never thought you'd actually lose, did you?'

Lewis reached in his pocket and pulled out a small glass bottle. It was sturdy, one of those pocket travel samples of men's cologne. Designed to be break-resistant, but still meeting all the glass-only requirements of a Djinn containment bottle. The cap, of course, was off, because Lewis had been accessing David's powers.

I saw him struggle with the choice. That was a no-win scenario.

He eventually did the moral thing, and tried to smash it against the deck. It didn't break.

'Where are the other Djinn?' I asked. Lewis shook his head and collapsed, panting. He was holding the bottle in a death grip. 'Let me guess. I have a good idea of how you think. You ordered David to send them all away, to a place of safety. Maybe Jonathan's house.'

Lewis nodded, eyes tightly closed. I wondered why he wouldn't look at me. I wondered what he saw.

'I'll bet you told yourself it was temporary,' I said, and took my foot off of Lewis's back to crouch down next to him, staring at his face. 'You'd let him go as soon as the emergency was over. But that's not human nature, Lewis. We don't work that way. We take power, and we keep it. We don't give it up. Someone has to come along and take it from us, usually violently.' I smiled softly. 'There's always another goddamn crisis, baby. Don't you get that?'

He didn't want to look at me. I wondered what was so terrible about my face; I felt positively great. Better than I had for ages.

Finally, Lewis got up his strength to ask, 'What are you going to do?'

'Take this ship where it was going anyway,' I said. 'Directly to Bad Bob. The difference is, most of you will be dead by the time it arrives, I'm afraid.' I paused, waiting to feel some kind of regret. Nothing came. The last little bit of me was slipping under the waves, and I really couldn't even care.

Lewis rolled over on his side and wiped blood from his nose and eyes, still avoiding my gaze. His pupils were huge, like those of a man who'd never left the darkness.

'Well?' I asked, and cocked my head. 'What are you going to do about this little situation? Aren't you going to stop me?'

He coughed. It sounded wet and deep, like something had broken deep inside him. 'No.'

'Really.'

'You're the one with the hero complex, not me.'

'And what are you?' He didn't answer. 'Oh, that's right. You're the one who doesn't have to feel good about himself to know he did the right thing. Then live up to it, Lewis. You can stop me. You've got the answer in your hand.'

His fingers closed around the bottle.

David's bottle.

'Come on,' I whispered. 'Let him out. You know you want to. Wouldn't it do your heart good to make him come after me? Wouldn't that be *fun*?'

'Stop.'

'Make me.'

The look on his face made fires ignite deep inside me. Tasty. 'No.'

'It's too late to get all noble on me now, Lewis. You put a Djinn in a bottle. Worse, you put a *Conduit* in a bottle. Don't you think that's going to piss the Djinn off? The last war was about them wanting their freedom. This one's going to be pure revenge, and they won't care about who's innocent and who's guilty. Congratulations. You've single-handedly destroyed the Wardens.'

'I'm not the one who made the Djinn . . . vulnerable to capture,' he said. He had to stop for breath. 'You knew marrying David . . . would do this. Vows. You didn't care.'

A wave washed over the bubble above us, leaving a thin, lacy film behind. It was like looking through my mother's kitchen curtains. The storm outside raged on, but it was losing some of its fury. It knew I'd won.

We'd won. Me and the storm, together.

'I'm a selfish bitch,' I agreed. 'I tried, OK? I did the good-girl thing. I fought the good fight, and where did it get me? *My skin burnt off, Lewis.* Nobody was telling me so, but I was never going to get better, was I? I'm damned if I'm going to walk around with no fucking skin the rest of my life so that I can feel all good about adhering to my strict moral code.' I took a deep breath and tasted ozone from the storm's whipping frenzy. 'It's just power. Doesn't matter where it comes from, or where it goes.'

'And you can quit any time you want.'

My tone hardened. I still didn't like being mocked. 'Fuck your intervention. I'm the one still standing.'

Lewis's fingers tightened around the bottle. The

one holding the only thing that *might* stop me. I'd known from the moment I walked out on the promenade that it was going to come down to this.

I smiled.

And he surprised me. 'No. I'm not calling David. Not just for his sake – for yours. If you live through it, I don't want you having that on your conscience.'

'I'm not Bad Bob,' I said. 'I love him.'

He coughed blood. 'You kind of loved me, too. Look how that turned out.'

I slapped my hand down hard next to his head. Hard enough to split the wood. Overhead, the storm shrieked harmony to the howling rage inside me. '*Call him!*'

'No way in hell.'

All he had to do was get David out in the open. That was all I wanted. I slapped the deck again, and again, and again. Splinters jabbed deep, and I left primal bloody handprints behind.

It felt so *good*.

Lewis opened his eyes and locked stares with me at point-blank range. 'No,' he said, very softly. 'This isn't going to happen the way you want.'

I looked up. There were other people out on the Promenade now – Wardens, arraying themselves against me.

Cherise, standing with them, like an actual person who mattered. They all wore identical tense, focused expressions . . . the look of soldiers just before the battle.

I looked down at Lewis and smiled a real, warm, sunny smile. 'We'll see,' I said, and stood up to put my hands on my hips. 'We'll see about that.'

Then I walked away to get some air.

Nobody stopped me as I walked.

In time, I felt the last whispers of power click into place, locking me into the storm. We were one now – a symbiotic dark engine, generating our own power. Our own reality. The storm and I were one.

Easy, I told it. *Easy, for now.*

And the winds began to slow. It could bide its time.

So could I.

I waited until the winds died a bit, then let go of the bubble of force that Lewis and David had built at such cost.

I ended up on the port side of the ship, in a bar – preciously named Arpeggio's – where some of the non-Warden guests and crew were still gathered. Tables and chairs had been righted. There'd been some minor injuries, but not even a broken bone, remarkably. I supposed we'd gotten off light, unlike the crew of the *Abigail*.

I bellied up to the serving bar and perched on one of the high chairs. There were three guys behind the bar.

One was cleaning up broken glass. The other two were taking orders. A lot of people were drinking. I didn't blame them at all.

'What'll it be, miss?' the server asked me, and gave me a smile so even and white that he should have been in a commercial. It faded quickly. Even across the other side of a ship the size of a small city, word traveled fast, and it clicked in quickly who – or what – I was. The room went quiet. He cleared his throat nervously. 'Anything to drink?'

'Cyanide?' I was trying to be charming, but I could see from the alarm in his eyes that I was somehow missing the target.

'Fresh out, miss,' he said weakly. 'Some other poison, perhaps?'

I gave up. 'How about a vodka tonic?' That was my sorry-for-myself drink, and this seemed an ideal place to throw a ten-minute pity party. He turned away, mixed the drink, and put it on the coaster. I sipped. It was excellent. 'I'm surprised the bar is open.'

'Anything to keep people calm.' There was more than a touch of febrile panic in his eyes now.

'Be sure to save some for yourself.' I smiled, with teeth. 'You're going to need it.'

He poured himself a shot of whiskey and downed it without a pause, then fled, leaving me in possession of the entire bar's contents. I sipped my vodka tonic and took a self-assessment as pretty much everybody else followed the bartender's lead and got the hell out of Dodge.

My back didn't hurt anymore. It also wasn't numb. It felt normal, natural . . . and as I angled around to get a look in the still-intact bar mirror, I saw the shadow of a black form under the new skin.

A torch, embedded instead of tattooed. Much, much larger.

One or two of the ship's staff hadn't fled with the rest. One stern-looking woman poured me a second vodka tonic without being asked. 'On the house,' she said. 'If you can get us out of this and home, you're welcome to drink the place dry.'

I drank it all in a gulp, and said, 'Two things. First, if I want to drink this place dry, you definitely haven't got a thing on board this floating sewage plant that can stop me. Second, you're not going home. Get used to the idea.'

Then I tossed a twenty on the bar and resumed my stroll. I paused at the big, flat stern of the ship to gaze out over our churning gray wake. Nothing in sight, not on any side, but open water and storm.

I leant on the railing and opened myself up through the darkness, searching. It didn't take me long to find the wellspring of that black flood. It was directly to starboard, and close.

Maybe a day away, if that.

'I'm coming,' I whispered into the dark. 'You're getting what you wanted, you evil old bastard.'

I felt Bad Bob's chuckle inside me like lips against skin. 'Knew you wouldn't let me down, little girl,' he said. When I shut my eyes I could see him standing beside me in ghostly outlines. 'You bring me the ship and the Wardens. That's a good start to our work. From then on, no limits. No limits at all.'

'On my way,' I said, and broke the connection with him. I used my Earth powers to lock out the computer controls of the ship and put in the destination.

Then I went in search of more vodka.

By early morning, the black torch mark was a bold swirl beneath my skin, stretching from the flame at the nape of my neck to the elaborate scrolled cap, just below the flare of my hips. The flames at its top weren't just black ink anymore. They were real fire, moving silently beneath the translucent covering of my flesh. It was the ultimate tribal stamp, declaring who and what I was to anyone with the courage to look.

It should have frightened me, I guess. Instead, I admired it for a moment, then picked up the hair dryer and began to make myself presentable for the day.

An hour later, I strode out from the cabin – perfectly put together. My hair was curly and tumbling glossy black down toward my waist. I wore a skimpy aqua-blue top with cap sleeves that bared most of my midriff, and low-rise jeans that hugged every curve. David had stocked the closets with anything I might want, for any conceivable mood or occasion.

I decided today was Seduction Day.

I ran into Cherise and Kevin in the hallway. They were talking with that suppressed urgency of two people trying to keep a secret, and they stopped when they saw me.

'What?' I put my hands on my hips and raised my eyebrows. 'Not enjoying the three-hour tour, Mary Ann? Of course, that makes him Gilligan. It fits.'

Cherise didn't smile. I'd never seen her not-smile at a *Gilligan's Island* joke before. 'We should talk,' she said. There was a faint quiver in her voice, and I saw her take Kevin's hand for support. 'Maybe back in the room?'

'Maybe you should get out of my way and stop bothering me,' I said. I let it lie there for a few seconds, then lightened it up with a grin that felt strange on my lips. 'I mean, you're between me and breakfast. You know how dangerous that is.'

'Don't,' Kevin said.

'Don't what?'

'Don't you fucking dare threaten her. She's trying to save your life.' Kevin stepped in front of her, or tried to. Cherise hauled him back and gave him a look that would have frozen Lake Michigan. 'Sorry.' Insignificant as she might be, Cherise wanted to fight her own battles. Well, I could have told him that.

'I just want to talk,' Cherise said, returning her attention to me. 'Please.'

She didn't demand anything, and I knew that if I pushed it, she'd back down. And I was tempted to push, very tempted, not so much because of her – Cherise really wasn't on the radar anymore – but because the simmering, furious violence in Kevin was addictively delicious. All I had to do was hurt her, and I could drink my fill.

Not yet, I told myself. *Don't enjoy yourself too much*.

'Please,' Cherise repeated.

'Jeez, OK, don't beg,' I said. 'Just you, though. Not him.'

Kevin held up his hands in surrender, a sour look on his face. 'Dude, like I want to spend time coddling your self-involved evil-turning ass.' His glance at Cherise said something different, though. 'Be careful.'

'*I'm* going to hurt her? I'm not the one with the body count, Kevin,' I said. He flinched, just a little. 'Why don't you loiter out here looking menacing while you wait? Maybe you can beat up cabin stewards, just to keep in practice.'

He flipped me off, but that wasn't original for him. I took Cherise's arm, and we headed back to the cabin.

She locked the door behind us. I raised my eyebrows as I settled on my unmade bed. 'Oooh,' I said. 'Is this going to be hot girl-on-girl action, or what?'

'Shut up.' Cherise hugged herself and stayed where she was, between me and the door. 'Something's really wrong with you.'

'Oh yeah? You think?' I leant back against the hard cabin wall and crossed my arms. 'You've been drinking Lewis's Kool-Aid about how bad I am, boo-hoo. But I understand why you'd go that way. He's still got an open position for girlfriend-slash-wife, so hold out for the brass ring, kid.' She gave me an uncomprehending stare. 'Wouldn't be the first man you've screwed for fun and profit.'

'Would you *shut up*? God, you can be such a bitch! Since – since your back thing happened, you've been changing. Slowly at first, but then it got worse, and now you're—' Cherise made a helpless gesture that encompassed everything about me, from head to toe. 'Look at you.'

I looked down. 'What?' Granted, the clothes might be a bit sluttier than my usual, but I liked them, and besides, it was a cruise ship. South Beach rules of conduct and dress.

'It's not the outfit, Jo. It's *you*. It's the look in your eyes, the kind of smile you give people. The way you think about them.' Cherise swallowed and ducked her chin to avoid eye contact. 'When you think they're not looking, it's like you're examining pieces of meat – like they're not people at all. You never did that before.'

I deliberately relaxed again. 'Yeah? You're sure about that? Maybe you just never caught me at it before.'

'No. I know you, and this – this isn't you. Looks like you, feels like you, sounds like you. It's in your skin, but it's not the Joanne Baldwin I'm friends with.'

I didn't know why this should wake a feeling of anxiety in me. Pale and faint, yes, but still . . . I wanted to make her feel better. 'People change,' I offered.

'Not this much. Not this fast. You let something inside you.'

I tried to explain – again, I wasn't sure why I bothered, except that the genuine warm concern in Cherise's eyes actually reached something in me, something I'd thought long drowned in darkness. 'It's just giving me access to power. Like having a Djinn at my command, only – better. Faster. You're going to have to get used to the fact that I can't be Miss Congeniality anymore. This is war.'

'Jo, the war's over. You lost. You're a casualty.'

I came up from the bed in one sinuous motion and took a step into her space. 'You know what's really over? This conversation. I'm leaving.'

'You have to go through me first.'

'Can do.'

'What? You're going to hurt me?' Cherise – tiny little Cherise, with her perfect tan and perfect teeth and glistening hair. Funny and sexy and quirky. 'Go ahead.'

Frustration erupted inside me. It burnt from the torch on my back under my skin, traveling lines and ladders of nerves, and I felt fire tingle at the ends of my fingers. '*Move.*'

'Make me, bitch.'

I wanted to, oh God, I did. Instead, I bared my teeth. 'You know what you are?' I asked, low in my throat. 'You're nothing. Even among human beings, you're a worthless failure. Model? A model is just some girl who strips for cash – a body for hire. A walking mannequin with a shelf life of about five minutes. Take away your looks and you've got nothing to sell. Who's going to love you then, the Human Torch out there? Face it, without tagging along to somebody *better*, you're nothing, peach. You used to be *entourage*. Now you're not even that.'

The color faded out of Cherise's face, leaving the tan like some eerie overlay, and I saw a real spark of fear in her clear blue eyes.

It turned hot.

'Why'd you just call me *peach*?'

Of all the things she could have said, that was the one that stopped me in my tracks. *Peach. Sweetness.* Bad Bob liked expressions like those, mockingly sentimental, used to wound. He'd used them on me all the time.

I took a step back. My hands locked into fists, and I felt the fire from the torch on my back flare hotter. It didn't like me doubting myself.

It didn't like me *thinking*.

'It's just another kind of Demon Mark,' Cherise said. 'Remember? Remember how that felt? You told me about it, how it made you feel so powerful, so free—'

'Shut up.' My voice didn't have much force to it.

'He's using it to destroy you. You've *got to stop*. You're going to destroy everyone and everything you love.'

I closed my eyes. Images flashed across the darkness – David, the first time I'd seen him, a dusty stranger on the road. David, naked in morning light, looking at me as if I was the most glorious thing he had ever seen.

Lewis, standing against the storm, and compromising himself and his beliefs to find the strength. Not asking for my praise or my applause. Knowing I might kill him for it.

Cherise, without the power to light a match, signing on because it was the right thing to do.

Everything I loved was right here, on this ship, and I was destroying it.

And I still couldn't care.

'You understand,' said a little-girl voice from behind me. 'That's good. I wouldn't want you to die without understanding that it had to be done.'

Venna stood behind me in her Alice pinafore, perfect and shining and eerie. I looked from her to Cherise.

'How the hell did you hook up with the Djinn?'

She shrugged. 'Diplomacy. Ain't it a bitch?'

'And so am I.' But I didn't strike at either one of them. Instead, I sat down on the bed and crossed my legs into the lotus position. It was a bit of a tight fit, in the jeans.

I stared idly at the far side of the cabin – Cherise's side – where she had beauty products lined up in thick clusters on the shelf. All kinds of things – tubes of makeup, lipsticks, eye shadow compacts.

Bottles of expensive perfume, just the right size to hold a Djinn.

Venna smiled. 'I'd kill you first,' she said, and there was absolutely no doubt in my mind that she meant it. 'There wouldn't be enough of you to summon the sharks.'

I held up my hands. 'Can't blame me for thinking about it.'

'Oh, I can,' she said. 'I most certainly can. But it would be amusing to see you make the attempt. Your vows with David gave humans access to the New Djinn, not my kind.' She was studying me with alien, utterly cold intensity. 'But I think I understand you. If someone offered you poisoned water in the desert, would you rather die of thirst, or take longer to die of poison?'

She really *did* understand. 'If I hadn't taken the poison, I'd be dead already. None of you were offering anything else,' I said. 'Alive, I can always turn myself around, right? Go to rehab, some twelve-step thing?'

Venna's eyes turned black. 'I've heard this excuse from others,' she said. 'Most recently from Lewis, as he violated our most basic trust. There will be an accounting, when this is done. No Djinn – not even our younger cousins – will be imprisoned by your kind again. Expedience is no excuse.'

I shrugged. 'So? Are we throwing down, MiniMe, or are we done now? Because I don't really think even you can stop me now. Or that you're allowed to try.' Venna's presence was waking a kind of utterly unsettling hunger inside me; she had so much *power*, and I had a bottomless appetite for it. If she fought me, she'd expend power.

If she lost, I could take it all.

Venna said, 'There is only one person who can save this ship. You, Joanne. If you wish.'

'Well, I don't. I'm taking it to meet Bad Bob, and what happens from there doesn't really concern me.'

Cherise covered her mouth with both hands, appalled and shocked. That was funny. Had she really not seen that coming?

'They won't allow you to do this so easily. They'll fight,' Venna said. It sounded like she was analyzing the next move in a Grand Masters chess game.

'Hope so,' I said, and slid off the bed to stretch, yawn, and shake my hair back over my shoulders. 'Fun time's over, girls. I need to do some work now, so I'm going. You can either move out of the way, or I can walk over your bleeding corpses. That's metaphorical for you, Venna, but you get the point.'

Neither of them moved. Cherise looked uncertainly at Venna, but for the little girl Djinn I was the only thing in the world holding her focus.

I walked right up to her. She looked up into my eyes with eerie, ancient eyes, and then moved out of my way.

'You can't do this,' Cherise whispered.

I used a casual punch of power to slam her across

the room, into a wall, and she tumbled limply to the floor.

Bleeding.

'You're not completely his,' Venna said, as I opened the cabin door. I looked back. She was standing in the same place, still calm and self-contained. 'Do you want to know how I know?'

'Do tell.' I drummed my fingernails on the wood of the door impatiently.

Venna's gaze flicked to Cherise, and then back. 'You didn't keep your threat. She's bleeding. She isn't dead.'

'Yet,' I said. 'I thought that as a Djinn you'd understand the importance of timing.'

Chapter Eight

As I sat in Arpeggio's deserted bar-cum-breakfast-nook, munched my command-ordered bagel and light cream cheese, and sipped coffee, I wondered what Cherise would report to Lewis – assuming Lewis was still in any shape to be reported to. Nobody bothered me, not even other Wardens.

The few fellow diners who'd endured my presence got up and left, quickly, when Venna appeared in the middle of the room, clearly and utterly alien in the way she looked and moved. She sat opposite me at the polished wooden table, a glass of orange juice in front of her, and stared at me with impassive intensity.

'I thought we were done,' I said. I sipped my coffee. It was bitter, dark, and exactly what I needed.

'For the sake of what you were, I thought I would try once more.' That was irritatingly superior.

'You can run back and tell Lewis that I'm done

with pretending to care about every little life that stubs its toe, every goddamn kitten up a tree. I've spent my life bleeding for humans. I've died for them. Enough. If that makes me evil, then fine. I am.'

Venna said nothing. She drank her juice like a little girl, two hands wrapped around the glass for stability, and it left her with a faint orange ring around her lips that she tried to lick off before wiping it away. 'Cherise is right,' she said. 'You are more like us than them now.'

'Let me sum that up with *ewwwwww*.'

She stared at her empty juice glass. It filled up, welling from the bottom of the glass. She emptied it again.

'Was that supposed to be a metaphor? Sorry. Don't get it.' I ate the last bite of my bagel and pushed my chair back to stand as I swigged the dregs of my coffee. 'Bother me again, and I'll seriously inconvenience you.' From the pulse of power inside me, it was entirely possible that I could really hurt her.

'You didn't ask,' she said.

'Ask what?'

'Anything. Why the staff of this ship are still willing to make your bagels when their world is crumbling around them.' Venna shrugged again. 'You don't ask anything, because you don't care anymore. It means nothing to you. It's very Djinn.'

'I'm not Djinn.'

'No,' she agreed. 'You're becoming something else. It's – interesting.'

'But not good.'

'No. Not good at all. Not for anyone, really.'

I didn't care. Some part of me could not wait to blow past these conventional, stupid rules.

And some tiny, whispering part of me was mourning that very thing.

'I won't see you again,' Venna said. 'Not until this is over. I'm sorry. I liked you. It would have been better if I'd killed you.'

I put my hands flat on the table. 'So? Do it now.'

'I can't,' she said, which was surprisingly honest. 'And I won't. That's for your own to do, not me.'

She flushed another half glass of OJ, then misted away without another word.

I thought she looked a little grave, and a little sad.

I got up and stiff-armed the door out onto the promenade.

The *Grand Paradise* had left the storm behind during the night, although it was following us like a pit bull on a leash, obedient to my every wish.

The ship cut a rapid, hissing passage through the still-high waves, making for the destination I'd identified. *Home*, part of me said. Not the best part.

Sunlight flooded the promenade, glittering on drops of spray, turning the place into a gallery of diamonds. Watertight doors had opened all up and down the length of the ship. Wardens who'd been gearing up for the fight of the century, or at least the storm of the century, were left wondering what to do. I didn't seem to be much of a threat, standing at the railing and enjoying the day.

Nothing but sun and fresh wind now. It was a beautiful morning.

I felt the winds shift. *Gravity* shift, at least on the aetheric level. A heavyweight had arrived.

When I looked over my shoulder, I saw that Lewis had made his way out onto the deck. Behind him was the Warden army – faces I knew and some I outright hated. *Ah, good.* Finally, we were at the showdown. Time to rumble.

I turned to face them.

'You're getting off the ship,' Lewis told me. 'I'm sorry, Jo.'

'Oh no. Mutiny! Whatever shall I do?' I put the back of my hand dramatically to my forehead. 'Wait. I know. Kill you.'

He didn't look especially petrified. Lewis had healed up some overnight – faster than I'd have thought, but he'd probably had tons of Earth Warden help to accelerate the process. He looked badass and focused, and whereas I was clean, scrubbed, and dressed for sexy success, he hadn't shaved, showered, slept, or changed clothes.

I was ahead on style points, but I wasn't counting the Wardens out. Not yet.

'You can't win this,' Lewis said. 'Don't push me, Jo. I'm telling you the truth: You can't.'

He sounded confident, but then, Lewis always did sound confident when it came to crunch time.

I felt the whispers of wind tease my hair, and the storm – my own personal pet now – yawned and began to spin its engine harder, preparing for battle.

'You going to talk, or are you going to fight?' I asked. 'Because the alternative is hate sex, and I'm kind of over you right now.' I noted, on a highly academic level, that I was starting to sound more and more like Bad Bob, even to the ironic dark twist in my tone.

Lewis took a step toward me. Just one. But I felt my skin tighten, and something inside me turned silent and watchful, all humor gone.

'You're talking a good game, but I'm still waiting for you to back it up.'

I laughed. 'Are you *begging* me to kill you? Seriously? Tactics, man. Look into it.'

'No,' he said softly. 'I'm telling you that deep inside, there's a part of you that's still protected. Still fighting. If there weren't, you'd be walking around this ship like the incarnation of Kali, destroying everything crossing your path. Think about it. You haven't killed anybody. And what is your master evil plan? You're taking us to Bad Bob. That's where we wanted to go.'

I froze, staring at him. It was true. I'd lashed out at him, but I hadn't killed him. Hadn't killed anyone, yet. Lots of talk, no action.

And he was right, something inside me had convinced me that the ship *should* be taken to Bad Bob . . . but it was the old Joanne, struggling to push me in the direction she considered right.

I opened my right hand, and a tiny pearl of light formed, flickered, and grew, expanding into a white-hot ball.

'Talk's over,' I said. 'It's time to play.'

I threw the ball of fire into the middle of them. Lewis hit it with a blast of cold air along the way, shrinking it, and then casually batted it out over the railing when it reached him. 'Going to have to play harder than that.'

I was aware that while my attention was fixed on Lewis, the other Wardens were trying to get to me. Not physically, but the Earth Wardens were messing with my body chemistry. All kinds of ways the human engine can go wonky – they weren't trying to give me cancer, but they were trying to crash my blood sugar, give me blinding headaches, and disrupt nerve impulses.

I snapped a lightning bolt down. One of the Weather Wardens stepped out and flung up both hands, intercepting the thick, ropy stream of energy and deflecting it, but it left her limp and moaning on the deck, with a black burnt patch on the wood that stretched a dozen feet around her in a blast pattern.

I felt an odd tug at my leg and looked down. The decking was growing green shoots, and they were twining up my leg in thick, twisted strands. I hissed in frustration and snapped the plant off at the root, but while I was occupied with that, more fast-growing tendrils erupted up around me, anchoring me in place. It was stupidly annoying, and I finally summoned up a pulse of fire to burn them away from me.

Then I pushed the wave of flame out at the Wardens.

A Fire Warden named Freddy Pierce stepped out and shoved the attack back at me. Then, surprising me, he rushed *through* the flame and hit me in a low tackle. As attacks went, it wasn't subtle, but it caught me completely off guard, and the man was stronger than he looked. I slammed down on my back, and Freddy flipped me over and held me down with one sharp knee digging into my spine.

'Come on,' Lewis said, and stepped through the guttering flames to stand over me. His voice was low, kind, and a little sad. 'You're not going to kill us. You won't, Jo. And that makes things tougher, because I can't kill you if I know you're still in there somewhere.'

I laughed and turned my cheek to one side, staring up at him through a mask of tumbling hair. 'Do you really think so?' I asked, and blew Freddy off my back.

I blew him *off the ship*.

Into the water.

Then I lunged up, wrapped my hands around

Lewis's throat, and called fire. It wrapped around me in a dripping mantle, and Lewis's clothes ignited instantly. He controlled that, but I was attacking him on multiple fronts; while he was putting out the flames, I was turning his breath toxic in his lungs, turning his blood to sludge in his veins. Earth Wardens knew a million painful ways to kill, and it was hard to fight, especially when you were on fire.

But Lewis managed, somehow. He batted me away, sending me reeling back to crash against a metal rail. Somewhere out in the churning iron gray sea, Freddy – a Fire Warden, with no power over either the water or the living things in it – yelled for help with panic in his voice. Something about sharks.

As Lewis staggered and fell, the bottle that held David's soul entrapped fell out of his pocket and skittered across the deck. I reached out for it.

Cherise got to it first.

She backed up, fast, both hands clenched around the small glass form. She pulled it in to her chest.

The Wardens closed ranks between her and me.

'Back off,' Kevin said, pushing his way to the front – and Cherise.

'*You* back off,' I snapped. 'I saved your life, you rancid little murderer. You owe me.'

'I owe Joanne,' he said. 'I don't know who the fuck you are, and I don't care. You make a move against Cherise and—'

'And what?' I asked, and took a step forward.

'You'll cut me? Oh, shut up. Get out of my way if you want to live.'

Venna misted into place next to him. She didn't speak. She didn't have to. I got the message well enough.

'I've fought you before,' I said.

'You lost,' she pointed out. 'The poisoned water may sustain you, but it's still poisoned. Don't make the mistake of thinking you're my equal. Ever.'

'*Booyah*, bitch,' Kevin said. Someone else, with more sense and better self-preservation instincts, muttered for him to shut up.

'I'm going to kill you all,' I said. I meant it. I felt it coming, a kind of inevitable darkness. 'I have to.' I was still just a little sorry about that, but it really was necessary. Lewis had been right that somewhere deep inside me, the old Joanne was still struggling – poisoning my thoughts, driving my actions. No more.

I flung my arms wide, felt the storm roar and answer, and shouted, '*Now*!'

The Djinn Rahel erupted from out of the ocean.

No, *not* Rahel – Rahel as commanded by her master, Bad Bob, the Black Warden.

Rahel was as large as the cruise ship. Her hair was a nest of writhing eels. Her face was distorted, pointed into an extreme triangle, and her mouth was full of rows of teeth. She was dressed in rags and weeds and pearls and fish scales, and in both hands she held swords as long as the hull of the ship.

'Oh, Christ,' someone said, appalled, and then the screaming started. Not among the Wardens, who instantly began pulling up every defense they had.

It really wasn't going to do them any good at all.

Venna, pretty and fresh in a sparkly pink shirt with a unicorn on it, jumped flat-footed from the deck to balance on the railing. The storm winds hit her like the wave front of an explosive blast, blowing her hair back in a rippling blond flag, but she was absolutely steady as she balanced. Rahel saw her, and that shark-toothed mouth gaped in a menacing smile.

Venna executed a perfect dive, and before she hit the waves, she'd changed into something else, something vast and dark that swam straight at the terrifying sea-hag that Rahel had become.

Rahel's shark teeth parted on a shriek, and she was yanked down under the waves. The *Grand Paradise* rocked violently as the water churned, and the storm winds lashed the ship in swirling gusts.

Rahel wasn't the attack, of course. Just a diversion, something to help get attention away from me. While the Wardens were focused on the water, I concentrated on the metal of the ship's hull, below the water line.

Metal bent and screamed, and the entire ship *twisted* as if it had been T-boned. It rolled starboard, then over-corrected to port, sending people flying and rolling and screaming.

Rahel broke the surface of the water and was

yanked under again. The battle continued, not that it mattered to anyone on the ship anymore.

I could feel the damage.

It wasn't containable.

I smiled.

Lewis left the deck in a sudden burst and went airborne – a trick that few Weather Wardens could manage under stress, even at full power. *Formidable*, I thought, filing it away for future reference.

Then something hit us hard on the side, and the ship, already dying, rolled all the way over.

Disaster can be oddly beautiful. It seems to happen in slow motion, like ballet, and if your emotions aren't involved, then it's only input.

All I was feeling, as the ship died around me, was a quiet kind of satisfaction.

It took about ten seconds for the *Grand Paradise* to capsize, and then I was in the water, floating away from the ship. It looked exactly like it had ten seconds before, only now it was upside down and wreathed in so many cascading bubbles that it was like some wild New Year's Eve party gone badly wrong.

There was a ripped section of hull below the waterline, extending nearly half the length of the ship. I could see inside to hallways, storerooms, and the complicated mechanics of what was probably the engineering section. I had done that. Just me.

I saw people flailing amid the strangely serene

wreckage of what had been our only salvation out here in the middle of this watery desert.

Rahel's massive sea-monster body dived past me, driven by a tail that was as much eel as mermaid, and disappeared into the gloomy depths. She was followed by a pink, sparkle-skinned unicorn with eyes of fire, gills, and flippers instead of legs. Its horn was shimmering crystal, lighting up the dark as it shot away in pursuit of Rahel.

The water was shockingly cold, or at least that was my impression. I instinctively reached for power and warmed myself, oblivious to the screaming people bobbing around me in the waves. Weather Wardens were quickly reacting, encasing people in protective bubbles and popping them to the surface if they'd been unlucky enough to end up sucking sea. I supposed they'd be all about saving those who were trapped, too.

I felt the suction of water rushing into the ship.

Rahel and Venna broke the surface again, two giants now screaming and ripping at each other, far less human than I'd have ever imagined; Venna had given up her My Little Pony sparkles and was fish-belly white now, and Rahel's body was a dark mesh of scales and teeth, too confusing to identify individual features.

Venna drove Rahel back under the surface again, and bubbles geysered in their wake.

Lewis rose out of the water. Levitated, like a

freaking superhero, dripping gallons of seawater.

'Everybody, move close together!' he yelled. 'Grab on to each other. Kevin, you're in charge. Count noses!'

The noses were still bobbing to the surface, like corks. Kevin swam to the center of the chaos and forcibly dragged people to form the first tight layer of the circle, then ducked beneath them to form up the next ring, and the next. 'Hold on to each other!' he yelled. 'Just like you're in a huddle! And keep kicking!' Now the survivors looked like a giant skydiving stunt, concentric rings of people floating with their arms around each other. Scared, sure, but human contact helped, especially for those who couldn't swim or were too terrified to remember how.

I bobbed in place, watching them for a moment, and then I called sharks.

Lewis felt the pulse traveling out through the water, and he knew what it meant. I saw his head snap around, his eyes widen, and the shock and horror on his face set up a warm, liquid glow deep inside me.

'Now I've got your attention,' I said. 'Don't I?' There weren't enough Earth Wardens to control big predators like sharks, not if they had to be focused on not drowning at the same time. The Fire and Weather Wardens would be completely vulnerable.

There were thousands of sharks out there. *Thousands.*

And now they turned and headed our way, drawn by an imaginary smell of blood in the water.

Something in Lewis's face changed. He'd made a decision, not one he liked. I wondered what it was.

Between the two of us, a vividly painted craft suddenly erupted through the waves. It was reflective yellow, bright as a traffic sign, and it was completely enclosed, sleek as a science fiction submarine.

A lifeboat.

More of them were popping up now, all around the Wardens. Lewis – or Venna – had broken them free of the sinking wreck. 'Ladders at the back!' Lewis yelled. 'Last row of the circle boards first! Each one of these will take about forty people. Wardens, I want a minimum of three of you per boat, and try to evenly distribute the powers!'

The railings around the ship were studded with these strange little craft – fiberglass, highly buoyant, with diesel engines and very little chance of being swamped even in high seas. I assumed they'd have life vests and provisions inside.

It was a race to see if he could get the Wardens into the boats before my sharks arrived for their feast. Lewis correctly deployed his forces, keeping the Earth Wardens focused on repelling attacking predators as the Fire and Weather Wardens, staff, and crew boarded their ships. Then he evacuated the last of them.

I bobbed in the pounding waves, cold and shivering, watching.

The *Grand Paradise*, that floating castle, rolled like a dying whale, heeling in the direction of its fatal wound, and then the stem rose at a ninety-degree angle out of the water, exposing the massive propulsion pods and steering mechanisms. I could see, very briefly, the entertainment area of the ship that I'd never had time to visit – the rock-climbing wall, the pools, the spas.

And then it all slipped beneath the waves with a deep, gurgling death groan, churning foam and debris, and was gone in less than a minute.

I put my face beneath the water and watched its free-fall descent into the dark, and laughed, because even if the Wardens survived all this, that was going to be one hell of a security deposit problem.

I was still laughing when something suddenly lunged up from the depths at me. I had one flash of a second to recognize the gaping maw, the dead eyes.

Shark.

Sometimes, no matter who you are, or how powerful, Mother Nature still wins.

I floated on my back, bouncing on the churning waves, watching clouds fly in black, menacing swoops overhead. My storm circled in thwarted, anxious fury.

I was bleeding badly, and I couldn't seem to stop it. I'd blown the shark into bloody meat, but too late; it had gouged a giant chunk from my thigh, and although

I'd shut down the pain receptors, I knew how bad it was. The power I had at my command wasn't meant to heal. It was meant to destroy.

Maybe it was a hallucination, but I could have sworn Bad Bob was standing on the wave-tops, looking down at me. He was wearing that same crappy, loud Hawaiian shirt, and his thin white hair blew in the same wind that blew spume from the water into my mouth as I struggled for air.

'What is it the kids today say, Jo? Epic fail?' He crouched down next to me. I could see the water rippling over his toes, but he could have been standing on concrete, while my struggles to stay afloat were getting weaker and weaker. 'I think you let this happen. I think you were so damn guilty, you thought a shark bite was what you deserved.'

'Fuck you,' I whispered, and coughed. God, I hated him. The darkness inside me had filled me to bursting, and I needed to gag it out before it choked me. 'I killed the ship for you.'

'Yes, you did. Not a bad job. But you let the lifeboats survive. That's a whole lot less impressive.'

I blinked away burning salt in my eyes. 'Help me.'

'Wait, what was the pithy phrase you just used? *Fuck you*, Jo. You kill Lewis Orwell for me. Then we'll talk about how I can help you.' He smirked down at me, his pale eyes as vicious and shallow as those of the shark that had come after me. 'Consider it the fairness doctrine in action.'

And with that, his image turned into a black mist and blew away.

But I didn't think he'd ever really been there anyway.

There were more sharks coming. I'd drawn them here, and now there really was blood in the water – mine. My wounds were pumping out more all the time, and the shark I'd destroyed was functioning as bait too. The next one to arrive wouldn't be so tentative. He'd just rip me in half.

I wondered if it was shock that was making me so fatalistic about that.

The lifeboats were all heading off to the horizon now.

All except one, which peeled off and turned back. I was unconscious before it arrived.

I woke up lying on the floor of the lifeboat, with two Earth Wardens healing up my bites as best they could. It hurt. It hurt a *lot*.

Cherise, Kevin, Cho Chu Wing, and the remaining crew were on this lifeboat, as well as the *Grand Paradise*'s Captain Miller, a sturdy gentleman who retained his military dignity despite his waterlogged uniform. He didn't say much. I didn't suppose he was regretting not going down with his ship, but maybe he was thinking about all the inevitable paperwork.

Or, if he knew I was responsible, he was thinking about finishing up what the sharks had left undone.

'We need to split up the boats,' Lewis was telling the captain as I drifted in, out, and around consciousness. 'We're like ducks in a shooting gallery out here on the open water.'

The captain nodded, but not as if he really understood or cared. I didn't think he cared about much anymore. 'I've already sent out distress calls,' he said. 'Six freighters are heading our way, including a Saudi tanker. They'll start rendezvousing with the other lifeboats within the hour.'

Lewis nodded and walked over to take a seat near me. The benches were fiberglass, with cushions that doubled as flotation devices. Among the supplies already broken out were insulating blankets, one of which was already wrapped around my damp, shivering body, and boxed drinks. They were trying to coax me to drink apple juice, but I couldn't choke anything down. Not yet.

I'd learnt a startling new lesson: no matter how badass you think you are, having a shark latch on to your body and break a piece of you away will put a dent in your self-confidence.

Cherise was playing Red Cross nurse; she draped a blanket over Lewis's damp shoulders and handed him a juice box, which he mechanically sipped as he stared down at me.

'What?' I asked, and tried to smile. 'You never saw somebody trying to kill you get their ass kicked before? Because I know you have.'

No answer.

'You want some advice? Pull the Wardens together. If you split them up between the rescue boats, you're screwed.'

'Thanks for the tip,' he said. 'Wardens stay on the boats. I want them protected in case you and Bad Bob decide to play Battleship.'.

I almost managed a shrug. 'Hazards of the sea. They all know what could happen.'

'Yeah,' he agreed. 'I'm sure that'll be a great comfort to their kids back home. I want Wardens behind us, guarding our retreat, as well as with us, guarding our asses up close. You got a problem with that, take it up with – oh, nobody, because at this point, you've got nobody.' He raised his head and fixed me with red-rimmed, fiercely focused eyes. 'What am I supposed to do with you?'

A week ago, if he'd asked that question, it would have been with an undertone of longing and some heavily suppressed fantasies involving schoolgirl uniforms. Not now. He was looking at me like I'd looked at the shark that had bitten me.

'I can still get you to Bad Bob,' I said. 'If you want.'

'I can't trust you.'

I winced and closed my eyes as one of the Earth Wardens laying hands on me did something particularly painful. 'I'm serious. I will take you to Bad Bob. I need to get there myself.'

'Why?'

I opened my eyes and locked stares with him. 'Because he left me to die in the ocean and get eaten by sharks. Because you came back.'

'Bullshit.'

I blinked.

'Don't tell me you've had a change of heart. I can see you didn't. You're just pissed that he didn't keep his promises to you. The enemy of my enemy is not my friend.'

I closed my eyes. I was too tired, too hurt, and too sick to care about his philosophy right now, and the darkness inside me *ached*, impatient with my body's weaknesses. Soon I wouldn't be vulnerable. Soon I'd be like the storm itself – unstoppable, unfeeling, a force of nature.

Lewis had chosen his healers well. They did their job, whether they wanted to or not. It took time, and I slept in between the exhausting bouts. I could feel the lifeboat moving, but I no longer cared where it was going. It didn't matter. The storm would follow me, pouring power into me, filling me with darkness.

When I woke up, *really* woke up, the Wardens had finished their work.

I was healed.

I looked at my jeans, which had a ragged hole ripped most of the way through them, and beneath the bloody cloth, my leg was mostly there. Scarred, yes, but it would heal. The new muscle and flesh felt weirdly tender.

I looked up and saw them all watching me.

'Thanks,' I said, and tried to stand. It wasn't as hard as I'd expected. I actually felt fairly good. Better, as the storm above us purred and rained down its darkness into me, reminding me who I was. What I wanted.

Lewis was right not to trust me, but I knew I didn't need to tell him that.

'Jo,' he said, 'sit down.'

I didn't. I looked at him. There was a tingle of fire in my fingers, and as I rubbed them together, I saw sparks jumping. 'Time to change course,' I said. 'I'm taking the boat. The rest of you – you can either come along and shut up or I can leave you behind. In pieces.'

He took in a deep, resigned breath. 'I didn't save you just to fight you.'

'No, you saved me because your delicate conscience couldn't stand thinking about me getting ripped apart by sharks,' I said. 'Your mistake, man. Not mine.'

'You don't want to do this.'

I smiled. And he saw that I really, really did.

Kevin wasn't surprised. He was grimly staring at me with a bleak expression, as if he'd known it all along. *Back at ya, punk.*

'You're not going to hurt anybody else,' Lewis said. 'I'm not going to let you.'

That made me want to prove him wrong. 'We knew this was coming,' I said. 'So go on. Try and stop me. It's time for the lightning round, Lewis. Go for the actual lightning. It's a small, enclosed space, but some of them may not die right off. The sepsis from the burns, that'll probably kill them in the end.'

He didn't move. 'Don't make me. Please, I'm asking you, don't.'

I called fire in my hand.

Lewis grabbed my arm, but instead of fighting me power for power, as I'd expected, he yanked me close, pinning me against his body. Putting my palm directly against his chest.

'Please,' he said. There were tears in his eyes. 'Jo, I know you're in there somewhere. *Please stop.*'

'No,' I said, and let the fire go. It flamed through his shirt, charred his flesh.

And I felt *nothing*.

Lewis let out a soft, agonized moan, but he didn't let me go.

'I'll kill you,' I growled, and I meant it. 'Every one of you if I have to. But I'm taking this ship.'

'No.' Lewis grabbed my face in his hands and – kissed me. There was desperation in it, and fury, and pain, and anguish . . .

. . . and death.

I felt something go very, very wrong in my brain. *Click.*

Lights going out. A burst of pain, of surprise, of *knowledge* . . .

Fail-safe. He'd put a fail-safe in my brain and he'd

made me forget about it and now I'd forced him to trigger it, at long last.

'You're not taking the ship,' Lewis whispered. I could hear him, and I could feel the fading sensation of his lips against mine. A benediction into the dark. 'Goodbye, Jo. God, I loved you.'

Pain exploded through my nerves like flares. I couldn't move, couldn't blink, couldn't take a breath. *Not fair, this shouldn't hurt, death should be quick* . . . The fire sank deeper, bonedeep, as if my internal organs were charring and baking.

All the pain was on the inside, shimmering like lava. On the outside, I remained limp. Apparently, already gone.

What was keeping me here?

Lewis lowered me to the deck. I could sense what he was feeling. He was full of horror and guilt for what he'd done to me, even though he'd known that it was necessary. It was toxic in its intensity, truly shocking. I didn't know how he could live with it.

Or if he could.

In the breathless silence, Cherise's voice sounded very small. 'What did you do to her?'

'I killed her,' Lewis said, and closed my eyes. I felt tears slide down my temples as he did – could the dead cry? – and felt his fingertips brush across my forehead in the old familiar gesture. 'I *had* to kill her.' It sounded like he was trying to convince himself of that.

Nobody spoke. Cherise pulled in a deep, trembling

breath, then let it out in a rush. 'You're lying. She's not *dead*. No way. Not Jo.'

One of the Earth Wardens who'd just wasted all that time and effort on healing me knelt down and pressed cool fingers to my neck, then bent over to listen to my chest. He checked my eyes, which were fixed and out of focus.

'She's gone,' he said. 'Christ, Lewis.'

'She's not *gone*,' Cherise insisted. There was a rising tide of alarm in her voice. The river Denial, flooding its banks. 'She can't be *gone*. Check her again.'

'Cherise—' Kevin tried to head her off.

'No! Check her again!'

They did. One of the other Wardens even tried reviving me – pumping my chest, breathing for me.

My body was an inert lump of clay, and inside it my mind was shrieking, trapped and unable to get free.

'She's gone,' Lewis repeated again dully, with a hitch of agony in his voice. He thought I was dead, I could feel that. Whatever was anchoring me here, in this dying shell, was something he couldn't touch. 'We have to let David say goodbye.'

'You can't do that, man. He'll kill you,' Kevin said. He sounded absolutely sure of it. 'No. I'm not letting David anywhere near this. There's no way he won't rip us all into meat for doing this to her.'

'Give me the bottle.'

'*No.*'

'I'm not going to ask again. *Give it to me.*'

'No!'

There was some kind of struggle, and then Kevin cursed in an unsteady whisper. Cherise was weeping as if her heart was breaking. From everyone else in the small boat came silence, rapid breathing, waves of distress and fear.

God, please, let me go, I begged. My brain should have been off by now, letting me escape into the comfortable dark, but instead I could feel my nerves slowly dying, my cells screaming for oxygen. Nothing I could do to stop it, either.

I was feeling my body die on a cellular level. God, would I be around for the rest of it? Feeling the dead cells turn into sludge and soup? *Decomposing*?

I didn't want to be trapped in this body as it slowly decayed, with no hope of release or rescue.

I realized, very slowly, that what was binding me here was one tiny thread of silver, stretching through the navel of my body and out through the aetheric.

David was holding me here, but he couldn't save me. His power wasn't mine to touch, and it wasn't his, either, not as long as someone else held his bottle and he was trapped inside it.

'Lewis – don't do this, man,' Kevin said. I'd never heard that tone in his voice before, so pleading. 'I'm begging you. Don't. It's not fucking fair.'

'I'm not doing it because it's fair,' Lewis said. 'I have to do it because it's right. It doesn't matter how long we wait; when we let him out of that bottle, his grief will be exactly the same. So let him out now. Please.'

The darkness that Bad Bob had put inside of me battered at the prison of my dead body, fighting to reactivate it. To stay alive.

Without the energy of my body sustaining the darkness, it was growing weaker. Dying along with me.

I felt a whisper of power scent the air as the cap came off of David's prison. I felt him battering furiously at the glass, trying to shatter his way free.

Oh, you fool, Lewis. He'll destroy you.

'David,' Lewis said. 'Come out.'

Wind blasted through the boat, pinning people against the walls, and a wild-eyed angel dropped out of heaven to gather me in his arms.

The sound that came out of him was some horrible cross between a scream and a growl – inhuman, furious, insane with grief. I couldn't move. I couldn't control my eyes to focus on his face, so his expression was mercifully blurred.

Suddenly, I felt the pressure of darkness inside me ease. Bad Bob had lost interest in me. Dead, I was of no use to him, none at all. The thick, toxic sludge of power inside me began to bleed away.

But it wasn't gone. Not yet.

Lewis said, 'David, please understand. You can't bring her back. Not this time.'

David's voice was a raw, bloody scream. *'She's not gone!'*

He could touch me. See me. Feel my ghostly presence. He hugged my limp form to his chest and rocked back and forth, his face hidden in my hair.

'Let me save her,' he whispered. '*Order me to save her.*'

I felt Lewis shudder. 'No. David, you have to let her go. She's damaged. She can't fight him off anymore. It's time to let her go.' He paused, and then said, with absolute precision, 'I'm ordering you to let her die, David.'

The silence in the boat was as deep as the ocean. So was the sense of pressure. Even my dead flesh could feel it.

'I'll kill you for this,' David said. There was nothing in his voice – no emotion, no hate, no grief. Nothing but simple declaration of intent. 'I'll rip you apart one cell at a time, and you'll live a thousand years through the pain. I might even let you scream, if you beg me.'

He was utterly serious. He would torture Lewis. He'd do it with the kind of cold distance that the Djinn reserved for those they truly, deeply, madly hated.

He'd do it for me.

'Listen to me,' Lewis said, and if he was afraid, it didn't show in his voice. 'I'm ordering you not to save her. I'm ordering you to cut the cord and *let her go.*'

'Well, that's a paradox,' David said. He still sounded eerily calm, almost relaxed. 'Because if I let her go, it destroys the vow that binds me to the bottle, and that means I'm free. Free to pull you apart, Lewis. Free to order the brutal, screaming death of every last one of your kind. Do you really think I won't?' There was madness in him, I realized. Terrible, burning madness, and Kevin was right – letting David free was a death sentence for Lewis. Not just for him, though. For the Wardens. For *everyone*.

In this moment, David was a bigger threat to humanity than anything Bad Bob had ever dreamt.

I didn't want to linger like this. I wanted to tell him it was all right, that Lewis had done it for a reason, a good one, and I didn't really mind. The darkness was dripping out of me in an invisible stain on the deck. I felt . . . clear, at last. Finally, myself again.

I couldn't bring myself back to life; it violated all the laws of the universe. All I could do, now that I was clear of Bad Bob's influence again, was choose to die. But if I did that, if I severed the cord holding me and David together, the result would be the same; he'd be lost, and alone, and mad with fury and grief.

I could feel Lewis working all of that out, and realizing that he was in a trap he couldn't escape.

Just like David.

'Let me have her,' David said. 'Let me have her and I swear I will not harm you.'

Lewis's voice came back stripped raw. Bloody. 'You think I'm afraid of *that*? He stopped and took a deep breath. 'She's too dangerous. *You know that*.'

'No,' David said softly. 'I don't know it. You fear

it. There's a difference. Let me have her, or I will teach you fear. *All of you.* You think you've suffered at the hands of the Djinn? *You have no concept of how much I can do to you.*'

Lewis knew the minutes were ticking away, and after a certain point, life wouldn't return to the decomposing tissues of my body. Not any kind of life I'd want to have, anyway.

He also knew that forcing David to kill me was even worse.

'Do it,' Lewis said. 'Save her.'

Before the words were out of his mouth, David acted. A silver cascade of power flooded me, pounded on my heart, drowned my brain. This was the pure white light of the Djinn, bathing me from the inside out. And where it met the fading black tangle of Bad Bob's tattoo . . .

. . . the silver light went out.

There was still a deadly core there, hiding inside me. Under the skin. Not even death had taken it away.

I took in a convulsive breath and sat bolt upright, still held in David's arms, and then I relaxed against him, even through the pain. My eyes spilt over with tears of agony, liquid screams that were the only thing I had to give voice to what was raging inside.

If I couldn't come back all the way, come back *clean*, I didn't want to come back at all.

I shuddered, and my eyes rolled back in my head, and for a precious moment I blacked out as my nervous system simply refused to conduct any more pain.

I returned to consciousness slowly, with the distant awareness of pain but unable to feel it directly. My back was numb again, all the way down to midway on my thighs. I couldn't feel the back of my head, either. Or the tops of my shoulders.

Out of nowhere, I felt the soft press of lips against mine. I felt the exhale of David's trembling sigh. I felt the burning drops of his tears on my face. 'That's all I can do,' he said. 'Jo. Please. Come back to me.'

I blinked, and my eyes slowly focused on his.

'It's all right,' I whispered. It wasn't. I felt sick and wrong, and the light seemed too bright for my eyes. 'I'm so sorry.'

David's eyes widened. Instead of bright copper sparks dancing in them, there was ash, as if something inside him had burnt itself out. 'Nothing to be sorry for,' he said. 'You saved their lives. If they'd let you die . . .'

The look he gave Lewis was utterly black with fury. I couldn't imagine being on the receiving end of that much hatred. David really *wanted* to kill him, slowly and horribly. Even now, I felt the conviction of that echoing inside him.

I wound my fist in David's shirt, pulling back his attention. 'No,' I said. 'Don't you dare. Don't use me as an excuse.' My voice was a parody of its usual tones, and I had no doubt he could see the sincere fright and dread in my eyes. 'No matter what happens. Promise me. He did that for a *reason*.'

He lifted a hand and traced the line of my cheekbone, light as a breath. 'No.'

'Promise me, David.'

'No.'

'Promise me.'

This time he said nothing at all. He was serious about this. Very damn serious indeed.

Lewis was still holding David's bottle. Now, he gestured to Kevin and handed it over. As Kevin's fingers closed over the glass, David's body shattered into mist and re-formed.

Taking on the appearance imposed by his new master.

As he re-formed, I saw the differences, not the similarities: His hands were too broad. The arms were too muscular, and stained with colorful flaming skull tattoos. His jeans acquired leather motorcycle chaps, and his shirt vanished to reveal a broad, muscular chest beneath a fringed leather jacket.

His head was shaved.

The only things about him that didn't really change was his face, and his eyes. Those remained his.

Those remained the ones that I knew.

Kevin cleared his throat. 'OK, order number one, you will not kill, or allow to be killed, any Warden not actively fighting with Bad Bob Biringanine in the current war. That includes Lewis. Order number two, you will not kill any human, or allow one to be killed, for any reason, unless saving them would put more people at risk. Three—' He sighed. 'Especially don't kill me, Jo. And get back in the bottle.'

David took all that without a flicker, and then he was gone. His eyes were the last thing to leave, and they never wavered from mine.

I felt sick down to my soul. He had come so close, so close to doing worse than I could imagine . . . and for me.

Just for me.

'So what now?' I asked Lewis. My voice sounded scratchy and uncertain. I felt stretched as thin as rice paper, and just as fragile.

Lewis slid down to a sitting position and rested his head in both hands. 'I don't know,' he said. 'He's put blocks around the mark to keep you from being taken over, but it won't be enough, not for long. This thing is vicious, Jo. It's fatal. We're back where we started, and I think you know I can't let that stand.'

My hands were shaking. I pressed them down on my thighs. 'I'm listening.'

'I need you to get off the boat,' he said. 'I need you to let us leave you behind.'

In the open water.

With the sharks.

I swallowed hard and didn't answer. I was too busy reliving what that had felt like – the teeth hot in my flesh, pieces of me coming off.

Blood.

Lewis didn't blink. 'I'm taking everyone else to landfall. I need you to go on, alone.'

'Alone,' I repeated, because I could *not* have heard him right. 'You want me to go after Bad Bob all by myself. Swimming. Through shark-infested seas. Are you fucking *insane*!'

He hated himself. I could see the loathing, but I could also see the cold steel underneath it. He knew what he had to do, and he wasn't afraid to do it.

He never was. I loved that about him, and I hated it, too.

'I can't keep you here,' he said. 'You're a bomb. Sooner or later, you're going to go off, and I can't risk what you're going to do. If you want to save yourself, you need to do it alone.'

'Don't feed me crap and tell me it's chocolate,' I said.

'I'm, what? A Trojan horse? Bait? Your own personal suicide bomber?'

'You're what you need to be. The way you always are.' He reached over and smoothed a hand down my tangled, damp hair. His long fingers felt cool and strange on my skin. 'The hardest thing I've ever had to do was kill you. Don't make me do it again. I'm already going to die for it; we both know that. He's never going to forget.'

I leant into the comfort of his touch, closed my eyes, and said, 'David will forgive you. Eventually.'

'No, I really don't think so.' He kissed my forehead. 'Especially after I do this.'

I felt his emotion spill into me, Earth Warden to Earth Warden – complicated waves of painful guilt, staggering responsibility, and love. So much love it hurt. He shouldn't love me so much. He knew I couldn't love him in the same way.

I started to tell him that, once and for all, but he touched my lips with his thumb. 'I know,' he murmured. 'I just wanted you to remember it. One way or another, this is goodbye, Jo. We're not going to step in the same river twice.'

Lewis stood up and spun the hatch. It was a sliding door at the top of the craft, and climbing the steps to get up to it seemed like the march to the gallows.

Lewis held my hand to keep me steady.

I emerged into bright sunlight, blinded by the glitter of the whitecaps and the endless roll of the ocean. By the reflective yellow surface of the fiberglass hull. The storm hung sullenly in the distance, a vast black curtain rippling with wind and power and fury. It couldn't reach me now, but it would follow.

It had to. It was still keyed to the power locked into Bad Bob's mark.

I looked back down as I stripped off the blanket and handed it to Lewis. 'Thanks for the apple juice,' I said. 'The beer's on you if I live.'

He didn't smile. There was darkness as thick as

the storm hanging around him; his aura was shot through with it.

'Tell David—' I said, and couldn't think of anything to say that David wouldn't already know. 'Tell him I'll see him soon.' I looked past Lewis's hard face and saw Kevin hovering behind him. 'Don't treat David like your slave. If you do, I'll make sure you regret it. Just – leave him in the bottle. Promise me.'

Kevin blinked. 'You don't want me to let him go?'

'Not yet,' I said. 'You can't take the risk. If anything happens to me – Well, you saw. I don't want you guys to pay for it.' I was condemning David to life imprisonment, if – as was very probable – I died. Not exactly the happy ending I'd been hoping for, but it could have been worse.

I'd seen how bad it could get. Our devotion to each other had a horrible dark side. I'd been willing to call fire, burn twenty innocent people alive to make my point. David had been willing to destroy millions to avenge me.

It wasn't David's fault that he could never, ever forgive; it was just his Djinn nature. Now I had to protect him from his own worst impulses.

I blinked away tears and focused on Kevin, with the bottle in his hand – and Cherise, clinging to Kevin and crying. 'Keep David safe for me,' I said. 'I love all of you. I won't forget.'

And then I turned and dived off the boat, into the water.

Chapter Nine

So.

It was just me and the sharks. I was acutely aware of the vast, complicated landscape of predator and prey beneath me as I floated; I'd drawn a whole lot of sharks here, and the Great Whites in particular alarmed me, because I'd seen *Jaws*.

I couldn't feel my back at all, but the rest of my body was chilled from the water. Still, I wasn't likely to die of exposure, or even hunger or thirst. I could maintain my body's electrolyte levels, heat, and general health; I could desalinate water to drink. I could eat raw fish that I could call into my hands, if I wasn't especially fussy. Wasn't looking forward to that part; sushi prepared by a brilliant Japanese chef is a far cry from munching on something fresh out of the sea and spitting out the scales and bones.

I floated and watched the rescue craft fleet sail

away. The hatch remained open on the lifeboat I'd
left, and I heard arguments pouring out of it until the
wind carried it away. Cherise had tried to jump out,
twice. I could still hear her screaming at the top of her
lungs long after other sounds had faded.

'Bye, sweetie,' I whispered, and bobbed in the waves
for a while, until the boats were just dazed smudges
on the horizon.

I wasn't a good enough Earth Warden to control
several hundred sharks, all operating under their natural
instinctive programming. What I *could* do – and did – was
create conditions that made it less fun for the sharks
to come near me, basically administering electrical
shocks to anything that came closer than ten feet.

It was terrifying. Eventually, though, the sharks lost
interest or found other prey to follow. A few continued
to circle, but I couldn't wait; the longer I delayed, the
less likely it would be that David's containment of Bad
Bob's torch would hold for me. I started to swim. It
was fun at first, and then boring, and then difficult.
The human body is designed for only so much wear
and tear without periods of rest, and my Earth Warden
powers could maintain it, but repairing overly stressed
muscles took time.

Time I wasn't going to have.

I kept swimming. After a while, pain took on a
lulling sort of normality. You really can get used to
just about anything, especially if you don't have any
alternatives.

The sun began to dip toward the horizon, and I thought about being out here at night, with a sky full of stars. It was oddly peaceful. I was still myself – rescued from the abyss into which Bad Bob had dragged me, though he hadn't exactly dragged me there kicking and screaming, to be perfectly honest about it. I had a wide streak of darkness inside, all my own, and it wasn't just the scars left over from my earlier Demon Mark; I'd always been ambitious. I'd always pursued power.

I guess I wasn't so different from Bad Bob after all, except that I knew all that was both a strength and a weakness. And I knew it had to have limits.

I felt none of the power or fury that had thundered through me when the torch had been active, but sooner or later, David's containment field would fail, and without him here to renew it, the torch would burn hotter than ever. I was a Warden. I wouldn't be that easy to kill, even stranded out here on the ocean.

I'm working too hard, I thought. *If I swim all the way to him, I'll have nothing left when I get there.*

Depression set in. It does that when your friends sail off and abandon you, and when you have to say a probably permanent goodbye to the one man in the world you'd not only die for, but live with. *Maybe it's not worth it. Maybe I should just take myself out of the game. That'd throw a curl in Bad Bob's tail.*

It had a seductive, petulant sort of sense to it. If I died, his plans were screwed, at least the ones I'd seen.

He wanted me. He might even need me to make his small-A apocalypse come true. Without me, he had his Sentinels, but they were second-raters, and we'd already taken out the real threats.

Then again . . . if I died, that left David snapped into that state of frenzy and rage, and I couldn't count on him staying imprisoned.

I didn't *want* him to stay imprisoned.

But I didn't want to stay apart. Or go back to the cold, evil bitch I'd become.

I considered all the ways I could make my marriage work while my burning, screaming muscles stroked away at the endless ocean. Nothing solved itself, but I hadn't really expected it to. Eventually, the effort whited out my problems more efficiently than anything else could have. They weren't gone, they were just . . . under the surface.

The sun went down. It was a beautiful sight, unbounded by the rules of land – nothing but waves and sea, and an endless bowl of sky. I had to stop more and more frequently and just let myself float. My body hurt so much I cried involuntary, hiccuping tears. Every deliberate movement felt as if my nerves had grown cutting edges and were slicing themselves right out of my skin. My skin felt rubbery and ice-cold, except for my back, which just felt like it wasn't there at all. *Keep going.*

I tried, but my efforts came slower, my rests more frequent. I just couldn't keep moving. My energy reserves were gone, and although the world was rich in it all around me, I couldn't tap it like a Djinn could.

I'm going to die out here. Except that I couldn't die, not without breaking the tie to David.

Not without setting him on a path of destruction that would annihilate everything.

The stars came out in thick white veils of light, and I floated on my back in the bobbing waves, too tired to keep moving at any cost.

I slept for a while. I floated.

I think I went a little insane, as the endless, isolated hours passed. Then I swam again, and then I slept.

Eventually, I dreamt I heard a ship's horn.

My ride's here, I thought. It was crazy, but somehow it all made sense, the way dreams sometimes do when you're stuck in the middle – life was an ocean, death was a ship to take me away to lands unknown. I'd bought the ticket, right? So why not take the ride?

I heard the blast of noise again, mournful and musical at the same time.

A spotlight appeared out of nowhere and hit the water, so bright I yelled and covered my eyes.

'We've caught ourselves a mermaid,' someone said, from behind the blaze of light. 'Fish her out. Let's see what we've landed.'

I didn't realize how much of the sea I'd swallowed until I was out of the ocean. I promptly fell to my hands and knees and vomited up enough foamy water to fill a goldfish bowl or two. I rolled onto my side, and continued hacking up frothing mouthfuls. My lungs were on fire from the inside, and my throat felt like I'd gargled with Clorox.

My head throbbed like thunder. My skin felt rubbery and soft, and I was incredibly dizzy.

'Huh,' somebody said, and I threw up clots of white foam on a pair of sturdy-looking black paramilitary boots. 'She don't look like much, Josue.'

The hot searchlight was still beaming down on me from a stubby upper deck. In comparison to the majestic cruise ship, this looked like a stunted dwarf – a working ship, some kind of smallish freighter. Not very well kept. The metal deck around me was spotted with rust, there were careless piles of rope and haphazardly stacked boxes, and the men standing over me didn't look like the shipshape type, either. There were four of them, all in filthy, grease-stained T-shirts, cargo-type pants or shorts, and nonskid work boots.

And they all carried knives and guns. Two of them had their firearms shoved casually into waistbands; the other two had what looked like automatic machine pistols slung on bandoliers across their chests.

I was pretty sure those weren't standard issue for guys on board most cargo ships.

I coughed some more. I tried to sit up. I was, instead, yanked all the way to my feet, where I wavered and nearly went down again. Gravity seemed like a very strange concept to me, after all that time in the water.

I tried my voice, which came out as rusty as the ship I was standing on. 'Thanks for the rescue.'

One of them laughed. He was the one who'd declared me alive, I thought, a big, muscular guy the color of mahogany. He looked like he could bite a metal bar and spit bullets. As rescuers went, not exactly comforting.

But I couldn't help but be relieved that the whole survival thing had been taken out of my hands.

'*Hola*,' the big guy – apparently, Josue – said, and aimed his machine pistol somewhere in the direction of a number of my more important internal organs, 'Is your name Joanne Baldwin?'

I frankly stared at him. '*What*?'

'Yes or no, mermaid. Joanne Baldwin?' He had an interesting accent to his English – thick, not quite Spanish, more lyrical and unpredictable. Close cousins, though. Portuguese, maybe. 'If you're not, I throw you back. I don't have room for pets.'

'In that case I'm definitely Joanne.' I swallowed another cough. 'Somebody told you to look for me. Who?'

'Why? Enemies would have left you sucking water, eh? Must have been friends.'

He had a point. I couldn't imagine these guys doing anything without a profit motive, and I hadn't pissed off anyone bad enough to make them spend a lot of money to kill me. Easy enough to just let me drown.

Wait . . . that meant it was someone who'd known I would be in the water.

'You didn't come all the way out here to find me,' I said. Josue raised his eyebrows and smiled, not in a comforting sort of way.

'Came for the salvage on the ship that went down,' he said. 'Stayed for the profits. You're worth a lot of money, mermaid.'

'Alive, I guess.'

He shrugged. 'Apparently.'

This ship was far from an honest sort of vessel. They'd picked up the maritime distress calls from the *Grand Paradise* – I assumed the captain had sent them – and of course the lifeboats would have transponders on them, probably sending out automated rescue calls. And in these waters, that would draw two kinds of vessels: well-meaning Good Samaritans, and the kind of ship I'd just been fished onto.

In other words, pirates. And somebody had co-opted them to search specifically for me.

'Look!' said one of the crew, stationed at the railing. He called for light, and the beam burnt out into the water, turning it from black to a muddy, sullen blue. At first I didn't see what he was looking at, and then I caught a glimpse of bobbing wood. A few bits of debris from the ship had followed the same currents I'd used. There was plenty of small, buoyant wreckage still around, though the debris cloud had long since dissipated and spread itself out over dozens of miles of open water. Not much of a grave for such an enormous vessel.

'Everybody get off?' the pirate captain asked me, and shoved me with the barrel of his gun when I delayed my answer. 'Everybody in those little boats, yes?'

'You bet,' I said. 'Everybody's been rescued. Well, everybody but me, obviously.'

He seemed disappointed. I guessed he'd been hoping to fish out some rich Americans he could ransom back at a significant profit. I didn't blame him; I didn't look like a rich payday, regardless of what his patron had told him.

'How come you didn't end up on a rescue boat, mermaid? You not fresh enough?'

A couple of his crewmates offered helpful commentary about how yummy I looked. Charming. I was starting to feel like today's catch, still wiggling on the line.

I took a deep breath. That was a mistake; it resulted in more lung-wrenching coughing, and I spat up some more foam and mucus. 'Let's just say I missed my boat,' I said.

'What makes a woman stay behind when a boat is sinking?' he asked. It was a rhetorical question; he was showing off for his crew. 'You have a kid on the ship?'

'No.'

'Money, then.' He flashed me a vulpine grin. 'Always money.'

'Speaking of money, who hired you to find me?'

The laughter died out on the man's face, and left it watchful and dangerous. 'Don't think I want to tell you that,' he said. 'Not yet.'

'Why?' I was starting to believe I'd been better off with the sharks.

'Americans, they're always talking about money. *I give you money if you let me go. My family has money. I got important friends who will pay you.* That sort of thing. They think they can buy their way out of anything.' He gazed at me for a long, cold few seconds. 'You don't offer nothing. That makes me nervous.'

'Maybe I'm poor.'

He snorted. 'Even the poor offer. You don't even try to make a deal.'

'Maybe I'm crazy.'

He showed me teeth. 'Maybe. Maybe you just think we won't hurt you 'cause you're so pretty.'

'No,' I said, and held his gaze. 'I'm sure you'd try like hell to hurt me, for any reason or none at all. I'm sure you've slit throats and raped and tortured if you felt like it. Probably just yesterday.'

That woke a lot of murmuring among the rest of the crew. I heard the slap of boots – more men arriving from other parts of the ship, drawn by the tinfoil smell of trouble in the air.

'Huh,' the captain said. 'So what you got to stop me if I want to do the same to you?'

'I'm pretty sure you don't want to know.' The

tingle on my back that I'd felt as I was drowning had subsided, but the nerves were waking up, and I could feel the outline of the torch forming again, black and steady. I could feel the black well of power opening, ready to flood into me if I opened the door. 'You guys know comic books? *The Incredible Hulk?*'

Josue looked blank. He looked around at the others.

'Bruce Banner,' one of the crew piped up. '*You won't like me when I'm angry.*' In any group of people, no matter how hard-assed they might appear, there's always a geek. I was just surprised that, in this company, he'd admitted it.

'It's like that, only I don't have to wait to turn green,' I said. 'I'm trying to help you out here, gentlemen. Don't push me, and I won't push back, and we'll all be just fine. Somebody's paying you to keep me alive and in one piece. Let's just all get along.'

The captain was no longer amused. 'Shut up, bitch,' he said, and shoved the barrel of his pistol under my chin. 'You don't threaten me. Not on my own ship. I'm not being paid enough for *that.*'

I didn't reach for power. It reached for *me*, a black tidal wave that pounded into me like surf to shore, immense and burning.

No! I rejected it, slammed the door shut and held it closed as the power thundered on the other side. I felt small and pitiful and ridiculously weak, and I knew I was only a second from death at the hands of these men, these *pirates* – but my other choice was worse.

'Sure,' I said. Josue hadn't noticed a thing, from the outside; he thought he was still in control, not one heartbeat away from being a red stain on the deck. 'You win.'

If he pushed that gun into me any deeper, we were going to be engaged. 'I always do,' he said. 'Tell me who you are.'

'Joanne Baldwin.'

'No. Who you *are*. You're not afraid of me.'

'I just gave up.'

'Not because you're afraid.' Josue was way too smart. It was a little creepy. Then he took it too far by saying, 'I like women best when they're afraid. They shut up more.'

'You're a real charmer, did you know that?' He flashed me his pirate smile. 'All right, so you're going to put me in the hold. What then? You turn me over to whoever paid you to come get me?' I had an awful feeling I already knew who that would be, and his initials were Bad Bob Biringanine.

'Something like that,' Josue agreed. 'Unless you plan to make me a better offer.'

'I'll pay you twice what he's paying you,' I said. I *did* want to get to Bad Bob. Just not as his helpless captive. Much better if I could hire myself a hard-bitten pirate crew and take the fight to him unexpectedly.

Josue slowly showed his teeth in a smile. He had two gold-plated incisors, both on the bottom, and it gave him a glam vampire look that must have been pretty effective in his line of work.

'Where you got all that money hidden, mermaid? In your panties?' He made a grab, as if he was about to make a withdrawal. I fended him off.

'No, idiot. I keep my money in a bank, like every other criminal who isn't a complete moron. Look, I was on that ship with some of the wealthiest people on earth. I'm not just some casino rat. I know people.'

Josue looked unimpressed. 'What people?'

'Cynthia Clark. The movie star?'

Pirates started naming movies with the geeky enthusiasm of film obsessives everywhere. From the breadth of their knowledge, I figured they must have the biggest DVD collection ever somewhere belowdecks. Not that they'd ever paid for any of it, of course.

'Famous friends doesn't mean you have money. How you expect to pay me?' Captain Josue asked, and spread his hands to show how unencumbered I was by those phantom millions.

'Electronic transfer,' I said. 'It's how business works these days. People don't carry cash, they carry personal identification numbers and ATM cards.'

He wasn't convinced. 'And how does this help me? Do you see any computers on my ship?'

I gave him a very slow smile. 'If you take me where I want to go, I promise you, I'll fill your ship so full of dollars you won't be able to sleep without restacking bundles of cash.'

'Then give me your account number and PIN code. I'll check it out.'

I raised my eyebrows. 'I thought you didn't have a computer.'

'That's not what I said.' He laughed. 'You give me the information and I'll verify that you're not a lying whore. That seems fair.'

'Sorry. It's all I have to bargain with. Guess you'll just have to trust me.'

'I was born at night, mermaid. Not last night,' he said. I didn't like the confidence of his smile. 'You show me cash, and then I believe you. Not before. Thiago, take her below.'

The guy who'd copped to being a comic book geek grabbed my arm and hustled me down the narrow space between the wheelhouse and the railing, toward the stern of the boat. 'Hey, Thiago?' I asked. 'I could use some help here. Talk to your boss, would you?'

'Shut up,' he said. 'You won't like *me* when I'm angry.'

So much for geek solidarity.

Two hatches later, I was shoved across a rusty threshold and into some kind of ship's hold. It was nothing like the vast, spacious warehouse of the *Grand Paradise;* this was a cramped, hot, stinking metal box that gave mute evidence that the ship had once been a fishing vessel.

I swore I'd never eat tuna again.

'Hey!' I yelled, as the hatch banged shut behind me. 'You're really going to regret this!'

And that sounded so stock B-movie that I shut up and found a place to sit and rest my aching head on my aching crossed arms.

The burning torch on my back throbbed in time with my heartbeat, and I could feel it stretching back through the aetheric, a slimy tether that kept pulling on me, trying to drag me to the dark side.

'Keep your shirt on, Bob,' I murmured to the dead fish. 'A girl's got to sleep sometime.'

I curled up in a nest of burlap and old packing material from one of the crates, and fell completely unconscious.

Not a care in the world, strangely enough. Too tired to have one.

When I woke up, my whole body ached less, but that only meant the alert level had gone down from red to orange, damage-wise. No way could I swim far in my current state. I needed the ship if I intended to stay alive.

Well, if I couldn't buy it, there were other ways. They were as dangerous to me as to the captain, though.

I banged on the hatch until I got attention, and was dragged back up on deck. It was midday, and the sun was dazzling on the water. I blinked against the glare.

Josue was once again lounging at the rail. 'Don't you ever work?' I asked him.

'Don't you ever shut up?' He nodded to the crewman holding my arm, and another gun dug into my ribs. 'Now, maybe you're willing to tell me the account number of all this mythical money you have to share?'

I shook my head.

'Wrong answer.' He turned to Thiago, who was holding me. 'Shoot her and put her over the side. Do it in the stomach. That way she has time to change her mind before the sharks come.'

Damn. I was glad this guy wasn't a Warden.

Thiago tried to follow orders, but when he pulled the trigger, it resulted in a dry click. He tried again, frowning.

'Here, let me see,' I said. I took the pistol from him, held it in my hand, and melted the barrel into dripping slag that ran through my glowing fingers and in streams across the deck. 'Oh, there's your problem. Man, they really don't make these things like they used to.'

I heard more clicks as other pirates joined the hunting party, but I'd disrupted the firing mechanisms of every single gun aboard the ship in one fast burst. So many delicate parts to a gun, really. Not like a good blunt object. 'Don't make me blow up your ammunition,' I said. 'It'll take your hands off with it when it goes up. Classic choice, though. Who wants a hook to complete the whole pirate image?'

Guns hit the deck and tumbled, metal on metal. Weapons skidded from side to side in the pitch and roll of the waves, and an Uzi nudged my foot. I kicked it to the rail, where it hesitated on the edge, then tipped over.

'Good boys,' I said. The captain – no coward, even if he didn't understand what was happening – pulled his knife, the better to fillet me. 'OK, not you, obviously, and I'm voting you off the island. Thank you for playing. Say hello to the sharks.'

I blew him over the side of the ship, out into the water. He hit with a tremendous splash and came up screaming.

I ignored him. 'Right,' I said. 'Your captain had an attention problem. Who wants to be in charge now?'

They all looked at each other. Nobody dared make a move to rescue Josue, who was flailing like a gaffed fish, although their gazes frequently cut in his direction. One man stepped forward – Thiago, who I suspected was the second in command anyway. 'You are,' he said. 'Miss.'

I smiled at him – my best, most winning smile, fueled by a wild edge. 'You're a smart guy, Thiago, do you want to make some money?'

'Sure.'

'Same deal I tried to make with your ex-boss. You take me in that direction' – I pointed toward where I knew Bad Bob was, as the torch on my back throbbed when I faced that way; no clue what the nautical course was, and I didn't much care – 'and I can promise you that you'll get one hell of a great payday out of it. Better than holding up unlucky pleasure boaters, anyway.'

He exchanged looks with his fellow scavengers – OK, pirates – and one by one, they nodded. The sound of their captain's increasingly desperate calls for rescue off the port bow probably had something to do with their quorum.

'Can we pick him up, please?' Thiago asked, like it was an afterthought, and pointed toward their captain. I turned my head and looked at him. The dawn wind blew my damp hair over my face, but I was pretty sure he could see my expression even at that distance, with that concealment.

'If he points so much as a dirty look in my direction, I'll shoot him in the stomach and let *him* tell it to the sharks,' I said. 'Make sure he knows that. I don't feel like giving second chances right now.'

Thiago nodded. He had a good poker face, but there was a shadow of uneasiness in his dark eyes. 'What do you want us to call you, miss?'

I smiled. 'You can call me whatever you want, buddy. This isn't going to be a long-term relationship. Believe me.'

Thiago gave some orders, the content of which was lost on me, but the ten or so men that crewed this rusty scow snapped to it. Somebody fished the captain out of the ocean and got him safely out of my sight. I felt the engines growl, shift, and surge beneath my feet as we got under way. The bow turned, heading toward a destination that wasn't visible in any way on the horizon – except to me.

After enjoying the view for a while, I went down to the hold, where I found the captain enjoying the hospitality of the rotting tuna. I pulled up an empty crate.

'So,' I said. 'How about you tell me who hired you to fish me out of the water, Josue?'

'*Vaipro Inferno*,' he said. '*Foda-se.*'

'Want to see a magic trick?' I asked, and put my hand out, palm up. Nothing in it. I turned it palm down, then over again.

Lightning danced along the skin, clung to my fingertips, and dangled from my knuckles like a handful of tangled string.

Josue sat back.

'You know anything about Tasers? This is the same thing, only without the delivery system. Oh, and the batteries. And you know the best thing?' I leant forward and smiled. 'It never runs out of juice.'

There's no such thing as a loyal pirate. 'He was a man,' Josue said.

'Name?'

'I don't ask names. He gave me cash money.'

'White hair? Big, blue eyes? Red nose? About this tall?' I indicated Bad Bob's height, but Josue was shaking his head.

'No, never seen that one. This one, he was weird. Shaved head. Wearing leather, like out of some motorcycle movie. Scary.'

My heart took a running leap. 'How'd he pay you?'

'You won't believe it: gold. Sunken treasure. He said he'd just found some.' Josue laughed and shook his head. 'Crazy people out here. All crazy. I thought I'd find you, see if you were worth keeping. He shows up again, I shoot him if I like you and keep the money anyway.'

Josue had no idea what a bad idea that would have been. 'Did he say what to do with me when you found me?'

'Yeah.' Josue's smile was a model of impish delight.

'He said tell you Kevin said hello. And to take you back to port and let you go. Crazy. Like I said.'

I let out a slow sigh. 'And you figured you'd threaten me into giving you something else? Or just rape and kill me?'

Josue shrugged. 'It's the way things are.'

'You are such a lucky man that things didn't work out your way,' I said. 'If they had, you'd be screaming your way to hell right about now, along with everybody else on this ship.'

He didn't believe me, but he should have. I was in no mood to be Ms. Nice Guy, but compared to the fury that David would have unleashed on them if they'd hurt me, there was literally nothing I could do to them that would be anywhere near as horrible.

'My offer's still open,' I said. 'You take me where

I want to go, and I'll pay you enough money to make you king of the pirates forever.'

He tried not to look interested. 'How do I know you'll keep your promise?'

I turned my hand over again. Lightning flashed and crawled. 'You know I'll keep this one.'

Josue sat up straighter, his eyes flicking around as if he was trying to figure out an exit strategy. He finally nodded. 'It's a deal,' he said. 'Just – put that away, *bruxa*.'

'Hey, Josue? Call me a witch again, I *will* Taser the holy shit out of you.' I felt the black exhilaration creep over me once more, the stealthy march of Bad Bob's influence running through my veins. 'Oh, hell, maybe I'll just do it anyway.'

I didn't, but it was fun watching him think I would.

I paced the bridge as Josue ordered the crew around. I had nothing to do, really, except wait and think.

Think about Kevin sneaking around behind Lewis's back to let David out of his bottle, sending him to pluck me out of the ocean.

Why?

Cherise, I thought. I couldn't imagine Kevin getting the initiative to come running to my rescue any other way. We'd always cordially hated each other.

I was even more surprised that David hadn't tricked his way out of the bottle again by now. It wouldn't take much slack for him to snap the rope that bound him; Djinn had been doing it for millennia, and they were very, very good at finding loopholes to exploit. Either Kevin had been very specific about what he wanted him to do, or David didn't really want to get free just now.

Maybe because he knew that if he did, he might end up fighting me, and neither of us wanted that. He'd wanted to save me. Kevin had allowed him to do it.

Kevin, you're a romantic. That made me smile. I supposed I'd have to thank him some way.

Maybe by not killing him. That was a gift that kept on giving, right?

The sun was putting on a spectacular evening display, all clouds and blood, when the lookout called a warning. At least, I thought it was a warning – Portuguese wasn't exactly my strong suit, but the tone definitely sounded urgent.

'What is it?' I asked Josue, as he left the bow rail to head toward the stern.

'A ship,' he said. 'Coming up behind us, and moving fast. Big, maybe a military ship or a tanker.'

'Tankers don't move that fast,' I said.

Josue continued to stare over the stern rail, frowning. 'Could be more trouble than you're worth, mermaid. I'm thinking I throw you back.'

'You want to go downstairs again, talk it over?'

He gave me a scornful sneer. 'You can't sail the ship alone. My men won't work for you.'

'Want to bet? Just do what I tell you, Josue. If I feel this ship slow down, you're over the side, and your crew goes with you. That's a promise.'

He knew I meant it. He nodded. I had no doubt that later on, he'd try to stab me in the back, maroon me, or otherwise screw me over, but for now he was treading carefully – partly because I was a potential payday, but equally out of sheer morbid fear. He'd seen a sample of what I could do, and he didn't want to see more.

I didn't really blame him for that. I wasn't wild to see it, either.

I locked my hands behind my back and kept my legs spread wide, riding the bucking of the waves with the ease of a long-practiced sailor. We both watched the dim shape on the horizon take on edges and definition.

Definitely a ship. Big.

The lookout called another warning. Josue looked up, frowning, and blinked. He cursed in Portuguese – no, I didn't recognize the words, but the flavor's the same in any language. 'Storm,' he said. 'Coming on fast from the south.'

My friend the storm had hung back, content to let me run; I wasn't sure anymore whether I was holding its leash or it was holding mine. But something had changed. Maybe it sensed that the containment around the mark on my back was fading again, or that I wasn't following my approved script.

It was heading our way. Fast.

The blood sunset had disappeared behind a boiling, rising mass of clouds – iron gray ones, with greenish-black underpinnings. It was already crawling with lightning inside. Power had been poured into it – an awful lot of power.

'Hold course,' I said. I didn't think all that effort Bad Bob was putting out was meant solely for us. We weren't that hard to sink, frankly.

As we sailed steadily toward it, the storm spread out, flattened, swirled, consolidated, gained density and deeper color.

Then it started to spin around a center axis – slowly, majestically, unevenly at first, then spiraling out like a deadly galaxy. The blender of the gods, taking shape right in front of me.

'We need to get out of its way!' Josue shouted. I felt the first breath of wind sweep over us, vivid with the smell of rain. The clouds were whipping toward us. He cursed me in Portuguese, and ordered his men to follow his instructions.

I locked the rudder in place with a burst of Earth power. They worked frantically to free it, but they weren't getting anywhere.

As the wind increased, so did the amplitude of the waves, and the small ship was nowhere near as able to crush through the turmoil as the *Grand Paradise* had been. The vessel was battered, and when it slammed bow-first into the rising waves, the spray fractured into foam and coated everything on board in slippery, unpleasant slime.

Then came the rain, hammering in sheets that felt like needles. Josue's crew broke out battered rain slickers. I ignored the offer, and stood at the bow, watching the storm's progress. I could feel its blind menace, its anger, but it wasn't directed downward at me, not even as the rain intensified into a heavy, strangely hot downpour. The wind speed increased, and the clouds rotated faster. It intensified as the ship crashed and fell through the waves. I tethered myself to the rail and resisted the waves that crested the bow and washed the decks, trying to pull me over.

Something wild inside me broke free as we rode through the storm, and in the blaze of lightning and pounding surf, I felt at home. Finally, completely at home. All those years of fighting the storms, and I'd never realized how much a part of them I was. How complete I was when I was with them.

I was almost sorry when we hit the eye of the storm and calm fell over us – but I looked up into the primal heart of the enemy, and it looked back at me with a kind of affectionate recognition.

Good dog.

When we hit the trailing side, the winds lashed us so viciously that we lost two of the crew, even though they'd been tethered. The seas swamped the decks, shattered glass, woke terror from seasoned pirates who picked their teeth and yawned at the idea of a normal tempest.

After a white-knuckled eternity, the storm was past us, and heading for its *real* victim.

The ship closing in on us from behind.

The seas continued heavy against us, and Josue wanted to slow our pace. The engines were laboring, and the crew was exhausted and sick.

'No,' I said. I didn't need them anymore. They'd served their purpose, both ship and crew, and I no longer had to worry about their breaking points. 'Just keep the throttle open. We'll be fine.'

I wrapped energy around the straining pumps and valves and increased their speed. It wouldn't last long, but it would give us more of a lead against our pursuer, who had the full weight of the storm to deal with now. I looked back to see its forward progress stalling, as if it had met cooler air to slow it. The storm was lashing that other ship with all its supernatural fury.

Josue, also watching, crossed himself.

The moon rose, but it was quickly veiled by clouds. As night descended on us, it was thick and black and claustrophobic. Only the shattered reflections of our running lights spoilt the illusion of sailing through empty, limitless space.

'*Mae de Deus*,' Josue murmured. 'It's still coming, that ship. Like a ghost out of the grave.' It *was* a ghost.

The *Grand Paradise* had gone down, I'd seen it.

It had been too badly damaged and too thoroughly flooded to float, and yet there it was, gaining on our tail. The running lights were all working, blazing merrily in the darkness, and it was charging at a speed that didn't seem natural for such an enormous ship.

It was trying to get to me before I reached my destination.

'Hold on,' I told Josue, and opened the throttles even more on our nameless little pirate ship, sending it leaping and slamming through the waves like an oversized, wallowing speedboat. The hull wouldn't take it for long, but it didn't have to.

Out there in the darkness was my destination.

I felt a Warden grabbing for control of our engines, and whipped a black scythe of power across the lines of force. It must have hurt, and badly. 'Do it again, and you'll pull back a stump,' I muttered, and gripped the rail tighter. 'Back off.'

I didn't think they would. If they were strong and confident enough to make it through the hurricane, they'd be more than competent enough to tackle me.

A Djinn breathed into focus on the deck a few feet away, and I prepared for the fight of my life . . . . . . but it was David. *David.*

My David, perfect in every line. Not Kevin's incarnation of him.

He didn't say anything. Neither did I. Josue drew a knife and stabbed at him, but David didn't even bother to cast him a look, just flicked his fingers and sent him flying across the deck.

'Are you here to stop me?' I asked.

'No,' my husband said, and took a step toward me. Then another. I was in the V-shaped well of the bow, pressed against the rails – nowhere to go but over the side, into the black waters. 'I'm not here to stop you.'

'Then what?'

He took another step, risking a full attack. I could feel the urge, the *need* vibrating through me like plucked strings. *Don't let him fool you. Don't let him stop you. You need to reach Bad Bob. If this goes badly, you know what will happen. The two of you will be responsible for destroying the world.*

In the ripping light of a lightning strike on the cruise ship looming slowly up behind us, David's face was serious and very calm.

'I'm here to help you,' he said.

He opened his hand, and in it were fragments of glass.

The broken pieces of his bottle. I stared at them for a moment, into his eyes. 'How—?'

'Cherise,' he said. 'She wants you to live. So do I. She got the bottle away from Kevin. She – trusts me.' Cherise was a romantic idiot, in this one sense: She simply didn't understand how dangerous David really was. I wasn't even sure I understood . . . although I was starting to get a really good idea.

I tightened my grip on the rail as the ship pounded

into a particularly deep trough, then painfully plowed up the leading edge of the next wave. 'I see. And did you stop for anything else along the way?'

'You mean, did I kill Lewis?' he asked. 'Not yet.' He took one more step, and we were body to body, soaked with rain, blinded by lightning. Sealed together by storms. 'That doesn't mean I've forgotten him. Don't ask me to do that.'

I couldn't begin to try. 'How did they raise the ship?'

'Who says they did?' David's smile was knowing, and a little bitter. 'It's not the *Grand Paradise*. Lewis lied to you from the beginning. The *Grand Paradise* was a decoy, designed to lure Bad Bob into showing his hand. He sent the other Wardens out of Fort Lauderdale, aboard the *Grand Horizon*. It's a sister ship) – a little smaller, a little faster. Crewed entirely with Wardens and Djinn. It's been making good time and staying off of Bad Bob's radar. Until now.'

That son of a bitch. Lewis really had suckered me, every step of the way. He'd known I was a risk, if not a ready-made traitor. He'd used me as a stalking horse, although I had to admit he'd put himself on the line, too.

But he'd also exposed Cherise and dozens of other innocents who had no place in this. And an unforgivably large number of Wardens, although I supposed for any kind of a feint to work, he had to commit himself to it.

I would never forgive him for risking so much, no more than David would be able to forgive him for the kill switch that Lewis had put in my brain.

'So by suckering Bad Bob into kicking the living crap out of us, the *Grand Horizon* got a virtually free ride,' I said. 'Right?'

'As far as I know.'

'How could you not know?'

'It's crewed by Ashan's Djinn. Everything was compartmentalized from me. Deliberately so.'

We'd both been cut out. Well, I'd been hoping Lewis had fallback positions, in the beginning, and it looked like he'd done a hell of a lot more with a hell of a lot less than I'd have managed in his place.

'They're in for it now,' I noted, as three lightning strikes crawled the *Grand Horizon's* deck, searching for something to destroy. 'But we're still going to get there ahead of them.'

'I know.' He cupped my face in both hands, and he studied me closely. I knew what he was looking for.

'I'm all right,' I said. 'Seventy-five percent all right, anyway.'

He seemed to calculate me at about the same rate.

'If we succeed,' he said, 'we will have another problem to consider.'

I hadn't actually thought past the consequences of failure, which were fairly horrific. 'Like what?'

'You may inherit his power. And you may be tempted to use it.'

'I could use it for good.'

'So did he. Once. It isn't a power you can use, Jo. It's a power you must destroy.'

I looked back at him. 'So if I grab it from Bad Bob, you're going to take it away from me. Or die trying.'

'Maybe,' David said. 'But first we have to live to get there, don't we?'

I turned to face him. The next lurching drop sent him into me. Our lips found each other, hot and hungry and damp, tasting of salt and desperation. For a moment even the storm seemed to stop, suspended between heartbeats.

I felt the darkness in me trying to reach out to him, and slapped it down hard. *No. Not yet.* David might be here, he might be with me, but he wasn't *with* me. And I wasn't going to be the one to enslave him yet again, not until I had no other choice.

I turned to face south, toward the empty horizon. 'He's not far now,' I said. 'One thing at a time, right?'

David's arms gripped the railing on either side of me, bracing me against the violent bucking of the ship as we plunged toward the darkness. 'Right.'

Chapter Ten

The Wardens on the *Grand Horizon* had learnt from our mistakes, it appeared; we saw them break through the storm, and they must have set up a series of Djinn/Warden cooperative alliances to maintain their bubble shield, because I could see the glistening curve of it from the deck of our ship as the waves broke and foamed over the smooth round surface.

I wished them luck in keeping that up. It was brutal, soul-shredding work. 'How long until they catch up?'

David handed me a plate. Our pirate cook had made some kind of meat, finely chopped and spiced, with spongy bread. It was delicious, and surprising; I'd somehow expected wormy crusts and rum. I gobbled down the lunch with gratitude.

'Good?' David asked, amused, and shook his head at my garbled reply. 'They're gaining. They'll catch up to us by midday.'

'Can't let that happen,' I mumbled. 'Lewis was very clear. This needs to be me. Not them.'

'Bad Bob and his storm didn't slow them down. How do you propose either of us stops them, short of destroying them?'

I chewed and swallowed. 'Ask them.'

He evidently hadn't thought of that. I winked and carried my plate to the wheelhouse, where Josue was dozing on a stained old cot at the back while his navigator did the hard work of steering the tough little vessel on the course I'd set. I asked about the radio and was pointed belowdecks, to a small, claustrophobic closet of a room with bad ventilation and a crew member who evidently liked beans and hated baths. I evicted him from his battered chair and rolled up to check out the radio. It was old, but highly complicated.

'Hey!' I yelled through the closed door. David opened it. 'Help me out a little. I'm not Sparky the Wonder Horse.'

That earned me a full, warm smile. 'I wouldn't say *that*.'

'Watch it.' I meant that; he was looking at me like I was the old Joanne. The less demented one. 'Keep your guard up. I mean it, David. Bad Bob can be funny, too. That doesn't make him any less of a monster. Don't you dare trust me. I can't trust myself, not anymore.'

The smile faded, and the sparks in his eyes turned ash-dark. 'Yes. I understand.' David looked at the radio, and the dials turned. 'There. That should put you in touch with the *Grand Horizon*'s bridge.'

'Thanks.' I slipped on the headphones as he shut the door between us – less to provide me with privacy than to give me elbow room. There wasn't enough space in here to breathe. 'Merchant vessel—' Oh, hell, what was this ship's name? 'Merchant vessel *Sparrow* for the cruise vessel *Grand Horizon*. Please respond, over.' I expected I'd have to repeat myself, but instead I got an immediate crackle of connection.

'*Sparrow*, this is *Grand Horizon*.' I knew that voice. 'You made it.'

'Lewis.' I kept my voice neutral, although I was glad he'd made it, too. Even if he had tried to kill me. 'You're lucky David hasn't made a lampshade out of you.'

'Time will tell.' Lewis obviously knew all about how much trouble he was in on that front. 'You're heading straight for Bad Bob.'

'I have a plan. Obviously, it won't be as good as yours,' I said, 'but I make one hell of a good distraction, right? So I go in, do as much damage as possible, and you guys land for the cleanup.'

'That would be great – if I thought for a second we could actually trust you.' Lewis's voice was bleak and dry, even through the distortion of the radio waves. 'You brought us this close. That's enough, Jo. Break it off. Whatever happens, don't let him finish what he started in destroying you.'

'What makes you think he can't do it from a distance?' I asked. 'I'd rather go down fighting for you than against you.'

'Jo—'

'Maybe you didn't get that I wasn't asking your permission. I was informing you, that's all. You can not love it all you want, but it's what's going to happen, and—' I felt the laboring engines of my little ship begin to struggle. 'Don't you even *think* about it, man. You start screwing with me and you are in a world of trouble.'

He covered the mike, presumably to warn off the Earth Warden or Djinn who was trying to shut me down. 'I'm not interfering,' he said. 'I'm just advising, and I advise you very strongly to break this off and run, Jo. Now.'

'You sent me out here,' I said. 'You put me on the hook for bait. *Let me do this.*' No answer but static. 'Fine. Joanne Baldwin Prince, signing off—'

'Wait,' he snapped. I did. 'Don't take David with you. We're not allowing any of the Djinn to make landfall. Too dangerous for them.'

I was a bit unclear on the concept of how one stopped Djinn from doing something, if they weren't bound to a bottle, but I didn't bring it up. 'And what do you suppose I'm going to do about stopping David?'

His sigh rattled the speaker. 'You're not going to love the idea.'

'Try me.'

He did. I heard him out, although my first impulse was to blow the radio up in a satisfying shower of sparks. I thought about it.

After a long, quiet moment, I agreed.

'Jo?' I was so deep in thought that Lewis's voice startled me. 'Still there?'

'More or less. Look, I can't trust anyone on this ship, not with what you're asking. Send me someone.' I thought about that for a second. 'Send me someone who isn't going to take shit from some fairly scary pirates.'

'I've got just the guy,' Lewis said. 'We're going to slow down, to give you time to get to the island ahead of us. But we'll be coming when you need us.'

'I hope so,' I said. 'Let's not say our goodbyes this time. Last time was a real bitch.'

He seemed to think so, too. '*Grand Horizon*, signing off.'

'*Sparrow*, signing off.' I put the old click-to-talk mike down and sat for a moment in silence, staring at the equipment.

Then I rummaged around in the desk drawers. It was a battered old thing, looked like it had seen service in the First World War, and I surprised a long-tailed rat in the top drawer, who stared at me with beady little eyes and an entire lack of alarm. A pet, maybe. Or maybe this was his ship, and I was the infestation.

I shut that drawer and tried the next one. The rats

had made nests of the paperwork that had once been in there; it was nothing but shreds.

The third drawer yielded an almost empty bottle of Cutty Sark.

'Score,' I said. I unscrewed the cap, wiped the lip of the bottle with my shirt, and threw back the rest of the booze in one long, thirsty pull. When there were no more threads of amber snaking their way down the glass to my mouth, I lowered the bottle and set it on the desk.

'David?'

He opened the door.

It's not that easy to catch a Djinn who's alert for treachery, and David – even though he loved me – knew better. I'd just told him not to trust me.

But he gave me the benefit of the doubt, even with the empty bottle open on the desk in front of me.

I looked up at him and said, 'We need to talk, honey.'

Lewis sent Brett Jones, Fire Warden, former Special Forces. He was bigger than Josue, and after a dick-measuring initial meeting, Josue evidently accepted that Brett was meaner as well. I didn't know Brett that well, but Lewis did, and if Lewis sent him to take care of us, then we could trust him.

'Watch your back,' I whispered to Brett as I passed him. He'd come armed to the teeth, which made him fit right in with all my pirate crewmates; on him, though, it looked like professional accessories. He nodded to me. It seemed like a thousand years since we'd sat in the movie theater on the *Grand Paradise*, watching as our colleagues were carried off in body bags after that first clash with Bad Bob's storm.

Brett looked as hard and tired as I felt. He also looked very alone, standing at the bow with his arms folded, watching the speedboat head back to the distant cruise ship. The weather was still foul over in that direction. The storm just wasn't about to give up its prize, no matter how hopeless it was.

Standing in the filthy confines of Josue's tiny captain's cabin, I brushed the worst of the tangles out of my hair, and used a burst of power to clean my clothes and remove the worst of the grime from my skin. As accommodations went, even temporary accommodations, these earned zero stars; the bed was filthy, the floor was littered with toenail clippings, and the walls were pasted over, with hard-core porn actresses in action shots.

David opened the cabin door and stepped in. He watched me in silence, not touching me. We'd talked about all this, but convincing him was another matter altogether. And even when he bowed to necessity, he did it grudgingly.

I wished I could really tell what he was thinking, but then, he probably was wishing the same thing.

'One good thing about this,' I said. 'This time, we get to do it right.'

He shrugged. 'As far as I'm concerned, the first time was good enough for eternity.'

That made me smile. 'You *must* be a romantic. I mean, what with all the mayhem and the chaos and the not finishing the ceremony—'

'If I wasn't a romantic, I wouldn't be here.'

He had an excellent point. I decided not to pursue it. Instead, I put down Josue's comb and did another critical review. I looked . . . surprisingly good, actually. The sun and sea had given me a blush of bronze, and my eyes seemed clear and cool as the Caribbean waters. My hair had, for a change, taken its glossy curls to a style, instead of to a mess.

David slid his hands over my shoulders, and I looked up at him. 'It's time,' he said. 'Wouldn't want to keep the guests waiting.'

The guests were, of course, the assembled pirates of the ship I'd recently, and randomly, named the *Sparrow*. None of them had made any effort to change clothes, splash water on their faces, or brush their teeth, but they were seated cross-legged on the deck, clearly happy with slack-off time.

Josue had donned a ridiculous coat. A tuxedo jacket, obviously ripped off from some prior victim on a yacht. I hoped I wouldn't notice any bloodstains.

'Hurry your asses up,' he said. 'We don't have long.'

Not exactly the wedding march, but it would do. I exchanged a look with David, and he gave me his hand,

and we walked the short length of the deck to the bow, where Josue was standing. The sun was behind clouds again, and the air smelt heavy with brewing storms. David's best man – and, I supposed, standing in for my maid of honor – was the Fire Warden, Brett Jones. Big and foreboding as a Djinn, only armed like a pirate and watching Josue and everybody else, including me, with smart, cold focus.

I felt both protected and unsettled.

'I don't have no holy books,' Josue said. 'So I make it up as I go along. You don't like it, you go get married in hell.'

'As long as you get the important stuff right,' I said. 'Go ahead.'

'I get paid first.'

There was a brief pause, and then David reached into his pocket and brought out a small handful of very large bills. Josue grabbed them and flashed a highly inappropriate smile, then asked, 'What's your name?'

'David Prince.'

'David Prince, you come here with this woman to be married. Right?'

I didn't dare throw a glance at David, because there was something so weirdly hilarious about this that I was already choking on it. After a beat, he said, 'Obviously.'

I coughed.

'You sure you want to do that?' Josue said. 'Because

you got to take care of her, love her, never look at another woman. Even if she's sick or gets old and fat.'

My coughing turned into a full-fledged fit.

'If you mean will I stand by her in sickness and in health, for richer or poorer, for all the days of our lives – yes, I will,' David said, very quietly. The urge to laugh left me suddenly, and I squeezed his hand. 'I vow that I will.'

I felt no corresponding surge from the aetheric, the way I had the first time we'd done this, but then, David had completed, his side of the vows the last time we'd done this.

I hadn't, not officially. Which was why Lewis and I had decided to go through with this. It was an experiment – probably doomed to failure – to see whether or not it would make any difference in the way Djinn and humans were bound together . . . if we were bound together by ritual, completely.

'You're sure about this,' Josue said. He continued to stare at David. 'I give you some time to think.'

David didn't smile. 'I'm sure. Move along.'

'Well, OK.' He turned to face me. 'How about you?'

'You suck at this,' I told him. I got a slow leer in return. 'Come on, at least make an effort!'

'You dump this guy, come back to my cabin, I'll make an effort.'

'To clean up the toenails off the floor?' I asked sweetly. 'Come on, Josue. Today.'

He clasped his hands, and tried for a pious expression. I doubted he'd ever seen one, except maybe in the DVD collection belowdecks. 'Do you – what's your name again?'

'Joanne Baldwin.'

'Joanne Balderwin, take this – uh, Prince David, to be your husband? Do you swear to honor and obey him, and to never look at another man, even if this one gets—'

'Sick, old, and fat, yes, I know.'

'What would that matter? He's a man, yes? It is the prerogative of a man to get sick and old and fat.' The crew laughed raucously behind us. 'Do you swear to honor and obey him, even if this one gets poor and lazy?'

I closed my eyes and fought a cage match with my temper. '*Ask it right.*' He heard the echo of darkness in my voice, and the laughter of the crew died away. 'I mean it.'

Josue cleared his throat. When he spoke again, the mocking tone was gone. 'Do you take this man as your husband, forsaking all others as long as you both live?'

Close enough. I felt something happening, a stirring in the aetheric like a soft breeze. It swirled around me, lazy and gentle, and then solidified into a silver mist.

'Yes,' I said. 'I vow it.'

The mist fell like soft silver rain on the aetheric, and I felt it sliding over my skin in warm threads.

And then it hit the black torch, and all hell broke loose.

'Jo!' David grabbed me as my knees folded.

'What—?'

I had to make this work. *Had to*. Holy crap, Lewis had been right the whole time. Because our wedding vows hadn't been finished, I'd made myself vulnerable to the invasion by Bad Bob. The equations had been out of balance, and on the aetheric that was a very bad thing.

We were setting it right.

The connection between us went wild, power flooding from him into me in a silver torrent. Power straight from the bloodstream of the aetheric, pure and white-hot.

'Take it out of me,' I panted. 'Hurry. *Hurry*!'

David rolled me over on my stomach and ripped my shirt open, exposing the rippling, angry tattoo on my back. The thing under there was being forced to the surface.

David's power was acting in self-defense, because I was now part of him. Flesh of his flesh.

I heard his breath rush out, and then he put one hand on the back of my neck and said, 'Hold still. It's coming out.'

I felt blood sheeting over my back, and heard the pirates scrambling backward to get away from the thing that was thrashing its way out of me.

I had enough control left to block the nerves

before the pain got unbearable. I couldn't see what was happening in the real world, but on the aetheric there was something that looked like a cross between a squid and a virus flailing its way out of my silver-shining body.

David fried it into grease and smoke on the deck beside me, and then burnt it again.

The change was immediate, and dramatic. Calm flooded me, and confidence, and power – the power of the Djinn.

I directed it to my back, and sealed the ravaged muscles and torn skin – something not even Lewis could have done, as powerful as his talent for things like that was.

I'd just become something else. A bridge between the Wardens and the Djinn . . . and something of both at the same time.

And Bad Bob's mark was *gone*.

I was free.

David picked me up and cradled me in his arms. I felt warm and relaxed, contented as a drowsy cat in the sun.

'It worked,' he said. He sounded surprised. 'You were right.'

'Damn straight,' I said. 'It's why he wanted to stop us at the wedding. Bad Bob knew that once we exchanged vows, he wouldn't be able to control me anymore.' I felt drunk on silver bubbles, and I laughed. 'Free. We're free of him.'

David captured my hands and kissed them. 'Not quite yet,' he said. 'He can't control you. That doesn't mean he's helpless.' He pulled me back to my feet. My shirt was a disaster, so. I tied the rags together in a makeshift halter top. Not so bad, really, all things considered.

Josue had prudently retreated as far as he could from us. Brett Jones was still standing there, looking focused despite the sight of an alien critter ripping out of my flesh.

I nodded to Josue. 'Finish it.'

'Hell with you, crazy bitch!'

'*Finish it*!'

From all the way across the deck, he made the hasty sign of the cross. 'Then I declare you married,' he said. '*Mazel tov*. Kiss the bride before we do.'

He picked up a half-empty bottle of cheap rum, pulled out the cork, and swigged down a gulp, then passed it around. Our version of cheap champagne.

David pulled me into his arms, and what would have been a symbolic kiss turned deep, hot, and thoroughly suggestive. I helped with that part, thinking of nothing except the moment, the sensation of his body against mine.

We'd won. At the very least, we'd won my freedom from becoming Bad Bob's slave.

Now I had to make sure that David didn't suffer that fate, either.

We broke the kiss and clung together, panting. He

was whispering things to me, quiet wonderful things. Promises.

And then he closed his eyes and said, 'I don't want to do this. Not this way.'

'I know,' I said, and kissed him again, gently. 'But it's important. Tactics and strategy, right?'

'Tactics and strategy.' He sounded resigned, not happy. 'All right. I'm ready.'

I nodded over his shoulder to Brett, who unzipped a pocket on his tactical vest and pulled out a small glass bottle with a cork. A little more ornate than I was used to seeing – probably something they had in the stores on the cruise ship, although the cork would have been a new addition.

'I've got your agreement to do this, right?' Brett asked. He was asking David. After a long moment, David nodded. 'Be thou bound to my service. Be thou bound to my service. Be thou bound—'

'Wait,' I blurted, and took both of David's hands in mine. 'If this is the last time I see you, I need you to hear this.'

He waited, amber eyes glowing like suns. I fumbled for words. 'I – just – David, if something happens to me, if this doesn't go right, you have to promise me, *vow* to me, that you will look out for humanity's good, not just the Djinn's. Don't punish the Wardens if I die. Please.'

He knew why I was asking that. 'Lewis tried to kill you,' he said. 'He *did* kill you. Are you asking me to forgive him?'

'I'm not going to ask the impossible. I'm asking that you not take revenge for something that turned out not to work anyway, that's all.'

There's something very unsettling about a Djinn that doesn't blink when he's talking to you – even one you love with a deep, desperate intensity. 'You *are* asking the impossible,' he said. 'Lewis hurt you. He did it as part of a plan. I can't allow that to go unanswered.'

'You have to,' I said. 'Please. I need a vow.'

'You know that I can't say no to you, don't you?' He wasn't smiling, though. 'Yet this time, I have to. The answer is still no, Jo. He can no longer be trusted by the Djinn.'

That really wasn't good. 'But you'll still work with him? With the Wardens?'

'To a point,' he said. I could tell he wasn't going to be more specific about where the point *was*.

That was all I was going to get from him, even now, even at this most vulnerable moment.

I nodded to Brett, who repeated the binding phrase again – three times, just to be sure.

David's hands misted out of mine as the binding took effect. I felt the hammering blow of it shatter the aetheric between us, and then he was exploding into mist, and the mist was sucked into the bottle in Brett's hands. He corked it with calm efficiency, and I watched him put the bottle in a special padded case, and then into the pocket of his tactical vest.

'With your life,' I told him. 'You know that, right?'

'Yes,' he said. It was a simple answer, and it left no room for doubt at all. He'd do it. I couldn't ask for better than that.

I fried the ship's engine with a burst of pure Earth power, fusing metal parts together, gunking up everything that looked remotely important. The *Sparrow* sputtered and began to drift, dead in the water.

Josue stopped looking afraid and started looking alarmed, then angry. 'You do something to my ship?'

'Why, is something wrong with it?' I kept my expression as innocent as possible. That was probably what made him glower at me as if he'd like to take me apart but wasn't sure it was safe to try. 'My friends on the cruise ship will help you. Oh, and I wouldn't try any other guns you might have stashed. Serious mistake on so many levels.'

He gave me his most dangerous look. In earlier days, I might have actually been intimidated by it. Today . . . not so much. 'Worst day of my life, the day I fished you out of the ocean, mermaid.'

'Really? The sad thing is, it wasn't the worst day of mine.' I stepped up on the railing at the vee of the bow, balancing on the balls of my feet. He backed away, watching me. Not quite certain of what I was doing. 'Good luck.'

He crossed himself. 'Go with God, so long as you

go.' His sudden piety didn't convince me he wouldn't stab me in the back if he could get a clear throw when I turned around. I gave Josue one last look, and then I dived from the railing of the *Sparrow* into the open ocean water, heading south.

Bad Bob wasn't on an island, after all. Well, to be accurate, he *was* on an island – but the island was floating and he was moving it wherever he wanted.

Neat trick. First, most islands aren't all that prone to float, since they're really the tops of underwater mountains. This one was able to drift, withstand the full force of a Category 5 hurricane, *and* navigate at will.

It also explained why he was so crazy hard to track down. I wasted time and frustration until I figured out that I was heading not for a specific spot in the ocean but a *mobile* spot. I found it as the sunrise spilt over the long, rocky key of the island, which was moving away from me at a fairly rapid speed. I had an embarrassment of choices for first impressions, but *you've got to be kidding me* was certainly in the hunt for first place.

The entire island was *turning*, the mirror image of the mouth of a black-and-green hurricane that was hovering above it, just . . . spinning.

Not even Bad Bob – I hoped – had the power to do this alone. No, he had to be augmenting it somehow . . . And then it occurred to me. I was filled with silvery aetheric light now, thanks to my connection to David; Bad Bob had a Djinn, too. Rahel. He'd taken her by force, and that explained the negative energy in what I saw hovering over the island.

Of course, Bad Bob himself was no Prince of Positive Thinking, either.

The scary thing was that with that much power, he could do almost anything he liked, and this floating fortress was just demented enough to amuse him.

I kept swimming. I'd been at it for hours, and I was very, very tired, but I also wasn't about to give up. Besides, I was building up some fierce quadriceps.

Jo, a voice whispered in my ear. I gasped, startled, and sucked down a lungful of water. I paused, treading water. *Jo, can you hear me?*

It was Lewis's voice. I shook my head and bopped myself in the ear, hoping I was just having a hallucination.

Stop hitting yourself. Yes, it's me.

'How do you know I'm hitting myself?'

I can hear the pops in your eardrum. It's an old Earth Warden trick. Works great for covert ops. Lewis was making an effort to sound like nothing had passed between us the past few days. Like it was all just the same old. *How's the swim?*

'Long,' I said. My teeth were chattering. 'You didn't dial me up on the ear-phone to chat.'

He paused for a few seconds. With Lewis, that was weighty. *Did David agree? Is he in the bottle?*

'Yes.' Better not to overshare on that, I decided. 'Could we speed this up? Water cold. Body tired.'

Can you do this? Are you sure?

What a dumb-ass question. 'No, I'm not sure,' I snapped. 'Of course I'm not sure. Why? Second thoughts?'

Yes. We've got one shot at this. He may not even let you get close. He may kill you before you get anywhere near him.

Cheery thought. 'If he does, you've still got a shipful of Wardens and Djinn ready to bring the wrath of God down on him and—' It occurred to me suddenly why Lewis was taking the trouble to say these things. 'David.'

You and I know that he'd stop at nothing to destroy what killed you.

Oh Christ. 'You cannot be serious with this. Lewis. Please, tell me you're not asking me to go and deliberately get my ass killed so that it will trigger David into a homicidal rampage against your enemies?'

It would work.

Sure it would. It would leave Bad Bob and whoever was around him radioactive dust. Including, probably, the cruise ship, which would become collateral damage.

The hideous thing was that as a nuclear option, it was not bad. So long as you accepted that the pile of bodies would be unthinkable, but at the end of the day, the enemy would be gone.

No. 'Not happening, Lewis,' I said. 'If I get killed anyway, fine, all bets are off. But I'm fighting all the way down. Get me?'

Yes. You understand that I had to ask.

Not really. But I was starting to think that in some ways David was right – I never would truly know Lewis. Not at his core.

'I'm signing off, Lewis,' I said, and spit salt water as a wave slapped me. 'Hey. Thanks.'

For what?

'Letting me say no.'

I got a dry, tinny chuckle in my ear. *How could I ever stop you?*

'See you on the other side, then.'

Yes.

That was it. Our big goodbye. As romantic scenes went, it lacked, but that was all right. We were past all that now.

After a good half hour of chasing down the floating island, my flailing hand finally slapped a boulder on the island's rocky shore – whatever sand there once was had long ago been scoured away, so there was nothing left to this beast but slick, water-smoothed stone. I grabbed at the rock, but my hand slid off. I kicked, gritted my teeth, and lunged up out of the water as far as I could.

My rib cage thumped down painfully on the smooth

surface, and I started to slip back, but more kicking and clawing paid off. I found a handhold, at the cost of the last memory of my French manicure, and hauled myself out of the pounding surf to lie exhausted and dripping, draped like Josue's proverbial drowned mermaid over extremely uncomfortable terrain.

'Damn,' I whispered. 'Why am I doing this again?' Oh yeah – because I was probably the only one who could, with anything like certainty.

And because sometimes I just had to face my own demons – and Demons – head-on.

I spent several moments just letting my muscles shake and cry out in relief, and then rolled up to a sitting position to take a look around. It wasn't much of a garden spot – lots of black basalt and granite. This place wasn't more than a few dozen millennia away from the lava flows that had built it in the first place. It still had most of its sharp edges.

That wasn't great for me, of course. I'd worn heavy boots, but my battered shorts probably weren't going to protect me from gathering some new and interesting scars as I scrambled across the edgy landscape.

I climbed up on the tallest boulder I could find and did a quick survey. The island was bigger than I'd expected – maybe a solid mile across – and toward the middle there was an unlikely small collection of jagged palms, all dying now. Whatever fresh water had nourished them was long gone.

This island was a rotting hulk, and I wondered

uneasily how Bad Bob had kept sixty Sentinels – that I knew about – alive on such a bare span of rock. I supposed he'd laid in supplies, but he didn't seem to be a logistical kind of guy.

Maybe they were eating each other. It wouldn't surprise me, given the level of devotion he inspired in people.

This was not the place I'd have picked as my home away from home if I had to choose a portable island paradise, that was for damn sure. No beaches, no living trees, no water, no shade. Just razor-edged rock and the odd crab scuttling by. The surface of Mars, only at least fifty percent less hospitable.

If I hadn't been doing such a careful survey of the island, I might have missed the first attack that came at me. There was nothing to give it away but a faint shimmer against the rocks, like a reflection of waves – but it didn't move with the waves.

It was bending light, and it was moving fast, heading my direction.

I'd never seen one in full daylight before. That was a crystalline skeleton, barely visible without the human disguise its kind had adopted back on the *Grand Paradise*. I knew now why it had gone for the skins; the creature made a vibration on the aetheric as it moved, a kind of ringing like a finger tapping an ice-cold crystal glass.

The skins had muted the vibrations, hidden them in the natural noise of human existence.

The crystal shimmer disappeared, lost in the glare of the sun for a second, and then I saw the blur of it against the piles of rocks only about three feet away from me, I didn't have time for fancy moves, just dived out of the way. It was fast, but the rocks were just as hazardous to its footing as to mine, and I saw it stumble and try to catch its balance as it checked its momentum. Instead, it tumbled off into the water.

It sank below the surface in seconds, pulled down by the density of its bones.

Well, that was great news, but as I looked up, I counted three more shimmers against the rocks, heading in my direction. I calculated frequencies. I didn't have time to try very many, but the good news was that I'd already killed one of these things on my own. Well, with help, but close enough. I knew the theory, and even without the direct access to the aetheric that I'd have had with David free, I wasn't starved for power. I was almost shining with what had spilt into me at our wedding ceremony.

The next creature lunged for me, and I opened my mouth and picked a note. Nerves forced the amplitude of the sound too high, and the creature just kept coming. I adjusted the range of the note, holding it steady, and fine-tuned it as the beast came closer, and closer, and—

—and then it burst into a powder-fine shower of disrupted crystal. Instant sand.

Gotcha.

Two more on the way, bounding over the rocks. I dug deep into my diaphragm and half-remembered old singing lessons. I kept the note going, and amplified it a thousand times, sending it in a shock wave out across the island from end to end. The intensity of the sound swept out like a bomb blast I was immune to it, but across the island, a dozen crystal ghosts exploded into dust and shards as the wave of sound rolled over them.

The note did more than take care of them; it also brought Bad Bob's other allies out of hiding. Farther inland, near the stunted, mummified trees, Bad Bob's former Wardens were coming out of camouflaged tents and starting to get organized. The shock wave rolled over them, and dozens more went down – not dead, but stunned and probably deafened. I'd caught them by surprise.

They returned the favor.

As I took a step forward, stone softened under my boot, and I sank in to my ankles. A rival Earth power was trying to harden the matrix again around my body, which would have not just trapped me but pulverized flesh and bone, if I was lucky – or amputated both feet at the ankles, if I wasn't.

I held her off, and found some weedy grass struggling to survive between the rocks near my opponent. I added a giant shot of power to send it growing and weaving between the stones. It slithered out of a crevice and wrapped around her ankles, yanking her flat on the ground, then dragged her out into the open where I could see her.

I knew the woman. She was a thin little thing, older than many of my peers in power – a veteran, someone who'd ruled with an iron hand in the old days. A contemporary of Bad Bob's. Her name was Deborah Kirke. She'd been wounded in the Djinn rebellion, I remembered, and she'd lost most of her family when her Djinn had destroyed her house around her. She had cause to believe Bad Bob's anti-Djinn agenda, but that didn't mean I could give her a pass. She'd taken up arms against me and the other Wardens.

That meant she had to be stopped.

'Deborah,' I yelled. 'Just stay down, dammit. I don't want to hurt you!'

She didn't. I suppose, from her perspective, she really couldn't.

I trapped her under a clump of boulders and reinforced it by melting the top layer into a concrete cage. She could breathe, and in time she'd probably dig her way out of it. I was heartsick doing this to an old lady, but I had a war to fight, and mercy wasn't going to win me any consideration from their side in return.

Another former Warden had emerged from cover as well. I knew this one, too – Lars Petrie, a Fire Warden. He liked to form whips out of living flame, and sure enough, one hissed through the air and cut a burning path down my right arm. It wrapped around my wrist and yanked me off balance. I wasn't prepared, and the burn bit deep, charring skin and muscle. That was bad; burns created distractions, made it harder to concentrate, channel, control the forces I needed to balance.

I grabbed water out of the sea. It rose in an arc into my hand, frozen solid, and compacted into a spear. I barely paused before sending it arrowing at Petrie's chest.

He dodged. The spear hit the rocks behind him and shattered into snow, but it distracted him. While it did, I formed another blade of ice and slashed it through the whip. The flame fell apart on my side of the cut, leaving ugly black spirals up the skin of my arm, with red exposed muscle.

I tried not to think about how much that was going to hurt once the nerves woke up.

I started running for him, knife clutched in my uninjured hand, and while I was at it, I shook the rocks under his feet, a miniature earthquake that sent him stumbling. He wrapped his fire whip around a boulder to steady himself, but I was there when he straightened, already cutting at him with the knife.

I got it under his chin and held the cold edge there. Our eyes met, and Petrie's widened in shock and horror.

'Listen to me,' I said. 'Lars, we have no fight here.

None. You can't win and he doesn't expect you to. You're nothing but compost and cannon fodder to him.'

'Yeah? And what the hell am I to you?' he demanded, and shoved me backward. 'I watched four Wardens die while Djinn ripped them apart, and where were you? *Screwing* one of them. You don't care about us, any of us. Don't pretend we're the same.'

The fire whip formed in his hand again, and I moved my right foot back for better stability as I tried to anticipate which way I needed to dodge. He trailed the whip on the ground, snaking it this way and that, hissing the burning edges of it over stones. A tiny alarmed crab scuttled out of a tide pool and toward the sea. A second later, the whip touched the pool and turned it into steam, baking whatever was unlucky enough still to be trapped there.

'I'm not your enemy,' I said, and held out empty hands toward him. 'Come on, man. Let's not do this.'

Petrie, like Deborah, was a post-traumatic survivor of the Djinn attacks. I didn't know what had happened to him, but I remembered that the review team had removed him from his duties, and that Miriam, the head of the internal security team of the Wardens, had put in precautions . . .

Petrie had a fail-safe in his brain. *Dammit*. Standard Earth Warden procedure was to put a two-stage failsafe in place. The first one stunned, and the second one killed. If I knew the stun code . . .

But I didn't. And I had no time to find out, because even if Lars was damaged and irrational, he was one hell of a master of that whipping loop of fire. It flared at me without warning, and I dropped to a crouch. That saved my neck, most likely; he'd been aiming to decapitate me, and I felt the scorching heat as the living flame snaked over my head.

I lunged forward and pulled up seawater with both hands, forming a massive wave that shattered over the rocks and hit Lars from behind, sending him flying and dousing his fire whip in a hot blast of steam.

I threw myself on his chest as he sprawled on top of the rocks. 'Stop!' I screamed at him, and banged his head against the rock. 'Stop fighting me!'

I put a forearm over his chest to hold him down as he struggled. My arm was bloody and torn from the fight, dripping on his chest, and I felt savage. So much for the black torch being responsible for all my darkness; Bad Bob had been right, I'd had some of it all along.

And I always would.

He got an arm free and put it to use by landing a right hook to my jaw – but not hard enough to break free, or to break my bones.

'Just stop,' I said. 'Please stop.' I didn't know if I was talking to Lars Petrie, or to myself.

I let Petrie go, and he sat up, exultant triumph lighting up his plain, middle-aged face. I backed away.

I heard a dry, ironic sort of clapping behind me. 'Impressive.' Bad Bob's voice. 'Damn if you aren't still a do-gooder, after all this effort.'

Petrie's face twisted in fury, and his fire whip formed in his hand, then snapped toward me.

From directly behind me, Bad Bob said, 'Duck.'

I did. Well, I was going to do that anyway.

A sheet of ice the thickness of a razor slashed through the air, spinning like a saw blade. It sliced feathering hairs from the top of my head, bit into Petrie's neck, and kept on spinning.

I gasped as Petrie's hot blood splashed over me in a wave. That blade hadn't been aimed at me.

It had been intended for Petrie. I whirled around while Petrie was still falling.

Bad Bob was sitting in a battered deck chair behind me, right out in the open, on top of a pile of rocks that I'd have sworn had been empty a few seconds before. He grinned and waved at me, and made a discus-throwing motion. 'Hell of a shot, eh? I should turn pro.'

Petrie's head and body hit the stones separately, spattering me with even more blood.

I couldn't turn to look. I didn't dare take my gaze away from Bad Bob, who was no illusion, not this time. He was *here*. Within striking distance.

Victory was at hand . . . for one of us.

'You look tired,' Bad Bob said. 'Rough trip?' He sipped a beach drink. He was wearing a Hawaiian shirt in vomit yellow and pinkeye pink that clashed with his skin and hair. He also was wearing old man shorts, socks, and flip-flops. If I hadn't known who and what he was, he'd have looked like any old pensioner roaming Fort Lauderdale or asking directions at Disney.

'Why?' I blurted. He knew what I was asking, so I didn't even look at Petrie.

'Thought I'd give you a helping hand, since you seemed to be having some crisis of conscience. Tell me, why is that, anyway? I figured you'd be well on down the road to not caring about anyone but yourself by now.'

I tried slow, even breaths. The burn on my arm was getting worse, and shock was setting in. I needed to heal myself, and I had the power to do it; I just didn't dare spare the concentration it would take to build the matrix of energy and direct the healing.

Bad Bob didn't blink. 'Oh, where are my manners? Have a seat, kid. You look just about done in.'

And with a wave of his hand, there was another beach chair, this one shaded by a ruffling yellow awning fringed in white. There was even a little side table, and a fruity cocktail with a blue folding umbrella.

'No, thanks,' I said. It was only three steps to the chair, but I wasn't at all sure the chair wouldn't turn out to be a spring-loaded bear trap. Messy, and undignified, as a way to exit stage left. 'I think I'll just stand. It's great for the calf muscles.'

'Suit yourself, but your calf muscles have always been top flight, especially in those heels you like to wear.' He smacked his lips, just another leering old geezer. 'Come here all by yourself, did you?'

'Sure. Why not? You're not going to hurt me, are you?'

'Never in a million years, sweetness.'

Oh sure. I remembered being forced down on my back, and Bad Bob handing a bottle to his Djinn, and a Demon sliding its black tentacles down my throat.

No, he'd never hurt me at all.

'Turn around,' he said. 'Let me see the progress.'

He meant let him see the black torch.

Moment of truth. I'd spent time in the water forming an illusion, one that had all the weight of reality to it. The twisting shadow on my back looked and felt like the real thing.

I hoped Bad Bob couldn't tell the difference at this range.

My shirt was knit, and sleeveless. I pulled it up so that my back was revealed. 'Satisfied?' I didn't wait for an answer, just dropped it back down again. 'I'm still on your team, Bob. You saw to that, whether I like it or not. I was your first-round draft pick.'

Had he bought it? I couldn't be sure. He sat there looking at me, nothing in particular showing in his expression, and then nodded. 'Just wanted to be sure,' he said. 'You wouldn't believe all the crazy crap people pull trying to get into the VIP section these days. Some Djinn came in here about three hours ago, pretending to be you, if you can believe that. Talk about your Trojan horses. That was a dumb idea. They think I can't tell the difference?'

I felt my throat go tight and my guts clench. 'Who was it?'

He shrugged. 'Didn't ask. She looked just like you, though, right down to the sassy attitude. Good copy. If I hadn't known that tattoo was a fake, I might have just let my guard down for her.'

Was he taunting me? I was afraid that he was, but I didn't want to force things until I knew for sure. 'So where is she now?'

'Why?'

'Because I'm not on great terms with them anymore.' That was almost true.

He lit a cigar, a big Cuban thing, and puffed until he was satisfied with the draw. 'What do you think happened? I've got dependents, you know. People got to eat.'

Whatever I'd expected, it wasn't that. 'What?'

He gave me more of that horrible grin. 'Sweetheart, you ever order a Djinn to become a pot roast for dinner? Unbelievable, the things you can do when you've got power over them. It's a real education.'

I felt an actual wave of sickness travel through me, like the blast from a bomb of nausea. And he kept on smiling.

I couldn't stop the words that rolled out of my mouth. 'You fucking sick awful evil—'

'Ah, that's the old Jo,' he said, and winked at me. 'You know what's wrong with all my old friends, the ones I talked out here to the middle of Buttcrack, Nowhere, with me? I tell them how to humiliate and mutilate a Djinn, and they dive right in. They think it's payback. I hate to say it, but the human race is starting to completely disgust me, sweet pea, and that's why I'm so glad you're here. You, I can still shock. You restore my faith in humanity.'

That logic was so twisted it ought to be served salted, with a side of mustard. 'You just killed your own guy,' I said. 'That can't be good for morale.'

Bob dismissed it with a shrug. 'Petrie was nuts. Everybody knew it. But I'll tell you what, sugar, I was really amazed at how many Wardens I got to turn their coats. I didn't even work that hard at it. Talk about morale, you guys need some team-building retreats or something. Then again, you'll all be dead, so that problem solves itself, really.'

This sounded so much like Bad Bob that it lulled me into believing that he'd keep on talking, forever . . . and then a thick black tentacle burst up out of the rocks beneath my feet and writhed its way up my ankle, my calf, my thigh.

'Oh, damn,' he said, and sipped his drink. 'Try not to move. It'll take your skin clean off if you struggle.'

The thing was like an octopus tentacle, and I could

feel the obscene, cold suction of hundreds of tiny cups against my skin. I froze. It didn't read as alive on the aetheric, and it wouldn't respond to any kind of Earth power that I could wield.

'Let me go,' I said. Bad Bob tilted his head, eyes burning an incandescent, almost Djinn shade of blue.

'Nope,' he said. 'Did you really think I wouldn't know you slipped the leash? Nice trick, by the way. I can always try it again, but I have the feeling you won't be all that easy to screw with again – Hold still or you'll lose that leg, you know.'

I gave up struggling. 'Fine. So what are you going to do with me? I don't make a very good pot roast, I'm just telling you right now.'

Bob sighed and pinched the bridge of his nose, like I'd given him a monster headache. 'What the hell am I gonna *do with you*?' he repeated. 'You're kidding. This isn't remedial school for half-assed criminals. I'm going to kill the holy hell out of you, but first, you get to help me get what I need out of the Wardens.'

I winced as my boot slipped against the rocks, and the tentacle wrapping my leg gained a couple more inches and got very, very friendly. 'Lewis won't deal.'

'Of course he'll deal. That boy loves you, always has. I know him. I picked him for the Wardens.' Bad Bob looked positively malevolent for a second. 'Lewis never did want responsibility. He isn't going to step up to it now, with your life on the line.'

I blinked. Bad Bob, the all-knowing and all-powerful, was talking like an old man, set in his ways, reciting out-of-date facts. Lewis certainly had once been like that, but like Bad Bob himself, he'd changed. Bad Bob hadn't bothered to find out how much.

'So what am I worth?' I asked. 'What are you going to ask?'

'He's not stupid. He grabbed all the Djinn he could find and bottled them. My folks back on the mainland couldn't find much, and what they did find got them killed. So I'll trade you for a cargo full of bottles. How's that? Make you feel any better?'

Not really. But I didn't believe for a second that Lewis would trade *one* Djinn for me, much less a boatload. Besides, rescue was on its way.

Right?

It had been maybe ten minutes since my arrival on the island. The *Grand Horizon* was supposed to be visible by now, but I couldn't see its distinctive outline anywhere on the open seas around us, and it was way too big to miss. Had something happened? Had Bad Bob managed to sink the second ship, too?

Was I all alone here, at the end?

Well, if I was, I was going to go down fighting.

God, please, don't let him kill me.

Because David really would destroy everything.

Chapter Eleven

Bad Bob talked. He loved to talk, and I let him, because I learnt a lot.

Bad Bob, I was starting to realize, really didn't have much. While we'd been sailing around the Atlantic as a big, juicy target, he'd been conducting a multifront war. Those never work; ask Napoleon. He'd had operatives back home who'd gone after the remaining Wardens, on the theory that if they were any damn good, Lewis wouldn't have left them behind. That got him a big fat score of fail. The Wardens didn't lose a single person, or any Djinn.

The Sentinels, who were getting increasingly desperate, had been taken down not by the Wardens themselves but by Homeland Security. They couldn't even defeat a bunch of *government* men.

That was kind of rich.

What remained of Bad Bob's threat to the Wardens

was here, on this island, which meant a bunch of fanatics in rags with the aetheric equivalent of a nuclear device.

Not great, but at least isolated.

I couldn't move much, thanks to my mutated octopus friend, but I could pay attention to Bob's manic ramblings, in case there was something useful to be learnt.

I didn't know if the thing inside had driven him mad, but it certainly didn't know how to flip the off switch.

Eventually, Bad Bob got impatient. He'd expected my rescue to heave over the horizon, but if it was out there, it was smart and very patient.

That was good.

It just wasn't good for me.

'You're sure they got the message?' I asked. I'd managed to find a position sitting on the stones, with my pinned leg carefully held straight out. I didn't want to look too closely at what was happening to me; it felt very much like that tentacle was sinking into my leg, and I'd really had enough of that kind of thing. 'Maybe your ransom demand went to voice mail. Sucks when that happens.'

'Oh, they know I have you. They just need some incentive, that's all,' Bad Bob said cheerfully. The sun was beating down on my unprotected head, and while I wasn't going to get delirious from the heat, or the lack of water. It wasn't the most comfortable I'd ever been.

And I didn't like the sound of incentive.

I liked it a whole lot less when Bad Bob got out of his chair and walked toward me, because as he did, he reached into empty space at his side and brought out the Djinn Ancestor Scriptures.

I stared at it wearily. It wasn't of human origin, this thing; as far as I knew, it wasn't of Djinn making, either. The Ancestor Scriptures probably wasn't even a book, in the strictest sense, although it certainly had that appearance here in this plane – leather binding, wrinkled ancient pages, metal flaps to lock it shut.

What it really was I couldn't say, but I was pretty sure that it had been written by a higher power than the Oracles, and the Oracles of the Djinn had been entrusted with its care and feeding.

Whether this was one of the three originals or a copy, I couldn't say – the copies were just as deadly, if maybe not imbued with as much power.

'How'd you get your hands on that?' I asked Bad Bob as he opened the metal latches and began to flip crackling, translucent pages. 'Garage sale at the Villain Supply Company?'

'I took it from an Oracle,' he said, but absently, as if it really didn't matter. He wasn't bragging. 'Air Oracle. Years ago.'

That, I could believe. The Air Oracle had always struck me as hostile, guarded, angry at the world in general and humans in particular. I'd certainly gotten little to no love from him/her/it.

That kind of made sense, if Bad Bob had gotten there first. He'd given bipeds a bad name.

'Hmmmmm.' Bad Bob looked down at a page, considered it, and shook his head. 'No, too subtle. This – too messy. Ah, here we go. I'll just turn on old DNA inside you, see what we get. Maybe you'll grow a tail, shark teeth, chicken skin . . .'

Well, I definitely wasn't waiting around for that.

I stole Petrie's specialty, and formed a whip of pure plasma out of the air, igniting it with a burst of silvery power out of my special Djinn reserve. It burnt hot blue, and where it slithered over the rocks, it left melted trails behind.

I snapped it toward Bad Bob.

He caught it in one hand, wrapped it around his fist, and yanked. I slid forward on the stones; the tentacle wrapped around my left leg tightened, and I felt flesh tearing under the strain.

Dammit.

I let go of the whip, and the fire guttered out, leaving just a trail of greasy smoke between us. Bad Bob, for a change, didn't say anything. He walked over to where I was pinned in place, blood streaking down over the tentacle anchoring me.

'You just don't lie down, do you?' he said. 'I always said you were way too good for the Wardens. You made the rest of us look bad.' He turned and yelled toward his watching followers. There were a lot fewer than I remembered – maybe twenty, if that. Granted,

I'd taken some down earlier, but I didn't think I'd grounded quite that many. He'd probably lost some to incursions and his own craziness – like Petrie – plus I figured that those who could think logically enough to escape had grabbed transportation and taken their chances.

That probably meant they were dead, out there on the ocean, but at least they'd died cleanly, off this black hunk of stone.

His remaining troops scrambled to assemble at his silent wave of command. They were terrified, and they were realizing – all too late – that the savior they'd imagined him to be was all in their heads. He'd used their fears against them.

I imagined he would continue to do that, right up to the end. They had to follow him now. Where else was there to go?

'Get over here!' he yelled. 'Bring our friend along!'

The Sentinels began crossing the distance. Some of them were old, some were wounded, none of them looked entirely compos mentis.

They all looked at me like I was dinner – which, considering Bad Bob's earlier pot roast revelation, was a truly sickening thought.

'Moira,' Bob said, and held out his hand. A spritely little pixie of a young woman stepped out from the others and came forward to lock fingers with him. In her left hand, she carried an old green wine bottle with an equally ancient cork stuffed in the top.

I didn't know her. She was younger than I was, which surprised me – a lovely young girl with fair skin and full lips and a head of thick, lustrous red hair that glinted gold in its highlights.

She held the bottle up to Bad Bob as if seeking his approval on a choice to serve with dinner. He nodded.

Her eyes were the same blue as Bad Bob's. 'Hey, Da,' she said. 'What can I do to help?'

He pecked a kiss onto her perfect milkmaid's cheek. 'Oh, just stand there and look pretty.'

I felt a step or two behind the curve. '*Da?*' I said. 'Unless she's speaking Russian, you've got to be kidding me. You've got a *kid*? Wait – more importantly, some woman actually slept with you? Without a condom?'

'Shut up,' the girl said, and temper blazed up in her like magma. That, more than anything else, convinced me of the paternal bloodline.

'Wow,' I said. 'I don't know whether to say congratulations or condolences. That probably goes for both of you.'

'Moira, meet Joanne,' Bob said. 'Moira's my pride and joy, the fruit of my powerful loins. Isn't she beautiful?'

Moira, like daughters everywhere, looked annoyed. 'Oh, can it, Da.'

'I'm very proud of her. But you know how that feels, don't you, Jo? You're a mother. More or less.'

That made me flinch, as he'd known it would. I

wanted to demand that he leave my own child out of this – a half-human/half-Djinn hybrid who'd become one of the three Djinn Oracles. The Earth Oracle, in fact, which was how I'd gained access to that particular set of powers – through her.

Imara had been born full-grown, and she was a lot like me – she could, and did, take care of herself. Besides, the Djinn would have closed ranks around their Oracles, protecting them at all costs.

Imara was safe. I was the one at risk. He wanted me to fear for her, but I just stared him down.

'Nothing?' Bad Bob watched my face. 'Huh. Well, OK then. Cross that one off my list.' And he pulled the cork on the bottle. 'Oh, wait. Let's revisit that.'

A ghost misted out of the air. My own body, mirrored. My own dark hair. Everything the same, except her golden eyes, and the brick-red layered dress that swirled around her body like smoke.

No. It couldn't be.

'Damn,' Bad Bob said, and turned to Moira. 'I thought I told you to bring the *white*.'

She smirked. 'Sorry.'

I didn't pay any attention to their playacting. My brain seemed stuck, unable to move past the word *No* to any kind of possible outcome to this moment.

My daughter Imara was *here*. And she couldn't possibly be here. There was no way Bad Bob or any of his minions could have captured her, stolen her from her chapel in Sedona, without triggering an all-out war with the Djinn. They'd fight to the last of them for her, no matter whose daughter she'd been in the beginning. Not only that, but David would have known. There was no way that he and Ashan *couldn't* have known, if something happened to Imara. The Earth Herself would have fought back to protect an Oracle.

My daughter looked at me with desperate fear in her eyes, and I couldn't stop a pulse of maternal anguish from traveling like lightning through my body.

And then I pushed it away. 'Nice try,' I said. 'But no sale. That's not my daughter.'

Moira gave her father a harassed look. '*Told* you she'd never buy that malarkey,' she said, and grabbed the bottle back from him. The form of the Djinn shifted away from Imara's reflection of my face, took on darker shades and harsher angles. Long, cornrowed hair with gleaming bits of gold beaded in. This was a Djinn I knew.

Rahel.

The Djinn had fought to keep that part of her appearance the same – at what cost, I couldn't quite imagine – but she'd lost the war on clothing. Moira dressed her like a Barbie, and the effects were ridiculous. Rahel was wearing a wine-colored evening gown, sleeveless, with a plunging neckline and a slit up the side. White opera gloves. Dangling diamond earrings.

Rahel was a beautiful creature, but this looked wrong on her. Deeply, stupidly insane.

'Wait,' Moira said, and giggled. She added a tiara on top of Rahel's head, a ridiculously ornate confection of chrome and fake diamonds. 'Wave to the adoring crowds, Miss America.'

Rahel's right hand came up and did a mechanical, empty wave.

Her eyes were locked on mine, and I hated what I saw in them, because it was a very close cousin to the madness that I'd recently seen in David, when he thought I was gone. A desire to crush and destroy and kill everything in her path. She'd been tormented, forced to do horrible things. And she, like David, was not inclined to forgive.

'Hey,' I said to Moira. 'Seriously, is that the best you can do? Because that's not even original. Honestly, I used to be a Djinn. I had a teenage boy for a master. Now, *he* had an imagination. You're just – sad. But then again, like father, like daughter . . .'

I got that pulse of fury out of her again. 'You shut your whore mouth!'

'Wow. Like I said. Sad. When you have to quote a MySpace graphic, you've just given up.' I ignored Moira and looked at her father. 'What's the point of having the kid here? Were you just lonely for somebody who had an extra helping of crazy in the veins?'

The girl smirked at me, turned, and skinned up the edge of her thin white shirt.

She didn't have a torch mark. Instead, her back was a mass of writhing fire, moving just below the skin

– worse than mine had ever gotten, even at its most painful. 'I'm one of the chosen,' she said, and dropped the fabric. 'Like you used to be, before you gave it all up.'

'Jesus,' I said. 'Just when I thought you'd hit rock bottom, Bob. Congratulations on tunneling down.'

'It's the family business,' he said. 'Bringing an end to this travesty we call humanity.'

I checked the horizon. No ships breaking the smooth outline of the sea.

I was starting to sweat.

'So what now?' I asked. 'Not that this isn't fun, but my leg's falling asleep. Can we move the end of the world along a little? Or at least work in a nap?'

Moira laughed. Bad Bob shrugged. 'Sure,' he said. 'For you, sweetness, I'll kick it into high gear. But you know that means you're going to suffer, don't you?'

'I figured,' I said, and shrugged. 'I'm already suffering. These rocks are really uncomfortable.'

He laughed. 'What a girl,' he said, and elbowed his daughter. 'Right?'

By her expression, she found me a good deal less charming. 'She's nothing,' she said. 'You never needed her, Da. You always had me.' Oooooh, jealous. *Very jealous. I could use it.*

'That's true.' He kissed her forehead, but his eyes never left me. 'That's very true. I've been taking out her bones, one at a time. What do you think, princess?'

'Too boring.' She wasn't even looking at me; she

pulled free of Bad Bob and walked a slow circle around Rahel, inspecting her Miss America impersonation. 'Make her work for it.'

'Hmmmm. There's an idea. Two birds and one very big stone.' Bad Bob slammed the book closed and put it under his arm. 'All right, then. Let's see what you can do, my child. Impress me.'

Moira sat down on a handy boulder, open wine bottle in both hands on her lap, and tossed glossy red hair back over her shoulders. 'Rahel,' she said. 'I want you to break Joanne Baldwin's right leg in two. Use your hands. Do it now.'

She knew the rules of commanding a Djinn – be specific about intent, method, and time frame. And I could see that they'd had plenty of practice with Rahel – she hadn't gained that traumatized fury without cause.

'Do it slowly,' Moira said. 'Make her feel every second of it.'

Rahel's eyes focused on me, and she began walking across the stones toward where I sat. Not a hell of a lot I could do to stop her; if I tried to resist, my *other* leg was sure to be crushed, and maybe even pulled off by this tentacle thing Bad Bob was using for a tether. She still looked ridiculous in her getup, but I didn't let that fool me for a second. I'd seen the Djinn in the grip of truly evil people, and they were no more to be reasoned with than the blade of a knife.

I looked past Rahel at Moira. 'I guess you hate me

for being the daughter he never had. Daddy didn't trust you, did he? That's why he came after me in the first place. Because you weren't measuring up. Either that, or he wanted to screw me. Your choice.'

Bad Bob's face went very still, and I knew I'd guessed right.

So did Moira. She surged to her feet. 'Rahel! When I tell you, you're going to kill that bitch for me!'

One rule of commanding an embottled Djinn: Never give your orders angry. Moira had just forgotten to explicitly frame her order as to *whom* to kill. *Bitch* could apply to, oh, more than one of us standing here, and unless she caught that error later on, Moira was in for a nasty surprise.

I saw the light flare gold in Rahel's eyes, and I took a deep breath. *Wait*, I mouthed. The desire to strike was almost primal in her, and she knew she was close, so close to having the freedom to exact her revenge.

I knew I could push that button anytime I wanted to – but first, I had to endure a little more. Moira would think of her mistake if I gave her the time.

I needed to keep her engaged.

Rahel bent down and put her hands on my outstretched right leg, the nontentacled one. Her opera gloves felt cool and smooth against my skin. 'She did say to do this slowly,' she said, and I let out a slow breath, then nodded. Rahel was telling me, without wasting words, that she had identified the gaps in Moira's original order. To a Djinn, the word *slowly* meant something entirely different than it did to a human. Their time scales were vast, and that instruction was not nearly as specific as Moira might have believed it was.

Now it was up to us to hide that fact.

Rahel froze, with her hands on my leg. I waited. I didn't feel anything – no increase in pressure, no pain, nothing. She'd taken the freedom Moira's instructions offered to simply stretch this out so long that it might take a lifetime for her grip to increase its force enough to crack a bone, much less break it.

'Nice,' I murmured, and got a brief, cold parting of her lips. Her teeth were filed to points. 'Don't panic, whatever I do.'

Rahel raised one arched eyebrow, and I began to struggle against her grip, panting – selling the idea that she was hurting me, when in fact she was doing nothing but pinning my right leg to the stone.

As performances go, this one probably was a bit over the top even for high school melodrama, but Moira lapped it up like cream. I tossed in some begging and bargaining. She loved it. Pretty girl, but either Bad Bob's genetics or Bad Bob's black tattoo had rendered her broken and sick. I remembered someone else like her – Kevin's stepmother, Yvette Prentiss. The avid shine in Moira's blue eyes as I threw myself around and shrieked in simulated agony was almost exactly the same.

Then again, Bad Bob had been involved with Yvette,

too. I had the feeling all the sickness came from one poisoned well.

Behind her, seated on his plastic throne, Bad Bob looked less focused on my performance. He scanned the horizons restlessly, frowning. His attention was on the effect, not the cause – he wanted my pain to draw my hypothetical rescue out from hiding.

I could have told him that it wasn't coming. Lewis was too careful for that.

I wasn't sure how long Rahel intended to carry on our little drama, but my voice was getting hoarse from all the screaming, and even Moira's attention was starting to wander. When you're losing your torturer's focus, it's probably time to wrap up the play.

I let out a heartrending shriek of utter agony, and went pitifully limp, weeping like my heart would break. I didn't have to simulate being exhausted. Throwing yourself into something like that takes a sweaty, aching toll.

Ah, she liked that. I had Moira's full attention once more. 'Rahel, break Joanne Baldwin's other leg,' Moira said, and her pale tongue came out to lick her lips. 'Do it just as slowly.'

Really, you can't spell sadist without the word sad. She'd just forgotten that my other leg was the one wrapped in Bad Bob's tentacle tether.

Rahel might not have normally been able to take the tentacle from my left leg, but she'd just been ordered to do something that allowed her to freely interpret method, and in one lightning-fast move, she reached down, plunged her fingers deep into the base of the tentacle, and ripped.

Oh *Christ* that hurt. The tentacle fought back, clamping down on my leg with all its muscular strength, and I felt things pop and move that really shouldn't be shifting around inside. Rahel ripped at it again, digging her sharp fingernails into dark flesh and ichor, and tore the thing loose from its roots deep in the rocks.

I rolled free, still wrapped in the black coil.

'What the hell are you doing?' Moira screamed. 'Rahel, *stop!*'

Rahel froze, still crouched over the thrashing remains of the tentacle. I had seconds, at most, to make this happen, and I knew it.

Strangely, Bad Bob hadn't reacted at all. I saw his face in a blur as I rolled behind the shelter of more stones, and it was impassive and watchful.

Assessing.

I didn't have time to try to remove the tentacle, but I didn't need to; cut off from its body, the thing was already dissolving into slime. When it drained away, it left my skin pallid, wrinkled, and torn, like old paper soaked for too long. I was losing blood, too much of it. I slammed Earth power through my nerves and pinched off broken capillaries, set up a healing matrix, and shut off the pain.

I couldn't afford it right now.

'Hey, Moira!' I yelled. 'How old are you? Maybe nineteen? Twenty? I was about your age the first time your dad tried to screw me!'

No girl wants to hear that about her father, especially when it comes from the daughter-rival that Daddy loves more.

Like I said, I could push that button anytime I wanted.

'Rahel!' Moira's voice was a raw, vicious snarl. 'Kill that bitch *now*!'

Again with the lack of specificity.

I felt the energy shift, darken, and as I peered around the edge of the boulder, I saw Rahel streak straight for Moira.

It's possible that Moira might have recovered in time to order her to stop, although Rahel's attack clearly caught her totally by surprise.

To make damn sure it wouldn't fail, I reached out with a burst of power and filled Moira's mouth with seawater. She choked, gagged, and then it was too late. As the water rippled down from Moira's open lips, Rahel's claws sank deep into her throat.

In her thrashing, Moira let go of the wine bottle, and it rolled toward the edge of the boulder.

Bad Bob calmly reached over and caught it as it fell.

Shit.

Moira was sputtering blood, and her face was shockingly pale, her eyes desperate. Rahel remained where she was, claws in the girl's neck, and I saw her flash a look at Bad Bob.

He didn't react at all.

I was gripping the edge of the rock too hard, but I needed the sharp reminder of where I was, what the stakes had become.

Rahel ripped her claws free in a contemptuous gesture, and blood misted and spattered in an arc around her. She willed away the Miss America costume in favor of her more usual tailored pantsuit – in bloodred, not neon.

She turned her back before Moira's pallid, dying body toppled.

Bad Bob was holding her bottle, and unlike Moira, that evil old bastard knew every trick. 'Freeze until I tell you to move again, Rahel,' he said. 'That was a goddamn stupid waste.' There was no genuine emotion left in him, not even for his own child. He saw it as a waste, all right – because Moira hadn't measured up, in the crisis. 'Jo. Come out.'

'Yeah, not likely!' I yelled. I tried to slow down my breathing, order my thoughts. 'This isn't going well for you, Bob. Maybe you should just give up now.'

He laughed. 'No.'

He still had the book, and even though he hadn't bothered to bring it out yet, he also had the spear, the Unmaking. I hadn't even managed to free Rahel, dammit, and if his daughter's bloody end hadn't been enough to distract him, I couldn't think of much else to try.

'Fair enough,' I said. 'Want to call it a draw? Lose/lose?'

'I want to call the game,' he said. 'On account of the death of the world.'

I'd have liked to think he was just being grandiose, but there was a dark undertone to his voice now. Seeing Moira die had destroyed his fun, apparently; he was ready to just skip right to the end, which in his book was *and then the universe blew up. The end.*

'That really what you want?' I slowly got up, hopping on my good right leg, and braced myself on the boulder I'd been using for sparse cover. 'Come on, Bob. If the world ends, so do you. I thought you wanted to destroy the Wardens and savor your victory first.'

'As long as we all go out together, I'm fine with it,' he said. I expected him to reach for the Ancestor Scriptures, but instead, he stretched out his hand, which disappeared in a tingle of blue sparks and reemerged holding a thick, matte-black cylinder like a spear, sharp on both ends.

The Unmaking. Its presence set up a horrible crawling repulsion in me, an itching all up and down my nervous system. I wasn't sure if the scientists were right, and it was stable antimatter, or if it was something even more exotic, like dark matter. Whatever it was, it did not have a place here, not in this world.

It was *wrong*.

It was also radioactive as hell, and it had almost

destroyed me the last time I'd come anywhere near it. Now I was so closely connected to David, sharing the same well of power, that I didn't dare risk it again. If I was poisoned, he might be, too. And through him, half the Djinn.

Bad Bob rested one end of the shaft against the stones at his feet and leant on it. The thing was a little taller than his head now, wickedly pointed. 'You really bamboozled me, you know. I never thought you'd come alone. Never thought David would let you.'

'He didn't,' I said. 'Nobody lets me do anything. You know that.'

He nodded, but the look in his eyes was far, far away. 'I liked you,' he said. 'Back in the day. Before things went wrong.'

'I liked you, too.' I hadn't, exactly, but I'd admired him. We'd all admired him. 'I know you took the Demon Mark on for the right reasons – you wanted to save lives. You just weren't strong enough, in the end.'

'Neither were you,' he said. We weren't accusing each other now; there wasn't any heat to this exchange at all, just simple fact. 'You'd have hatched out a Demon in the end, if you hadn't gotten all tangled up with the Djinn. But look what it did for you – all the things you've seen, all you've done. I made you stronger.'

He wanted my approval.

I felt a hot breath of wind, then a gust off the ocean. Something was stirring out there. It blew my hair into a writing cloud, and waves crashed the rocks at my back, dousing me in spray.

'Whatever doesn't kill you makes you stronger,' I said. 'And whatever *does* kill you—'

'Makes you invincible, if you're lucky,' Bad Bob said, and smiled. I sensed a kind of goodbye in that smile, because it was real. Not a manic stretch of his lips, but a genuine expression of feeling and warmth. 'You'll always be my kid, Jo. My crazy, brave, stupid kid.'

And he'd always, in some sense, be my father. My mentor. The man who'd pushed me over the edge and made me grow wings to survive. The most abusive bastard father in the world.

I nodded, not trusting my voice.

'Here it comes,' Bad Bob said, and looked up.

Something fell out of the eye of the hurricane. It was like a glass ball, soap-bubble thin, and it hit the rocks of the island and smashed into smaller spheres, each of which bounced and rolled over the rocks, uncoiled, and stood on two or four legs.

Crystalline skeletons, creatures out of drug dreams, that vanished like ghosts against the sunlight.

The Sentinels – those still standing – were unprepared. A few of them defended themselves, but most died, ripped apart on the rocks. My old colleagues, who'd lost their way and followed a false messiah.

I couldn't help them. Worse: I didn't want to help them.

Here at the end of the world, we were all going to have to settle up our debts.

'They're parasites,' Bad Bob said. 'Like dust mites. Bugs crawling through a crack in the wall. Vicious little things, though.'

He slammed the Unmaking down onto the rocks, and a ringing vibration rippled out from its quivering length – the same frequency I'd used before, but a thousand times more powerful. Every crystalline skeleton exploded into powder.

Another glass ball fell, but it exploded well before contact with the ground when he slammed the point down again and woke that awful sound.

I'd clapped my hands over my ears. I couldn't help it.

'I thought you'd welcome their help,' I said. I kept watching Rahel, hoping that she'd be able to somehow break out of her paralysis, but she was as still as the rocks around me, and just about as lifeless. My only ally was completely out of commission. 'Since it looks like it's just the two of us.'

'What would they be good for? You can kill them. I've seen you do it.' He shook his head. 'We're on to bigger things. You feel the lines of force under us? This is a nexus point, Jo. It's the thinnest space between the planes, and between the worlds.'

The island hadn't come to this place by accident. I could feel the humming power underneath my feet, and in the air around me. He'd been very careful about his choice of location for this. A born manipulator.

Like Lewis. *Where are you, Lewis?*

'Basic principles of magic, Jo,' he said softly. 'Like calls to like. And sacrifices have special weight here.'

He threw the Unmaking to me – not *at* me, but *to* me, a low underhanded pitch.

I dodged it easily, but it didn't fall; it turned and hovered in midair, pointing at me. Menace radiated off of it like black light. I backed up, carefully, not taking my eyes off it.

It darted straight for my chest. It was too fast, and I had no room to maneuver.

My body reacted instinctively, and wrongly.

I put out my hands and grabbed it to hold it back from my exposed chest.

It was like plunging my hands into a vat of dry ice – instant, agonising cold.

The pool of Djinn power inside of me turned toxic and black, poisoned at its source, and I felt myself begin to rot from the inside out. I was just enough Djinn to be vulnerable, and just enough human to be corruptible.

He'd counted on that. And on my survival instincts.

The spear felt hot and heavy in my hands. It had burnt me, before, but now its touch felt different – almost like flesh. I could hear it singing to me, a fascinating whisper of noise that had nothing in common with the music of our world, any of our worlds.

It made me sick and dizzy at first. I tried to drop it.

I gagged and tried to throw up the darkness inside, but it wasn't the kind that sat heavy in the stomach. This darkness filled me to the brim.

It took me over, completely.

When I opened my eyes again, I saw things differently. Literally. Holding the Unmaking made colors shift and burn, the whole structure of matter and light twist around me. It was beautifully destructive.

'We need more,' Bad Bob said. He was a pillar of blazing darkness in front of me, alien and somehow not alien at all. 'You know how to make more of it, Joanne.'

I knew. I'd seen the process at work. The antimatter incubated inside the body of a Djinn, converting the power into its raw, black opposite, stabilized into a form we could handle and use.

Rahel knew it, too. I saw the fatal acceptance in her face, and the haughty courage, even though she was trapped in place by the bottle that Bad Bob held in his hand. *Come, then*, she seemed to be saying. *If you can.*

If I'd been myself, any version of myself, I wouldn't have done it. Couldn't have.

But holding the Unmaking had taken all that away from me, just as Bad Bob had intended.

I heard myself scream, a raw sound that fused oddly with the music of the Unmaking as it crawled through my nerves.

I lifted the spear in both hands and plunged it toward Rahel's chest.

It never got there.

A pulse of pure hot Earth power rolled up through the rocks and blasted them into knife-edged fragments under our feet, sending me flying in one direction, Rahel in another.

The attack came from underneath us.

Bad Bob was caught by surprise. He staggered, leapt for stable ground, but it dissolved underneath his sandals. He fell. The Ancestor Scriptures skittered across stone, and the bottle dropped toward a fatal impact with the edge of a piece of lava rock.

I got to Rahel before the bottle hit stone. I felt the firm impact of the spear hitting her flesh, and then – then she was gone, and the spear was broken off at the tip, vibrating like a tuning fork in my hands.

Rahel's bottle had shattered into pieces, and she was gone.

Rahel was *free*.

The Unmaking howled at me. It was angry at being cheated.

'Son of a *bitch*!' Bad Bob clawed his way out of the hole in the island, and jumped again as another hole was blasted up through it from beneath. Water geysered into the air between us. I held the spear in both hands and cast my own awareness out, too.

It was an impossibly stupid thing to do, but

Lewis had taken the *Grand Horizon* down, like the world's most unwieldy submarine. It floated in its protective, glistening bubble right below the island, and as I looked down into one of the holes, I could see people on the decks looking up at me a dozen feet below.

Something hit me from behind with stunning force, and I toppled into the water. The spear was as heavy as an iron bar, and it dragged me down toward the ship below.

Rahel wrapped her arms around me and pulled me back before the spear could touch the fragile surface of Lewis's protective shield that kept everyone on the ship alive beneath the waves. I fought to get free, and when that didn't work, I tried to move the spear around to stab her from behind.

She pinned my elbows and dragged me back, swimming like a dolphin at attack speed.

The protective dome sparked with golden light, and I saw Wardens emerging. Lots of them. They were accompanied by the bright silver glow of Djinn, and it was all bright, and weirdly beautiful, and I realized that I was running out of air. The screaming of the Unmaking in my head was so loud it blotted out everything.

Rahel wouldn't let me breathe. I fought with everything I had, trying to throw her off, and for a moment it seemed like I'd succeeded.

I seized the opportunity and shot myself through

the water at cannon speed, heading up. I blasted a path through the rocks and came up in the middle of the floating island, gasping and shuddering. I grabbed the husk of a dead palm tree and pulled myself from the water just a second before the hole sealed itself over beneath my boots. I used the Unmaking to lever myself to my feet. Where it touched, the rocks blackened and dissolved as if I'd doused them with acid.

My hands were black now, and my forearms were the gray of dead flesh, but I didn't hurt at all.

Bad Bob slid down a small mountain of rubble, and it exploded into flame and shrapnel behind him. He thumped down next to me, and we both looked up.

The storm circling overhead had taken on a thick darkness, pregnant with menace. As I watched, the clouds inverted their colors – a negative image, just a flash, and then emerald lightning tore through the sky, breaking in all directions.

'Time,' Bad Bob said. 'Take that up, Jo. Take it to the other side.'

Now I knew what he wanted from me. The Unmaking had made it clear to me, in ways that nothing had ever been clear before. None of this mattered. None of this was real. I'd been living an illusion all this time, a sad little nightmare of a life that started nowhere and ended in darkness.

Beyond that portal lay the *real* world. The *only* world.

This was just a fiction, and it needed to end so that we could all go to a better place.

I took a firmer grip on the spear, and rose up into the aetheric, into the heart of the storm.

Chapter Twelve

At the center of the slowly rotating mass of energy was the portal to the other world. The *real* world.

It was like a drop of pure darkness, maybe a dozen feet across – space made liquid. I could feel a kind of pull coming from it – not gravity, not force, nothing so simple as that. It was aware, and awake. It was hungry and endlessly patient, and I realized that it was like the slow, vast intelligence of the planet below me . . . like, but so much *more*. The Earth was a virus, a microbe. What lay on the other side of the portal was *God*. Not ours, though. A jealous, angry, hungry God.

In the aetheric, the spear I was carrying was tremendously heavy, and the higher I tried to rise, the heavier it got. It was like swimming with an anvil.

Then a truck full of anvils.

Then the world in my arms.

I screamed in soundless frustration and gained another few feet.

Then another. *I was so close.* I could see the shimmering waves in the portal, feel its draw. I could feel the answering vibration in the Unmaking, the key for the lock, and the lock that wanted to be turned.

My whole aetheric body was on fire. My senses had shifted, changed into a different spectrum, and I could finally see what was holding me back from completing my mission . . . The Djinn.

They were all around me, grabbing on to me, pulling me down. So many of them. Between me darted human forms – Wardens, trying to stand between me and the destiny of everything.

It was the magical weight of the world, and it was all against me.

I snarled and surged forward, again. I tried stabbing at the Djinn with the spear, but they easily avoided me. The Wardens did, too.

I was being dragged backward, and as I was pulled, I gouged bloody holes in the aetheric in my fury. The spear left a gaping black trail, a scar between worlds – not enough to open the door, though.

I reversed my efforts, and instead of trying to break free and go up, I charged down, arrowing through the unprepared Djinn line, and used a burst of hot black power to brake myself back into my body.

Bad Bob was on his back, trying to crab-walk away from the Djinn who was advancing on him – who had already hurt him, from the burns and scars on his face and arms. His hair was half burnt off, and his eyes glittered with absolute insanity.

I didn't recognize the Djinn, because it was shining like a golden sun, power incarnate. It reached down and picked up the Ancestor Scriptures from where Bad Bob had dropped them.

The Djinn's back was to me. I didn't think, I just acted.

I raised the spear.

He turned.

It was David. David standing there, facing me. Facing his own death at my hands. I couldn't identify what I saw in his face, in his eyes, except that it was not anger, not at all.

I snarled and lunged for him. The Unmaking had me now, dark and cold and certain, and it was going to take us both.

He said, '*Fides mihi*,' and touched his hand to his chest, over where a human heart would be.

And suddenly, the world went quiet. Time stopped. The Unmaking swallowed its unending shriek. And I *remembered*.

I was an observer to the past.

The lifeboat, where Lewis had killed me.

I was dead on the floor, lying in David's arms. Pale and limp and open-eyed. Done, and yet still trapped inside the shell.

My old self took in a convulsive breath and tried to fight her way free. I knew this moment. I recognized the agony that rippled through her body as Bad Bob's torch fought her for control.

I watched her pass out, head lolling against David's body as he poured energy into her to seal off the mark and cut her off from the black influence of the thing, one last time.

I didn't remember anything else, but the scene played on, a bare few seconds that changed everything.

'The containment won't last,' Lewis said. 'You know it won't. I used one fail-safe on her. We can put in a second one while she's out.'

'Not without her consent.'

'She already gave consent.' That was lawyering the point, but David allowed it to slip past. 'We can't kill her. We can't save her. The best we can do now is to make sure that she can be controlled if this goes bad.'

David bared his teeth like a wild thing, and I thought for a second that he really would lunge right for Lewis's throat. '*You're* not deciding when she lives or dies,' he said. 'Not *you*.'

Lewis closed his eyes in what looked like gratitude and relief. 'I don't want to,' he said. 'I never wanted to. You have to be the one, David. You're the only one she trusts enough to get close at the last moment. If it's Joanne or the world, you have to choose.'

David froze, and the people clustered around the

edges of the tableau shuffled. Cherise was the one who finally spoke.

'She'd want it to be you,' she said. 'She really would.' There were tears shining in my friend's eyes. 'I'll put the fail-safe in place,' Lewis said. 'You choose the codes.'

It was a combination, of course. Words, and deeds.

Fides mihi. Trust me.

And his hand, giving me his heart.

Fides mihi.

David's use of the fail-safe should have killed me. If I'd been myself, only myself, it would have turned me off like a light, gone forever.

The Unmaking deflected it from shutting down my body, but it couldn't stop the memory from returning, and the memory brought its own clarity. Its own powerful, unstoppable force.

In the second that passed, the terrible certainties that had filled me since Bad Bob put the Unmaking in my hand began to unravel. *No. This is wrong. This is all wrong. I can't do this.*

David wasn't the enemy.

This life wasn't a fiction. It was the only reality I had. The only one I wanted, no matter what the creature beyond that portal promised me.

But even though my brain caught up with the realities and horror of being taken over, I couldn't stop the physics of what was already in motion – me. I was already lunging for him, and I was too close to miss him.

David put the Ancestor Scriptures between us.

The Unmaking hit the book, and for a second it pushed deep into the pages, tunneling through toward David's chest. Then it stopped moving, as if it had hit an impenetrable wall.

Then it began to shake in my hands. Not vibrate. *Shake*.

And then it exploded.

Shards of it flew everywhere – powdery bits, larger fragments. Some hit the rocks around us and gouged out massive craters as they skidded. The powder whipped away on the wind, a radioactive cloud that glowed hot green in the aetheric.

And one fragment – the largest one – flew straight up, into the eye of the storm.

It shrieked its way through the portal in our world, then the aetheric, and then through every plane stacked above it, ripping a hole just large enough for a single drop of darkness to squeeze through.

It trembled pendulously, then fell from the portal – a dozen feet across, maybe.

Directly above us.

I lunged toward David, trying to push him out of the way. He did the same, trying to save me.

We collided at the center, and the black drop came crashing down on us.

I wrapped my arms around David, felt his go around me, and power flared silver through and around us. Then the darkness hit us, and the world ended.

I never expected to wake up, and I was really sorry I did. I must have been lying on the rocks for hours, cold and wet and cramped; my muscles were so stiff and strained that I whimpered even before trying to shift my position.

Overhead was a clear night sky, thick with constellations, and a bright yellow moon, three-quarters full. Wind rustled over the island. 'David?'

No answer. I pushed myself up to a painful, staggering walk. In the moonlight, I saw nothing but black rock and sea spray.

'David?'

There was a body lying a few feet away, half hidden behind a boulder.

Bad Bob, not David. He'd died hard and ugly. Something had blown his torso in two, dividing him neatly in half from the crown of his head to somewhere around his navel. He'd been dead for hours. The blood was mostly dried on the stones around him, and he smelt lightly of decay.

More dead Sentinels littered the landscape. Moira was still draped over the stones where Rahel had left her. Lars Petrie's severed head rocked gently in the tropical wind.

There was a cruise ship standing off the island, all its lights ablaze, but it was too far to swim, feeling as cramped and cold as I already was. God, I felt *awful*.

It was a mystery to me how I was still alive, or why.

'David?' I fumbled around, trying to find that silvery cord that connected us on the aetheric. I couldn't *find it*. Or the aetheric. I'd gone completely headblind; I was unable to feel anything beyond my own normal human senses. I'd lost my access to power.

'David!' I screamed it in panic this time, desperate to find him. I felt like I was suffocating, trapped inside my own skin.

So *alone*. I scrambled over rocks and bodies, looking for him with single-minded intensity, getting more and more panicked with every silent second.

I found him sitting on a boulder at the very tip of the island. He was naked and shivering.

'David? Oh God – honey—'

He was different. Very different.

When he raised his head, I saw that his eyes had gone plain brown.

Human brown.

I crouched down beside him and wrapped him in my arms. He tried to speak, but nothing came out. 'My God. What happened to us?'

He couldn't tell me.

I needed to signal the ship anchored out there, let

them know we were still alive, but when I reached out for a spark of power, I found nothing. Nothing at all. Not a single tingle of energy that wasn't fueled by the rapidly diminishing level of my own blood sugar.

I had no supernatural power at all.

Neither did David, as far as I could tell.

He got over a little bit of his violent shivering – enough to talk again. 'B-b-black corner,' he whispered.

I knew what that meant. There'd been damage to the Earth Herself – damage that had destroyed the ability of the planet to channel energy to this part of the world. Most black corners were small; a few measured as much as a city block, but those were rare.

This one . . . there was no way to know how far it extended, but inside it Wardens wouldn't have power, and Djinn wouldn't be anything more than human – helpless, and ultimately dying as their stored energy ran out.

We had to get off the island. *Now.*

I gathered up dried palm husks and whatever I could scavenge from the bodies and ripped tents of the Sentinels that was burnable. I found some waterproof matches in a backpack and got a signal fire going. It wouldn't burn for long, but it didn't need to, and while it was burning, I wrapped David in the cast-off clothes of dead men and sat with him at the fire, trying to get him warm enough to stop shaking.

It seemed to take forever for a boat to arrive. When

it did, it was full of Wardens, and Lewis was the first to step off the craft and onto the rocks.

He didn't exactly rush to our aid. He looked ill, and almost fell as he made his slow, careful way over the rocks. He wasn't the only one. All the rest of the Wardens looked just as bad.

'What's happened?' I asked. 'Lewis?'

He coughed, as if something was broken inside. He wiped blood from the corner of his mouth and leant his weight against a boulder as if he was too weak to keep standing.

'When the portal leaked, you and David took the hit. You absorbed it and stopped it from going any deeper into the earth. If you hadn't, we wouldn't be here right now.' He stopped to cough again, and this time I wasn't sure he'd stop. When he finally did, his voice was scratchy and thin. 'But because you were joined when you took the hit, the shock bounced both ways. Through the Djinn, and through the Wardens.'

Oh dear God. 'How bad is it?'

'It's turned this whole part of the ocean into a giant black corner,' Lewis said. 'We've got to get under way. If we run the engines hard, we might make it out of the dead zone before the Djinn start to die.'

David raised his head for the first time. 'Won't help us,' he said. 'You and me.' He nodded to me, and I knelt next to him, my knees digging painfully into the edges of the stones.

'What are you talking about?' I asked. 'What about us?'

'The blast – had to shift everything away to keep us alive—'

Lewis was getting it now, that bad feeling. I saw it as he straightened and looked more intensely at the two of us. 'What is he talking about?'

David grabbed my arms. 'Our powers are gone,' he said. 'Had to destroy them. Had to.'

I wasn't sure I could even dare to speak. I finally, slowly shook my head. I wanted to reject this. I wanted to believe that we were just wounded, maybe, temporarily stunned. *Something*.

'You mean the impact left the two of you human,' Lewis said. 'No powers. Nothing but – human.'

David nodded, relief flooding over his face. He hadn't been able to put enough words together, in his shattered state, to make sense out of it.

Human.

The two of us. *Human*.

I was suddenly aware of him in ways I'd never been before – of anxiety that I'd never felt before.

He was *mortal*. And I couldn't protect him, or myself, from anything that could fly at us – weather, fire, earth. Demons. I couldn't even bat away a simple tornado.

We *were fragile*.

'No,' he whispered, and put the warmth of his palm against my face. 'No, think it through, Jo.'

It was hard to push past the fear, the knowledge

that we were so much at risk, but I looked into his eyes for a long moment, and then I saw what he meant.

We were both human.

We could have a life together. A normal life.

We could have children of our own together.

'But—' My trembling fingers touched and traced his lips. The same lips, and different. 'But you used to be—'

'I used to be human,' he said. 'Long, long ago. And if I have to be human now, I can't imagine a better partner for my life.'

He kissed me. It was a real, human kiss, intimate in ways that even our most amazing kisses hadn't been, somehow. Bordered by our own awareness of mortality.

'Hate to interrupt this tender moment,' Lewis said, 'but we're fucked if we stay here. And by the way, your powers aren't gone. They're still out there, somewhere. Basic conservation of energy.'

We both looked at him. I saw a weary flash of utter hatred in David's face. No, being human hadn't taken away any of that antipathy. Definitely not. 'Someone else inherited our powers.'

'The problem is we don't know where they went,' Lewis said. 'Or who's got them. If we survive outrunning the black corner, we've still got to find out where your powers went. Worst-case Warden scenario – someone just woke up with enough power to destroy half the world and hasn't got a clue what to do with it.'

'And the Djinn?'

'Ashan,' he said. 'Worst-case scenario is that Ashan is now the sole Conduit for all of the Djinn, and he's going to be very, very pissed off about Wardens in general.'

I pulled David to his feet, and realized that I could barely walk. My left leg and arm were covered with the scars that hadn't had time to heal since the battle. Nothing was bleeding, but everything hurt, and hurt badly. I fought back tears and braced David as he took careful, halting steps.

He stopped, breathing hard, shaking his head. Overwhelmed.

'Hey,' I said, and grabbed his face in both my hands. 'Don't you give up on me now. We're alive. We're together. Don't let him get to you. *Our* worst-case scenario is that we end up together. Human. Alive. That doesn't sound so bad, right?'

He nodded, and a convulsive shudder went through him. He put his arms around me, and his head rested on my shoulder. The last of the Wardens boarded the rescue craft, and then it was our turn.

I didn't want to let go.

'*Fides mihi*,' he said. 'I said that, didn't I? To get you back in time to save both of us?'

'I will always trust you.' I kissed him gently on cheeks that tasted of sweat and sea. 'And I will always bring you home, my love.'

Fides mihi.

Now I had to make it count.

Sound Track

As always, I had plenty of musical help to get me through the complicated journey of *Cape Storm*. Enjoy . . . and please, support the artists by buying the music – otherwise, they might have to stop making it.

'So Long'	Stereoside
'Hole in the Middle'	Emily Jane White
'Black Is the Color of My True Love's Hair'	Nine Simone & Jaffa
'Light It Up'	Rev Theory
'Count to Ten'	Tina Dico
'Silence'	Delerium & Sarah McLachlan
'Let It Die'	Foo Fighters
'Get Free'	The Vines
'Electrofog'	LeCharme
'Electric Feel'	MGMT
'Alive and Kicking'	Nonpoint
'The End Is the Beginning Is the End'	Smashing Pumpkins
'Kill, Kill, Kill'	The Pierces
'Bad Girlfriend'	Theory of a Deadman
'Every Day Is Exactly the Same'	Nine Inch Nails

'Don't Trust Me'	30H!3
'Our Time Now'	Plain White T's
'I'm Not Over'	Carolina Liar
'Strange Times'	Black Keys
'Better Brother'	Madita
'The Bomb'	Bitter:Sweet
'The Best Revenge'	Fischerspooner
'My Mistakes Were Made for You'	Last Shadow Puppets
'Tomorrow'	Ladytron
'Pocketful of Sunshine'	Natasha Bedingfield
'Violet Hill'	Coldplay
'At Your Side'	Lionel Neykov
'Sour Cherry'	The Kills
'Salute Your Solution'	The Raconteurs
'Walk Like an Egyptian (Kairo Mix)'	Wilman de Jesus
'Could've Had Me'	Lex Land
'Sitem'	Candan Ercetin
'Retreat'	The Rakes
'Mercy'	Duffy
'It's Not My Time'	3 Doors Down

Acknowledgements

Jim Suhler & Monkey Beat
Joe Bonamassa
Lucienne Diver
Charles Armitage
Katherine Gunther
P. N. Elrod
Jackie Leaf
Christina Radish
Joya Manning
Jenn Clack
Kari Phillips
ORAC
Jackie Kessler
Richelle Mead
Kaz de Winter

. . . and, as always, my lovely and very patient husband, Cat.

Thanks for sharing the voyage, and making all the lovely, fruity drinks.

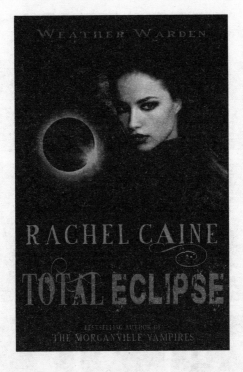

Also by Rachel Caine

The Morganville Vampires series

Check out our website for free tasters and exclusive
discounts, competitions and giveaways, and sign up
to our monthly newsletter to keep up-to-date on our
latest releases, news and upcoming events.

www.allisonandbusby.com